SECRET LIVES

Nadia Mason

Copyright © 2020 by Nadia Mason

All rights reserved. This book or any portion thereof may not be reproduced or used in any manner whatsoever without the express written permission of the publisher except for the use of brief quotations in a book review. This is a work of fiction. Names, characters, businesses, places, events, locales, and incidents are either the products of the author's imagination or used in a fictitious manner. Any resemblance to actual persons, living or dead, or actual events is purely coincidental.

Published by Amazon

First Printing, 2020

FOR JOHN AND SOPHIE

My life. My world. My sunshine.

With special thanks to Gareth Lane for the precious gifts of love and time. Without either, this book would never have been finished.

Thank you Drew Berry for your help and patience.

PART ONE

The future is not some place we are going, but one we create. The paths are not found, but made, and the activity of making them changes both the maker and the destination.

John Schaar

CHAPTER 1

The Country Swinger's Club was actually just that. Not in the sense of obscure country bumpkins swinging each other around a barn and square dancing until they all pissed themselves on the local cider they'd been drinking – but a 'double entendre', *take your clothes off,* free for all.

Jack had always led everyone to believe that when he wasn't here working for Tom at the insurance company, he and Cheryl, his voluptuous thirty five year old wife, were running the local country dancing club at weekends. They had founded it three years ago (he had told everyone in the office) and their commitment to it was as strong as ever. However, word had been flying around Brandley & Baxter Insurance Co. of late, that the only 'swinging' involved was probably from the nearest chandelier.

Jack was thirty nine, the same age as Tom. They had lived next door to each other as young children and had walked to school together every day until sixth form had ended. The young, handsome and dark-haired Tom Baxter had gone onto college to do a degree to please his parents and impress his friends, while the young, red-headed, lanky and spotty Jack Preston, had found himself a not so impressive part time job working at the local dry cleaners. It had eventually led to full time hours but it was to be six whole years before Tom, then twenty three, and even taller and more handsome than before, had gone in there to pick up a suit. Finally the two of them had come face to face once again. It had been great catching up on the 'good old days', although mortifying for Jack to admit he had been at the dry cleaners since leaving school and was struggling to make ends meet. Within ten minutes Tom had offered Jack a job at his own insurance firm, back then called Baxter Insurance. Jack left the dry cleaners that very week and had stayed with Tom in insurance ever since; sixteen years to be precise. The small but comfortable office was just a few minutes' walk from the bustling high street that he had become so accustomed to. He remembered well the time that Tom had first mentioned Angela; about how he had finally found someone to invest in his small business and that the name of the firm would now become Brandley & Baxter Insurance, 'Oh, and by the way, did I mention, she has great tits?' Tom had told him way back then, that one day 'that sexy little bitch with the high heels and cute butt (oh and by the way, did I mention that she has great tits?) will be my wife. Just see if I'm wrong, mate.' Of course Tom hadn't been wrong. Tom was never wrong. They had married soon afterwards and Tom was as happy as a pig eating his own shit. Unlike himself, who so elated that four years ago someone had finally taken notice of him after thirty five years of unintentional celibacy (that surely would have even impressed the pope), had jumped straight into bed with Cheryl, proposed within five minutes of orgasm and hot-footed it all the way to the registry office two months later. OK, so he had the Country Swinger's Club every Saturday evening, where he and Cheryl had an agreement of sorts; the same four or five couples came every weekend, quite literally, but with whom was not pre-arranged. They would *go with the flow* and see what chemistry and hormones allowed for on the night.

To begin with, the club had been held monthly, but Cheryl's appetite for a varied sex life grew so much that she soon changed it to weekly for those who wanted it. Half the time at least, that meant all of them. Although it had been Cheryl's idea to begin with, the club actually suited Jack nicely. With almost no sexual experience before Cheryl had come along he felt he was now owed his dues. However within six months of marriage, Cheryl had cut their private sex life down dramatically to once a month. At best. He had felt cheated in the beginning but it wasn't long before Jack came to the conclusion that anything was better than 'practically nothing'. Even if it did mean sleeping with another member of the Swinger's Club in order to have that vital physical contact with someone. Even so, it was no substitute for the settled, happy, love-filled marriage that he had always dreamed of; the kind that Tom and Angela had.

"Penny for them!"

Jack looked up from his desk into the powder blue eyes of Maxine Carter; the office's general dogsbody.

"A cup of strong coffee should sort you out," she chirped brightly. She slammed his chipped mug down in front of him, causing tiny splashes of coffee to spill onto his mouse mat. "I'd love to know what you're thinking about this time," she giggled, pushing both sides of her smooth blonde bob behind her ears. "If only I could get inside that head of yours."

"If only I could get inside that *bed* of yours!" he muttered back as she nonchalantly turned on her black, court shoe heels and slinked off back to the filing cabinet.

"Hey, Max," he called out excitedly, "I read somewhere once that according to esoteric teachings, every orgasm that a man has inside a woman's body leaves an energetic imprint that stays there for three years. *Three bloody years!* Can you believe that?" He pushed his tongue out as far as it would go and wiggled it at her slowly and obscenely. "So... what d'ya reckon then, you up for it? I'd only have to stick it in the once, have a quick 'jiggy-jiggy' and I'll be a part of you for years to come." He sighed pathetically while she laughed at him and raised her new microbladed eyebrows suggestively in reply.

Jack smiled. *There were no 'sexual harassment lightweights' in THIS office. No #metoos here.* Time had stood so still at Brandley & Baxter's that he could almost fool himself that it was still the free and easy nineties. He doubted he would make it past probation in another company in this day and age.

For the tenth time that day he took in Maxine's long slim legs, short black skirt and large breasts straining against her blouse buttons, and he wistfully smiled to himself. Then, suddenly remembering Cheryl, he turned back to his computer screen and made a mental note to stop day-dreaming quite so much.

CHAPTER 2

The dark blue Mercedes swept into the impressive circular driveway and made a crunching sound on the gravel. Seconds later it came to a complete stop near the stone steps that led up to the huge house. Jessie bounced excitedly in the back while Angela climbed out and unclipped her from her seat.

The late August sunshine beat down strongly on them as Angela walked to the boot of the car and took out the numerous shopping bags. Jessie tugged wildly on her mother's spare waiting hand and they walked slowly towards the house. Once they had climbed the few steps, Angela dropped the heavy bags at her feet and, before going into the house, she looked all around her as she had done so many times before.

Nearly six years ago, having just married Tom and feeling on top of the world, she'd had no idea of the many dark months of mourning that would lie ahead. In Fiji with her husband of just two days, her parents had been killed in a car crash back home. She and Tom had ditched the honeymoon and flown straight home to go through the motions of heart-wrenching grief and funeral organising. Only two weeks later, she had decided to move back into her parent's empty house and fill it with all of the love and laughter that her parents had previously bestowed upon it when she had been a young girl growing up here. Tom loved the six bedroomed

Georgian house with its huge hallway and sprawling double staircase. He knew that it would make him feel incredibly important to live here and so he had agreed without a second thought.

Angela bent down, scooped Jessie up into her arms and looked around at the view. She raised her head, closed her eyes and let the sunshine warm and refresh her. After a moment she opened them again and took in the two acres of land that surrounded Brandley House. Even now, six years later, it was hard to believe that all of this was now hers. *Well, hers and Tom's*. She breathed in the heady smell of the fragrant pines that lined the little private road that led to the house. A gentle breeze had brought the scent right to her front door and she wanted to stay there and inhale it forever.

Jessie's persistent tugging on the shoestring strap of her summer dress brought her out of her short reverie. She put Jessie back down onto the top step and gathered all of the shopping bags together in one hand, quickly smoothing down her long glossy chestnut coloured hair.

"Come on then, Princess," she chirped happily as she straightened up, "time to find that daddy of yours."

Tom was in his study. He picked up the phone. It was Jack calling from the office. Again. One of their biggest rivals, Webber & Son, had been slowly enticing old customers back to them with special deals and discounts. Jack had been trying to come up with some ideas of his own to prevent any more of their customers from leaving, but Tom hadn't been too keen on any of them up to now. It was always the same, Tom thought wearily; every time he decided to work from home to get through piles of paperwork the phone didn't stop ringing.

"What's up now?" Tom asked him. His voice was full of the strains of a fifth phone call in as many minutes. "He what? Look Jack just tell him that I'll phone him myself later, OK? I'll take him out for a meal, try the old sweeteners, works every time. Tell him that I said don't do anything until he's spoken to me, OK?"

Tom cut Jack off abruptly and slid the phone across his desk. He rubbed his temples vigorously with his fingers and sighed. Jack was Tom's 'second in command' and Tom knew that he could trust him to look after things when he wasn't there but sometimes he had the worst business ideas he had ever heard. Tom had begun to called him Boris. 'What? After Boris Johnson?' Jack had complained the first time his new nickname had come to light. 'I'm nothing like him. He's short and blonde for a start and I'm tall and ginger!' 'five foot nine is NOT short,' Tom had replied, 'But OK, you're a tall, ginger Boris.' 'But he's a twat!' Jack had countered, 'A complete liability!' Tom had laughed and left it there but the name had come up many times since.

Tom knew deep down that Andy and James, the office twins, had more business acumen than Jack could dream of, but Jack was his best mate and so Tom had continued to let things slide. He had a great team working for him, better still, they were all such good mates. What could possibly go wrong? It had worked so far. Despite that, Tom wondered if maybe he should call into the office today after all; Jack had seemed distracted and had been verging on 'unreliable' for the last few weeks now.

Andy and James were twins, not identical, thank goodness – Tom had enough on his plate without customers getting two of his employees confused with each other. They were thirty five now, but only twenty five when he had head-hunted them from Webber & Son, of all companies. They were the best in their field and Dave Webber never let him forget it. He had told Tom that he would never forgive him for taking them away and keeping to his word, had tried to make his life hell ever since. Normally Tom would let it roll off him, unaffected, but sometimes it was too much. At the end of the day he just really hated the guy.

"Daddy, daddy, I love you daddy," Jessie sang, screeching like a misguided sixteen year old at an X-Factor audition.

She flew past Angela and burst excitedly into the room, breaking into Tom's thoughts in an instant. He stood up just in time for her to run into his arms.

"Baby!" he cooed, scooping her up and covering her with dozens of tiny kisses. "Had a good day?"

Jessie squealed 'yes', wriggled straight out of his

arms back onto the floor, ran into the hallway and up to her bedroom, disappearing as quickly as she had arrived. His eyes fell on Angela and the amount of shopping bags in the study doorway.

"Oh," he laughed. "Looks like you've had a *great* day."

Angela smiled and, leaving the bags where they were, walked into the space that had previously been occupied by Jess. She reached up and kissed the tip of his nose softly.

"You're just what the doctor ordered, Angel," he sighed. "My day's been a right bitch."

"I'll get us a coffee and we can have a chat."

"Sorry, babe, I can't. I've gotta go into the office, there's a problem with that old git, Webber. Jack just called. You know the firm 'Oasis' – we insure about eight hundred of their employees? Well Webber's only offered them a forty percent discount if they move back to him. Oasis' owner, Mark, has just been on the phone telling Jack it's too good a deal to turn down. He's stealing a pile of our liability insurances too!"

"What? Well what are we going to do?"

"I don't know. I told Jack to phone him back and tell him not to do anything until he's spoken to me. I'm gonna have to think up a good one this time."

"Either that or lose them."

"Exactly. But I don't want to lose anything else, not to that bastard anyway."

When he looked at her again, she was pouting like a

child. Her brown eyes were wide and she had tilted her head to the side. He smiled, defeated.

"OK. I'm too exhausted for decision making anyway. I'll put the kettle on instead," he laughed.

Angela smiled and grabbed him playfully. "Listen you, get your butt down to that office this minute, check everyone's OK, phone Mark to sort out lunch, and then get your gorgeous bod back here to me, pronto."

Tom laughed. He knew she was right; he should get down there and sort this out as soon as possible, it would only hang around his neck like an over-sized albatross otherwise.

"OK. But I won't be long then, I promise," he said, kissing her quickly. He turned to leave but stopped when he got to the doorway. "I love you," he whispered. He raised his eyebrows and smiled. "And I just *love it* when you tell me what to do."

Then he winked at her and left the room, narrowly missing the cushion that she threw at him.

***

Jack had passed the job onto Andy. Andy tried Oasis' number again. Nothing.

"Shit," he shouted to anyone who was within hearing distance. "The bastard's been ringing *all* morning and the minute I try to call *him*, he does a Reginald Perrin and disappears off the face of the sodding earth!"

"I wish *you* would bloody disappear off the face of

the sodding earth," James replied curtly, who was as fed up with his brother by now, as he was with the whole Webber/Oasis saga. "Then we'd all get some bloody peace around here!"

Andy tried hard not to look offended. He slammed the receiver down with great force and began fiddling with some papers on his desk, mildly embarrassed.

James was only two minutes older than he was, but anyone who didn't know they were twins, would think there were years between them, decades even. James looked older, dressed older and acted older. Andy pushed the papers away and looked at his brother who was typing away furiously on the keyboard of his computer. Receding and greying hair, an oversized collared shirt fresh from the seventies, teamed with blue corduroy trousers. *For chrissake, he looked more like sixty five than thirty five.*

Andy got up, left the office and went to the toilets. Turning on the cold tap he splashed his face furiously, trying to cool himself down but it didn't help. He looked up and studied his own face in the mirror.

"Good grief," he said aloud to his reflection. "Am I *really* related to that man out there?"

Andy was thirty five and *looked* thirty five. His short brown hair had flattened at the front, so he rubbed some water between his palms and ran his fingers through it several times to make it stand up. His eyes were a soft green and his chin had just the desired amount of stubble on it. Not the 'hipster' look that all the younger guys were sporting nowadays, he hated that look. No, he preferred the classic 'Beckham' look.

Andy had had all the girlfriends when he and James had been growing up - that was just the way it had always been, right up until eight months ago anyway. For eight long months now there had been no girlfriends and Andy had actually surprised himself to realise that he quite liked it like that. No more hassles. Bliss. There *had* been Susie. That was until she had found out about Rachael and so had promptly slashed every item in his wardrobe before doing a mini bunny-boiler 'show' with his mate's daughter's hamster, that he had happened to be looking after at the time. Then there had been Michelle... until she found out about Joanna and camped outside his front door all night. She had stayed there half the morning too, until he let her in, only for her to beat the crap out of Jules, who had been moving from his bed to the wardrobe for most of the night, every time she thought she heard a noise downstairs. He had decided he'd had enough of the lot of them and he wasn't going back there again for a very long time. Samantha had been the last in his huge string of muddled 'relationships' and the only one that he still thought about. She had been just about the most perfect girlfriend he had ever had, and he had blown it big style. He was embarrassed thinking about it. He had used her terribly, only seeing her when it suited him, and shagging just about anyone else he could at the same time, he had lost the only girl who had ever really meant anything to him.

His mobile buzzed in his trouser pocket and he snatched it up instantly. He knew who it would be. Thoughts of Charlie began to fill his head but he tried to blank them before opening the text message, reading the lewd contents and hating himself for smiling at it. Fiddling with the collar on his crisp, white shirt and straightening his purple silk tie, he took several deep breaths and returned to the office.

When he got there, Tom had arrived and was in a deep and animated conversation with Jack. Keeping his head down, Andy made a beeline for his desk and resolved to get on with his work quickly, so that he could clear off home as soon as was physically possible.

CHAPTER 3

Jack looked at his watch. Ten minutes until the raucous entertainment would begin again. He could hardly believe that Saturday had arrived already. His thoughts drifted back to last Saturday night, when he had become overly familiar with Sue... for the fifth weekend running. Cheryl had given him a look that had said something along the lines of *'If you're falling for her, mate, I'll cut off your piddly little appendage and shove it up your goddamn arse!'* before walking past him and into a spare room with Jackie's husband, Rob. He shuddered slightly as the memory washed freshly over him, before allowing his thoughts to return to Sue.

He liked Sue. In fact he more than liked Sue. He dreamed of being with Sue all the time, spending endless days wrapped in her arms and rodgering her stupid like an over-testosteroned teenager. He knew that would be breaking all the rules, but you can't be in control when the signals from the brain to the todger decide to divert via the heart, he reasoned. But Jack knew only too well that if he and Sue chose to become *overly familiar* again tonight, then his feelings for her might become all too obvious to everyone else in the group – if they hadn't already. Sue's husband, Alan, generally tended to be on another planet altogether and seldom paid any attention to whom his wife was currently cavorting with, so there were no problems there. No, the only problem he could see was Cheryl. That woman didn't miss a trick. Especially after the 'look' last week.

"For the third time, Jack, DID YOU PUT THE FUCKING PRINGLES OUT?'"

Cheryl was shouting with a face so flustered that he momentarily wondered if she would have a seizure. *Would she ever treat him with the respect that he wanted and deserved? Probably not.*

"Yes! They're with the cheese sticks in the front room."

Hearing the kitchen door slam loudly behind him, he turned quickly to follow her.

"So... um... are we all ready then?"

Cheryl turned to face him, her honey-blonde hair falling softly around her shoulders as she tilted her head and smiled at him. She looked beautiful tonight he had to admit, in her pale pink, low cut top and her 'just a tad expensive' ripped designer jeans that clung to her every curve. He was sure they were meant for teenagers but he quickly removed that thought.

"Yes, babe, all ready."

How could she do that, he wondered? She had the ability to turn from demon to saint within seconds and he knew that he would never quite understand it or even want to. She smiled at him; the picture of tranquillity as she walked across the room and pecked him on the cheek. She seemed to glisten and gleam somehow, to sparkle and shimmer as though an inner sunbeam was radiating from her very being.

Jack found his arms instinctively encircling her, as she leant heavily into his chest. He closed his eyes and began to stroke her silky hair. He *did* love Cheryl, he knew that. And he knew that she loved him too. But if he truly loved her, then why did vivid images of Sue, straddled across him in her birthday suit, constantly flood his mind?

Most people would question their love regardless if they really knew what went on in their house on a Saturday night. People wouldn't understand, he thought. When Cheryl had first mentioned the idea of a swinging club to him, he hadn't understood himself. He had been momentarily horrified. But then they had talked about it in length and Cheryl had explained how she believed that it could 'enrich' their marriage. Whilst they would be sharing their bodies with other people, she had said, it would be open; no secrets, no lies. It would be in *their* home with *their* rules, with the same couples each weekend and there would be no cause for jealousy because they would *know* that they loved only each other. The arrangement was purely physical, she had said, and all parties were consenting, what could possibly go wrong? Jack had thought about it for a while (but not for long) before deciding that this was probably most men's dream come true. Certainly his, he quickly realised. A week later they had advertised on the internet as discreetly as was humanly possible, for couples who lived locally and felt the same way, and stopped when they had found half a dozen other couples.

And so the club was formed. For two and a half years now they had been slipping onto assorted mattresses in assorted rooms, with assorted people and it had *never* been problematic in all that time. Until now. *You weren't supposed to become attached. You weren't supposed to fall in love with one of them and think about them morning, noon and night. It was breaking the rules that they had made a long time ago. It was sticking two fingers up and saying, 'Oh well, love, what the fuck did you expect? And hey... it was your idea anyway!'*

There was nothing else for it. He would have to be a man and fight it. *Hey, they're only feelings after all,* he told himself. *There's five other women walking into this house in a couple of minutes and you've slept with them all countless times. Where's the problem? Just cast your eyes in the direction of the others and make out Sue isn't even there.*

Suddenly the doorbell rang and Jack rushed to the toilet, leaving Cheryl alone to answer it.

CHAPTER 4

The cork hit the ceiling with a loud bang and Angela burst out laughing as Tom grabbed the champagne glasses and began expertly pouring the golden, bubbly liquid into them.

"Cheers, Angel," he said, handing her a glass. "Happy anniversary. Six years. Unbelievable."

She clinked her glass against his and took a sip, enjoying the fizzy coldness on her tongue.

"I've got something for you," she smiled.

Tom downed his entire glass, topped them both back up and then turned to her, raising his eyebrows. "Promises, promises."

"Hey, you know what I meant." She laughed and narrowed her eyes at him and then walked over to the walnut cabinet in the corner of the living room. There, she retrieved a small package and then sank back onto the huge cream sofa next to Tom.

"Go on, open it."

He looked at her with boyish excitement on his face and began to unwrap the small present.

"You shouldn't have, I didn't think we were buying anything."

He opened the box and was momentarily speechless. It was the watch he had been looking at for the last two months through the window of 'Jacques', the jewellers in town.

"Angel? What the hell? I've been staring at this thing for months! I swear, that's crazy!"

"Really? Wow I'm so good." She smiled and downed the rest of her glass. She had known of course. Jacques had tipped her off when she had gone in a couple of weeks ago for some ideas.

"I take it you're pleased then?"

"Babe, I'm thrilled. I love it!"

Angela smiled as he discarded his old TAG Heuer watch and took the new steel Breitling one from its black, leather box. He fiddled with the clasp and put it straight on, holding his arm out and admiring its beauty.

"And that's meant to be for *best*," she laughed.

"Hey, every day with you is *best*," he grinned, pulling her closer to him and kissing her passionately on the lips.

Angela already knew what Tom had bought for her. She had found it a couple of weeks ago in the study inside the bottom drawer of his desk. It had been tucked right back behind some letters she had been looking for. She knew that she shouldn't have opened the box but the urge had been too strong and she had picked up the tiny blue ring box and taken a peek there and then. Inside was a gold band with six pink rubies set into it. She had only intended to take a quick glance and put it straight back but the rubies had held her gaze for an age. Finally, unable to restrain herself any longer, she had slipped it from the box and tried it on. It had fitted perfectly. She loved Tom so much; he always got it just right. As she finally returned it to its box, she noticed the tiny engraving on the inside. '6 xxx'.

With tremendous guilt washing over her, she had quickly put the ring back, re-covered it over with the letters and tried to forget all about it. So where was it now, she wondered? Maybe he was waiting for the right moment, but you couldn't get more 'right' than now, surely?

"Hey, Angel," he said, cupping her face with his smooth hands, "fancy finishing this bottle upstairs?"

Angela smiled. She loved being wrong.

CHAPTER 5

Andy turned his key in the lock and opened the door. It was a nice apartment; quite the 'Batchelor Pad.' James had moved into one first and Andy been so taken with it when he had visited, that he had made James promise that as soon as another became available, he would let him know. He hadn't had to wait long. Two months later James gave him the good news and helped Andy move in the following week. Andy had wished that it hadn't been quite so close to his brother's apartment (immediately above it), but they had promised to keep out of each other's hair and had amazingly stuck to it. Working with each other was quite enough brotherly bonding for either of them, they had agreed. Andy loved it here. Already beautifully furnished when he had moved in, he hadn't had to do any decorating at all. OK, it was pretty expensive living this close to the town but the fact that he was so close to all the local amenities, coupled with the amazing view of the Old Abbey and its surrounding land, alone made it worth it. And anyway he didn't have anything else to spend his money on. He had lost count of how many girls he had brought back here in the two years he had now been here. He had kept it immaculate for that very reason. Lynn, the cleaner was worth every single penny that he paid her, and more. No Mandy, Carol or Samantha (oh, Samantha) was going to be impressed if they were constantly tripping over skid-marked boxers every time they went to the loo. Oh no, he wasn't that stupid. And whilst he had tired of the women in his life, he hadn't tired of having a spotless flat, so Lynn the cleaner had been kept on regardless of his recent lack of lady friends.

After taking his coat off and tossing it onto the sofa, Andy walked into the kitchen and pulled a plate from the cupboard. He was starving. Starving and knackered. Work had been hectic all week and judging from the amount still sitting in his inbox, next week wasn't going to be any easier.

Quickly tipping the Chinese from its foil box and onto the plate with one hand, he grabbed some cutlery from one of the drawers with the other and then made his way back into the lounge area. He sat himself down in front of his new 55" flat screen TV and looked at the time. Eight o'clock. Eight o'clock on a Saturday night and all he had going on was the television! He was too tired to go anywhere anyway, even if he did have somewhere to go... which he didn't.

But then there was Charlie. He knew he couldn't stop Charlie from breaking into his thoughts no matter how hard he tried. He thought about Charlie's deep, piercing brown eyes and the wicked sense of humour that they shared. The unexpected feelings for Charlie mocked and confused him. *Where had they come from?*

He and Charlie had met three months ago at a mutual friend's wedding. They had been placed next to each other at the reception, on 'Table 9'. After a lot of laughs (mainly at the expense of the other guests) and a lot to drink, they had discovered how much they had in common. As the day came to an end, Andy assumed that their paths would never cross again, but unbeknown to him at the time, Charlie had managed to wangle his mobile number off the best man, and had rung Andy several times since to arrange a night out. Andy had gone too, eventually, and they had had a great time, but it was only last week when they had met for the third time, that he had found out how Charlie *really* felt about him. He had felt completely foolish for not realising that Charlie's feelings for him were not platonic. He had got so used to blocking out any sexual motive on his part that it was a shock to realise, when he stopped to think about it, that he actually felt the same way. He had tried everything to get his head straight but the constant flow of late night phone calls and innuendo-filled text messages had excited him more than he cared to admit and he knew that they would meet up yet again. It was as plain as the nose on his face.

Flicking repetitively through the channels with one hand and shovelling forkfuls of greasy Chinese food into his mouth with the other, he knew he was hooked. He had invited Charlie here, to his home, Monday night for a bite to eat. *Actually, hadn't he said 'supper'? Shit. Supper? What did he do that for?*

"What the hell constitutes a supper?" he asked

himself aloud, suddenly panicked. *Cheese and biscuits? Or would a cooked meal be expected?* Suddenly feeling replete, he walked into the kitchen and scraped the rest of his Chinese take-away into the bin.

***

Washing up at the sink, James could hear his brother in the apartment above him, swearing for the third time in thirty seconds. *What the hell could be wrong*? James knew he couldn't have burnt his dinner because he had seen him out of his front room window twenty minutes ago, carrying something in a brown paper bag that definitely resembled a take-away. Again. Checking that the front door and windows were locked, James made his way slowly into the bathroom and shut the door. Once in there, he shaved, washed and sprayed himself liberally with the new body spray he had bought at the local supermarket earlier that day.

"ARE YOU COMING OR WHAT?" shouted the voice from the bedroom on the other side of the bathroom wall.

James sighed and looked at his tired and grey reflection in the bathroom mirror and wondered what on earth he was doing; Charlie was going to do nothing but bring chaos into his wonderfully comatose life, and he knew it.

"Yes, I'm coming, Charlie," he mumbled defeatedly. "Keep your wig on!"

CHAPTER 6

"More wine anyone?" Cheryl did her usual parade of the living room, with a bottle of white in one hand and a bottle of red in the other. "Or are you sticking to Prosecco, Sue?"

Jack had been putting off a trip to the bathroom for fifteen minutes now for fear of being followed by Sue. He was desperate to relieve himself but unfortunately, since seeing how Sue was dressed tonight, it was in more ways than one. As usual she looked amazing. Her shiny brown hair bounced perfectly on her shoulders and her green eyes were hypnotic as always. She wore a pair of low cut, faded jeans and a white see-through top with a white, lacy bra visible underneath. He wished just for once that she would turn up in an old parka and wellington boots, but even then he thought, thoroughly frustrated now, she would still look stunning.

She had arrived with Alan at the same time as the others, so it had been easy to do as he had planned and avoid all eye contact with her... in the beginning at least. Now though, two hours later, it wasn't that simple. He could see from the corner of his eye that she was trying to catch his attention at every possible moment.

Apart from that, the evening had started the same way it started every Saturday. Cheryl clucked around everyone, handing out the nibbles and alcohol that had been brought along and making sure that everyone was happy. He knew the routine well. Soon everyone would start pairing up and eventually find a room in the house where they could be alone. There had never been any group sex in the house and Jack thought it unlikely that there ever would be. Were they the only swinging group to behave that way, he suddenly wondered? Jack and Cheryl's bedroom was the only room in the house that was out of bounds on 'Swinger's Night'. All other rooms that were available for a not so discreet lust-up, had a sheeted mattress specially placed on the floor and a covered duvet spread out on top of it. Cheryl being Cheryl, liked everyone to be as comfortable as possible.

Jack glanced at his phone and noticed with surprise that he had been talking to Amy, Jackie and Rob, for nearly an hour now. The red wine he had been guzzling at a ridiculous speed since eight o'clock, had long since gone to his head and he realised that if he didn't get to the bathroom within the next few minutes, there could be an embarrassing repeat performance of the 2017 Christmas work's do. Making his excuses, he quickly left the room and ran up the stairs three at a time to the bathroom. The relief was instant and he groaned as the painful pressure on his bladder began to lift.

"Hey! What's with the silent treatment?" Sue whispered, standing behind him.

Jack's heart stopped for an instant before re-starting seconds later at double-speed. As Sue locked the door behind her, Jack turned around quickly before realising a second too late that his manhood was on full display and that he was now peeing on the floor. He felt stupidly embarrassed and hastily tried to shove himself back into his boxers.

"What are you *doing*?" he hissed, incredulously. He might have slept with this woman countless times, but to just follow him and walk in while he was having a pee was an entirely different matter.

"I wanted to see what you were doing," she replied, giggling now and holding onto the bathroom radiator to steady herself.

"Well what do people normally do when they go to the bathroom?" he answered, dumbfounded. *Jeez, what the hell would Cheryl say if she walked in now?*

Sue giggled again; the effects of her 'Prosecco-swigging' all too obvious.

"Well now," she cooed, sashaying closer towards him, "I suppose that sort of depends on who you go to the bathroom with, doesn't it?" Her hungry eyes trailed over the now wet bulge of his boxers and he quickly yanked his jeans back up.

OK. This was it. His speech had been mentally prepared for use in an emergency situation such as this and he knew that right now it was time to download and deliver it.

"Sue... the thing is, we've..."

At that moment Jack's legs gave way and a sharp blow

to the back of his head quickly followed, leaving him lying on his back on the bathroom floor, with his head bent forwards, forcing his chin onto his chest. He opened his eyes and realised that the back of his neck was pushed against the base of the toilet. This soon became irrelevant when seconds later a sharp pain began coursing down his spine.

"What the...?" Jack tried to move his legs but couldn't. Sue had clamped herself down heavily on top of them and showed no immediate signs of moving.

"Shit! If I'd have known that yanking your jeans back down would nearly kill you I'd have got you to change your will first," she giggled.

"You... you're trying to tell me," he uttered in disbelief, "that the reason I'm in this... this *position* is because you *tried* to yank my jeans down?" He cast his gaze southwards. "Oh... you *did* yank my jeans down!"

He realised it was now or never. He would say what he had to say and she would damn well listen to him.

"Sue, listen to me right now. You know I think the world of you... OK, I *more* than think the world of you... but..." The sharp pain continued to shoot down his back but he carried on regardless. "But you know, these feelings, our feelings, they've gone way beyond what they should have. I'm flattered if you feel the same and you know as well as I do that if... SUE! Sue, what are you doing? *Aaahh aaaahhhhhhhh!*"

A small smile began at the corners of Jack's mouth

and then spread rapidly across his entire face. The pain had vanished.

***

Cheryl poured herself and Rob another glass of Malbec, plonked her full glass into his spare hand, winked at him and told him that she would be back 'in a jiffy'. Walking from the room with as much grace as she could muster for somebody who was half cut and bursting for the loo at the same time, she made her way to the downstairs toilet. As she got there she witnessed Alan's pale blue shirt sleeve as it disappeared behind its door a second later.

"Damn!" she muttered, annoyed at the thought of having to dash upstairs to relieve herself.

As she reached the top of the staircase, deep groans that sounded very much like Jack's, drifted across the landing and into her line of sound.

"Bloody hell!" she screeched in a high-pitched voice from the other side of the bathroom door. "You bunged up *again,* Jacky-Boy?" Hearing only the sound of Jack's persistent groaning, she rapped heavily on the door. "The fibre sachets are in the left hand side of the cabinet, you dozy old sod! I told you to take one earlier, you never listen to me!"

And then turning around quickly, she ran to the last place left that she knew would be available to pee in. Their en-suite shower room.

CHAPTER 7

Jessie kissed her mother and ran off into her classroom without looking back. The rain poured down heavily, mirroring the feeling inside Angela's chest. She hated September. It was the month that stole the summer. It was the month when the cruel world had taken her parents from her and killed them in a car crash. She hated the red and gold leaves that brought with them each year the painful memory of her parent's car overturned, as more and more of those hateful leaves fell slowly down on top of their temporary metal grave. This September's pain had doubled. Jess had started school and a new sense of loss was merging with the old one. One week of classroom life and already her five year old baby had changed. September had changed her into a school-girl. Yes, once again September had stolen something from her and changed her life and she hated September all the more for it.

Angela climbed back into the car and fingered her soaking wet hair. The rain was driving down even faster now. She gazed out of the window and focused on the rain soaked parents running to their cars. Despite the sadness inside her, her thoughts drifted to Tom. *Why hadn't he given her the ring?* When Saturday night had become Sunday morning, she thought that he must have simply forgotten, after all they had been busy that night and had had other 'more important' things on their minds. But by the time Sunday evening had arrived and there was still no sign of it, she was itching to ask him if he had forgotten something. Desperate to drop a few hints, she kept having to remind herself that she wasn't supposed to know about it in the first place. How could she let on without exposing herself as a snoop?

Tom had left for work early this morning, no different to any other Monday morning, and she had darted into the study the moment his car had pulled out of the driveway. She had opened the drawer, pulled out the letters and saw nothing. No box. No ring. Confused, she had slammed the drawer shut and then realised that maybe he was planning on giving it to her tonight instead. *Talk about clutching at straws. What was she? Stupid? Today was her parent's memorial and he wasn't exactly going to give her the ring today, was he? Or maybe he was; maybe he thought it would cheer her up?* He *had* seemed a bit preoccupied this morning, she had to admit. Thoroughly fed up, the thought of going home depressed her further. She would only end up searching the entire house for the ring and that would be insane. No, she would much rather wander around town for a bit, even if the rain clouds weren't showing any signs of stopping just yet.

Finally reaching the town centre, Angela parked up and clambered out into the elements. It had eased off slightly now but she pulled out her black umbrella regardless and headed off in the direction of the dry cleaners. Tom had asked her to collect two of his suits that had now been waiting patiently for their owner for over three weeks.

She opened the door and a little bell rang. A young girl of about sixteen years of age appeared from around the back and walked up to the counter. She was chewing gum loudly. Angela fumbled around in her purse looking for the ticket as the girl tapped her fingers impatiently on the counter. Finally finding it, she handed it over to the girl who ran her eyes over it lazily before disappearing around the back again.

"There you go," she said, still chewing, as she came back into the shop and folded the bagged-up suits in half. "Oh, and this was in one of the pockets. Dunno whevver it's important or not."

Angela peered at the slip of paper that the girl had given her. It was some sort of receipt, so she put it inside her purse and thanked her. Stepping back outside into the grey, wet day, she deliberated over whether it would be right to go shopping today. Shouldn't she be slopping around at home all day crying her eyes out? After all that's what she usually did on the twelfth of September, wasn't it? No, she needed to be outside today, to feel free; not to be trapped in four walls with timeless grief and memories suffocating her.

Feeling positive for the first time that day, Angela headed for the high street shops, thinking that she might even call into the office later and hijack Tom for lunch. Now there was an idea. They hadn't done lunch in months.

***

Maxine closed the door to Tom's office and then walked the ten feet or so to her own desk. It sat in the spacious open plan office that she shared with Jack, James and Andy, except while their desks were cluttered, hers was clean and organised.

Her stomach rumbled for the fifth time that day and she remembered that she had skipped breakfast this morning and was now paying the price for it. She would have to eat something soon. She had a banana in her drawer but she couldn't for the life of her think why she had bothered bringing it. She knew she wouldn't eat it; she had tried eating them before, but in an office full of men it was impossible. Every time the banana went to her lips, all eyes became fixed on her and all mouths dropped open. She couldn't bear to go through the humiliation again. She glanced at her watch. *Thank goodness it was only an hour until lunchtime.*

Maxine became aware of someone approaching her desk. It was Jack. She had already noticed that he looked particularly smart today and instead of his usual mismatched jackets and trousers, he wore a black suit and tie, with a crisp white shirt. He smirked at her as he licked his finger and ran it along one of his eyebrows. He positioned his fingers to look like a gun and pointed it towards her.

"Bond. James Bond!" he said in his most serious Daniel Craig voice.

"Off. Piss Off!" Maxine replied, before dropping her eyes back down to her work.

Jack feigned offence by pulling an imaginary dagger from his chest and groaning. "What's up with you, heartbreaker? Bad weekend?"

Feeling guilty she looked back up at him and smiled warmly to make amends. "Yeah, I'm sorry, Jack, bad weekend."

"No worries, I..."

Jack stopped as Maxine's mobile buzzed on her desk and she covered the screen quickly with her hand to hide the incoming message.

"Look sorry, Jack, we'll speak later, yeah?"

"Oh... yeah sure, no probs. But I see you got your mobile screen fixed, blondie. It looks good."

"Hey? Oh yeah," she replied, trying to hide the screen even more. "Um... sorry Jack, I'll get the one you lent me back to you tomorrow. It was a lifesaver, thanks so much."

"Nah, no problem, keep it in case you ever need a backup, I've got two others at home."

Maxine smiled weakly and turned away, leaving Jack to walk back to his desk feeling not dissimilar to one of those girls he had driven past on a Sunday morning with their party clothes still on. He tried to remember the name for it. *Wasn't it the 'walk of shame'?*

Jack flopped back down into his chair and fiddled with some paper clips that sat idly in a box in front of him. He fancied Maxine, sure. He would admit that, no problem. OK, so on the scale of 'Sue' she came nowhere near, but she was pretty, blonde, with amazing legs and tits – of course he imagined what she wore underneath her duvet at night. Fighting thoughts of Saturday night in the bathroom with Sue, he watched Maxine grinning at her phone like a love-struck teenager. She was excitedly bashing out a reply and pushing her blonde bob behind her ear while trying not to giggle. He scanned the office quickly. Andy was furiously tapping away at his keyboard while James was on a heated call with a customer. Jack turned his head and looked back at Maxine. He had seen the name 'Tom' flash up on her phone when the message had come through – she hadn't covered the screen as quickly as she thought she had. He frowned. *He hadn't known that Maxine had a boyfriend. She hadn't mentioned it as she had in the past when there had been any potential suitor on the scene.*

Feeling uneasy, he watched her a little more. He hoped he was wrong but somehow he didn't think he would be. It would take only a few seconds to confirm his suspicion. Grabbing a letter off his desk he stood up, walked towards Tom's office and very quickly knocked twice before walking straight in. Tom quickly dropped his mobile to his desk and looked up awkwardly.

"Everything OK? he asked.

"Yeah," Jack replied, disappointed at the sudden

confirmation before him. "Just wondered if you fancied a cuppa.

CHAPTER 8

The sharp, cold wind whipped Angela's face as she pulled her coat sleeve up with a gloved hand and glanced at her watch. 11.45; a bit too early to drag Tom to lunch yet, but even so, she was wet and cold and needed to sit down somewhere warm. And she wasn't going home.

Nicco's as usual, was warm and serene. Only the hushed tones of friendly chatter could be heard from the few people inside. The calm ambience, helped along by the restaurant's dim lighting, seemed out of place with the hustle and bustle of town life outside its walls. Tom had proposed to her in this little Italian restaurant that was only a two minute walk from his office, and it had been their special place ever since. They didn't get to eat here very often nowadays; once Jessie had come along it had grown more and more difficult to find the time. Today though they would eat here again, she decided.

Finding a table tucked slightly away, she sat down and looked for Nicco but there was no sign of him. She hadn't seen him for a good year now and she felt a pang of disappointment at the prospect of another year passing before she might again. He was a family friend and she had missed seeing him, laughing with him and sharing news. And he always talked about her parents, which she loved. Within moments, a young Italian waiter that she didn't recognise appeared at her side smiling.

"Buongiorno signora, may I take your order please?" he asked, in a gentle voice.

She ordered a black coffee and took off her coat, scarf and gloves, relaxing herself as he disappeared from view. She took the interim to view the internal deco of the place for what must have been the twentieth time in her life. Apart from a fresh lick of paint every couple of years, it hadn't changed in all the time she had known it. The same black and white pictures, most of them old movie posters of Hollywood classics, hung only inches apart from each other, adorned the walls. In the little alcove where she was seated, Gene Kelly splashed in his famous 'lamp post' scene alongside a poster of David Niven, Cary Grant and Loretta Young in The Bishop's Wife. She looked for her favourite and there it was beaming down at her from its black frame; James Stewart and Donna Reed in an original movie poster from Frank Capra's 'It's A Wonderful Life.' That film could lift her spirits on even the dullest of days. Even today maybe.

At that moment a bell rang and she looked across to see one of the waiters walk towards the kitchen to collect someone's food order. When he came out with the two plates and placed them in front of a couple seated at the table next to hers, she was sorely tempted to shout out, 'Every time a bell rings, an angel gets his wings!' but decided that if they didn't share her penchant for Jimmy Stewart films, the sentiment would be lost on them and they might just think she was deranged.

The good looking waiter brought the black coffee to the table and placed it down in front of her.

"Thank you. Oh, and I need a table for two in about an hour, is that possible?"

He raised his eyebrows, smiled at her and slowly waved his pencil around the room.

"This will be no problemo, Signora, as you can see we are not busy today, so anything is possible."

Feeling pleased with herself, not only for her idea of lunch but also for her good fortune in it being so quiet in Nicco's today, she picked up her coffee and took a sip of the strong, hot liquid. It slid down her throat smoothly, warming every fibre of her. This was truly the first time today that she had felt relaxed; not just in the physical sense, but mentally and emotionally as well. She closed her eyes for a few seconds and let the gentle hum of conversation around her and the dull clinking from the kitchen, wash over her. This was all the therapy in the world that she needed. She could quite happily sit here like this forever.

A new voice edged itself into her mind, joining the others. It was a light, giggly voice that had just arrived from the bitter cold outside. She heard the door slam shut. A happy voice. A happy voice that belonged to a happy person; someone like herself maybe who was only too glad to be entering the warmth and comfort of Nicco's. Another voice joined it, but it was so quiet that she could only just make out that it was male. Angela kept her eyes closed and carried on taking in the relaxing smells and sounds around her, contented to let them continue washing over her. This was such a nice place, she thought drowsily. Such happy voices. Yes, this was a place for happy voices that belonged to happy people, who had happy lives.

"Signora, you OK, signora?"

Angela opened her eyes only to find the handsome Italian waiter's face inches away from her own. The force in which she jumped in her seat, knocked over her cup and its entire cold contents all over the tabletop, which then began dripping onto her jeans. The waiter began what Angela could only assume was apologising profusely in Italian, whilst grabbing handfuls of paper serviettes from an empty neighbouring table and desperately mopping up the spillage. He pushed some of them into Angela's hands, so that she could tackle her own legs.

"Mi dispiace, mi dispiace. Non l'ho fatto apposta!"

"Please, please, don't worry about it, it was completely my fault." Angela felt stupid and embarrassed. The coffee on her legs felt very cold. "I must have fallen asleep. I'm so sorry." Her watch said 12.10. She had been out cold for a good twenty minutes.

"Signora, I bring you another coffee, this is no problem, we pay," and with that he scurried into the kitchen, muttering more Italian anguish under his breath.

Angela finished mopping at her jeans and then, throwing the wet serviettes onto the table, leant back into her seat and let out a small sigh.

A light giggly voice, the very same one that she remembered hearing before she had fallen asleep, drifted across the restaurant to her table again, and she instinctively turned around this time to see where it was coming from.

Although the lighting was dim and Angela could only see the side of the girl's face, she could tell that this female was two things; young and beautiful. Angela felt compelled to watch her for a few more moments. The girl was throwing her head back and giggling as she pushed her blonde hair behind her ears. *Wasn't it Maxine from the office? It certainly looked like her. No, it couldn't be.*

Angela strained her neck for a better look. Maxine had certainly never looked like this whenever Angela had gone into the office to see Tom. If anything, she had always thought Maxine as a cool and sulky girl.

"Another two coffees please, Paolo," came the man's voice next to her, "then we really must go."

Angela moved her head sharply to take a look for the first time at the man sitting opposite the blonde beauty. It was Tom! And the girl *was* Maxine after all. Angela smiled. Should she just go over to them or sneak up behind him and put her hands over his eyes? She could imagine Maxine laughing as he tried to guess who had temporarily blinded him.

Before Angela had a chance to get up from her seat, Tom had reached into the inside pocket of his suit jacket and pulled out the blue box that Angela recognised instantly as the one she had seen in his study. He was smiling and holding it out towards Maxine, who in return and with a flushed face, took it from him.

For a few seconds Angela felt paralysed. Her lips parted in disbelief and her heart thumped so violently inside her chest that she thought it would kill her. It wasn't long before the numbness of her body was replaced by involuntary shuddering of disbelief and incomprehension. *There was no way this could be real, no way this could be really happening*. Angela felt her face crumpling, her mouth turning dry and a sickness in the pit of her stomach that was threatening to erupt out of her. She tore her eyes away from the scene but within a couple of seconds they had pulled themselves back, needing confirmation that this wasn't a bad dream. Her breathing was now short and heavy and she was acutely aware of the bile rising up into her throat and the sudden urge to throw up right here in the restaurant. She fought it and shrank back into her seat, not wanting to be seen. Within a few seconds Angela shifted slightly forward again, just in time to see Maxine deftly open the box. Tom took the box back from her and plucked out the beautiful ruby ring, turning it around in his fingers a couple of times before sliding it with ease onto Maxine's dress ring finger.

"I told you I'd get you something special," he beamed, oblivious to anyone else around them. "Six rubies for six special months."

CHAPTER 9

Andy was, to put it mildly, crapping himself. He had been all day. He had spent the morning desperately trying to clear some of the backlog that had been nestled cosily (almost to the point of being comatose) in his 'in tray' since last Thursday but every time he managed to settle down and focus on something, his mobile would buzz and it would be Charlie again.

The text that came through just before lunch had wholeheartedly promised him a night that he would never forget. Subsequently his lunchtime break had been spent rushing around Tesco trying to find something more suitable for 'supper' than his previously ridiculous idea of cheese and biscuits. He had then spent the entire afternoon trying to banish all scenarios of fucking up the food, from his mind. However, no matter what he tried to think about, images of serving up charcoaled chicken on a bed of congealed rice to Charlie, with flames licking the walls of a smoke-filled kitchen behind them, kept creeping their way into his already highly panicked brain.

Andy looked nervously at his watch. Five to eight. He didn't know whether it was nerves or excitement. *Maybe it was both?* He cast a quick, final glance around the room to check for absolute flawlessness.

"Fuck, fuck, fuck!" he stammered in disbelief.

In the far corner of the room, he caught sight of a

stray clump of soggy tissues hanging out from behind one of the sofa cushions. He grimaced and rushed over to pick it up between his thumb and forefinger before depositing it into the bin.

"Fuck me!" he scolded himself out loud. "The door's about to go any second now and I've got wank rag hanging out of my sofa! Stupid prick!"

This only served to send Andy into an even higher state of panic as he realised why the tissue was there in the first place. Racing as quickly as he could, he reached the television stand and grabbed his ebay collection of pornographic DVDs with both hands and shoved them under the sofa, just as the doorbell rang.

***

The noise from upstairs had made James stir for the fifth time that evening. He shifted in his armchair trying to get comfortable but to no avail. *Why was he so shattered anyway? It was only Monday for chrissake and he hadn't exactly been run off his feet at work today.*

Tom had phoned up in the morning to say that he wouldn't be in and probably wouldn't be back for a few days. He had told James that he had some important things to take care of and that Jack would be in charge while he was away. That didn't make any difference to the amount of work that he himself had to get through this week but he had noticed that Andy had mounds of paperwork sitting on his desk and throughout the day it had stayed much the same size. As James dealt primarily with new claims (and for the last week there had been a distinct lack of them) and Andy more with the ongoing cases (and for the last week there had been a distinct *increase* in people wanting to know '*When the fuck am I going to get my money, arsehole?*'), he guessed this was the reason why. Whilst everyone in the office dealt with their own sections, it had always been the office etiquette to muck in and help each other out whenever possible. If someone looked snowed under and you had jack shit to do – bar seeing how far you could ping an elastic band across the office (bonus points for catching someone in the face and nearly taking their eye out), then of course you would help them. Tom had made sure they all knew each other's jobs inside out anyway, for that very reason. In an office as small as theirs it only took one person to be off ill for any longer than a few days and all hell would break loose. But this was different; *why wasn't Andy wasn't working his balls off to plough through as much of his own backlog as possible? If Andy couldn't be arsed to help himself then why should James give a monkey's gonad?* Every time James had looked over towards his brother, Andy had been staring blankly at the pile of paper on his desk. Under those circumstances, James couldn't see why he should help him out at all. *Bollocks to that on a Monday!* Hence his easy day.

James looked at the clock. Five past ten. *What the*

hell was going on up in Andy's apartment anyway? The noise was really starting to piss him off so he tried his old trick of banging the broom handle against his living room ceiling three times. He waited. Silence.

Just as James reached the bathroom to get ready for bed, the noise started up again. Loud voices and laughter, along with a screeching cat. *How was anyone supposed to sleep with that racket going on?* There was only one thing for it, he decided. He would give it another half an hour and then he would go up there himself. This was late for him and no one was going to stop him getting his sleep.

***

Andy smiled nervously at Charlie as they sat together on the sofa like a couple of kids. He couldn't believe this was happening. Everything had been going well and the likelihood of anything going tits up now seemed as likely as the din in the flat next door to him suddenly subsiding. He had even gone and knocked on their door himself a while back and asked his new neighbours if they could please quieten down (he had thought the lie about a young nephew staying overnight with him might have helped), but all he had got in return was a mouthful of abuse and the door slammed in his face. He hoped James didn't think the noise was coming from *his* apartment.

Regardless of the racket next door, in the last hour

Andy and Charlie had become so engrossed in their conversation that they were almost oblivious to anything now other than each other's childhood memories. The food had turned out perfectly too (even if he did say so himself). He had remembered to chill the wine and clean the bathroom but he hadn't changed the sheets on the bed. He didn't have to; he knew that nothing was going to happen in that department, not with Charlie, not tonight and not ever. Yet here they were, dined, wined (just finishing off the second bottle) and unable to take their eyes off each other.

Charlie had kept him captivated for the entire evening and, when the wine had started to take effect, had had him in stitches. Did that mean Charlie could only make him laugh when he was intoxicated? They *had* been drunk at the wedding when they had first met. And they *had* drunk quite a bit when they had met up twice since.

Moving to the floor ten minutes later, they lay on the black rug that Andy had bought only two months ago. He realised that he had let Charlie talk for most of the evening, and while he had listened (or had he hung on?) to every word, laughed in all the right places and genuinely enjoyed the company, he hadn't given much back in terms of actual conversation.

Doing a quick memory scan, he decided to balance the scales with a detailed account of James' seventh birthday party. Every time the children started to sing Happy Birthday to him, James would run from the kitchen to the bathroom with an urgent case of diarrhoea, resulting in them singing it nine times in total.

Andy laughed and clutched his aching stomach as he finished the story, relaying every last detail of James pebble dashing the kitchen floor as the children's ninth rendition of Happy Birthday slowly faded out, and all twelve small faces screwed up in horror and disgust.

"I'm sorry," he chuckled guiltily, "but that story kills me every time I tell it."

For the first time that evening, Charlie wasn't laughing with him. Andy saw that something had changed. He *felt* it. Felt it around him and inside him.

"What's wrong, did I upset you? What did I say?"

"Take me to bed," Charlie blurted out.

"What?" Andy stared back, his jaw dropping open at the completely unexpected request. He laughed nervously. "No way... I..."

"Take me to bed, Andy," Charlie said again, reaching out for one of his hands and gently stroking it. "Please?"

"I can't." Andy replied, so quietly that he thought he could barely hear the words himself.

"What do you mean, you *can't*?" Charlie looked hurt and Andy could see the deep brown eyes searching for an answer in his confused face.

"I just... *can't*."

"I don't understand. I thought you wanted to? I want to."

Andy stared at Charlie's face as it came down closer

and closer towards his, until their lips were just touching. Pinning Andy to the floor, Charlie began kissing him passionately and within what seemed like seconds, had successfully removed both of their clothes and flung them carelessly across the room.

"Shit, Charlie, STOP IT! I've never done this before..."

Charlie wasn't listening and, pulling him up by the arms in one swift movement, threw a naked Andy down onto the sofa with such force that both he and the sofa moved three foot closer to the window, leaving the previously hidden pornographic DVD collection lying scattered across the floor in full view. Charlie stopped still for a second before bending down to pick one up.

"Girl Next Door?" he read out, raising his perfectly manicured eyebrows. "Who the hell watches DVDs anymore?"

"Listen, Charlie, will you? I've never..."

Charlie picked up another, again reading the title aloud. "The Mechanic's Tale?"

"*I've never been with a man before!*" Andy shouted. He stood up and paced the floor, nervously. "I'm sorry," he continued, shaking his head slowly. He felt pathetic and awkward as he cupped his hanging genitals. "But I've *never* done anything like this before."

Charlie stared at him blankly for a second but no matter how hard he tried, he couldn't stop a small smile from breaking out onto his lips.

***

Andy stared at the ceiling, confused thoughts running through his mind. What the hell had they just done? This was wrong. *Completely* wrong. He wasn't gay for chrissake. How the hell could he be gay? He had slept with so many women that he couldn't begin to count them all, and he had never felt this way about a man before, never even *thought* about a man like this – not before Charlie had come along anyway. *What on earth had he done? How the hell had he let this happen? He had to get Charlie out of here as soon as possible and pretend that this awful event had never happened. Only then would he be able to get on with the rest of his life.*

Charlie stepped out of the bathroom and padded lightly into the bedroom, re-joining him in the bed, but Andy pulled the duvet back and swung his legs out of the other side. He was ready to end this right now (albeit a little too late).

"What are you doing?" Charlie asked, confused. Leaning over, he tried to pull Andy back into the bed.

"This is a terrible mistake... I feel sick. I'm sorry."

"Oh great, charmed I'm sure! No one's ever made me feel so good about myself."

Charlie's voice was shrill and camp – *why had he not noticed that before?*

"Come back to bed, come on," Charlie cooed. He waved his arm around the room dramatically. "We're in this wonderful bedroom, let's not waste it."

Andy stared at Charlie. Really stared at him. His dark, floppy hair hung over his pale, gaunt face like a gothic curtain across a baby's unblemished skin. Suddenly 'dark, handsome and mysterious' looked 'scary, strange and weird'. Charlie had told Andy at the wedding that he was a Professor of Art but right now Andy thought he looked more like a professor of the Dark Arts, straight from the pages of a Harry Potter book.

Andy groaned as he put his head in his hands and tried to dispel all of the images of Professor Snape that now danced around in his mind. It was true that Charlie looked 'deep' and 'dangerous'. *Maybe that had been part of the attraction? Chrissake! Now he was even more confused.* He felt his stomach churning so much now that it was all he could do to stop himself from hurling right there and then. The last thing he wanted was to hurt Charlie's feelings so he forced himself to lie back in the bed before closing his eyes and putting his head in his hands again. He had to try and figure out what to do next or at least try to make some sense of the situation.

"Look," Charlie sighed, "if it's any consolation, I was the same when it was my first time. It's confusing and..."

"First time?" Andy interrupted. "First and *last* time, Charlie. FIRST AND LAST!"

Andy pulled his aching body out of the bed again and walked into the lounge where his clothes lay.

Before he could reach them Charlie had followed him and grabbed his arm to turn him around.

"Please don't treat me like this, And, it's not fair. I know how you feel, I really do but just think about it for a moment. No one's died! It's not the end of the world! You were bi-curious, it's no biggie!"

Andy looked at the ceiling. Only minutes ago he had been with this man; shared something with him that he never thought he was capable of, and now... now he didn't know what to think, except that they were only inches apart, both naked and there seemed to be a strange sound at his front door.

"Did you hear something?"

Charlie looked bewildered and shrugged his shoulders. "I don't think so, no."

A second later Andy heard his brother's voice coming from the other side of the front door.

"Andy! Will you please be quiet! All evening I've put up with it – what are you even doing in there? I'm trying to go to sleep!"

"It's not me, it's next door!" Andy hissed but it was too late.

The door flew open and James took one uninvited step into Andy's unlocked apartment before stopping abruptly at the sight before him. Unable to stop his mouth from falling open, James stared from left to right at the two naked forms.

"*Charlie*?" James whispered. "What the... what the *hell* are you doing here?"

Charlie looked from James, to Andy, down towards his stiffening penis and then back up to James. He bit his bottom lip like a naughty schoolboy and said nothing.

James pulled his gaze away from Charlie and looked back at his brother, as the reality of the scene before him began to sink in. Dazed incomprehension was now turning into a sharp realisation.

"What the actual hell?" James asked Andy in disgust.

"It's not what you think!" Andy protested.

James ignored him and turned back to Charlie, who now looked strangely excited about the dramatic scene that was playing out before him. His dark eyes were lit up in mischief and he looked like he was about to stifle a giggle.

"What are you doing up here with my brother?" James asked bewildered.

Charlie began opening his mouth to answer but James stopped him in time with a hand in the air.

"NO. Don't answer that! It's blindingly obvious what you're doing." He had tried to ignore the fact that they were both naked but it was impossible.

Andy had now cupped his genitals in his hands but Charlie stood confidently and defiantly with his pale hands on his bony hips, without saying a word.

"I told you my brother lived directly above me. Why would you do this?" James shook his head in confusion.

"Wait... hang on a minute!" Andy spun around as he finally came up to speed. "You two KNOW each other?"

He felt a jolt that instantly killed any embarrassment he had previously felt and he moved his hands to his throbbing temples. "How the hell do you *know* each other?" he whimpered, as the world closed in around him.

Andy waited for a reply but none came. James glared at Charlie and then turned and left the apartment.

CHAPTER 10

"You're gonna be late, Jacky-Boy!" Cheryl screamed up the stairs at the top of her voice for the second time in two minutes. "Your toast is getting cold."

"Who cares, I'm the boss today remember? I deserve a lie-in," Jack shouted back downstairs to her.

Grabbing the heavy duvet with one hand he pulled it over his head, while continuing to work his manhood vigorously with the other.

Sue's perfectly heavy breasts bounced up and down on top of him, in his mind's eye. As she leaned forward they dangled joyously in his face. Jack groaned with intense pleasure, burying his head between them so that they enveloped him like a giant pair of soft, warm pillows. He was lost in that silent and special place which no man should ever be without; the cleavage. The rhythm of her slow deep stroke began to speed up – as if by magic she knew his yearning for a change in tempo to aid his climax. Jack was well aware, somewhere in the dark recesses of his conscious mind, that he had merely increased the speed of his hand on his stiff tool, but he desperately pushed this annoying realisation away.

Flicking the duvet away with a swish of his left hand, the warm offerings landed gently on his belly.

"Are you coming or what?" Cheryl shouted up the stairs impatiently.

"I certainly am, Chez," he chuckled to himself, as he reached under the pillow for the tissues. "I certainly am."

***

The shrill ringing of the telephone broke through the heavy silence that had settled around the office, like a canary at a wake. Jack had already decided that there was no way he was going to answer it again.

"What the hell is wrong with everyone today?" he shouted out into the deathly open space. "It's like working at a bloody morgue for fuck's sake! Have I missed the Dementors flying in from Hogwarts or something?" He examined the ignorant faces around him.

Maxine's usually bright and bubbly demeanour had somehow been snatched away overnight and was replaced with something heavy, dull and cold. She was barely recognisable to him as she sat slumped in her chair like an unloved rag doll. She was evidently struggling to get through each minute of the day and it was only ten o'clock. She stared at her computer screen doing nothing. Her normally sleek, shiny hair looked tatty, dull and lifeless, in tune with the depressed aura around her. Suddenly she moved, checked her mobile for the fifth time in two minutes and then, disappointed, placed it back down onto her desk to return her gaze to the computer screen. Jack carried on watching as she took a crumpled tissue from the palm of her hand, to dab her eyes with. *What on earth was wrong with her?*

Next he looked across to James. James was James (he always looked drab, grey, old and miserable) but today he had excelled himself. His suit was grey, his face was grey and he hadn't spoken one word since he had arrived at work. As for Andy, there sat the biggest transformation of them all. The normally smart, sharp Andy, sat behind his desk looking like he wanted someone to kill him. Every so often his hand would move involuntarily, as if an electric shock had coursed down his arm, making it hit out. Other than that his body seemed to have no will to move at all. Andy kept his head still as his eyes glazed over, ignoring the work in front of him. Suddenly he would blink and look around the office as if to check where he was, before returning to his previous trance-like state.

Jack realised that the phone had stopped ringing and not because it had been answered by any one of the three depressed misfits in front of him, that was for sure.

"Right, that's it!" he called out, trying to instil a modicum of authority into his deeply pissed off voice. He pushed his chair out from behind him and stood up abruptly. "You lot know that Tom's not going to be in for a few days and that I'm in charge while he's away, right? So come on, stop taking the piss! There's an office here that needs running and there's a shitload of work to do, so can we all just get on and do it, please?" Jack looked around. Not a single head looked up or indeed moved.

"James!"

Nothing.

"Helllllooo!"

Nothing.

"Fuck's sake, JAMES! You're more grey than 'Fifty Shades' at the best of times!"

Nothing.

Jack looked at the others for a reaction. He felt sure Maxine would find that funny; she always laughed at his lame jokes.

"You're more like a hundred shades and that is NOT a compliment."

Nothing.

He hated doing this but someone had to take control or absolutely nothing was going to get done today.

"Well..." he carried on regardless, "you know that I don't like acting the big 'I am' when Tom's away and I don't even use his office, I mean, I'd much rather sit out here with you guys and carry on as normal."

Nothing.

"It's probably only for a day or two. But for fuck's sake you lot, what the shite's going on? Have I missed something?"

Nothing.

"Is it Brexit?" He was sure that would raise a smile. "Because we've got months of negotiations yet before we find out if we're getting our blue passports back so let's stay cheery, eh? I say 'fuck it' myself, too much shit-shagging hassle to change it."

Silence.

The phone began to ring again. Nobody moved. Jack threw his arms out in front of him and shook his head in disbelief.

"You lot are taking the piss. Come on guys, what can I do to make things better?" he asked.

"Answer the phone!" James replied.

★★★

Jack spun himself around in Tom's executive leather chair. He felt slightly guilty and, if the truth be told, slightly dizzy. He had never actually worked in here before. As he had said to the suicidal bunch only moments ago, he would always much rather stay in the main office where the banter was (usually) rife and the laughter (usually) flowing. Today however, he knew he would want to top himself if he had to stay in there with that lot for another five minutes. Why couldn't everyone just be happy like he was? Happy and floaty and unable to get the ridiculous smile off his face every time he thought of Sue (which was every couple of minutes).

On the night of the bathroom incident he had had an epiphany; he loved Sue and she loved him so why the hell shouldn't they spend time together if they wanted to? Well OK, yes they were both married and that did make things slightly awkward he guessed, but for heaven's sake, they shagged other people didn't they? Every weekend, didn't they? *For two and a half years, hadn't they? If they were doing that and that was OK, then what could be so wrong about spending some extra time with each other?*

One solitary and very annoying cell in his brain (which would later come forward and admit to being his ever so weeny 'conscience'), instantly spread the idea to all the other brain cells, that actually there was everything wrong with it. Cheryl knew about and was indeed the instigator of the Swinger's Night, but to sneak around behind Cheryl's back and see Sue whenever he could in private... well that was a different matter entirely. And deep down he knew it. Once again, he pushed the thought to the back of his mind and, putting his feet up on Tom's cluttered desk, closed his eyes and let the memory of Saturday night take over. They had stayed in the bathroom for most of the night and when they had finally pulled themselves apart and gone downstairs at around midnight, they had become aware of the moans and groans of the rest of the group, behind various doors around them. Jack smiled, remembering the way that Sue had grabbed his hand and pulled him into the kitchen and how they had drunk coffee alone and talked for a good hour before they were interrupted. They talked in hushed voices about their growing feelings for one another. She wanted to see him more often. He wanted sex with her more often; more than just once a week on a Saturday night with his wife in the next room. They had quite simply discovered that they both wanted the same thing; to spend more time together. Sue had then stepped out of her skimpy black knickers, plucked up the blue biro from the pot on the side and written 'text me! X' on the tiny white, wash care instruction label that was stitched inside them. 'And I don't mean on the group chat,' she had giggled. 'You know... just ME. You've got my number – message me.' She had smiled and pulled the waistband of his jeans out, shoving them down the front of his black Calvins. It was only moments later that Rob and Cheryl came out of the living room, chatting excitedly and walking towards them. Sue giggled, licked her lips and quickly mouthed, 'TEXT ME!' behind Cheryl's back. And so of course he had.

Coming round from his daydream, he picked up his mobile from the desk and began punching in his third text of the morning. How he wanted to be back in that locked bathroom with her, feeling her on top of him, down between his legs again.

It was no good. He couldn't even *try* to resist her. And he acknowledged again what he had known since Saturday night. Sue was well and truly under his skin.

CHAPTER 11

Steam began pouring out from the lip of the kettle moments before it switched itself off with a gentle click. Tom filled the two china mugs to the brim, took them through to the lounge and placed them down on the coffee table next to Angela. A part of her couldn't help wondering why he had bothered; the two coffees that he had made an hour ago were still sitting next to them, untouched.

She didn't move. Lying out on one of the deep squashy cream sofas in her dressing gown, was the only comfort that she could feel right now. Tom walked over and sat down in one of the matching armchairs beside her and waited for her to speak. But she didn't speak, and when a further fifteen minutes had passed and all that could be heard was the faint ticking of the grandfather clock coming from the huge hallway, Tom desperately needed to break the awful silence.

"Please, Angel, say something. Anything."

Angela continued to lie on the sofa in a semi-conscious state. She felt drugged, lifeless and worse still, like she could give up on life altogether. She was aware of her heart beating faintly somewhere deep inside her but other than that she felt completely numb. She didn't want to talk to him, she didn't want to drink his shitty coffee and she didn't want to see his mournful face. She didn't want him anywhere near her. Part of her mind and body had closed down and she knew she was 'just existing', sunken in the comfort of the sofa. Angela also knew it wouldn't matter what he said to her now – the clever way he might try to spin his words to encourage her to see the situation in a different light. She felt completely indifferent to him and the emotional wall around her body felt tall and impenetrable.

Tom got up and walked across the room to the french windows that looked out onto the vast amount of land at the back of the house. Jessie's swing rocked in the gentle breeze and he could see the sun trying to break through the thick white clouds overhead. It was having more luck than he was having trying to break through his and Angela's own dark cloud. *But what could he say to her that he hadn't already said yesterday?*

The moment he had got home from work he had known instinctively that something was wrong. The normal 'hustle and bustle' of the house had been flattened by a bulldozer of negativity that was quite alien to him. It wasn't until Jessie had been bathed and tucked up into bed, that his worst nightmare was finally realised. She had flown, really flown, *literally* flown at him, firstly with two vases and a picture frame, and then with her tongue. He hadn't known what had hit him as her words whipped and tortured every fibre of his being. He had been rooted to the spot, waiting in vain for the moment when he would wake up and silently thank God over and over for the fact that this had all been just a terrible dream. He had never seen Angela so angry and upset, before. To say he had been taken aback to learn what she had witnessed was an understatement and when she had waited for his response he had been stunned to find that he didn't actually have one. This wasn't something that he could just wave away and declare was a figment of her vivid imagination. This was as real as it got. *She had seen him with Max for goodness sake, what the hell could he possibly say to make things any better?* Angela had gone upstairs that night with more mascara and snot on her face than Katie Price with Swine Flu. She had emerged this morning from the locked bedroom like Julie Andrews on Rohypnol. He turned his head to look at her again. The face that had been red and crumpled the night before was now pale and expressionless.

Looking back out through the french doors he took in the beautiful view. Beyond 'Jessie's garden' which was right outside, was the main garden with its stunning array of tall, colourful flowers either side of a long and winding flagstone path. He had lost count of how many times he and Angela had walked that path together. They would keep on walking until they reached one of the many ornate iron benches hidden in its beauty and then they would sit there, sometimes for hours. They would look out at the beautiful grounds around them and talk about how lucky they were. Tom looked back at Angela again and wondered sadly if they would ever walk through those gardens together again.

He felt sick. *What the fuck had he done?* He dragged his fingers though his short dark hair and remembered the text message that he had sent Maxine that morning. He had told her very little – just that Angela had seen them together and that things between them had to end right now. He had told her not to ring and not to text, but of course she had replied. Several times. And instinctively he knew that – despite the fact that his mobile had remained turned off since. His brain felt scrambled but he knew one thing for sure, he wanted to be with Angela. He loved her absolutely and knew that he would stop at nothing to win her round and keep their marriage alive.

"Do you love her?"

Tom jumped as Angela's unexpected question broke through the silence of the room.

How the hell was he supposed to answer that without breaking her heart further? He *did* love Max, well he *thought* he did. Could it have just been lust and desire with a bit of addiction thrown in for good measure? If it wasn't love then it had certainly fooled him. It must have at least been a kind of love. He didn't care who said you couldn't love two people at the same time; people who said that had never experienced what he had. They were fools who didn't understand. But as for 'how much?' that was an easy one; he thought about her all the time. He couldn't tell Angela that, she would never understand. *Could he lie to save his marriage? That was a stupid question; he had been lying for the last six months, hadn't he?* No, it was no good, if there was to be any chance of a fresh start with Angela then there could be no more lies.

"I'll take your silence as a 'yes' then," Angela said coldly, before he could say what he was still computing in his head.

She dragged herself up from the sofa and, pulling her white towelling robe around her, walked slowly towards the living room door. Tom raced across the room to block her exit but was too late.

"Go to hell, Tom," she muttered, slamming the door behind her.

***

Tom heard the car pull out of the driveway. He had heard Angela run upstairs half an hour ago only to see her come back down scrubbed, dressed and made up. Now she had driven off to God knows where. For want of anything better to do, and to try to take his mind of things, he began building up a fire in the marble fireplace. Once he had it burning at a steady pace, he let himself fall back into one of the armchairs. It would be a while before its warmth would heat the room but he tried to relax nonetheless. Then he remembered his mobile nestled safely in his pocket like a dormant explosive. Taking it out carefully as if it might suddenly explode in his hands, he turned it on. Within ten seconds it vibrated and Maxine's seven messages waited impatiently to be read.

He read them all, one after the other. They were pretty much what he had expected; she wanted to know more, *needed* to know more – *What the hell was going on? Surely they could still see other? He could tell Angela they had ended it, couldn't he? She would never know. Maybe they could just have a break and in a few weeks when everything had blown over they could pick back up. Couldn't they? One day at a time? What do you think? Are you going to have the decency to explain to me properly what the hell is happening? When are you coming back to work? Don't you love me anymore?*

Tom read them several times before deleting them. Surely things were better left alone now and to reply would only make things more difficult for them both in the long run. He tried to clear his mind but his head was flooded with images of Maxine's worried face. *Maybe he should just block her? Or maybe he should reply first?* It's not like this is even Maxine's fault, he reasoned. She wasn't the one who had started the affair and it certainly wasn't her fault that Angela had caught them together yesterday. He had been sleeping with her for the last six months – surely the least he owed her was a proper explanation?

Tom glanced at the new watch on his wrist. Maxine would be at work. *He couldn't call her now. How could he trust her to stay in control – what if she completely broke down on him and shouted his name out? The entire office would know what was going on and things would really spiral out of control. But hadn't they already? On the other hand he couldn't be a complete bastard and do nothing.*

Tom tapped out a long message, explaining in more detail what had happened yesterday evening, what had happened this morning, how he was feeling and what he thought was the best way, or rather only way, out of the mess that he was now in. He knew as he sent it that she wouldn't agree but that was the way things were going to have to be from now on, and that was that.

* * *

"Hey, Angela! I didn't know you were popping in. How's Tom feeling... any better?" Jack dropped the file he had been carrying onto Maxine's desk and walked over to kiss Angela on the cheek.

At the mention of her name, Maxine's eyes tore themselves away from Tom's message and were greeted with Angela's fixed smile.

"Oh, he'll be fine thank you, Jack," she replied, without taking her eyes off Maxine. "He'll be back next week, I'm sure of it." Her voice was warm and syrupy, and her smile too wide to be sincere.

"Now..." she continued, as though she were about to ask a huge favour, "if you could lend me Maxine for an hour or so I promise to tell Tom it's high time he officially promoted you to Deputy Manager."

Jack grinned soppily at her, and without waiting

for his reply she smiled back, silently mouthing 'thank you' to him.

"Come on then, *you*," she grinned at Maxine, the false smile even wider now. "I believe we've got some catching up to do." She gripped her hand tightly around Maxine's upper arm.

Maxine froze in her seat, her blue eyes wide open in a combination of shock and fear. Her mobile was shaking in her hand with Tom's message still illuminated on its screen. Any attempt of Maxine's to make the kind of eye contact with Jack that said, 'For fuck's sake tell her I'm too busy... tell her *anything*,' failed miserably. Jack's eyes were firmly locked onto Angela's pert breasts, that were outlined by the soft fitted fabric that gently hugged them.

Maxine watched helplessly as Jack's head tilted, his eyes slowly moving down Angela's long, slender legs. '*For fuck's sake, Jack!*' she screamed silently in her head, '*why are you always such a fucking perv?*', but oblivious to everything around him, he continued staring at Angela and bit his bottom lip lecherously.

"Oh yeah!" he said suddenly. "Take as long as you like." He winked playfully. "As long as I'm next on your list of 'take-outs' it's all good!"

"Thanks Jack."

By this time Angela had managed to pull a rigid Maxine from her seat. Angela's fingers were digging into her arm now as she began guiding a very pale and sick looking Maxine out of the office door.

Jack walked slowly back into Tom's office and closed the door. He had always thought Angela was stunning for her age, and whilst he would never truly think of her as anything other than his best mate's wife, (apart from the odd 'boob peek' when she wasn't looking), he still loved any excuse to have a legitimate flirt with her. Strange though how he had never noticed before that her and Maxine were such good friends.

CHAPTER 12

Maxine shifted uneasily in the leather seat. Every attempt she had made to get Angela to say something had fallen on deaf ears. She didn't mind admitting that she was absolutely shitting herself and felt so close to being sick that she had even gone so far as actually envisaging the clash of last night's pizza on the Mercedes' soft cream leather seats.

"Just tell me where the hell we're going," she barked shakily.

She had asked the same question, in vain, five times already. She had also tried to get out of the car at the first set of traffic lights they had come to but the child safety locks were on and the door had refused to budge. Maxine took a deep breath and turned in her seat to try and see Angela's expression but it was impossible to read. Her face was a blank canvas, looking straight ahead at the road, showing no emotion at all. This only served to scare Maxine all the more.

Looking out of the car window properly for the first time, it occurred to her that they were heading towards Tom and Angela's house. She knew of course exactly where Tom lived - she had been inside the house on several occasions when Angela had been away, and in their bed too come to that. She bit her bottom lip and panicked. *What the actual fuck? Angela couldn't do this; wasn't this kidnap? You couldn't just hold some-*

one against their free will!

"Let me out!" she screamed, panicking. "NOW!" Maxine could feel the bile rising in her throat and began taking slow, deep breaths to try and steady herself. Angela ignored her and kept her eyes on the road ahead.

Maxine knew that resistance was futile. There was no way that Angela was going to suddenly turn around and take her back to the office. Defeated, she sank back into the soft seat and tried to calm her trembling hands in her lap. They travelled on in silence and before long they had reached the beginning of the long, private road that led to the huge house. This was the longest ten minutes that she had ever known and the disgusting smell of the pine trees was doing nothing to ease the sickness that was still whirling around in her stomach.

Finally, Angela turned off towards the circular driveway to park next to Tom's silver Mercedes. She brought the car to a jerky stop and swiftly climbed out.

Maxine slowly followed; the sooner she got this over and done with, she realised, the sooner she could get the hell out of here. *What had Angela said to Jack at the office again? Something about them only being an hour, or something like that?* She couldn't remember exactly now but that had to be a positive, surely? It at least meant that she wasn't going to be here for long.

As she started following a mute Angela towards the

house (her cheap heels sinking into the gravel with every step), everything in front of her began to swim out of focus. She stumbled on the first of the steps that led up to the front door and paused for a moment, putting a pale hand onto her frazzled head. She thought about telling Angela that she was about to throw up all over her beautiful driveway but at the same time she wanted to hide the fact that she felt so petrified.

"I'm not going in there with you," she spat, with a confidence that she didn't own. "Anything you've got to say to me you can say right here. I'm not going any further!"

Angela turned the key in the door and glanced back at Maxine, looking her up and down slowly and shaking her head. "You're pathetic," she said finally. "You're a girl who's young enough to be Tom's daughter for heaven's sake. Do you know I even liked you, Max, and you know what? I never thought for one minute that I would ever have any reason not to trust you. Now... get your cheap little cheating arse into my house this minute or I *will* drag you in there my bloody self!"

Flinging the door wide open she stepped inside and waited for Maxine to follow her.

Maxine's white face turned an insipid grey. Swallowing slowly, and then taking in a deep lungful of fresh air, she reluctantly followed her in.

***

Everything looked exactly the same as it had when Maxine had last been here. The huge entrance hall floor shined immaculately under the bright hallway lights, gleaming within an inch of its life. Maxine scowled. She was certain that irritating things that appeared in other people's houses, like dust and crumbs, never came calling to people like Angela and Tom.

Angela turned and walked into the living room where Tom was still sitting, deep in thought, oblivious to her return. When he saw her, he stood up anxiously.

"Angela? Are you OK? Where have you bee..."

The sight of a tearful and extremely dishevelled Maxine appearing behind her just outside the living room door, stopped him mid-sentence and tore at his heart.

"Max? What the hell..." *Why the hell was she here?*

He had never seen her look like this before; so hopeless, helpless and so bloody scared. The love he still felt for her made him want to rush over and hold her in his arms.

"ANGELA! What the hell's going on?"

Angela grabbed Maxine by the arm and pulled her into the room towards Tom. "Here she is. This is what you want, isn't it?"

Maxine trembled. She felt like a piece of meat, thrown into an arena; a cow at a farmer's auction - the prize cow to be won, or the disaster of the herd about to be cast aside.

"What are you talking about?" Tom blustered, "I told

you, it's over." He pointed towards Maxine. "I sent her a text this morning telling her everything. She knows it's finished. She can show you the message. *I can show you the message!*"

"Oh, that's big of you," Angela replied sarcastically. "That's not the impression I got earlier, Tom. If you love her then you'll want to be spending *more* time with her, not less." She couldn't stop the coldness from cutting into every word.

"I told you no such thing, what are you talking about?" Tom turned and looked guiltily at Maxine as he finally felt the weight of the betrayal he had heaped on both women.

"When I asked you how much you loved her you didn't reply. But your face said it all."

Maxine's face lit up. 'Hope' had appeared to her like a heavenly beacon through the dark, grey clouds above. *Maybe she WAS the prize to be won after all? He couldn't even deny their love to Angela! He was going to choose HER, surely? Angela had practically said so herself. She was handing Tom to her on a plate! This was fantastic. They could finally be together properly. A real couple in a real relationship. She could update her Facebook status; her friend, Tina, wouldn't believe it!*

Maxine smiled at Tom nervously, trying to quell the excitement that she now felt rising inside her body. Tom looked from Maxine to Angela, then back again. He wanted to tell his wife that 'of course it wasn't love', that he loved *her* and only *her*, that it didn't mean anything, that it was just a one off. *Really? Just a one off that had somehow lasted six months? A 'one off' that was worth a pretty expensive ruby ring? Shit.*

He looked at Maxine again. Her blonde hair was falling in greasy strips around her bare face. Her eyes were red and puffy, her face was grey, and one solitary tear was sliding slowly down her right cheek, but she was smiling with the hope of a child on Christmas Eve. How could he say any of those things to Angela without hurting Maxine even more? And anyway, none of it was true; he wanted to wipe away her tear, hold her close and tell her that everything would be fine. But more than that, he wanted his wife.

"Well, this is nice and cosy, isn't it?" Angela folded her arms calmly and looked at them both, amusement dancing across her face. "Do take your time, Tom. Don't let me rush you," she added sarcastically.

"I don't know what you want me to say and I don't know what you want me to do." Tom looked helplessly at the ceiling to avoid both of the women's eyes. They were boring into him and he couldn't stand it any longer. "This isn't Jeremy fucking Kyle, Ange, what do you want from me?"

"I WANT," Angela replied angrily, "for you to CHOOSE, Tom. RIGHT HERE, RIGHT NOW!" She jabbed her finger downwards, towards the floor. "I'm not having you telling me it's over, only for you to sneak around behind my back again with your little tart!"

Maxine flinched. This was just about the most humiliating situation she had ever been in and Tom wasn't helping any! *Why didn't he just tell her? Tell her she was boring. Tell her the marriage was over. For fuck's sake, why didn't he just say it?*

"She's a *kid* for chrissake, Tom! A fucking kid!" Angela continued. "Well, we're *both* here, we're *both* waiting and we're *both* listening. If it's over with this... *girl*, then you can tell her now... properly. In front of me!"

Tom stared in disbelief. Maxine had shuffled forward even more, her eyes wide and silently pleading. They both stood in front of him waiting for his answer – Angela with her arms still folded across her chest waiting impatiently, Maxine smiling ridiculously, her eyebrows raised in hope.

"Shall I get us a coffee while you're thinking about it?"

"Oh for heaven's sake, Angela, stop it!"

Angela walked over towards one of the sofas, sat down on it and made herself comfortable. She felt sick to the stomach but there was no way she was going to let it show.

Tom looked at her and then at Maxine. This was going to kill him but he knew he had no choice.

"I'm sorry, Max," he said barely audibly, "it's over... I'm sorry."

For a moment Maxine did nothing. His words were vague and dreamlike, unexpected, and she couldn't compute them. And then they hit her, like a baseball bat, squarely in the face. She frowned and shook her head, confused.

"Wh... what?" Maxine stared at him as her pale face crumpled before him. "What are you *talking about, Tom*? No!"

"I'm sorry, Max."

"NO! WHAT ARE YOU ON ABOUT, TOM?" she screamed, "We can finally be together!"

"Don't." He shook his head. "It's over."

Maxine blinked slowly. *He was actually choosing his wife over her?*

"NO!" She shouted again. "Don't say that, you know you don't..."

Before she could finish, Angela flew out of the chair to Maxine's side, like a vulture sweeping towards the shoreline to scavenge on the remains of a carcass. She threw out her right hand.

"The ring. Give it to me."

"YOU WHAT?" Maxine asked, stunned.

"I said, give me the ring."

"No way," Maxine answered, defiantly. "It's *my* ring and it's staying where it bloody well is!"

Angela didn't wait a second longer. She grabbed Maxine's hand and ripped the beautiful ring from her finger with one sharp yank.

"Oh no, dear, it's *my* ring. *My* husband bought you the thing and *my* money paid for it, so believe me, it's *my* ring. Now get out of my house!"

Maxine looked at Tom in a last-ditch attempt for help and in ridiculously vain hope that he might suddenly change his mind, but he looked at her helplessly and lowered his gaze to the floor.

Hurting more than she had ever felt in her life, she turned and left. When she reached the last of the steps at the front of the house she began to run. She ran so fast that her heart felt like it was beating outside of her chest. The tears streamed down her face freely and she sobbed loudly, oblivious to anyone she passed in the streets on her way. She ran and she ran and didn't stop until she reached her smart two bedroomed apartment in town – paid for by Tom. And Angela.

CHAPTER 13

James followed Andy to the sandwich bar across the street at just gone one o'clock. Jack wasn't happy to be left in the office on his own and was in an even fouler mood because Maxine still hadn't returned. He knew he'd told Angela to take her for as long as she liked but he hadn't really meant it. They were busy and he needed her! What the bloody hell was going on? She had said that they would only be an hour and it had been over three.

Andy paid for his sandwich and turned to find James standing behind him.

"Oh... you," he mumbled.

"Yeah, me. Ands, we've got to talk, you can't avoid me forever you know."

"Just get out of my face and leave me alone."

James put a hand out to stop him leaving the small sandwich shop but Andy barged past him and everyone else who was queuing up behind them, and made his way out onto the busy street. James ran after him and grabbed him by the arm.

"You never told me you were gay, bro!"

James had shouted it loud enough for the entire queue to turn around and swap amused faces with each other. He had barked it out loudly on purpose in a bid to slow Andy down and it had worked. Andy stopped and turned around, his handsome face growing dark and angry as he noticed the staring eyes of the silent crowd around him.

"Get off me, arsehole."

Holding tightly onto Andy's flailing arm, James dragged him around to the side of the sandwich bar and down the alley, throwing him into several of the shop's filthy bins that lined the graffiti ridden brick wall there. The stench of rotten food and urine lined Andy's nostrils, and he wondered where the usually sedate and mellow James had suddenly got this strength, this 'life' from. With the smell, came the memories of when he had brought Samantha here two years ago in the middle of the night for a quickie against the wall. He had been just about as drunk as you could get without falling down in a sad heap and pissing himself, but he'd had more important things on his mind that night; like getting inside Samantha's skimpy knickers. He had succeeded too – until he had sicked his curry up all over her hitched up dress.

"TALK!" James shouted at him. "You're not ignoring me anymore, so just TALK!"

Andy could barely hear him. He was still thinking about the night with Samantha and the second eruption of spew, which that time had covered the ample bust that was spilling over her low cut dress.

James' hands suddenly grabbed him and bashed him into the filthy wall, hurtling him back to reality.

"Now tell me, And," James asked quietly now, "what

were you doing with my boyfriend? ...I mean apart from shagging him."

Everything swam back into focus. *Had he just woken up halfway through somebody else's conversation?*

"What? What did you just say?"

James released his grip on him and let him fall onto the cold, damp paving slabs beneath him.

"I said, why were you..."

"Your *boyfriend?*"

They stared at each other, both of them now panting for breath.

"Yes." James looked him squarely in the eye. "My boyfriend."

"What the actual fuck, James?"

Andy felt his brain begin to implode. He stood up and turned to face the brick wall, resting his hands to steady himself. His head was filling up with what felt like huge wodges of cotton wool trying to blot out a lifetime of comfort and stability. *What was James talking about?* Andy shook his head as if that might suddenly help him to think straight. *How could James be gay? How could he have not known that? He had known James for thirty five years. Longer! Since fertilisation for fuck's sake! He had lived with him for twenty one years.*

"You're *gay?*" Andy managed to finally utter the words.

"Very perceptive of you."

"I... but... I never knew. How could I not know?"

"Oh. Then not so perceptive."

"But you... you can't be."

Andy looked around and shook his head again in disbelief before noticing a lad of about fifteen years old standing ten feet away. He appeared to be recording them on his phone and now looked disappointed that the 'show' was ending. Andy raised his eyebrows and glared at the lad.

"REALLY? I mean fucking *REALLY*?"

The lad stared back then shrugged his shoulders, put his phone in his pocket and started to walk away. Andy watched him for a few seconds more and then turned back to James.

"What about Ruth? What about Jane?" he asked. His legs wobbled beneath him so he slid himself back down to the ground. "What about..."

"They were friends. I'm allowed to have female friends, aren't I?"

"But... I thought... I thought you were... you know."

James tried to fight back a smile but it appeared anyway. "I've always been gay, And. I've known since I was five." The words flowed from him easily. These words had waited thirty years to do this and there was no stopping them now. "What about you?"

Andy looked up at him, his shocked face becoming indignant. "*Me*? I'm not gay! Is that what you think?"

James moved closer to Andy and sat down on the damp concrete beside him. "Well," he said calmly, looking mildly entertained, "if you're not gay then what were you and my boyfriend doing bollock naked in your living room?"

Bile shot up into Andy's throat and he gagged but produced nothing. "Oh shit," he swallowed. "*You*? You and *Charlie*?" The realisation that he and his brother had slept with the same person, worse still, a man, and worse still... *Charlie*, hit him properly for the first time. "No. No way, no *fucking* way!"

"Well how did you think I knew him?" asked James, still amused.

"Well I don't bastard know, do I? I don't know! I didn't know you were a... a bloody faggot!"

"Well," James continued calmly, "from one faggot to another, I haven't been able to get hold of him since, so do you mind telling me how he is?"

Andy summoned all of his strength and jumped to his feet, kicking James as hard as he could between the legs. "I AM NOT A FUCKING FAGGOT!" he screamed, thick veins now appearing at his temples. He could feel the tears prickling at his eyes and turned away in the hope that James wouldn't see.

James was too doubled up in pain on the filthy paving slabs to know anything other than that *this* was why he had never talked about his sexuality before. He had never been picked on at school - simply because no one ever suspected him of being gay. He wasn't effeminate and so hadn't lived up to the kids' images of a stereotypical 'gay boy'. It was incredible but he had managed to live all of his thirty five years without friends or family ever suspecting the truth. He thought about all of this now, as he lay on the cold, wet, stinking slabs. He had dreaded this day his entire life but now he felt lighter, freer. The only pain he felt right now was the physical one between his legs. The huge emotional weight that he had carried around for thirty five years had been lifted from his shoulders by good old fashioned honesty and, despite the pain, he smiled at how good it felt. Andy, his twin, now knew the truth – it simply couldn't get any worse than this. Things could only get better now.

Andy looked at his brother. They had always been the best of mates, always there for each other - how had it come to this? Regret was eating at him and he felt tortured and confused. It felt ironic now that James was the *one* person who could help him to feel better. He walked over and slumped down next to him, furiously wiping away at the tears that had finally released themselves.

"I'm sorry, Jay, I'm so sorry. I don't know what else to say. I'm *not* gay. Well... I *wasn't* gay. Charlie's the first man I've ever... well, you know."

James eased himself up but didn't speak.

"I've slept with, shit, I don't know how many girls," Andy continued. "Too many. It was a mistake with Charlie. He's a great bloke, very funny, but... shit, how is that even possible? How could I DO that? Do you know what I'm even trying to say? Tell me, Jay, how is it possible that I can get to thirty five being straighter than Ronnie O'Sullivan's snooker cue and then meet one guy... just ONE guy who made me feel differently for a while? That's not possible, is it? Well is it?"

Andy's tears continued and James put an arm around his shoulder, but still he didn't speak. He didn't want to interrupt his brother while he was on such a therapeutic roll.

"The truth is," Andy continued, "I haven't seen him since yesterday either. After you stormed out, he threw his clothes on and just left without so much as a *cheers, great first attempt!*'. When you recognised each other at the door I thought he was a mate of yours or something... I had no idea that... oh shit. What the hell have I done? I feel sick, I feel so bloody..."

Andy started to turn away from James but it was too late. The first eruption burst out and splattered the front of James' dark brown, suit jacket. The second caught James right in the face.

***

Jack looked at his watch for the tenth time in two minutes and decided to move away from the window. *Where the hell was everyone?* This was way beyond a joke now – it was three o'clock and *still* no Max and *still* no sign of James *or* Andy. Andy had said he was only popping over the road for a sandwich, and as for James, he hadn't even seen him leave. Just as Jack pressed the green circle on his mobile phone to call Tom, he pressed the red one quickly to cancel it. *What on earth was he thinking?* He couldn't phone Tom - how incompetent would that make him look? He had only been in charge for a morning and he could just imagine Tom's face if he rang him up to say that he didn't know where any of the staff were.

    Jack looked around at the empty office. In the last hour the phone hadn't rung once. After the crazy morning and lunchtime he'd had, the office now felt eerie. The silence was deafening and he didn't like it; it felt like a morgue and it unsettled him. Not one client had called in either, and all he'd had for his time were three very suggestive text messages off Sue. The last one had said something about Alan being away at a conference in Bristol for the day. Opening WhatsApp he re-read the message and then looked at his watch. Five past three. If he locked up and went now, he would have a good few hours with Sue before he would have to leave and go home to Cheryl. Now there was a thought! In his mind the deal was done. He raced from desk to desk to shut down the computers as quickly as he could but as he shut down the last one, a noise outside made him stop.

    He listened. *Nothing. Good.*

    Running into Tom's room, he grabbed his jacket from the back of the chair and started searching for his keys. When he reached the main office, he noticed a strange smell that had seeped into the room from nowhere. *What was it? It hadn't been there before, had it?* He glanced around briefly and sniffed a few times but couldn't tell where it was coming from so, shrugging his shoulders, he quickly snapped off the office lights. Another noise, the same as before, was now coming from the other side of the door so he quickly flicked the lights back on just as the office door burst open.

Andy and James stood before him. Their hands, faces and clothes were streaked with dirt, blood and something indistinguishable. They stank of rubbish bins, vomit and piss.

"What. The. Actual. Hell?" Jack grimaced. "What on *earth* happened to you two?" His mouth gaped open and his wide eyes raced over their dishevelled bodies. "What in heaven's name happened?"

Before either twin could answer, Jack pointed to the vomit on James' jacket and moved two steps backwards as the strong stench caught at the back of his throat.

"Is that... what the hell?" Jack continued, horrified now, "is that what I think it is?"

"Um... yeah, it is," James replied, fighting back a grin at seeing Jack so disgusted.

"Look we'll explain later, Jack," Andy interrupted, "but we've seriously got to go home and get cleaned up. I think some little shit recorded most of it anyway so I expect you'll see it on Facebook soon enough." Andy and James looked at each and smiled.

"See what?" Jack's eyes were still darting over them both from head to toe and back again. He couldn't imagine what on earth could have happened for them to end up like this.

"We'll get back as quickly as we can," Andy added as he and James turned to leave.

"NO! WAIT! Look... don't worry," Jack interrupted, smiling now. *This was perfect, just absolutely bloody perfect.* "Just get yourselves home and sort yourselves out, OK. I'll see you tomorrow, you can tell me all about it then."

Andy and James glanced at each other.

"Are you sure? Thanks mate," Andy said gratefully, "I could really do with a long hot soak in the bath right now to be honest."

"Amen to that!" James added in agreement.

"It's fine," Jack went on. "It's been as dead as Trump's hair follicles in here. There's more chance of Oasis getting back together than the phone ringing. To be honest I was just about to take some work home and lock up," he lied.

Andy and James exchanged more glances that telepathically screamed that Jack had gone completely mad. This had never happened before. They both knew that they were thinking the same thing - *what would Tom say about this?*

"Well... if you're sure then thanks," James cut in, before Jack could change his mind, "that's great." An image of a hot, soapy bath dangled tantalisingly in reach in James' mind, exactly as it was in Andy's.

Too true I'm bloody sure, thought Jack happily. No one, but *no one* was going to stop him getting his achy little hands on Sue this afternoon.

CHAPTER 14

The sex had been the best so far. Jack glanced around to check his watch against Alan's silver Sony alarm clock. 17:55.

"Are you OK?"

Sue lifted her head from his chest and laughed. "Of course I'm OK, why shouldn't I be?"

"I just thought that, well, I mean it's not every day you make love with someone else in the marital bed, is it?"

She didn't answer.

"Oh. Or is it?" he asked, suddenly feeling hurt.

"Huh? Oh no, don't be silly." She laughed again, and Jack breathed a silent sigh of relief.

"Well, don't you feel bad about it?"

"Do you?" she asked, raising her eyebrows.

"No."

"Good then, nor do I. Hang on, won't be a minute."

Jack stayed spread out on the double divan as he let his eyes take in Sue's curves before she disappeared, completely naked, through the bedroom doorway. Did he feel bad about it? Maybe just a little. And it was a very small 'little'. He closed his eyes and thought again about Andy and James. What on earth could have happened to get them both into that sort of mess? Whatever it was, he was thrilled it had happened or he wouldn't be lying here now, having just had amazing sex with the woman he had lusted after for so long. It was funny how different it had felt making love to Sue this time around. It had surprised him, shocked him even; they already knew each other's bodies inside out, so why should it have felt any different this time? But it had. Completely. And it wasn't just the fact that there weren't a dozen other people only feet away from them, behind closed doors of their own, though that had helped, obviously. But it was more than that. They were here together, just the two of them, because they had chosen to be. They had arranged it without anyone else knowing and whilst he knew it was wrong, it was, he had to admit, incredibly exciting too. Yes, despite the fact that they had spent countless Saturday nights having sex together, this was, he realised, the first time they had really made love.

"Are you joining me?" The sound of running water, along with Sue's mellow voice, called him from the bedroom and into the bathroom.

She was standing under the shower and for a moment he just stood and watched, mesmerised. Her eyes were closed and her head tilted upwards as the hot water fell onto her face and body. Droplets of water clung to every inch of her and she opened her mouth to let the bubbling liquid fill it and eventually spill out over her lower lip and onto her chest.

"Jeez, don't *do* that," Jack groaned.

Cupping his tackle, he quickly joined her, taking the soap from the sink with him as he went. Soon he was moving the slippery bar over her in slow, circular motions. It glided easily across the silky skin on her back but she took it from him almost instantly and pushed him underneath the spray. She lathered the soap onto his smooth chest and stomach before dropping to her knees and rubbing it across his pubic hair. Within seconds, her hand dropped lower still.

"That's some lather you're working up there," he sighed, watching her on bended knee. "I'm not sure if I can again... you know... so soon."

Sue stood up, reached for the shower head and pulling it back down to the bottom of the shower with her, she resumed her original position.

"Open your legs," she giggled naughtily.

"What? Why?"

"Don't ask silly questions, just do it."

Relaxing into the subservient role, he did as he was told. Before he knew what was happening, she had turned the shower head upside down and was spraying firm jets of water up between his legs. With the other hand she continued working up a lather, slowly and deliberately, until in no time at all Jack's knees buckled and he groaned yet again. His back slid down the wall of the shower and he flopped, wet and crumpled, on the shower tray below.

"Arghh, Sue," he panted. "I'm beginning to think you've got a thing for bathrooms."

CHAPTER 15

Jessie came running down the stairs with her new friend, Eva, with as many dolls in their little clenched fists as they could hold. Eva, like Jess, was a pretty little thing, although the complete opposite to Jess in every other way. Where Jess' hair was strawberry blonde and wavy, Eva's was black and poker straight. Where Jess was loud and confident, Eva was quiet and shy. Angela thought they complimented each other perfectly.

Angela and Eva's mother, Maria, had got to know each other quite well at the school gates each morning, when they'd been dropping the girls off. Angela realised that she still hadn't got around to asking Maria where they were from. Sometimes she thought they looked Spanish or Portuguese, but she really wasn't very good at guessing things like that, so guessed they could be from anywhere in the world. As the diffident Eva refused to tell her, she decided that she would definitely ask Maria when she came to pick Eva up.

"What are you playing?" Angela asked them, smiling. she hid the pain of Tom's betrayal so well that she felt some kind of award was deserved.

"They ignored her and threw the dolls onto the floor before rushing past her to fetch some more.

"Girls, Eva's mummy will be here soon so don't go getting anything else out."

Oh well at least they were happy. And when would she ever be happy again? Could she ever be happy again? And shouldn't there be at least a grain of happiness inside her right now? Tom had finished things with Maxine. She had won, hadn't she? She certainly didn't feel as if she had won anything. Only two days ago her life had been perfect, or had at least felt perfect, so was it any surprise that she couldn't quite get to grips with the fact that it now lay in shreds around her feet? Her perfect bubble, popped so cruelly.

"I thought we could get a take-away tonight."

Angela jumped. She turned to see Tom pulling a stool out from under the kitchen counter and proceeding to sit down on it. Ignoring him, she busied herself with some washing up and clattered the plates around as noisily as she could.

"Well, what do you think?" Tom asked.

Angela suppressed a cold laugh. "I'll tell you what I think, Tom, shall I?" she spat. "I think that I can't believe you're sitting there like nothing's happened and that you expect me to sit down and eat a bloody meal with you!"

Tom looked up with a pained expression that made Angela even angrier. How dare he look at her like that – as though she had no right to be treating him badly?

"You're right – how stupid I am. I'm sorry," he said, getting up and pushing the chair back under the counter. And then he left the kitchen.

***

Maria De Silva was Portuguese. Angela was secretly tickled that she had been part right about her nationality and wondered if all Portuguese people were as beautiful, warm and kind as Maria appeared to be. She was just the kind of friend Angela needed right now and she promised herself that she would make every effort to deepen their friendship.

Maria's long black Mediterranean hair shone brilliantly as the weak September sun began setting. With her strappy tan coloured sandals and long flowing tie-die skirt on, she looked like she had walked straight out of a Spanish hippy market. Angela thought she could feel a mystical air around her. She couldn't decide if it emanated from Maria's face or her clothes, or was simply a by-product of her personality. Either way she enjoyed being around her, basking in her sunny aura. It made her feel good.

"Yes, a cup of tea would be wonderful, Angela," she said in her soft accent. "I 'ave no plans for tomorrow, so where we meet?"

"You know your English is very good for someone who has only lived in England for a year."

"Well you know, we speak Eengleesh too in Portugal," she said with some amusement. "Though not much in the village where I come from."

Angela laughed foolishly. "Yes. Of course you do."

"So, you come to me, yes? I give you my address and

you come in the afternoon?"

"Yes, that's great," Angela replied a little too enthusiastically.

She couldn't help it. The thought of getting out of the house and away from Tom and their problems, even if just for an hour, lifted her immensely.

Maria delved into her straw bag, pulled out a little card and handed it to her. "My address is on this. It's easy to find, yes? You shouldn't 'ave a problem. You can Google it, no? I see you at one o'clock then?"

"Yes, one will be perfect," Angela replied happily. "I won't be late."

CHAPTER 16

Andy fetched one of the clean, dark green bath towels down from the airing cupboard and wrapped it around his waist. That felt better, he thought, looking at himself in his bedroom mirror. The person looking back at him was unrecognisable from the person who had been there a couple of hours ago. The filthy, crumpled and smelly 'tramp' from the back of the sandwich bar had been replaced with a clean, shaved and after-shaved hunk. He smiled. Noticing the time, he threw on some clean jeans and a blue faded Ted Baker t-shirt from his wardrobe and padded barefoot into the kitchen to get the plates and cutlery ready. It had been ages since he and James had eaten together, so he was chuffed that on the way home James had suggested bringing round the chilli he had made yesterday. They could share it, he had said, just like in the good old days when Andy had first moved into the same apartment block; they shared a lot of meals back then. There was no denying that after their talk this afternoon Andy felt closer to his brother than he had in years and he was keen to continue strengthening this new found bond.

Andy's mobile beeped on the kitchen worktop beside him and he leant over to pick it up. It was a message from Charlie. He stared at the screen in surprise. He wasn't expecting to hear from him again and it unsettled him. He hadn't been able to avoid the first few lines that had flashed up for a few seconds. It had said something along the lines of 'Hey gorgeous, how are you? Sorry I left the way I did...', but there was no way he was opening it up now to read the rest of it. No - Charlie could wait until much later. He sighed and rubbed his forehead. *The cheek of him. Who the hell did he think he was?* It buzzed again at the end of the worktop but Andy ignored it and busied himself tidying the kitchen until there was a tap on the door.

James was standing in the apartment block's communal corridor with the promised chilli in a huge, white ovenproof dish.

"Wow, who else have you invited?" Andy laughed when he said it but he was secretly pleased.

He hadn't eaten since breakfast. He wondered what had happened to the sandwich he had bought at lunchtime but it must have got lost in the fight. *Maybe 'video kid' had nabbed it? Little shit!*

"It's boiling so no need to heat it up," James said, placing the heavy dish down onto the kitchen worktop.

Grabbing a serving spoon, Andy wasted no time in ladling some of the chilli onto the two plates that he had laid out. He carried them to the table, where James had already helped himself to the sliced garlic bread.

"You were right about not cooking any rice," Andy laughed again, "there wouldn't be any room on the plates to put it!"

Within fifteen minutes, the large, white dish that James had carried the chilli in was empty. Andy stood up, leaving everything where it was and flopped down into an armchair.

"So... still not heard from Charlie?" he asked as nonchalantly as he could, suddenly wondering if 'cocksure Charlie' had messaged him too.

James got up and followed him to the living room area before sitting himself down on Andy's sofa. He looked across at the television with a frown on his face.

"No. Why, have you?"

"Nope," Andy replied coolly. "Nothing." He told himself that as he hadn't opened the message up to read the full contents, this technically wasn't a lie.

As if it had been listening, Andy's mobile buzzed on the kitchen worktop. In perfect synchronised movement they looked in the direction of Andy's phone, and then back to each other.

"Oh, that'll be Lynn, the cleaner," Andy lied.

"Often send you text messages does she, your cleaner?" James quipped, his eyebrows raised.

Andy fidgeted. He was keen to get back onto the subject of Charlie. He wanted to know how long he and James had been seeing each other for. How had they met? *Where* had they met? But then again, did any of it matter now? Not really, but still, he'd like to know.

"How did you meet him?"

James pulled his eyes away from the 'serial killer' documentary on Netflix.

"Who?"

"Who do you think? Charlie of course." Andy suddenly remembered something else from last night. "Hey, hang on, didn't you say that he *knew* you had a brother living in the flat above you?" *The shit! That bastard had known damn well what he was doing. He had known Andy was James' brother!*

"I really don't want to talk about Charlie, can't we change the subject?" James sank further into the sofa and fixed his stare at the rug on the floor beneath his feet.

"Not really, no. He was... he was, you know... with *both of us*. Doesn't that make you feel sick?"

"Not at the same time he wasn't." Still James refused to meet his brother's gaze.

"Of course not at the *exact* same time, but he was still with both of us!"

"Look, I don't really want to think about it, OK? I came here for a nice evening and I don't want it ruined talking about a complete shit-head. And anyway, I could ask you the same thing."

"What do you mean?"

"Well did *you* ever tell him that you had a brother living in the flat below you?"

Andy chewed the inside of his cheek. 'No' was the simple answer. He had never mentioned it. But why hadn't he? The truth was that he hadn't even thought about mentioning it. Right now it seemed like the most obvious thing in the world, but he had only seen Charlie four times, why would he mention it? *Wait! Hadn't he told Charlie the diarrhoea story of James' birthday party when they were kids? Had he mentioned it then? It was irrelevant now though, wasn't it?* The fact was that James had told Charlie, so Charlie had known anyway.

Andy looked at James again who was now far more interested in Fred and Rose West than he was in 'Professor Snape', so he resigned himself to the fact that for tonight at least, he wasn't going to find out anything more. Maybe it was better this way – maybe it was better to just put the whole sorry episode down to experience and get on with his life.

He belched loudly, reached for another can of lager and watched with James as Fred and Rose West's grinning faces disgraced his television set.

***

"Thanks love, that was great." Jack pushed his plate away and took a swig of the Cabernet Sauvignon that Cheryl had poured. "I'm sorry again for being so late."

"So basically, you've no idea *when* Tom's coming back then?" she asked slightly annoyed. "It's not fair you know, Jack, you could be left holding the fort like this for weeks for all we know. Will he pay you any more money?"

"Angela said that she thinks he'll be back next week, but I guess we'll just have to wait and see. He's the boss so he can take as long as he wants I suppose.

And I already get paid more, remember?"

Cheryl took the plates to the sink and began washing up. "Well I hope you're not going to be a slave to that office and come home late like this every night this week."

Jack looked at his watch and thought of Alan. He would be home from his conference by now.

"No, love," he said flatly, "tomorrow will be back to normal. I'll be home by six."

***

James looked at the time and got up to leave.

"Cheers, it's been a good night. I always did beat you at chess."

"Yeah, you're not kidding there," Andy mumbled. "You always made a better chilli than me too."

"Sorry it's so late, And, I didn't realise the time."

11.30pm wasn't late for Andy; he didn't usually hit the sack until gone one in the morning, but he decided not to mention that to 'Ten o'clock James'.

Andy's sleepy brother turned to leave but as he reached for the door handle, there was a knock on the other side of it. He stopped, startled, and looked enquiringly at Andy.

"Bit late for visitors, isn't it?" he said, before yanking open Andy's front door.

James stood before the unexpected visitor with his

mouth wide open in disbelief and threw the door wide open, so that Andy could see the face of the late night caller.

"Charlie?" Andy shook his head. "What the hell are *you* doing here?"

Charlie looked from Andy to James and back again. "What do you mean, '*what am I doing here*?'? Didn't you get my text messages?"

***

Andy looked at the clock as he drained the last few drops of lager from his can. It was nearly midnight and his mind was buzzing from Charlie's bombshell.

"Hang on a minute, let me get this straight. You're telling me that you've left your *wife*? I didn't even know you *had* a fucking wife!"

James said nothing, but while Andy had Charlie here, he was determined to say his piece.

"And NO! You *can't* stay here, no way! No fucking way! You must have dozens of friends whose houses you could stay at. I'm sorry but not a chance. It's not happening."

"But there isn't anywhere else I can go." Charlie protested. "Everyone else I know is happily married with kids. And they don't want an unstable bi-sexual on the loose in their house!"

"And I don't want one in mine either!" Andy shot back quickly.

"Oh that's just great. Thanks for nothing, duck!"

"Listen," Andy continued, glancing surreptitiously at his brother, who was listening with mild interest at the scene playing out in front of him, "you can't stay here! Things are awkward. I really don't want you here, Charlie, not after... well, after everything that's happened."

Charlie began pacing the living room floor. Some colour had returned to his face since Andy had seen him last and he wondered momentarily if it was make up.

"Well, I simply can't believe this, guys!" Charlie breathed angrily. He swished his sleek dark hair away from his face with a dramatic head shake and was wringing his hands together in mock anguish. He stopped abruptly in front of James and stared at him; his dark brown eyes narrowing, as they tried to burrow deep into his conscience.

Nothing.

"Right... well then..." he said, dramatically rolling his tongue around inside his cheek, "I suppose that's that then!" Charlie clapped his hands together in an attempt at a grand finale.

James returned the stare and Charlie twitched his eyebrow quickly and angrily before turning away from him. He walked back to the table and took the last cold swig of the coffee Andy had made him and placed the mug back down noisily. Walking to the front door Charlie bent down and swiftly picked up his holdall.

"You can stay at mine if you like..." James blurted

suddenly.

The words sliced through the awkward atmosphere like a machete attacking Andy's jugular.

"What I mean is, well it won't be a problem for me - not really."

Andy's lips parted in disbelief. What the hell was his brother playing at? He shot James a *what the actual fuck?* stare.

"I just meant that he..." he began proffering to Andy but Charlie was already onto it and interjected before James could change his mind.

"REALLY? Oh amazeballs, Jay, thank yooou!" he sang, like a five year old who had just been given a twenty pound note as pocket money. "Thank you sooo much!"

Childlike joy had returned to his dark eyes. "I promise I won't be any trouble at all, you won't even know I'm there!"

James looked across awkwardly at Andy and then stood up to leave. Within seconds Andy had grabbed his arm and pulled him back.

"Hang on a minute, what the hell's going on, what are you talking about? You're not seriously going to let him stay at yours?"

"Yes I am," James replied curtly. "You heard him, he's got nowhere else to go."

"I don't fucking believe this, Jay, you're not serious?"

James pulled his arm away. "I'm deadly serious. You might not want him," he added quietly, "but I *do*."

James walked towards the door and glanced at Charlie. "Are you coming then?" he snapped.

Charlie glanced at Andy, a huge grin spreading across his face. He was beaming like a fat kid with five huge slices of cake.

"Well! Night then, Ands," he grinned, holding up a triumphant hand to wiggle five bony fingers at him in a camp farewell before strutting off towards James.

"Oh surprise, surprise. All trace of suicide gone now then, has it? Just like that?" Andy glared at him.

Ignoring him, Charlie followed James to the door. Once James had opened it and walked out, Charlie quickly turned back to Andy and blew a sneaky kiss.

"Night night, ducks," he said smiling. "Sweet dreams!"

CHAPTER 17

"What are *you* doing here?"

Jack quickly pulled his feet from Tom's desk and stood up with an embarrassed grin on his face.

"Cheers, Jack, good to see you too."

"Sorry, mate, it's great to see you but Angela said that you wouldn't be back until next week that's all. You're feeling better then?"

"Not really, no," Tom replied. "To be honest I've just popped in for a few things. I'm going mad at home, you know what it's like."

"Oh, right."

It dawned on Jack that not only was there very little work for Tom to take home, but also that Tom's office would still be his for the rest of the week as he had hoped. *Maybe there was some way he could smuggle Sue in one evening for a quickie in the dark, over Tom's desk?*

"Then again," he said aloud, "maybe not."

Tom looked puzzled. "Maybe not *what*?"

"Eh? Oh. Sorry, nothing. Just talking to myself."

"You feeling alright, Jack?"

"Absolutely. Mind's a million miles away, mate, that's all."

"Where's Max?" Tom jerked his head in the direction of Maxine's empty chair. The question came out with a lot more urgency than Tom had hoped.

"Actually I was hoping you'd be able to tell us the answer to that one," he replied, noting the worry etched on Tom's face. "Is everything alright? I mean, well, Angela came in for Max yesterday, said that she would only be an hour and no-one's seen hide nor hair of her since. I've tried her at home but she's either not there or not answering." Jack raised his eyebrows quizzically as he waited for a response.

Tom closed his eyes and ran his fingers through his heavily waxed hair and said nothing. The realisation that Max wasn't coming back, instantly killed all other thoughts whirring around inside his aching head. *Duh! Of course she wasn't going to come back!* What sort of dickhead had he been to expect to see her sitting at her desk working away as if nothing had happened? She had lost her job and he hadn't even stopped to think about that.

"Is everything alright?" Jack tilted his head worryingly and Tom shook his head slowly.

He could ring her but what good would that do? Well it would at least mean that he could check that she was OK, wouldn't it? He felt sick with worry for her.

"You've been seeing her, haven't you?" Jack blurted out. He couldn't hold it in any longer and now seemed a good a time as any.

"You what? Tom looked up sharply.

"I said, 'you've been seeing her'. Maxine."

"Don't be ridic..."

"I *know*, mate. You can't hide it from me. And you

don't have to worry, I haven't told anyone, before you ask."

Tom groaned and put his hands into his faded jean pockets and walked to the little window of his office that looked out onto the town below. Pulling at the blinds he could see that the shoppers were out in their droves, looking for last minute bargains in the early autumn sales. He looked back to Jack.

"I had no idea it was that obvious," he whispered.

"Well maybe not to anyone else, but not much gets past me, mate."

"Angela knows too," he confessed, looking at Jack for support.

"What? You're kidding? But yesterday she... oh. OHHH!"

He stopped mid-sentence as Angela and Maxine's sudden 'close friendship', and Tom's mysterious sickness, all fell into place.

"It's a bloody nightmare, Jack. You should have seen her."

"Who? Angela or Max?"

Tom looked exasperated.

"Both! I can't believe what's happened in the last twenty four hours. Angela practically kidnapped Max and dragged her to our home for a showdown."

"She took her to your *house*?" Jack stared in disbelief.

"She even swiped the ring I bought her. Whoosh straight off her bloody finger!"

"*You bought her a ring*?" Jack's head was pounding. He didn't know how much more new information he could process in the space of sixty seconds.

"I've never seen her look so bad, she looked bloody awful."

"Who? Which one?"

"Both."

"Hang on, you're not making any sense. How did Angela find out?"

"Hang on a minute. Never mind Angela, how the bloody hell did *you* find out?"

Jack took his mobile from his pocket and waved it.

"You heard us on the phone?"

"Saw your name on a text."

"James and Andy don't know?"

"No. Like I said, I haven't told a soul. I Wouldn't. But can I ask you something? Why? You have Angela and she's amazing. I just don't get it - I've been puzzling over it since I found out. What's it about, mate? The sex?"

Tom didn't reply but looked away ashamed and Jack realised it was really none of his business.

"Listen, forget the details, I just want to know that you and Angela are OK, that's all."

"You and me both, mate," Tom muttered. And then without taking any work with him, he turned and left the office.

Jack watched Tom from the office window, winding his way through the heavy traffic of shoppers.

"Lucky bastard," he whispered aloud to himself. "I bet she was absolutely banging in the sack too."

CHAPTER 18

Tom rang the doorbell for a second time and cast a slow glance over the front of Maxine's 'new build' apartment. The curtains were closed and he couldn't hear any noise coming from inside. It was half past nine so she should be up by now, he thought worriedly. Ringing the doorbell for a third time he finally heard the distant patter of bare feet on the laminate floorboards.

"Thank God," he muttered under his breath.

When Maxine had started working for him two years ago, he had become smitten with her almost instantly. Despite not even being seventeen, she had flirted mercilessly with him from the word go and once she had turned eighteen, after eighteen months of self-restraint (and with an ego that had gradually been inflated to the size of Kim Kardashian's underwear) he had caved in. Completely and utterly. The next six months had been two seasons of sheer excitement, bare lust and wild sex. He had felt younger and more alive than he had in years. Now though, he felt older than he could ever remember feeling before. He felt like a dirty old man who had been caught with a schoolgirl and he hated himself. She was eighteen and a half now but that was little comfort to him now. Like Angela had said - he was still old enough to be her father.

The door finally opened and Maxine's puffy eyes took

a moment to focus in the bright daylight that flooded in.

"Tom! What are you...?"

"Are you OK? I was worried about you. Can I come in?"

Her eyes scanned the street behind before pulling him into her small hallway and slamming the door shut.

"Tom!" she cried out excitedly, flinging her arms around him and sobbing dramatically into his chest. "Oh, I'm so glad you're here. I didn't know what to do."

He could feel her tears begin to wet his shirt, and he felt stupidly useless. Lifting her head towards his so that he could take a proper look at her, he saw that her face was crumpled, just as Angela's had been - he had known it was from crying all night, he had heard her in the next room. *Had Max been crying all night too?*

"Look at you, Max, you're not even dressed. Have you eaten? Did I wake you up? Are you OK?"

She pulled away from him quickly, suddenly aware that she was still in her nightclothes, had no make-up on, and must look a far cry from the Max that he knew and loved.

"I've spent the last thirty six hours crying and feeling sick, Tom, of course I'm not OK!" She rubbed at her red eyes and looked away.

"Go and get dressed and I'll fix you something to eat," he replied, trying to placate her.

"I'm not hungry."

"Please just do as I say. I'll still be here when you're finished, I promise."

When Maxine came down half an hour later, washed, dressed and even with a little make up on, Tom was sitting in her kitchen nursing a cold coffee. She glanced around and could see that he had tidied the kitchen up for her and had also tackled the two day old washing up in the sink. She looked over at the bacon and eggs in the frying pan, that she had smelt as she had come out of the bathroom.

"I'm sorry. The place was a bit of a mess, wasn't it? A bit like me really. Does Angela know you're here?"

Tom laughed through his nose. "Of course Angela doesn't know I'm here, Max. She'd bloody kill me!"

"Of course. I'm sorry."

He put the bacon and eggs onto a plate and placed it down on the table in front of her.

"Come on, eat up. I'll get you a coffee."

She looked at the greasy food in front of her. It smelt wonderful, it even looked wonderful, but the thought of eating anything made her stomach cramp and the nauseous feeling returned again.

"Come on, eat," he ordered gently.

She knew better than to argue with him, so picked up her knife and fork and gently slid the food around on the plate. Tom returned with two fresh coffees and sat down next to her at the little white breakfast bar.

"You haven't been in to work then?" he pried tentatively.

Maxine looked astounded.

"What the hell do you think, Tom? Does it look like I've been to work? And excuse me if I'm mistaken but I *had* assumed that I didn't *have* a job to go to anymore."

"I didn't mean it like that – it came out wrong."

"Well what did you mean then?"

"I just didn't think." He looked around the little kitchen awkwardly. "Well what the hell are you going to do for a job? Is there anything I can do to help?"

Dropping her cutlery she looked up at Tom once more, as two fat tears slid down her reddened face.

"I don't bloody well know, Tom!" she shouted incredulously, "What the hell *AM* I going to do? *You* tell *me*!"

"Hey, come on, we'll sort something out I promise," he said calmly. "Everything will be fine, trust me."

"But it won't be, will it?" she whimpered. "How can it be alright? Things are never going to be the same, you know that as well as I do. Oh no, does she know about this apartment? Has she found out?"

"No she doesn't know. And anyway I only paid the deposit remember? You're the one making the monthly payments. It's *your* apartment."

"*Only* paid the deposit! £50,000 is a lot of money for a deposit, Tom. Well it is to someone like me anyway. And you know damn well that the extra money you give me each month in my pay goes towards the monthly repayments. There's no way I could afford it otherwise." She shook her head bewildered. "How can she not have noticed?"

"Look, I've told you before. Angela knows that I invest a lot of money in different ways. She doesn't question me like that, she trusts me. Well... she *did* trust me."

"Crikey, you two must have a lot of bloody money if Angela doesn't notice the odd fifty grand going missing every now and then!"

"Once, Max, *once*! Not every now and then. And I do have money of my own you know, I work as well remember? It's partly my business too! I told you, it's not a problem so don't worry about it."

She laughed hysterically and hated herself for it; it made her sound mad and crazy. She didn't know why she should be so surprised that Angela hadn't missed the money anyway – she had known from the moment Tom had first taken her to their home that this was the scent of serious bucks; fifty grand must be spare change to people like that.

Tom got up and paced up and down her small kitchen several times before stopping again in front of her. He was so close to her now that she could smell his aftershave fighting its way up through her blocked nostrils, bringing back memories of special times together.

"Oh, Tom, I miss you so much, please stay," she begged. "I don't want you to leave."

Tom studied her face. She looked so fragile, like a

delicate flower; her petals battered from a huge rainstorm. She needed to be cared for, to be loved, but he knew that if he stayed now it would never end. He would want to see her again, to feel her body against his and touch every part of her. How could he do that to Angela all over again? Closing his eyes and taking a deep breath, he tried to find the words to let her go.

"I love you, Max, and please believe me when I say that, I never wanted you to get hurt. But if I stay now... well I'll only hurt you again and I couldn't bear that."

"No, it doesn't matter," she cried out loudly, wanting him more than she had ever wanted him before. "Please just stay with me, you won't hurt me I promise you. Please, Tom, don't go."

Tom wiped the tears from her mascara-stained cheeks with his thumbs and pulled her to him, kissing the top of her head. He thought about Angela and when he had tried to kiss her this morning, how she had said that they would talk tonight. She had tried to smile at him; a sort of hopeful, sad, desperate smile and he had kissed the top of her head just as he had kissed Maxine's. He thought of Jess. She didn't understand and miraculously hadn't even noticed the different atmosphere that had invaded their home less than two days ago. Even so, he knew he had desperately let her down too.

"So," Maxine smiled confidently, as she sniffed the last of her tears away, "will you stay?"

He looked into her eyes. They were anxious and full of hope but he shook his head slowly. "I'm sorry, Max," he whispered.

And not trusting himself to stay another second, he turned and left the apartment for the very last time.

CHAPTER 19

"James, phone call. I'll put it through."

Jack pressed the relevant buttons on his office phone, waited for him to pick it up, and then replaced his handset.

Andy stopped working and watched James muttering quietly into the mouthpiece. *Was it Charlie on the other end? If it was, wouldn't he have called James' mobile phone instead?* Either way it made him feel sick to his stomach to think about it.

He had tried so hard to get some sleep last night, too hard in fact, so that sleep had merely scarpered off every time he had tried to chase it. He had spent the entire night caught between staring at the ceiling and trampling ever decreasing circles into the pile of his bedroom carpet. *How could he possibly sleep when his brother had taken Charlie with him downstairs into the flat right beneath him?* Most of the night had been spent straining his ears, trying to pick up any type of sound, long after the two familiar voices had died down. He had then tortured himself with lurid images of the two of them in bed together, although he really doubted that anything like that had actually happened. Looking across at James now though he couldn't be so sure; his head slightly bent as he spoke in hushed tones into the mouthpiece and all the while a faint smile dancing across his lips. Finally, James caught sight of Andy's gaze and, with a handful of whispered farewells, finished the phone call quickly.

Andy had to get out. Faking a 'cake run', he pushed his chair back, grabbed his jacket and left the building.

***

The sun shone brilliantly for mid-September and as he tilted his face towards it, Andy noticed for the first time that day that there wasn't a single cloud in the azure blue sky. The heat of a beautiful summer's day had cheated Autumn and he found himself wandering through the local park just two hundred yards from the shops and offices, so that he could take advantage of it. When he had found a good spot, he lay his jacket on the grass and let himself fall on top of it. He glanced around at the empty park; adults at work, children at school, and only one mother at the far end, pushing her baby along the pathway in a three-wheeled buggy. Silence, except for that faint therapeutic whirring of the distant wheels on the paved path. He needed this silence. Charlie had caused a tsunami of feelings inside of him the last few weeks and now tidal waves of confusion, chaos and drama were slowly beginning to ebb away. He tried to relax, determined to make some sense of the last twenty-four hours - and what a twenty-four hours it had been. He had slept with Charlie, who unknown to him had been his brother's boyfriend. *Did that mean that he was now bi-sexual? Or was he allowed to play the 'curious' card? The 'Get Out of Jail Free' card? And his brother was gay for heaven's sake. And sleeping with Charlie. And Charlie was married! And Charlie had left his wife! And now Charlie was staying in his brother's flat, while he himself had to sit a few feet above them and suffer the lurid images that danced revoltingly in his head.* For all he knew, Charlie was making himself right at home in James' flat – he didn't know for sure but he would bet money that James' generosity would extend to more than just one night. His mind ticked on. James was at work and Charlie would be at the apartment on his own. He could go right this minute and see him; they could talk – argue even? But did he *want* to see Charlie. Right now he couldn't think of anything worse. He didn't want to see James either but hey ho, they worked together. *Could he really blame James for any of this anyway? He was as much a victim in this as himself; they had both been cheated by Charlie.*

Andy thought about the phone call James had just taken. If it *had* been Charlie on the other end of the phone then James had quite obviously forgiven him. *He wouldn't take him back surely? Not after he had slept with his twin brother? Had James known that Charlie was married? What had James said last night before leaving his flat? 'You might not want him but I do'*?

Andy thought back to how he had felt when James had caught them together; sick and embarrassed, among other things. But he had felt like that *before* James had seen them too, he remembered – in the bedroom in the aftermath of the deed that had changed his life. *Had he forgotten that he had regretted it instantly and had felt overwhelmed with repulsion? Hardly the emotions of a man who had just been with someone he loved!*

As Andy realised for the first time since last night that he didn't actually *want* Charlie, he smiled. *Why had he been getting himself into knots over this? It was embarrassing, sure, and bloody awkward but he didn't want him!* The realisation brought a beautiful and blessed relief to Andy's shattered mind. The pressure that had been in his neck and shoulders lifted instantaneously and he took a slow, deep breath in through his nose. He could seal off that chapter of his life now, lock it up and throw away the key for good. It was strictly 'girls only' from now on.

Suddenly he laughed; *was his bisexuality the shortest on record? Maybe not. Maybe there were others just like him who had 'holidayed' one night in 'Bangkok' and then been as repulsed as he was? But what was life for if not for making some mistakes? No, if James wanted Charlie then he could have him. He really didn't care.*

He now had complete empathy for his brother and the life that he had led. James had spent most of his life being ashamed of something that he had no reason to be ashamed of and Andy hoped that he could now live his life no longer caring what people thought.

As he tortured himself with the finer points of the tangled mess, sleep began to pull heavily at his eye lids. He fought it, just as he fought everything else in his life and tried to stay focused but from nowhere, Samantha's image appeared beneath his eyelids and he didn't want to fight it anymore. He was back in the alley at the side of the sandwich bar, two years previously. The stench of urine and vomit was as strong in his imagination as it had been in reality, and Samantha was standing there again, beckoning him towards her as she pulled off her vomit soaked, floral dress. As the dress fell, so too did the curtains of consciousness in his weary mind.

***

When Andy arrived back in the office two hours later, Jack was more disconcerted to see there were no cakes in sight than the fact that he had been one man down for most of the afternoon.

'What happened to the cream slice?' he asked deflated. He had been waiting for it eagerly so that he could send Sue a photo of his tongue in the cream centre and tell her exactly what he was thinking about while eating it.

"Sorry, mate," Andy replied, feeling refreshed and now guilt free, "cream's off. Curdled and lumpy like an old slapper's..."

"DON'T!" Jack put his hand up to stop him. "Please, just don't." His face contorted into a look of disgust and he turned back to his desk slowly, all thoughts of

Sue slowly being replaced by Cheryl.

CHAPTER 20

The cottage could have come straight from the pages of a fairy tale book. Just a two minute walk from the main road, Angela could hardly believe that she had walked near here many times and never noticed this little narrow lane before. Just a hundred yards down the lane, the tall but sparse larch trees loomed into view before she had noticed the beautiful cottage nestled sleepily amongst them. As she got closer however, all thoughts of fairy tales vanished. The 'white' paint of the house greyed before her, along with its dried flakes that had begun to peel away. It had grown old ungracefully and was yearning for the love and care that the previous owner had failed to bestow upon it. Still, it was remarkable. Ivy grew, covering much of the front but parted almost magically around the little leaded windows, which too were badly mottled with age.

When Angela reached the wooden front door, she stopped in front of it and let her jaw drop open at its beauty. It was old and knobbled but had an intricate pattern of swirls and tiny squares carved into it. The more she looked at it the more she saw. Carved mice were being chased by carved cats, and tiny carved ladies chasing the cats and mice all the way around the door. Angela put her hand on it and gently ran her fingers over its incredible features.

"You have such a beautiful house, almost surreal,"

Angela said, as Maria poured them another cup of tea from a delicately patterned china teapot. "And such beautiful things inside it too."

"Ah yes, Angela, but eet is very old and needs lot of work, yes? Eet is small too you know, but I think big enough for me and Eva. And these beautiful things are not mine, they were here when we arrived."

Angela took the opportunity to find out as much as she could about Maria's life.

"So there's no 'Mr De Silva' then?" she pried.

"Ah, no. Eva's father, Adrio, he is in prison in Portugal. He bad man Angela, very bad man."

"Oh. Oh dear, that's awful. What happened?"

Maria shifted uneasily in her wicker chair and then leant forward to reach for her tea. She wrapped her small hands around the china cup to warm them.

"He was never a gentle man, even before Eva was born, 'ow you say, he was violent, yes?"

Angela nodded her on.

"When Eva came along I thought eet would make him a gentler person but things got worse. He drank more and worked less and wouldn't come home for days. I don't know where he went. I told my mother and when he found out he went mad. You understand what I say?"

Maria narrowed her eyes slightly and Angela knew that she was deciding whether or not to carry on. Without warning she smiled, and as if her decision to trust Angela was confirmed, she continued.

"He beat me and smashed up most of our possessions.

The beatings, they carried on. Eet took us years to replace everything and just when we had, without warning..." she paused and swallowed before carrying on, "he kidnapped Eva."

Angela's jaw dropped open in disbelief.

"He *kidnapped* her?" she repeated loudly, unable to believe what she was hearing.

"Eet took us nearly a year to find her but he had not gone far, only to western Spain, but eet was only luck that I found her at all. My family, they have many friends in Spain and they helped us after we heard they had been seen near Valencia. He was caught and sent to prison, but he told the Portuguese officials that I was planning to kidnap Eva myself and that he only took her as... last..." she struggled to find the words. "Last resort? Is this right?"

Maria paused, a look of fear creeping into her eyes. "He will be out soon," she continued shakily, "and that is why we are here, Angela. I cannot go home – if he finds us then he will take Eva away for sure and God knows where he will go this time. Somewhere I will never find them. This is what he has told me."

Angela realised her mouth was still gaping and closed it quickly. "I don't know what to say. I can't believe what you've been through. I'm so shocked. Poor Eva. And poor YOU!"

"I am fine. He cannot find us here. Eet is, 'ow you say... a needle?

"A needle in a haystack?" Angela finished.

"Yes, that is eet. I feel safe here."

For the rest of the afternoon Maria talked about her family and friends back at home. She told how she'd had to lose all contact with them so that Adrio would not be able to find them when he was released. Then she explained how she had taken with her only enough to fill one small case, before starting her new life. And then she had cried, talking about the close friends she had left behind, and her mother who she had now not spoken to for nearly a year.

"My mother could be dead for all I know," she continued sadly. "She was very ill the last time I saw her. But I am sorry, here I am talking about myself. Please, tell me, how are you and your wonderful family?"

Angela picked up her cup and drank down the lukewarm tea in two mouthfuls. She could really use a friend to confide in right now but Maria had enough on her plate without having *her* problems dumped on her too.

"We're fine thank you, Maria," she said smiling brightly. "Just fine."

CHAPTER 21

Jack put the phone down, pulled out Andy's empty chair and waited. It had been easy to lie to Cheryl on the telephone; no glaring eyes boring into his and burrowing searchingly into his soul. He thought that his voice had stayed exceptionally sincere when he had told her that he was as fed up as she was about having to stay on and sort out Maxine's untouched work.

"Well is she OK? Is she sick?" Cheryl had questioned. "I mean, fancy not ringing in to explain what's going on – that's outrageous. Have you told Tom?"

In that moment he came very close to spilling the beans about Tom and Maxine's affair, and it was in fact only the thought of having to stay on the phone for a further half an hour while Cheryl picked every minute detail from him that prevented him from doing so.

"Yes, Tom knows, love. I think it must be a virus or something."

Telling her he would be home as soon as was possible, he slammed the phone down quickly to get ready for Sue. Within seconds his mobile vibrated in his pocket and he snatched it up to read that Sue was on her way.

"Bingo, bloody bingo," he cheered, running into the staff toilets to wash down his nether regions at the sink.

By the time he had finished and returned to the office a car pulled up outside and, peering through the blinds, he watched excitedly as Sue got out of it and opened the main building's door below. He could hear her ascending the stairs at great speed and within seconds the door next to him burst open and she rushed straight into his open arms. For a short while they didn't speak, they just kissed, but several minutes later they began tugging frantically at each other's clothes. As she unbuttoned his shirt, he began pulling her jeans down.

"No knickers!" he gasped excitedly. "Ooh, that reminds me."

Jack unzipped his trousers and pulled them down to his knees, standing eagerly to attention in his modest grey underwear. A corner of black lace protruded from his waistband, nestled comfortably against his auburn pubic hair.

"Are they my bloody knickers?" she laughed, yanking them out of his underwear.

"I forgot they were down there to be honest. I've shoved them down my pants every day since you gave them to me. They make me smile every time I go to the loo. They make me horny too."

"You haven't? she laughed, "You're such a fibber!"

"Honest! Ever since you wrote on them for me." He waved them at her and smiled. "Can't bear the thought of giving them back to you though, are you sure you need them?"

"I've been thinking about you non-stop, Jack," she whispered, suddenly serious.

"Ditto. I've thought of nothing else but you. Well, apart from your little lacy knickers between my legs, been thinking about that quite a lot."

"I mean it, Jack, it's been awful. I can't sleep or anything," she frowned, annoyed that he had made a joke while she was opening her heart to him.

"Sue, I'm nuts about you. Honestly. It's killing me too."

Before he knew what was happening she had grabbed him with both hands and pushed her tongue into his mouth so forcefully that he gagged. He pushed her back and yanked her top off over her head and in seconds had unclipped her cream, satin bra. He pulled the straps down from her shoulders and threw it to the floor to join the other items of clothing that lay there in abandon. Burying his face into her neck, he breathed her in and then stroked her collarbone with his thumbs.

"You're perfect," he whispered, working his way downwards, cupping and kissing her DD-cup breasts and rubbing his face across them, as he had done many times before.

Jack's tongue traced a line from her cleavage to her belly, before he lifted her up and carried her across to the row of desks.

"What are you doing?" she giggled excitedly.

He laid her across the cluttered desks, pushing her legs apart with his hands.

"I'm going down, baby," he said, raising his eyebrows, "and you might *never* see me again."

***

He had had the roughest sex with her that he had ever had in his life. He hadn't intended for it to be that way – it had just happened. Raw, sexual desire had risen to the surface and completely taken him over. The need to be inside her, taking her, had overcome all of his other thoughts and feelings, and with every thrust he wanted her to know how much he was enjoying it.

As they lay post-coitally across his and James' desks, with telephones, staplers and folders of paperwork strewn all around them (not to mention James' computer monitor digging into the back of his head), he stroked her hair and kissed her gently on the lips.

"I love you," he whispered. The three words had almost spoken themselves straight out of his mouth, for all the ease it took to say them. He looked at her nervously but Sue smiled at him and told him that she loved him too.

"I do, Jack, so much, but I have to get back. Alan will never believe that yoga classes last three hours."

"Yoga classes?" Jack laughed. "Is that what you told him?"

"Hey, I've got to explain the sweat somehow haven't I, unless you're offering to take me home and shower me off?"

"Chrissake, I wish I bloody could," he groaned. "Somehow though, I don't think Cheryl would be too thrilled about it."

Once Sue was dressed, she leant forward and kissed him hesitantly.

"Jack... about Saturday."

"What about it?"

"What are we going to do?"

"What do you mean 'what are we going to do?'"

There was a sadness shooting through her eyes and he wondered what on earth she was going to say next.

"You know what I mean." She scanned his face cautiously. "I mean, *the others*." Anguish dotted itself in specks all over her fine features where moments before there had been only pleasure.

"What about the others?"

"You know, we're going to have to be... well, sensible. We've got to think about them too."

Jack felt himself tense as the true meaning of her words sank in.

"You know as well as I do that Alan and Cheryl are going to get suspicious soon," she continued. "Alan's already joked about us two being joined at the pelvises and there aren't many women sharper than your Cheryl."

He looked down at the office carpet and let her words do their worst to his head and heart. He knew that she was implying they should sleep with someone else next weekend for appearance sake but he didn't even want to think about it. He didn't want to sleep with anyone else and he certainly didn't want Sue sleeping with anyone else either. OK so she slept with Alan, but he was her husband and there wasn't much he could do about that. Well at least not for the moment anyway.

"Jack? You know what I'm saying, right? Are you OK with that?"

Still he didn't speak. Thoughts and images rushed through his mind like high speed trains darting around his brain cells daring to collide with each other. *This was ridiculous. What was the matter with him? They had slept with everybody else on a Saturday night a multitude of times. Wasn't it about the physical, the variety and the spice? Hadn't that been the whole point of the club in the first place? It wasn't meant to be about love.*

Jack clenched his jaw and smiled at Sue, feigning a maturity that he simply didn't occupy. "Yeah... sure. Of course. I understand."

"After all, we'll know it doesn't mean anything, won't we?" She looked at him with the same hurt in her eyes that he felt washing over his body.

"Yep," he lied. "Of course we will."

Sue stood at her car door and blew a kiss up to him at the top of the building before driving away. Jack thought about Saturday, and he knew that the jealousy would drive him insane.

CHAPTER 22

"Tea's up."

James shuffled his slippered feet into the kitchen to join Charlie at the table.

"Thanks, this is great," James said, meaning it.

Dinner after a hard day at work normally came from one of the local take-aways or the freezer. One thing it never was, was a fresh roast chicken with home-made roast potatoes and fresh vegetables. He couldn't help but feel that sitting down to a roast dinner on a Thursday evening was quite lavish and he wondered upon Charlie's reason for cooking it.

"Chilli's just about the only decent dish I can make from scratch," he told Charlie in a shamed voice.

"Nothing wrong with chilli, doll," Charlie smiled back. "It can warm the bits that roast dinners can only dream of. Besides, I'll bet your chilli knocks the socks off Andy's." He looked up at James and smiled. "Not that I've tasted Andy's, of course."

James stared at Charlie for a moment before dropping his head back down; his face suddenly focusing on the dinner plate piled high in front of him. It was the first time that Andy's name had been mentioned since he had brought Charlie to his apartment last night but he knew that the avoidance couldn't last forever.

"So," James continued nonchalantly, "how long do you think you'll be here for? Have you spoken to Paloma yet?"

Charlie sucked his cheeks in effeminately and raised his head proudly as his dark hair fell around his face. He flicked it away like it was an oversized insect crawling over his perfectly pale features.

"Tried to call her but she slammed the phone down on me," he answered abruptly.

"Oh. Do you want to talk about it?"

Charlie slammed his cutlery down hard on the table and looked James squarely in the eyes.

"You want to know why I left her?"

"Well... as you're staying with me... I suppose it would be good to know. That's if you want to tell me, that is."

Charlie picked his cutlery back up and busied himself by chopping up bits of potato and stuffing, and then mashing them together with his fork. He clanked his cutlery against the patterned plate so loudly that James thought it might break at any moment.

"She caught me," he blurted out finally. His lips pursed tightly together again as soon as the words were out.

"Caught you?"

"Threw me out. She came home early from work and found me. Standing there in her hold ups I was – with her satin Ann Summers garb on."

For a moment James was speechless. He had no idea that Charlie liked to dress up in women's clothes and the confession had astounded him.

"But... but... *why?*"

"Because it feels nice," he shrugged indifferently.

"Do you, do you often...?"

Charlie could see where this was going and quickly changed the subject. "Thanks for offering to put me up for a few nights. I phoned up my work today, told them I've got a virus. You won't know I'm here, duck, I promise." Once again, his lips knitted tightly together as soon as the last word left his mouth.

"There's obviously quite a lot I don't know about you," James said, trying to change the subject back again. "Want to talk about it?"

Charlie looked up, annoyed. "Does it look like I want to talk about it?" he replied abruptly. "Anyway there's nothing else to tell you. Paloma found me dressed up in her stuff and threw me out. End of story."

James watched him carefully as he sliced into the chicken breast with his knife, doused it in a puddle of gravy and placed it carefully into his mouth. For the very first time he had an overwhelming need to know the extent of his 'relationship' with Andy. He thought about his brother in the flat upstairs, alone, messed up and screwed up over one night of homosexuality, and how he had knowingly made things worse by inviting Charlie to stay here with him.

"How could you do it?" he asked Charlie, flatly.

"Do what?" Charlie forced more food past his thin lips.

"I told you months ago that my brother lived in

the flat above me. You *knew* that. How could you do it?"

"Oh, that."

"Yes, *that*."

Charlie chewed his food thoughtfully for several seconds and then put his cutlery down again.

"It wasn't intentional, Jay, if that's what you're thinking. I met him at a mate's wedding in June. Graham Duke. Do you know him? Oh, well you weren't there so I guess not." This last bit he added on with a chuckle and James knew that Charlie was relishing the fact that he had now let on that he had known Andy for three whole months. "I know that you told me your twin brother lived above you," he continued flippantly, "but so do ten other people, Jay - it's a block of apartments. It's not as if you two actually look anything like each other now, is it? I swear I didn't know who Andy was until the other day when he invited me to his place and I saw a picture of you in his living room. I mean, I've never seen him when I've been here at yours, have I? It's not like you have any photographs of him here or anything. Anyway, we'd only been texting each other and stuff, met up for a drink a couple of times, you know the sort of thing. The other night - well, that was the first time that..."

"Yes, I know."

"You've spoken to him about it?"

"We *are* brothers - yes, we've spoken about it."

"Oh." Charlie sounded almost disappointed that he hadn't been the one to deliver the news and plucked his cutlery back up haughtily. "Well then, there's nothing else to tell you. Sounds like you know all there is to know. I don't know what else you expect me to say."

"How about how you could sleep with him when you'd just found out who he was? You just said that you realised when you saw my photo there. He's my brother!"

"It was too late by then, Jay. Emotions were running *way* too high." Charlie had put on his campest voice and was flailing his arms into the air dramatically, gravy splashing off his fork onto the table.

James looked back to his full plate and wondered where his huge appetite had vanished to. There was still more he wanted to know. *Would Charlie have ever told him about his time with Andy if he hadn't caught them together?* There was no point in asking him – of course Charlie would say 'yes'. *Anyway, wasn't that irrelevant now?* James pushed his plate away and stood up to leave the kitchen.

"Where are you going? You haven't eaten anything!"

"I've got a headache," James said wearily. "I'm going to bed!"

"BED? Fucking *BED*? It's seven o'clock, Jay!"

"I'm well aware what time it is but I can't deal with this right now!"

"That's *exactly* what you're going to do!" Charlie snapped, standing up and grabbing James' arm. "We've been together for what? Almost six months now? I've told you everything in that time, absolutely everything! And I would have told you about Andy too if you hadn't caught us. You've always known about Paloma. And you've always known I have an eye for a hunk."

"You didn't tell me you liked to dress in women's clothes," James countered. "And I'm not a hunk!"

"No, of course *you're* not a hunk," Charlie stifled an inappropriate giggle behind a small clenched fist, "I'm with *you* for your brain not your looks... obviously!"

James felt indifferent. Charlie's words couldn't hurt him because he knew all of this already. What else would someone like Charlie see in him? He took in Charlie's fine porcelain features. He was wearing a beautiful black Italian shirt with white buttons, white cuffs and subtle white piping along the shoulder. His skinny black jeans were ripped at the knees and he reeked of his usual Prada aftershave.

"We just don't go together, Charlie,' James continued, "I'm a hermit and you're a party animal. I dress like a sixty year old and you... well you dress like an Italian gothic fashion designer. It's crazy." He stopped for a few seconds before carrying on. "You need to go home to Paloma and sort things out."

"Don't be so ridiculous!" Charlie laughed, once again exaggerating his already highly effeminate voice. "You need to get the fuck over this, Jay. It was a SHAG! Nothing else." His voice was high pitched and screechy and James worried Andy might hear from upstairs.

James looked at him for a second longer and then

turned to leave.

"WHERE ARE YOU GOING?" Charlie demanded angrily, "we're talking!"

"I already told you, I'm going to bed."

Charlie watched him leave the kitchen and, not knowing what else to do, threw his hands onto his bony hips.

"Looks like it's the bloody sofa for me then!"

★★★

They were supposed to be talking. *Isn't that what she had said; that they would talk later?* Tom carried the two teacups into the front room and gently kicked the door shut. Putting them down, he joined Angela on the sofa. He had decided against opening a bottle of wine for the simple reason that he didn't want Angela becoming more emotional than she already was. This had resulted in him making them both the third cup of tea in less than an hour. And still she wouldn't drink it. And still she wouldn't talk.

CHAPTER 23

Everyone turned and gaped in surprise as the familiar figure walked through the doorway.

"Morning all," she said brightly. "Anyone missed me then?"

"Bugger me!" Jack breathed heavily.

Maxine laughed. "You never give up do you, Jack Preston?"

"Hey, you know what I meant," he said laughing too, despite the shock of seeing her. He walked over and gave her a big hug.

"It's so good to see you, hun, you look great. Really."

Andy looked up from his work and smiled.

"Hey, Max, how are you feeling? The place hasn't been the same without you. When are you coming back?"

"No, it really hasn't," James joined in. "This place has gone to pot without you. Just look at the state of my desk!"

Jack wished James hadn't mentioned his desk. He thought about himself and Sue sprawled across it last night. He looked at the files in disarray and the skewed computer monitor on James' desk; all that remained of his and Sue's frantic lovemaking. *Wow, it had been good. No, it had been more than good - it had been great.* He looked away nervously and cleared his throat. He felt hot and flustered and ran an index finger around the now tight collar of his blue shirt.

"Ahh, you guys!" Maxine said, unaware of Jack's unease. "I didn't know you all cared that much." She batted her eyelashes theatrically. "C'mon then, aren't any of you going to make this lady a coffee?"

"I thought that was *your* job?" Andy replied cheekily.

"C'mon," Jack said, taking her chivalrously by the arm, "if the lady wants a coffee, then she shall have one! After you." He held the door to Tom's empty office wide open and smiled at her.

Maxine looked at him suspiciously and hesitated for a second before entering and closing the door behind her.

"You could have made me one in the staff room you know," she said, her narrow eyes on him.

He walked to the corner of the room, filled up Tom's small kettle with water and switched it on.

"Yes, I could have. But I wanted to talk to you without any chance of being interrupted every two minutes by one of the goddamn Chuckle Brothers."

Maxine laughed. "Oh Jack, I've missed you, I really have."

"Seriously, hunnie, how are you feeling?" he asked, scooping instant coffee into two mugs.

She looked at him through beautifully made up eyes and sat down in the spare chair.

"I'm fine, Jack," she replied quietly, touched by his concern. "I've just come to get my stuff really, that's all."

"Come to get your stuff? You mean you're not coming back then?"

"I've been offered a job at Webbers," she lied. "I can start whenever I like. More money, better hours – you know the kind of thing."

Jack sucked the end of his rollerball pen thoughtfully and let his gaze blur into the patch of carpet behind her. Several moments passed before he focused back onto her face. Tom had already filled him in on his visit to Maxine's flat but regardless of that, Jack knew her only too well and could see behind the veil of her bravado. She might look like a composed and beautifully strong lady to anyone else but to his eyes she was fragile. One gust of wind in the wrong direction might just snap the brittle strands holding her heart together. Like an African Violet, he knew she needed just the right amount of everything right now to keep her steady and he wasn't sure what he should and shouldn't say. The last thing he wanted was her losing it in Tom's office.

She was staring at him now, with her wide powder blue eyes boring into his soul and he thought she had never looked so small. Small and alone, behind her delicate blue eyes. He reached out and took one of her cold, pale hands in his and curled his fingers around it protectively.

"Jack?"

Jack shook his thoughts away and blinked. Maxine

was glaring at him.

"What on earth do you think you're doing?"

"What? What's wrong?" Snapping out of his daydream he became horribly aware that he was stroking her hand seductively.

"You're looking at me as if I were a frenzied furniture-slashing monster on diazepam, Jack, that's what's wrong!"

"Oh shit. I'm so sorry." He dropped her hand quickly. "I don't know what I was thinking. I'm sorry, Max. You just looked upset."

"OH. MY. SHIT!" The realisation hit her body like a defibrillator delivering a thousand volts to her heart. "YOU KNOW, DON'T YOU?" she panted, suddenly realising why his body language screamed '*emotionally wrecked woman present – beware!*' "YOU BLOODY WELL KNOW, JACK! HE TOLD YOU!"

Jack tried to speak but his tongue had momentarily stuck to the roof of his mouth.

"Oh great! That's just bloody great!" she cried out loudly. "And can I ask just *how long* you've known? I bet you've known all along, haven't you? I'll bet you and Tom have had a right laugh talking about me. I don't believe this!"

"No. I mean yes. Well, Tom only told me the other day. Well actually he didn't, I sort of guessed, but you know, he kind of..."

"Jack, you're talking shit. Did he tell you or not?"

"Yes. Kind of."

"You know everything?"

"Yeah. Kind of. I think so. Sort of."

She looked around at the closed door behind her and thought of James and Andy on the other side of it.

"OH NO... do they know too?"

"No. They think you're off sick. I think."

"I AM OFF SICK," she cried, frustrated at the injustice of it all. "The trouble is I can't bloody well come back, can I?" She could feel the first prick of tears stinging the back of her eyes but held her head high, hanging desperately onto any last threads of dignity she imagined she had left.

"Thanks for the coffee that never was, Jack, but I'd better just get my stuff and go."

"What are you going to do?" Jack couldn't let her go. Not like this.

Her clear eyes were now glazed and reddened – no amount of make-up could mask that kind of hurt. If your eyes were windows to your soul, then hers had been completely and utterly destroyed, he thought.

She looked at him for a moment and then put her head into her hands. She desperately needed someone to talk to. Sure, she had talked about it with her best friend, Tina, on the phone, but Jack was 'here and now'. Tom had confided in him and he was maybe the only person Tom had told. *Maybe she could use this to her advantage? Maybe he could help?*

"Jack..." she said, calming herself, "what did he say to you? When did you last see him? Please tell me what's been happening." She sat herself back down and was looking pleadingly at him.

"What are you asking *me* for? I know less than you do."

"Please, Jack. Anything at all. He came round yesterday morning to my apartment and I haven't heard from him since." The bravado gone again, more huge tears came from nowhere and slid down her cheeks shamelessly.

"I haven't seen him since yesterday either. He came here first thing and then left. That's the truth."

"Well what's he been doing? WHERE THE HELL IS HE?" She screamed.

"I don't bloody know!" Jack felt suddenly irritated; *Max only had herself to blame – she had known Tom was married.* "Probably at home with Angela trying to save his marriage, where do you think?" It had come out crueller than he had meant, but he had said it now.

"OH THANKS! Thanks for that Jack. I really wanted to hear that!" The tears were streaming now, leaving tram lines in her foundation.

"Well she *is* his wife, Max. What do you expect me to say?"

"DON'T YOU JUDGE ME!" she screamed. "HOW DARE YOU, WHO THE HELL DO YOU THINK YOU ARE?" Her tear-stained cheeks were flushed and her mascara had smudged below her eyes where she had furiously tried to rub away her tears.

Jack got up, walked over to the kettle and began filling the two mugs with the boiled water.

"I'm sorry, mate, I'm not judging you. Who you decide to shag is none of my business." It was facetious and disrespectful, but it was too late, he had said it. "Max, you asked me a question and I answered it that's all. I'm sorry if it wasn't the one you wanted to hear."

When he turned back around she was gone.

***

Jack drained the dregs of his second coffee (Maxine's) and put the empty cup on the desk next to the first. *How could she think that he had been judging her? He hadn't meant it to come across like that. Good grief, who was he of all people to judge somebody else over extra marital affairs?*

His mobile buzzed and flashed as the James Bond theme tune brought it to life, and he snatched it up without a second thought. It was Sue.

"Darling, guess what? Alan's going to Swindon next week for a two day seminar!"

"You're kidding me, right?"

"No, honestly."

He beamed. She sounded as though she could hardly contain herself. He compared it to a child who had just seen the first snowflakes of the year outside her bedroom window.

"Two days, Jack! I can't believe it either. Well... what do you say?"

Jack paced the office floor running his fingers

through his red, straggly hair. His mind buzzed frantically.

"Shit. Are you saying that you want me to stay the night?"

"It would be fantastic, wouldn't it? Just think, we can lie in each other's arms all night! I'm so excited. Please say yes!"

He tried to collect his thoughts. On one hand there was nothing to think about; he would be there alright, like a rat up a drainpipe. But what would he tell Cheryl? What if Alan came back early? Could they really do this and get away with it?

"Say something, honey," she squealed excitedly.

"Shit, of course I'll be there. Just say when."

"He's going Wednesday morning and gets back Thursday night."

"So you want me to stay Wednesday?"

"Oh I can't wait. I just can't *bloody* wait! What will you tell Cheryl?"

Jack chewed the inside of his cheek and felt his insides churn around. It felt heavy and cold, like he had the contents of a cement mixer whirring around inside him.

"Leave Cheryl to me, honey. I'll sort it, I promise."

CHAPTER 24

Andy gave the alarm a quick thump. He had forgotten last night when he had gone to bed that Saturday was on the other side of midnight and that no alarm was needed. He could feel the coldness of the bedroom closing in around him as his senses threw off their heavy cloak of slumber. He shivered and grabbed the duvet, pulling it tightly around him, trying to recapture the warmth of sleep.

The darkness of the mid-autumn mornings had finally arrived, along with its light patter of rain against his window pane. Thank goodness it was the weekend he thought, still half asleep. There was no way he would be able to pull himself from his bed this morning. If it wasn't for the bright red digits on his black radio alarm clock glowing 07:00 at him he would have sworn by the gloom around him that it was around three in the morning.

Suddenly voices cut through the silence; good humoured banter with the odd chuckling thrown in for good measure. The trouble with the conscious mind, he thought, is that it wanted to receive information constantly. Sleep was its only respite and the moment that was interrupted it came alive again like a sleeping Black Mamba being prodded with a sharp stick.

The voices belonged to James and Charlie and it was the first sign that Andy had had since Tuesday night that Charlie was in fact still in the flat downstairs with James. Sure, Charlie had rung James every day at work but that didn't mean anything. He could have been ringing from the satisfying warmth of his own home for all Andy knew; his wife smiling at him as he chatted to an 'old friend' – all forgiven. Now though, that appeared not to be the case.

The two brothers hadn't spoken since their Tuesday 'chilli' night, when James had taken Charlie downstairs with him to his apartment. This was partly because Andy couldn't see the point and figured that it would only end in an argument of sorts anyway. James, out of embarrassment or indifference, he couldn't tell which, had made no effort to speak to him either. And so it had continued that way; the pair of them sitting opposite each other at work throwing furtive glances when they felt sure the other wasn't watching.

The chuckling became louder and more frequent and Andy knew there was more chance of Donald Trump giving out American visas at the Mexican border than he had of getting back to sleep.

He lay there for another ten minutes until he could bear it no more and then got up, threw a clean pair of boxers on and trudged into the kitchen to boil the kettle. Lynn, the cleaner had been and gone, leaving his flat, whilst terribly lonely, 'show-home' immaculate.

CHAPTER 25

Cheryl double-checked her make up in the dressing table mirror.

"Do I look alright then?" she asked, as Jack bent down and kissed her on the cheek.

"Yeah, you look fine. You always do."

"What about my top? Does it go with this skirt?" She smoothed her short black leather skirt down with her hands, her eyes willing him to say yes.

"It's fine, it's only a Saturday night," he said, puzzled. He wanted to add, 'none of it will be staying on for long anyway', but thought better of it.

As Cheryl gave her already loaded lips another coat of colour, the doorbell rang. "Oh go get it love, will you? I'm nearly finished here."

Jack looked out of the bedroom window and saw Amy and Richard waiting under a huge black golf umbrella, on the doorstep.

"Still pissing down out there," he said, feigning interest.

He glanced up and down the road but couldn't see any sign of anyone else. Maybe Sue and Alan wouldn't come tonight. That would solve all of his problems – for tonight at least. He remembered what Sue had said about not wanting to arouse suspicion among the group. The decision had been made that they should avoid each other tonight and have sex with someone else in the group. He was dreading the entire evening and could think of nothing else other than getting it over with as quickly as possible.

"Well come on then, don't keep them waiting, Jacky-Boy," Cheryl squawked excitedly. "Let the riot begin!"

***

"Really? Two days?" Jack queried it with fake interest and tried not to smile.

"Yep. Seminar in Swindon," Alan muttered. "Bloody thing."

"Right, well... uh, another top up?"

"Great, cheers."

Jack wanted to wipe the smug look off Alan's face and tell him that not only did he already know all about the seminar in Swindon but would also in fact be pleasuring his wife for him while he was there. Instead he walked over to where the drinks were displayed and filled Alan's wine glass to the brim. Talk of Swindon was doing nothing to calm his lustful thoughts of Sue and he hoped that Alan would get so drunk tonight that the last of his problems would be to notice whom his wife had gone off bonking with. And if that was the case, then it might just be him after all.

So far, tonight was no different to any other Saturday. The nights often produced lots of laughter as each of them began to finally unwind after their hectic week at work, and anyone looking in on them would have thought that they had all known each other since childhood and not from an internet ad three years ago. They were all so easy in each other's company, like siblings at a weekly family (albeit a rather incestuous one) supper.

As he picked up his third can of lager, he noticed that Sue was already in deep conversation with Amy's husband, Richard. No matter how much he tried to ignore it, he could feel the first stab of jealously piercing at his heart. *Richard. Fucking Richard.* Of all the people in the room why did it have to be 'Pricky Dicky' (*he had heard all about Richard's super ten inch penis from Cheryl... many times*) who would steal her away from him tonight? There was nothing else for it, he would go over and talk to her and hopefully Richard would back off.

Up until now, he and Sue had only said hello to each other, when she and Alan had arrived. He had taken their coats and fetched them some drinks but since then they had made a concerted effort to avoid each other. He scanned the room quickly. Cheryl's arm was draped lazily around Rob's waist, and Rob's wife, Jackie, was giggling quietly at something Alan had just said to her. Picking up a half empty bottle of Sue's favourite prosecco, he filled a fresh flute and headed towards her.

"Hey, you trying to get her drunk, Jack?" Richard laughed, pointing to Sue's already full glass. He raised his eyebrows slimily. "Ha! Sorry... beat you to it, mate."

Jack held his stare. He wanted to say, 'I'll fucking 'mate' you in a minute, you bastard cock-freak,' but he refrained. What had he meant by 'beat you to it'? *Beat him to what? Filling Sue's glass or bagging her as a bed-mate?* Either way it was eating him up inside and it was as much as he could do to not rip Richard's smug head from his shoulders right there and then.

Sue smiled. "Thanks anyway, Jack. Nice to know that I'm being so well looked after."

Jack looked back to Richard and gritted his teeth. He felt completely unable to cope with the jealousy that now seeped through his entire body, contaminating his veins and arteries with its poisonous green liquid.

"How's Amy?" he asked through still-gritted teeth. "I haven't had a chance to speak to her tonight yet. Are you two still talking about moving away next year?"

"She's fine," Richard replied heartily. "Saw her chatting to Jackie and Rob earlier but God knows where the dozy beggar's got to now."

The laugh that followed was more of a deep snort, the sort that you produce when you have a huge wad of green phlegm stuck at the back of your throat.

"And what's all this about moving away, we never told you that, did we?"

Jack wanted to tell him that no, he had never said any such thing and it had been purely wishful thinking. He looked back to Sue. Her cheeks were flushed. It was definitely warm in here but he had a suspicion that it was as much from the amount of prosecco she had been drinking as it was from the heating.

"How much have you had?" he murmured quietly to her.

"What's all this, mate? You her mother now, are you?" Richard laughed.

Shit. He had heard him.

"It's very warm in here tonight," Sue said, rescuing the situation. "I think Cheryl might have overdone the heating a little. Couldn't check it could you, Jack?"

Jack looked at her flushed face. He wanted her so badly that he physically ached. He wanted to grab Richard around the throat and tell him to keep his grubby little hands (and his ten inch cock) off her, and then he wanted to declare his love for Sue in front of everyone in the room. Instead, he took a deep breath.

"Yes. I think you're right. I'll go and turn it down." He looked her in the eyes for just a second more and then turned and walked into the kitchen.

Finally on his own, he looked at the ridiculous setting on the thermostat. "Effin' hell! I know she wants everyone to get their kit off but this is taking the piss!"

Feeling hot, angry and jealous all at the same time, he turned the dial down to a more comfortable level and then bashed his fist down angrily on the kitchen worktop. He could quite happily stay in the kitchen all night by himself, to be away from everyone else, away from their communal thoughts of lustful 'free for all' sex. Suddenly the idea of what they did on a Saturday night repulsed him; an epiphany borne from jealousy.

"Fucking Pricky-Dicky-Bastard," he muttered out loud. "Keep your fucking hands to yourself, you wanker."

"This yours?"

Amy stood behind him with his beer in her hand. He had no idea how long she had been standing there for.

"Oh, um, cheers, Amy."

As he took it from her he felt the colour drain from his face. *Shit! She must have heard his comment about her husband, it would have been impossible not to.* Surprisingly, she smiled and then wrinkled her nose at him cutely. *Great – maybe she hadn't heard him?* He gulped down the remaining lager in one go, and then belched absentmindedly.

"Oh no, I'm so sorry. I really shouldn't drink lager!"

"Not a problem. You should hear Richard if you think that's bad."

Shit. Richard! "I'm sorry, darling. I just have to get something from the other room. I won't be a minute."

He moved quickly past her and made his way out of the kitchen and into the living room, just in time to see Richard leading Sue up the stairs. Jack stopped in his tracks as Sue's head turned in his direction and she locked her eyes onto his.

"No," he mouthed at her, shaking his head. But Sue pulled her eyes away from him and carried on walking up the stairs.

***

Amy bucked beneath him with every thrust, flailing her arms around her and wailing with unnecessary volume when she came. Jeez she was annoying, he thought for the first time ever. Her small breasts sat like poached eggs on her chest and beneath them her ribs strained against her flesh, making them jut out at an awkward angle. She was painfully thin – why had he never noticed that before? He thought about Sue's voluptuous body; the soft, gentle curves that hugged her bones so perfectly, the satin smoothness of her skin and the hunger in her eyes.

He came quickly and deftly rolled off her, collapsing back onto the mattress.

"What's up?" Amy asked disappointedly. "You look troubled. Not like you to be done and dusted that quickly."

Opening his eyes, he looked at her lying naked beside him. Poor Amy. She was OK really, he thought guiltily. She was a pretty little thing with a pixie face, short dark hair and too much make-up. She was also the youngest one in the group.

Amy and Richard had met at college. He had been her tutor and was fifteen years older than her. Jack had never understood what she had seen in him and guessed that she must have been swept away by his air of authority... not to mention his ten inch dick.

"Was it something I said?" Amy looked at him with

worried eyes. Her pale, impish face had lost its earlier abandonment and she looked conscious of her very being. She pulled the duvet up, over her skinny frame and looked away embarrassed.

Jack felt more guilt towards Amy in that moment than he had ever felt for Cheryl and he knew he wasn't being fair to anyone. He had slept with Amy countless times and had always enjoyed it, she was lively and great fun to be with – it wasn't her fault that tonight had been different, that tonight he only wanted Sue.

"I'm sorry. It's not you, Amy. Please don't take it personally. I don't feel too good, I think I'm coming down with something." He wiped the palm of his hand over his forehead to add weight to his poor excuse.

Amy sat up and frowned. She reached forward for her clothes, annoyance beginning to creep into her tiny features.

"Yeah, me too," she said flatly. "I believe it's called 'Pricky-Dicky-Syndrome.'"

CHAPTER 26

Angela hugged her coffee to her and looked at the clock. They would be home any minute now. She walked into the conservatory and sat down on one of the soft chequered sofas there and thought about yesterday. Tom had, unbeknown to her, arranged for Jessie to go to Eva's for a few hours to play so that they could talk. When Maria had dug deeper, Tom had told her that he and Angela really needed some time together. Alone. Maria didn't need or want any more details and told Tom, without any hesitation, to pack some night clothes for Jessie so that she could stay the night. 'It would be my pleasure and Eva would just love it,' she had told him. Angela had assumed that Tom was at home looking after Jess, while she had been out shopping, but he had been busily cooking a wonderful meal for the two of them. By the time she had got home, the table had been set, the candles were lit and he was just pouring her favourite wine out into crystal glasses. Her heart sank when she realised what was going on and that this would mean they would finally have to face the truth and talk. She could leave, she had thought (there was nothing to stop her from turning around and walking straight back out of the door) but common sense told her that they would have to talk sooner or later, and when Tom announced that Jess was staying at Eva's for the night she realised that tonight would be as good as, if not better, than any other night. The three course meal (she had to admit, though only to herself, that he had done an amazing job) was consumed in near silence. He had tried every few minutes to talk to her but she wanted to scream at him. Just because he had cooked a bloody meal it didn't mean that she had to talk to him, or that everything was going to be OK. She carried on eating though, properly for the first time all week, and looked at him through red eyes every time he spoke. She could think of nothing to say in return. When they had finished the meal and Tom had carried the second bottle of red wine into the lounge with him, he tried again. He told her that he adored her more than anything in the world and would make this up to her, even if it took him the rest of his life to prove it. Angela had burst into tears as the wine began to take its toll and, finally they began to talk. They had stayed up until three in the morning listening to each other, and when she had begun yawning and rubbing her puffy, swollen eyes, she told him that she was going to bed. He had asked if he could come with her. She hadn't answered but he had followed her anyway, and the two of them had fallen asleep on the bed, fully clothed, in each other's arms.

***

"Thanks again, Maria, you're a star," he shouted from the half wound down car window.

Maria smiled and waved before taking Eva back inside with her.

Within seconds Jessie was asleep in the back seat. Maria had said that the girls hadn't slept much. They had been far too excited at the prospect of their first sleepover and when they finally did close their eyes, one of them would wake the other within the hour, every hour. They would giggle for five minutes before their heavy eyelids dragged them back to sleep again.

Tom watched her in the back seat, in the rear view mirror and smiled to himself; she looked just like Angela when she was sleeping. As he turned the corner and stopped at a red light, he thought about last night and allowed himself another little smile. Finally things were beginning to work out. OK, it was only the start, but it *was* a start, and he couldn't be happier.

As the lights turned green and he pulled away again, he remembered all the things that he had said to Angela last night. He had meant every single word. He wanted Angela for life, no one else. If he had learnt anything at all from the last six months then it had been that. It was time to put Max to rest, he told himself. He had to keep her out of his life altogether now and focus only on the future.

* * *

As the car pulled up, Angela rushed to the door to meet them. She could see that Jessie was asleep and she watched smiling as Tom bent down to pick her up from the back seat. Her outstretched arms flopped down by her sides as he gently kicked the door of the car shut with his foot and walked slowly across the gravel towards her.

"She's knackered," Tom smiled. "Maria says they were up all night talking and giggling."

Jess opened one eye sleepily. "Was not!" she croaked, making them both smile together for the first time in a week.

Angela reached out and took Jess from him. Smiling at her and stroking her hair away from her face, she kissed her cheek.

"Come on young lady, you need a little nap or you'll never last the day."

As Jess began to complain, Tom plucked her back from Angela's arms and ran through the house and up the stairs with her. The two of them laughed as he hit his knee on the five foot statue of Hera, the Goddess of Marriage, that stood at the top of the staircase on the first floor, where it had been since Angela was a little girl.

"Daddy, you hit Hera!" Jess laughed.

"Oh she's an ugly moo anyway," Tom whispered back conspiratorially as they reached Jess' bedroom. "But don't tell your mother."

Jess laughed so much that she began hiccupping.

"I'm going to tell mummy, I'm going to tell mummy."

"Not until you've had a sleep first, Princess," he

said as he laid her on her bed and closed her curtains.

"I love you, daddy," she said, crawling underneath her duvet and rubbing her eyes. "Does mummy still love you?"

Taken aback, Tom sat down on the edge of Jess' bed and stared at her for the longest time. "Yes, honey," he said at last, tears stinging the back of his eyes. "Why would you even ask that? Of course mummy still loves me."

CHAPTER 27

The clock said 08:15. Maxine got up and ran herself a bath and then padded into the kitchen to check her mobile. Nothing. Bastard! How dare he just ignore her? She had sent Tom half a dozen text messages in the last few days and he had ignored every single one of them. When there had been no reply to the first one, she had known somewhere deep down in the depths of her empty heart that he would probably never text her again but she had kept on trying nonetheless. She didn't want to give up on him, not yet. She was sure that if she could just say the right thing then he would come back to her. Maybe not now, but in a few weeks when things had calmed down with Angela, who knew?

Feeling the rejection slicing into the last shreds of her already frail self-confidence, she hurled her phone at the kitchen wall and screamed. *What was he thinking? What was he doing? Was he even thinking about her?*

She went back into the bathroom, slipped off her satin bathrobe and immersed herself into the hot mixture of water and bubbles. He must be thinking about me a little bit at least, she thought desperately. *You don't just bed someone for six months and then feel nothing for them.* She tried to dispel the negative thoughts in her mind that told her it had just been a game to him; a bit of fun that had helped to pass the time at work. Maybe that was all it really *had* been? She scolded herself and remembered all the loving things he had said to her and the ring that he had put on her finger (that the bitch wife had *stolen* off her). No. She *knew* that it had meant as much to him as it had to her. It was 'bitch wife' poisoning him, that's what it was! The bitch had probably threatened him with everything he had; the house, the kid, even his livelihood – she owned the majority of the insurance firm after all, not him.

Unable to believe that she had been so blind, she allowed herself a little smile of realisation. The mist had gone. Oh yes. She had been so blind that she hadn't seen the wood from the trees, but not anymore. He wanted her as much as she wanted him and she wasn't going to give him up without a fight. Bitch Wife had probably thrown his mobile away and told him it was for the best; (*you don't need that little tart when you have everything you could possibly want here*). Arghhh! She could imagine Angela saying it.

Maxine dunked her head beneath the frothy water and held her breath for as long as she could – until the pain in her lungs hurt her more than the pain in her heart. She spluttered as she came back up for air, promising herself that she would get him back. Oh yes, even if it goddamn killed her... she would get him back.

She washed quickly, got out of the bath and looked at herself in her wardrobe mirror. Her eyes were puffy and red – had been for a week now. Her curvy figure was already beginning to diminish under the slavery of an unintentional diet and her hair was limp and lifeless. If she wanted him back then she had been going the wrong way about it. *She wasn't going to get him back looking like this!* Things were going to have to change. She needed a job for a start, then she might actually look like someone he would want to be seen with and not the pathetic, straggly, unemployed mess that glowered in the reflection before her. She quickly scanned through a couple of YouTube tutorials on how to get rid of red, puffy eyes and then a further one that popped up as 'related' on 'how to get your ex-boyfriend back'. Looking at her miserable excuse of a make-up collection she frowned then sighed. It would have to do.

Over an hour later a glowing face smiled back at her, and after another hour on her hair, she beamed at her reflection. She quickly scrolled through local job vacancies online for another hour, and by 12.30pm she was outside the job centre, just across the road from Brandley & Baxters Insurance Company.

***

"And I was just getting used to having an office of my own, you bastard," Jack joked to Tom. "Tell me you're not seriously putting me back out there with the god-damn Chuckle Brothers?"

Tom laughed. "Sorry, mate, but it's you or me, and

put it this way... it's not going to be me."

He passed a coffee across to Jack and sat back down behind his desk. "Anyway, James and Andy are alright. What's the problem?"

Jack took a sip of his coffee and sat in the chair on the other side of Tom's desk.

"Oh I dunno. Just got used to working in peace for a change I suppose. I got kind of used to this little room you know."

"And used to sitting on the other side of the desk?" Tom finished for him.

Jack laughed. "Well yeah, that too."

Tom frowned at the enormous pile of paperwork on the desk in front of him. "Jack, did you actually get *any* work done while I was away?" He checked the date stamp on a couple of letters at the bottom of the pile. "Some of these are a week old."

Jack swallowed hard and quickly gulped down another mouthful of coffee. "There's been Max's stuff to do too you know," he offered in defence. "You're going to have to hire someone, we're knackered without her."

Tom chewed the inside of his mouth. He knew that her name would come up sooner or later but he hadn't expected it to happen so quickly. He looked towards his closed door, wondering about the twins that sat behind it working at their desks, and about the empty chair where Maxine sat no more.

"They still don't know anything if that's what you're worried about," Jack said, broaching the subject again.

Tom took a deep breath and gulped down his coffee. "Right. Good. I'll get an ad put on the jobs website then, and in the local paper. I'll phone up, get it in there for tomorrow afternoon."

He saw the look of surprise on Jack's face.

"What's the problem?"

"It's Max. I should really tell you, um..."

"Tell me what?" Tom looked worried.

"She came here while you were away."

"WHAT? What do you mean she came here? What for?"

"Well I don't know really. Said she'd come for her stuff. Ended up in here screaming at me. She said something about me judging her or something."

"Oh shit, that's all I need." Tom got up and walked to the window, pushing the opening wider still to aerate the now stuffy little room.

"And did she?"

"Did she what?"

"Did she get her stuff?"

Jack tried to think back. "Shit, mate, I dunno. Like I said, she sort of ended up screaming at me and the next thing I knew she was gone. I don't think she did, no."

"Didn't you check?" Tom asked in disbelief. "Bloody hell, mate, you only have to go out there and open a couple of drawers to see if her stuff's gone!"

Jack felt incensed. "Hey hang on a minute. Regardless of what you might think, I *have* been working you know. It might be important to you, but to be quite honest I don't give a shite if Max took her stuff or not! It really wasn't on the top of my 'To Do List'!"

Tom put his hands over his face and rubbed his forehead vigorously. "OK, OK. Ignore me. I'm just worried she's gonna come back again that's all. I don't think I could handle it, mate. What day was she here?"

"Thursday I think. In the morning. Look, I'll go and check the drawers now, just give me a sec." Jack disappeared. Within thirty seconds he was back, a paperback book in one hand and her spare make-up bag in the other. "This is all that's left. Looks like she took the rest."

Tom groaned. "Why the hell did she leave *that*? Why didn't she take it all? If she's coming back again I don't want to be here."

"Maybe this stuff isn't important to her. It was in the top drawer and everything else has gone. Maybe she wanted us to bin it."

"Have you ever known make-up not be important to Max?" Tom felt uneasy.

"Makes no odds, mate, surely? She's quite obviously got more make up at home. She's gone. She won't come back."

"AND HOW WOULD YOU KNOW?" Tom turned away from him and began pacing the small office floor. His heart was thumping and his mind was racing. He stopped abruptly and looked back at Jack.

"She's been texting me non-stop. I don't know what

to do. I read them, delete them and then the next one comes along. I just can't bring myself to block her."

Jack remembered the text that Sue had sent him early this morning. He had read it and then deleted it straight away, just as Tom had done to Maxine's. He had been too hurt and angry thinking about her night with Richard to reply to her, but now, thinking about her once again, his resolve was already weakening.

"Well I can't say I'm surprised," Jack said, trying to ignore his own problems, "she was pretty bad when she was here the other day. Wanted to know if I'd seen you, where you were, all that sort of stuff. Maybe if you speak to her you could sort it out properly? Let her know where she stands. Pretending she doesn't exist isn't going to sort out anything."

"Already tried that," Tom replied, "she knows exactly where she stands." He sat back down and started chewing a fingernail as he thought about his brief visit to her apartment on Thursday morning. *She must have come straight here after he had left?*

"Anyway, I suppose I'd better get some work done now that the boss is back," Jack joked, looking at his watch. He walked towards the door and grabbed the handle before turning back to Tom. "What if the messages keep coming, mate? What will you do?"

Tom looked at Jack over the mound of paperwork in front of him and shook his head. "Block her I guess."

***

Maxine looked up at the building. *She had seen him!* Albeit very briefly. He had come to the window to open it wider and had momentarily looked down at the street below. *Had he seen her?* She didn't think so. Just the thought that he was there did strange things to her insides; churning them around like clothes in a washing machine on a fast spin and then splattering them back against the inside walls of her body. *He wanted to speak to her, of course he did. He was trapped like a fly in a web, unable to move in any direction, waiting for her to rescue him from the Bitch Spider Wife.*

Maxine walked around the corner and out of sight into a quiet side road and then took another turning into an alleyway. Pulling out her iPhone from her tiny black handbag, she scanned the conversations in her WhatsApp list. She scrolled past the 'Team Twats' conversation (the work's group chat, where James and Andy had been asking again when she was coming back) and also past her best mate, Tina, who she had messaged before leaving the house, before stopping at Tom's name. There was no point calling his mobile again or messaging him; he obviously no longer had the phone. She thought for a moment and then went into her telephone contacts list, stopping at the entry that read 'Tom's Office'. She took a deep breath and called the number. It only rang twice before he answered.

"Hello, Tom Baxter speaking," he said, in what Maxine called his 'sing-song voice'.

She faltered, taken aback by the speed at which the

call had been answered. His beautiful voice was right there, on the other end of the line. She was rooted to the paving slab beneath her, unable to move or speak.

"Hello?" his voice came again, more serious now. "Brandley and Baxter's Insurance. Can I help you?"

Maxine could feel her heart pounding ferociously inside her chest. She held her breath and swallowed, afraid and unable to make a sound.

"Hello, who is this?"

She pressed the phone closer to her ear and closed her eyes. Her churning stomach and tightening chest threatened to engulf her, but a sudden panic overwhelmed her at the thought of him putting the phone down before she had even spoken to him.

"Hello," she said finally, in a cracked whisper.

The line went quiet as Tom took on board the identity of the caller. She waited for a response but he stayed silent.

"Tom, I need to see you. Say something, anything."

There was further silence for a moment longer and then the finality of the click, as he put down the telephone.

CHAPTER 28

"It was a disaster from the moment I got there!" he said, throwing his denim jacket down onto the kitchen table huffily.

James switched off the T.V. and gave Charlie his undivided attention. Charlie had been gone for three hours and if the truth be told, he had been more than a little worried that during that time things between him and Paloma might have been going a little *too* well. Now though he tried to stifle the feeling of joy that had begun to rise in his chest and, he could now feel creeping onto his face.

"Come on, it couldn't have been that bad," James said, hoping that in fact it had been.

Charlie walked over to the fridge and pulled out the Bacardi he had bought earlier. "I'm telling you, Jay," he said slamming the fridge door closed, "it was like confronting Simon Cowell in drag. I couldn't have been more scared if Marilyn Manson had walked in and started shagging me up the arse!"

James laughed. "I daresay that wouldn't scare you at all."

Charlie ignored the quip and joined him on the sofa with the bottle still firmly in his hand.

"You know, you'd think that after all these years we've been married we'd be able to, well you know, talk about things in a civilised manner at least, wouldn't you? But, oh no! I mean, is that too much to ask?"

"Never been married. I don't know about these things, but it's understandable I suppose. She's probably still in shock, you can't blame her."

Charlie downed his drink and looked back at James.

"I s'pose you're right." He filled his tumbler with another Bacardi. "Anyway, I've got quite used to being here with you. I feel sort of settled now." Charlie gave James his best coquettish smile.

James thought about reminding him that this was only a temporary arrangement and that there was no point in making himself too comfortable, but as he opened his mouth to speak, the words remained stuck in his head, never making their way to his vocal cords. He hated to admit it but he was really enjoying Charlie being here and if the truth be told, the thought of him packing up his holdall and going back home to Paloma filled him with an agonising dread. He swallowed hard, fully aware of what was going to come out of his mouth next.

"I have to admit that I've kind of got used to you being here too." He could see no reason to deny it any longer.

Charlie looked up in surprise. "You have? Ooh duck, you're getting me all excited!"

James smiled and remembered Charlie dumping his bag in the living room a week ago as he 'crashed' at his apartment, just as any 'mate' would do. Not once Charlie made any move to pursue their previous sexual relationship; the one they'd had before the 'Andy' saga had started. Not once had he tried to touch him, kiss him or in fact even say anything mildly suggestive. It had caused a clash of feelings inside James; respect that Charlie hadn't assumed any such thing would happen when he moved in, and hurt, that maybe after Andy, Charlie just didn't want him in 'that way' anymore. The words were rising again, the stifling hadn't worked. They were pushing harder this time and wrapping themselves around his voice box, like tiny boa constrictors threatening to asphyxiate him. James sighed in defeat.

"There's something about you, about you being here, I... oh I can't find the words. It doesn't matter."

Charlie looked offended. "Hey it *does* matter. It matters a lot. To me anyway. More than... I don't know... being shagged up the arse by Marilyn Manson!" He smiled cheekily. "It *matters*, Jay, so tell me."

This was the attitude that had endeared Charlie to him more than ever over the last week. James had thought about it carefully. His grey and uneventful apartment had coloured and come alive since Charlie had graced its rooms. It buzzed with excitement; every room becoming brighter and more auspicious as he moved about them. A feeling of panic washed over him at the thought of all that ending.

"You can stay as long as you like," James told him, trying not to sound too keen or worse, plain desperate. "I just wanted you to know that, that's all."

A broad smile swept over Charlie's face.

"You know, I'm really glad you said that, Jay. I

really am."

***

James carried a Bacardi and Coke and a cup of tea into the room and, handing the Bacardi to Charlie, climbed back into the still warm bed.

"I just knew you wouldn't be able to keep your divine hands off me for much longer," Charlie quipped cheekily, slipping even further beneath the warm duvet. "Reverse psychology see – works every time!"

James looked at him blankly, unable to follow. "What?"

"Well, you thought I didn't want you, so it made you want me even more." Charlie grinned, looking ever more pleased with himself.

"You mean you were playing games with me?" James asked, suddenly feeling stupid. "How could you do that? I don't do mind games, Charlie, never have and I'm certainly not going to start now. What you see is what you get."

"OK, keep your sticky condom on," Charlie laughed. "I'm only winding you up."

James looked at him and despite himself, smiled. He moved himself closer to the warm body beside him and then slowly disappeared below the duvet.

"Oh, hang on a minute," came the muffled voice five seconds later. "What about Andy?"

Taking a deep breath, Charlie let his head sink

further back into the soft pillows, his smile spreading wider across his already contented face.

"Andy?" he breathed. "Darling, who the fuck is *Andy*?"

CHAPTER 29

Filling up her wine glass for the third time in less than twenty minutes, Maxine brushed the tears from her eyes and took another huge glug of red wine. Why on earth was Tom doing this to her? *What had she ever done to him to make him treat her this way?* She had fallen in love with him that was all. And what sort of fool was she to have fallen for all that shit anyway? *Love! What a load of bollocks that was!* She could feel the rage still burning in her chest, borne from the humiliation of it all. She tried to fight it but couldn't stop herself from re-living the nightmare of the last few hours. How many times had she gone over it now?

When Tom had hung up on her while she had stood in a stinking alleyway, she had rung him straight back – her feet still glued to the same inch of pavement beneath her. Why would he hang up on her? *Maybe he hadn't recognised her voice. Maybe there was someone in the room there with him and he hadn't been able to talk to her?*

He had left it longer to answer the second time and then his voice had been there again, soft and silky, coating the line.

"Max, what do you want?" He had said it with annoyance in his voice - an annoyance that she had not been on the receiving end of before.

"Oh, Tom, I'm missing you so much. Can you talk?

Was there someone there with you before?" Her voice had become fluffy and light; he was there on the other end of the line – as close to her it seemed, as if he were standing on the pavement right there beside her. It thrilled the very essence of her.

"No. No one was around," he had answered shortly.

She had been surprised and disappointed by his reply.

"Oh... oh OK. Well... how are you? Tom, I've missed you more than I've ever missed anyone in my life. It's been hell. When can I see you again?"

If Tom had been momentarily stunned by the first call, then this one had stripped him naked, tied him down and whipped him in the testicles.

"Max, what are you on about?"

"I need to see you, when can you call round?"

"Max, I came round last week. I thought we'd been through all of this, I thought you understood. Didn't I make it clear?" He paused, fully aware of the extra shot of pain he was about to inject into this poor girl's life. "Max, I'm sorry, it's over. I'm not coming round. I told you, I have to make this work with Angela, I *want* to make this work with Angela."

"Angela?" she had whispered numbly. "I knew it. She's poisoned you against me."

"What?"

"Please, Tom, I'm begging you," she had wailed, exposing her sad desperation. "I can't let you go, I just can't do it. I want you. I *need* you! You can't just turn your feelings off, I *know* you want me too."

Unbeknown to her, Tom had held the phone tightly in his hand and with the other rubbed his eyes furiously. This was hell. An absolute living, torturous hell. Maxine was right, he couldn't just turn his feelings off; she hadn't just been someone to pass the time with, he had really cared for her, really wanted to look after her. Hearing her plead down the line like this, crying and begging, made him want her all over again. In the next few seconds his mind's eye played him just a handful of their 'bed scenes' he had stored away in its dark corners. His heart and groin ached simultaneously. Then he had looked down at the picture of Jess on his desk and twirled the wedding ring on his finger.

"I'm sorry, Max, I really am," were the only broken words that would come out.

Of course she had rung Tina and told her all the details and it was at this point in the re-telling of the story that Tina had not so helpfully interjected, 'You stupid dumb-ass bitch. They *never* leave the wife, Max!'.

"That *bitch* wife of yours!" Max had ranted on at him. "I hate her. I fucking HATE her!"

"Max, stop it," Tom had shouted. "None of this is Angela's fault and you know it."

At that moment something inside her was damaged beyond repair. Like a band that had been stretched too tightly or a balloon that had had one too many lungfuls of air blown into it. '*It*' whatever '*it*' was, was broken.

"How can you stand up for her? You don't care about me!" she had stammered. "All the time I thought you really cared and all I ever was was just an extra shag whenever you could get it!"

"That's not true, Max, and you know it."

"Yes it *is* true, otherwise you'd see me." The tears were streaming down her blotchy cheeks now with a life of their own. "Otherwise you wouldn't say those things to me, Tom. Otherwise you'd leave the Bitch Wife and live with ME!"

"That's enough! I'm not leaving Angela, not for anyone, but that doesn't mean that I didn't care for you. DO care for you." He could feel the tears stinging the back of his eyes.

"Then prove it, Tom, fucking prove it!" Maxine had screamed.

"You know how I feel and that'll have to be enough."

"Well it isn't enough. It might be for you, but it isn't for me. It's NOT enough!"

Tom had felt completely helpless and bereft of any ideas to get out of the horrendous situation that he was now in. He had taken a deep breath and bitten down so hard on his bottom lip that within seconds he could taste his own blood.

"Stop calling me," he had said at last, and then for the second time that day, he put the phone down on her.

Twice more she had phoned Tom back but he hadn't

answered.

Now Maxine glanced around her dimly lit living room and wiped her eyes. She didn't want to think about the day's events anymore; they were pounding into her precious memories like a jackhammer churning up bits of broken pavement. She poured the last of the wine into her glass and drank it down before reaching for the cigarette packet that she had bought earlier. She hadn't smoked since she and Tom had started seeing each other (he had hated it and she had packed it in for him willingly without a second thought – without him even asking her to). Today however, she had bought them as a 'two fingers up' to him. '*Yeah, fuck you!*' she had said, as the cashier had put the change into her hand. The cashier had looked at her with a horrified expression. '*Oh no, NOT YOU!*' Maxine had gasped. '*I meant... oh it doesn't matter.*'

She pulled a cigarette out of the near empty packet, lit it with relish and then tearfully looked around her dark living room; the place where they had first made love.

"YOU WANKER!" she shouted out into the empty space around her. "YOU FUCKING WANKER, how dare you treat me like this! I hate you, I hate you, I FUCKING HATE YOU!"

She wiped her snotty nose on the back of her hand and took another long drag on her cigarette.

"You just wait, you heartless bastard. You haven't heard the last of me."

CHAPTER 30

Wednesday had come around quickly enough, too quickly in fact. Jack never thought that he would ever think that way about a date 'of sex' with Sue, but he was thinking it now as he walked down the concrete path that ran along the side of hers and Alan's red brick house. He walked through the gate and opened the back door. It was unlocked, just as she had said it would be.

The 'rear entry' arrangement (which was quite different to the one that he was used to) was supposed to draw attention away from any prying eyes in the neighbouring semis which might otherwise, by chance, see him at the front of the house. However, he couldn't help feeling that the nosey bags would be a lot more suspicious if they should see him right now walking straight through the back door of her house without knocking.

As he stepped into the dining room he saw Sue standing there waiting for him. Her face was lit up and she glowed from within as if sunbeams were shooting out of her. Without any need for words they fell into each other's arms holding on tightly, content to just be together. He breathed in her scent deeply and then let out a long, quiet sigh as he fingered her hair. He couldn't help wondering if Richard had held her like this on Saturday night; had breathed her into his lungs and let it fill him up or had buried his face in her hair. He doubted it. Saturday night was just what it was for everyone, what it used to be for him – just sex, for the sake of sex.

Since Monday, he had managed to push Richard to the back of his mind, but now he was here with Sue again, it was all he could think of.

Before he could speak she held her hand out to him and led him into the front room where an open bottle of Rioja was waiting alongside two large wine glasses. He noticed they were filled and that one of them already had her familiar lipstick mark around the rim. She plucked them both up and handed the one without the mark to him, and then moved over to the soft, brown leather sofa at the edge of the living room.

"Come on, Jack, what are you waiting for?" Unable to stop herself, she began giggling. "I'm so excited, aren't you? I've waited and waited for tonight. Stupid really I suppose, but hey – *you're staying the night!* I feel like a kid on Christmas Eve!"

Jack smiled as a warm tingle invaded him. In all of his life he couldn't once remember having ever felt so severely flattered by a single comment. All thoughts of Richard on Saturday, and Alan at his Swindon seminar, evaporated.

He quickly made his way over to the sofa to join her, his mind suddenly flooded with an onslaught of questions. *Why did he love her so much*? Was the reason purely because he loved the fact that she wanted him so much? Did he crave that feeling *that* much? Was he *that* hooked on 'needing' her to 'need' him that he would hit rock bottom and go to pieces like a drug addict, without it? Was this *feeling* nothing more than *his* drug, *his* fix? Did that make him 'sad' or just 'normal'? Did that mean if she told him that she no longer needed or wanted him, he would in effect become worthless? Or at least feel worthless, until he found someone else to replenish him and make him feel whole and 'priceless' again?

"Ooh, I forgot to ask – what on earth did you tell Cheryl?" Sue blurted out breathlessly, breaking into his thoughts. "Hey, didn't you bring a bag, babe? Won't you need fresh clothes for tomorrow?"

Jack looked at her flushed, excitable face. She was right; she *was* like a kid on Christmas Eve and he couldn't remember ever having seen her look that way before. She glowed and sparkled in a way he never knew existed. That was enough for him. Enough for now.

"Don't worry your head about anything," he grinned. "I don't need anything. Just you."

★★★

The wine bottle empty, Sue fetched another from the stainless steel wine rack and took it upstairs. Jack was standing at the foot of the bed waiting for her, just as she had told him to.

"What on earth's this lot for then?" he asked when she got there. He was oblivious to her reddened face as he fingered the selection of scarves and ties that were laid out on the bed before him.

"Having a clear out?"

"What do you think they're for, Jack?" Her eyes lit up like fairy lights again.

"Haven't got a clue, that's why I asked."

She laughed at the child-like confusion on his face and, putting the bottle down on the bedside table, picked up one of the ties and began wrapping it around one of his wrists.

"Give me your other hand." She waited, amused, for him to comply, and when he did she noticed the confusion still sitting ill at ease on his face. "Don't tell me you and Cheryl have never... you know... tied each other up before."

Jack was, for the first time that night, speechless. The truth was that he and Cheryl had never done 'a lot of things' before and tying each other up was just one of them. Unless he counted the time he and Cheryl had entered a drunken three legged race at the town's charity auction two years ago. Somehow he didn't think that he could. He felt himself smiling back and pulled his tied up hands above his head, playing along with her game in earnest.

She slid his polo shirt off and pushed him backwards onto the freshly made bed, and within minutes had removed his jeans, pants and socks. Quickly, she tied his legs slightly apart, to the curled metal at the bottom of the bed frame.

"Hey, hang on a minute," he protested weakly – all acts of servility quickly disappearing. "I'm gonna need a lot more bloody wine if I'm going to go through with this Fifty Shades malarkey."

Obligingly, Sue scrambled to the bedside table and re-filled the two wine glasses. With Jack still lying flat on his back, she held his wine glass a few inches away from his mouth and slowly dripped some of the wine down into his waiting, open mouth. Within seconds his mouth was full and the burgundy liquid was overflowing and dribbling over the sides of his mouth and over his ears. She ignored his splutterings as he tried to swallow the wine, and instead eyed the red stains that had appeared instantaneously on her pristine duvet cover. Raising her eyebrows and saying nothing, she reached for more ties.

"Gawd, al-bleeding-mighty," Jack complained, "don't you think I'm trussed up enough, babe? Don't go getting too power-crazed on me, I feel like a friggin' Christmas turkey as it is!"

He wriggled on the bed trying to loosen the ties on his legs but they tightened themselves further in evil rebellion. Flinging his tied hands back above his head in defeat, he knocked his wine glass off the bedside table, causing the remaining wine to fall onto the edge of the cream duvet cover.

"OH JACK! Look at the mess you've made of my clean bed," she exclaimed, playing her part to perfection. "You're REALLY for it now."

Reaching for a scarf and stifling a giggle, she covered his eyes and lifted his head off the pillow for a few seconds while she tied it securely at the back.

"There, that's better," she breathed, sounding pleased with herself.

"What's that for, what are you doing?"

"Punishing you of course," she said matter-of-factly. "What do you expect when you trash my John Lewis duvet cover?"

"I think," he replied slowly, "that I've led a bloody sheltered life, that's what *I* think! Take this bugger off my face, honey, come on. I don't trust you when I can't see you."

Sue smiled and crept gently off the bed and over to the dresser where she pulled out a black leather belt from beneath some of Alan's socks.

"Now if you're good this won't hurt a bit."

It sounded to Jack as though she had mustered up the best dominatrix voice she could find within herself. But it didn't work; Sue was too kind and gentle to be a good dominatrix and he knew she wouldn't hurt him.

"You WILL be good, won't you, Jack?"

"Oh sure, sure. Of course," he humoured her.

She walked back over to the bed and gently swept the belt over his semi erect penis.

"SUE?" he called out from beneath his blindfold into the now silent bedroom. "What the hell are you doing? Stop it, it's not funny anymore. I'm bloody crapping myself, so unless you want an even bigger mess on your duvet cover you'd better pack it in now!"

"Don't be so silly," she said, addressing him as though he were a child. "Come on, turn over, it's just a bit of fun."

"Sue, you're evil. This isn't funny you know. I know what you're thinking, so don't even go there. I don't do pain!"

"Oh shut up and turn over, you big wuss."

"How am I supposed to do that when you've tied my legs to the bed, eh?"

Sue quickly untied his legs and took off his blindfold, and not wanting to ruin her fun, Jack turned over willingly and wiggled his backside at her invitingly.

"Come on then, baby," he said smiling now, "What are you waiting for? Never let it be said that Jacky Boy's afraid of a little... *OOOOWWWWWW*!"

He turned his head around just in time to see Sue bringing the black belt down across his rump for a second time. Although the initial whack had shocked him, it hadn't been quite as bad as he was expecting. Sue raised her arm for a third time.

"SUE! NO! Don't even think about it!" But it was too late and Alan's black belt cracked his buttocks again.

The sting turned to burning and Jack flipped himself over and pulled the duvet over himself for protection.

"Well, what did you think?" she asked him, eyes wide and waiting.

"You're fucking mental is what I think! Don't ever do that again." And then he kissed her before making the best love he had ever made.

***

Cheryl looked at her watch, sighed and got up from the floral settee to turn the television off. It was midnight. She expected Jack would be off his head by now, unable to walk properly and probably being sick in a toilet cubicle somewhere. Serve him right.

How come she had never heard him mention Dan before when he had talked about his old days at the dry cleaners? Still, it was nice that they had kept in touch for all those years and that he had thought of Jack when planning his last minute stag do. When (slightly disappointedly) she had asked Jack why they hadn't been invited to the wedding, he had told her that Dan and his bride-to-be were legging it off to St. Lucia on Saturday to get married on an exotic beach somewhere. No family and no friends, just the two of them. How romantic, Cheryl thought dreamily. It meant that the Stag Night had to be mid-week which was a bit of a nuisance for him, but as Jack had said to her yesterday – it was a small price to pay to keep an old mate happy.

CHAPTER 31

Maria looked around the small coffee shop. She had never been here before, although from the sounds of it Angela was quite a regular. She and the girl behind the counter had called each other by name and the girl had even asked her how her family were. 'The usual, Ange?' she had then asked, when they had finished with the pleasantries.

Maria was thrilled that she and Angela had become such good friends. Since moving to England she had found it difficult to make any friends at all let alone trust someone with the things that she had trusted Angela with. The things she had found herself confiding were things she had never told a living soul but there was something about Angela that made her feel safe enough to do it. And now it seemed that she was returning that confidence by opening up to her in return. She had told her about Tom's affair with his secretary, Maxine. Maria had been shocked (Tom just didn't look the sort) but she had tried not to show it. Tom had seemed like such a nice man when she had met him, she had liked him straight away and, she decided, she still did – mistakes happened in life after all.

"And so things are good now, yes?" Maria poured them both another cup of tea from the china pot and smiled warmly.

"Yes, things are good," Angela smiled back. "He's

so sorry, Maria, I know it sounds crazy but he really is. I believe him when he says it's over and that it won't ever happen again."

"He is a good man, Angela, I know these things. Believe me, he is feeling bad at what 'as happened. He will not do this again, I am sure."

"You don't think he's just feeling 'bad' at being caught out then?" Angela couldn't help but sound a little bitter.

"No. I don't think this. He loves you and he doesn't want to lose you. He would do anything. He 'as more sense, you will see."

Angela smiled gratefully for the support and took a sip of her tea. Since Maria had confided in her about her husband, Adrio (not to mention the beatings and the kidnapping of Eva), Angela felt that the bond between them had strengthened and that she could now consider her a close friend. She felt that if she couldn't trust Maria with her and Tom's problems then she couldn't trust anyone – and right now she just had to trust someone.

CHAPTER 32

Tom walked to the window of his office and looked out at the people scurrying about below. The wind had really picked up now and, spotting the dark clouds overhead, it looked as though rain was on its way too. He sat back down at his desk and picked up his new mobile phone, running his fingers over the shiny new screen protector. He had wanted a new number (the calls and texts off Maxine had been getting ridiculous - in number and content) and he had been due an upgrade anyway so had decided to change the entire thing. If he was to focus on the future as he intended to, then the old one simply had to go.

She had stopped calling the office phone days ago, after he continued to hang up on her. Even so, she could see that he had still been reading her messages and so she had carried on sending them – with a vengeance, until he blocked her. Now, his new phone offered him a fresh start, a new beginning. He could finally put the past behind him.

Sally, Maxine's replacement, knocked lightly on the door before bringing him in an afternoon coffee in a yellow mug.

"There you go, Mr Baxter," she said smiling confidently.

"Thanks, Sally, but I told you before you don't have to do that, that's what that's for." He pointed to the small kettle in the corner of his office.

"Oh sorry, I keep forgetting," she said tutting, "I'll get used to it."

Sally was different to Maxine, which was first and foremost why Tom had hired her. Her short black hair, pale un-made face and long skirts belied her true age of only twenty two. He promised himself as soon as she walked through the door at the interview that she would be the one to get the job, even before he had heard about her first class references or seen the next four girls waiting in line for their interview. She was plain and she was serious, not flirty and playful like Max. Right there and then, to Tom, she was perfect.

Back in the main office, Jack beamed at Sally.

"You sure know how to make a good cuppa, girl." He was about to add, 'if nothing else,' but stopped himself just in time.

He missed Max a lot. He missed her being in the office, missed the laughs they used to have and the base, un-PC jokes that they would share, but even he could see that Max could never come back. Not now. He had messaged her a few times to see how she was (did she want to go for a coffee or a 'proper drink' to talk about things?) but she hadn't replied.

He let his thoughts drift back to the early morning when he and Sue, for the first time ever, had woken up in each other's arms. It had been bliss. If only he was still lying next to her warm body - what a change it had made to his usual mornings at home with Cheryl.

Sue had made him breakfast in bed and then she had washed him all over in the bath before giving him a quick massage, and it hadn't ended there. She had even gone on to dress him for work. He wondered (rather stupidly) if she did the same for Alan. Probably not, he guessed, as common sense prevailed; it was just a 'mistress thing', wasn't it? Cheryl certainly never did that for him and never had, not even in the early days. He looked down at his creased shirt and smiled at the memory of Sue pulling it from his body thirteen hours earlier. He had forgotten to take a change of clothes and hadn't had time this morning to pop home first; he had arrived for work ten minutes late as it was.

Smiling, he twiddled with a small pile of paperclips that were tangled up in front of him and thought about his impending fortieth birthday. Events such as that were usually turning points in life, weren't they? *What was it exactly that he wanted from his life anyway?* He didn't know the answer to that one anymore. *Had he ever?* All he knew was that before Cheryl there had been 'nothing', but *with* Cheryl there had been 'something'. That 'something' had been enough for him before so why wasn't it anymore? That was a question that he did know the answer to; never before had he felt the kind of love that he felt for Sue. Jeez, how sad was that, he thought depressingly – nearly forty and what had life given him? Not a lot. Not a lot until Sue. His long forgotten teenage visions of a bleak and unfulfilled future were resurfacing as he reflected on his life.

He used to think he had it all worked out, thought he would be with Cheryl forever, celebrating their Ruby Anniversary quicker than he could turn around and say 'thank you for saving me', but now... now he wasn't so sure. What about the children he had always wanted to have someday? What about his desire to spread his wings and start up a business of his own? What about the 'deep and meaningful marriage' he had always wanted but had never had with Cheryl? The one that Tom and Angela used to have. Might still have. Were all these things handed out deservingly by some great Creator in the sky? Or did you make your own luck and have to take the bull by the horns to get what you really wanted from life, before Mr Reaper called to wipe the smile off your face and plunge you six feet under? Had Cheryl merely been a stepping stone until it was time for true love to walk into his life? And why hadn't he and Sue talked about leaving their spouses, to up sticks and get a place of their own together?

He scolded himself. Maybe it was a bit early into their 'relationship' to be thinking about things like that; just the thought could be enough to send Sue running twenty kilometres in the opposite direction. Far better to wait, he thought. *But time was fast running out wasn't it, so what the hell was there to wait for?* They were crazy about each other. They had risked everything to be together and they were already planning the next time that they could see each other.

Jack put the paperclips down and tried to concentrate on the work in front of him. *Forty. What the hell? FORTY!* There was a time in everyone's life when some life changing decisions had to made and, Jack realised, the time for his was now.

***

"Brandley and Baxter, can I help you?" Andy hurried the words into the mouthpiece.

He was so busy he didn't have time to fart let alone answer the phone - at least that was what he had said out loud the last time the phone had rung. Sally had glanced over at him with a look of disgust on her nondescript features and scribbled something onto a notepad before carrying on with her work. Andy had ignored her and carried on musing over how work could swing the way it did. One week they would be scratching around for stuff to do and other weeks not even have time to grab a sandwich.

"Hello?" he repeated, as the line remained quiet. "Can I help you?"

"Andy?" The familiar voice broke the silence. "Um... it's Charlie. How are you, duck?"

Andy felt himself freeze in his seat and he silently groaned. The two of them hadn't spoken since the day Charlie had followed James out of Andy's apartment and walked straight into James' below him. God only knew how they had managed to avoid each other for this long, but circumstances had, for once, been kind. Until now.

"I'm fine." Andy squirmed.

Silence opened up between them like an unwanted guest at a dinner party. What did Charlie expect him to say? Hearing Charlie through the thin barrier of the two apartments was bad enough but to have him on the other end of the line where there was no escape, was nothing short of agonising.

"What do you want?" Andy asked finally, determined to punch said silence in the face. "James?"

"Ah... yes please. I'm sorry, duck, this is bloody awkward I know, but James doesn't have a mobile at the moment, it's broken, so I've got no choice but to ring his work number. I guess you were bound to pick up on me sooner or later. I hope there isn't any uneasiness between us there doesn't have to be, you know." His voice was low and he sounded uncomfortable.

Andy closed his eyes and took a deep, silent breath, through gritted teeth. "Of course not," he replied with as much good grace as he could muster. "But he's left early today, dentist I think, so I can't put you through." Andy took a badly chewed pencil from the corner of his mouth and continued. "I'd tell him you called but I'm sure you'll see him before I do."

Andy didn't know why he had said it but the comment was deliberate. In that moment he had wanted to inject even more ill-ease into an already uncomfortable situation. If Charlie noticed anything he didn't say.

"Oh... OK, well thanks anyway. Oh, and chick, before you go... why don't you join me and James for dinner tonight in the apartment?" His voice changed from awkward to self-assured and high pitched. "*I'm cooking – chicken in white wine with the best taters you've ever tasted!*"

"Sorry," Andy tried to clear his head, "but are you taking the piss?"

Sally looked up, added something else to her notepad and then looked away.

"Certainly not!" The offence in Charlie's tone was rife. "We're all grown-ups after all. I'm sure we could sit through a little meal together, you just said yourself there's no need for any juvenile awkwardness."

"No, *you* said that, not me. I just agreed. And stop calling me 'chick' or 'duck', I'm not an animal."

"C'mon, And, don't you think it's time we all moved on a bit? This can't go on forever, babes, can it?"

"Look, really I can't. I'm... washing my car tonight... or something."

"Well I'm not taking no for an answer. We'll see you at eight."

Charlie rang off, leaving Andy staring blankly ahead, the phone still resting in his hand.

CHAPTER 33

"What do you mean you invited him for dinner?" James looked up at Charlie's incorrigible face. "I really hope you're winding me up."

"Not at all, he *is* your brother after all so what's wrong with that?"

"You know damn well what's wrong with that, don't be so facetious."

"I'm not being facetious." Charlie flicked the dark hair from his eyes with one sharp jerk of the head and sucked his cheeks in, trying his best to look offended.

"Well there's no way he'll turn up," James said calmly, "so don't bother laying the table for him."

"How do you know?"

James tilted his head to the side and stared at Charlie's face; a canvas of innocence.

"You're a pain in the backside sometimes!"

"And don't I know it!" Charlie smirked.

"Oh, very good! Nice one."

"Look, we can't carry on like this, Jay, it's ridiculous. I'm here for God knows how long now and he's going to see us together sometime, so get it over and done with, that's what I say."

James thought about it. It was true enough that they would have to face Andy as a couple sooner or later, if indeed they even *were* a couple. Maybe Charlie was right, maybe sooner would be better. Andy had been fine at work the last few days, it certainly seemed as if he had got used to the idea and was finally moving on with his life. He had even talked to James today about how he'd been thinking of contacting his ex, Samantha, to see if she fancied meeting up sometime for a drink.

"OK I guess you're right," James said finally. "But I still say he won't turn up."

***

Andy looked at the kitchen clock. It was 8.15pm. He had heard the chairs scraping on the kitchen floor in the apartment below him half an hour ago and wondered if they would really lay out a place for him. *Had James known that Charlie was going to invite him for dinner? Had they sat down and planned it together or had Charlie just come out with it on the spur of the moment?* It was irrelevant anyway; there was no way he was going. It was a miracle that he and James had spoken to each other in the last few days at all considering the mess they had inadvertently created between themselves. But they *had* spoken and maybe he had walked a lot further away from this whole sorry saga than he had given himself credit for. He looked at the clock again. 8.16. *Would they be talking about him right now, trying to figure out what his absence from their dinner table might mean?*

Andy flicked through the television channels to find something to watch, so that he didn't have to think about it anymore. One of the cable channels was showing a film that he had once taken Samantha to the cinema to see. He felt his stomach lurch as once again the memory of her began to swamp him. Maybe he *should* contact her again; he had told James today that he was seriously thinking about it. If he was honest with himself he hadn't thought about anything else for weeks. His eyes wandered back to the television set briefly before plucking up the remote control and switching it off. It hurt too much to think about her and the way that it had ended.

He asked Alexa to put on his favourite Killers album and then tried to drift off to sleep but Samantha wouldn't leave him alone. If he had learnt one thing in the last eight months it was that the cliché 'you don't know what you've got until it's gone', was true. His pride, his ego, whatever you wanted to call it, had always got in the way, especially when it came to his love life. It had an unsubtle way of marching right in there and screwing things up for him every time. Well he had had enough of cutting off his nose to spite his face, his ego wasn't going to win anymore.

With his eyes closed he could feel Brandon doing his stuff in the background. He reached out and felt the phone there beside him. He would give himself just five minutes to psyche himself up and then he would ring Samantha.

***

It rang only three times and a woman with a 'rougher' voice than he remembered Samantha having, answered the phone.

"Yeah, this *is* Smanfa," she said abruptly, when he had asked if she still lived there. "What d'ya want?"

Shit. Bugger. She sounded positively scary. Andy could feel his well-prepared conversation deserting him.

"Ello? I said, 'what d'ya want?'"

Fuck. Bollocks.

"Do I know you?" she continued, annoyed at the silence.

Go on, you stupid git! Hurry up or she'll put the phone down and then it'll be too late.

"Hi, um... it's Andy."

"Andy?"

"Yeah, don't you remember me? It wasn't that long ago that..."

"Oh, *Andy*!" she said at last, registering his name. "What do *you* want?"

"Well, I, um... I thought that maybe, if you fancied it... well maybe we could... um, meet up and..."

"Meet up? Wiv you? I wouldn't have thought so! You gotta be fuckin' joking! What sort of stupid twat do you take me for, eh?" she belted out, astounded. "I ain't never known such a tosser in my 'ole life, so why on earf would I wanna meet up wiv you again, huh? ...*Well*?" She waited a second for an answer that never came, before continuing. "You swan off wiv oo-ever you want, whenever you want, treating me like shit the 'ole time we was toogever, and then fink you can just pick up the phone eight munfs later when you've got bog all else to do and ask me out on a date! Do you fink I'm fucking desperate or sumink? Well do ya?" She continued like an unleashed dog that had been chained up and muzzled for eight months.

"I adored you, you pig! I would've done *anyfing* for ya, only you were too fuckin' stupid to notice, or to care! Fort you could just mess me about and I would be 'ere waiting for ya, again and again. You couldn't believe it when I told ya I wouldn't stand for it no more, could ya?" Her voice was rough and frenzied, her pronunciation unrecognisable from the sweet, soft voice of the Samantha he had known and loved. "Ya want a date, huh?" Well I'll give ya a fuckin' date! How about tonight? Come round 'ere right now, I got a great new chair for you to try out. All I gotta do is plug the fucker in!"

Hand shaking, he slammed the phone down in horror, but it rang back straight away. He ignored it, but it wouldn't stop, it just kept ringing and ringing... and ringing... and ringing...

Andy jumped. He was lying on the sofa in his living room, the television remote control on the floor next to him and The Killers had stopped playing. His mobile was ringing persistently and he realised with immense relief that he had just been saved from possibly the worst dream he had ever had. He snatched up the phone, silently offering thanks to whoever it was on the other end.

"Andy, it's James. Is everything alright?"

"Um, yeah, everything's fine. Why?"

"Well it's 9.30 and you haven't turned up for work."

***

"What with you not turning up for dinner last night too, I thought something had happened."

Andy waited for Sally to move out of earshot and watched her walk back to Maxine's old desk before continuing.

"It was a bloody *nightmare,* Jay, I'm still trying to convince myself that it was just a dream."

"Well ring her. It's the only way to be sure."

"Oh for fuck's sake don't say that. I couldn't possibly ring her now, could I? I was scared enough *before*, but now I'm bloody petrified."

James laughed.

"Seriously! You should have heard her voice. I'm never watching Eastenders ever again!"

"You don't watch Eastenders!" James exclaimed, "but you *should* watch Emmerdale, it's really good now."

"Don't mess about, Jay, I'm still shaking, look." Andy held out his wobbling hands for him to inspect.

James bit his bottom lip and despite himself, Andy smiled. His dream had taken over all other thoughts and now for the first time, he felt bad about not mentioning the meal he had turned down.

"Jay," he said tentatively, "I didn't 'not' turn up on purpose last night you know. You do believe me, don't you? I was going to come... it was just that..."

"It's fine. You don't have to explain."

"If the offer's still open I could always join you both over the weekend instead."

James looked up in surprise.

"Oh. Well yeah, that's fine. Oh no, hang on, sorry. Charlie's away this weekend, but Monday would be good. Only if you're really sure you want to though, you don't have to do this you know, And."

Andy thought about his dream. Despite what he had said to James it had made him more determined than ever to get in contact with Samantha again. He knew one thing for sure – her voice would still be as soft and sweet as it always had been, even if she did shout and bawl at him. And if she was going to scream and swear at him, then let her - at least he would know what to say to her in return. He would be prepared for it properly. Like a knight going into battle, his armour would be in place and he would be ready for anything. He would let her spew out her madness, frustration and anger and he would fight it off. And then do whatever he had to do to win her back. He wanted her. He *needed* her.

He looked at James' face. It was ashen and tired, and his worry lines were etched deeper than ever before.

"No, Jay," he said smiling at his brother across the desk. "Monday will be great. I want to do this, I really do. It's time to move on."

CHAPTER 34

Turning the heater up to high in her car, Maxine continued watching the house from a safe distance. Lights came on and were then turned off randomly. The little girl had come out to play for a while earlier on before it had got dark but she had been so engrossed in her own little game that Maxine doubted she would have noticed her if she had jumped out of the car and run around naked beside her.

Another light came on and Tom's unmistakeable profile drifted past the living room window. Maxine let the imaginary visions of him and Angela cosying up on the sofa eat into her heart. He wasn't going to get away with this. He couldn't just drop her like a hot potato when the going got rough. How dare he put the Bitch Wife first? What happened to his previous cries of 'my wife doesn't listen to me' and 'she doesn't have time for me anymore', or 'you're more important than anything else right now'? 'Right now' when? 'Right now' in his office during her lunch hour, when he was about to put his hand inside her knickers? 'Right now' as he made love to her on his and the Bitch Wife's living room carpet?

It had been the worst week Maxine could ever remember having and she could feel her frustration and anger bubbling up more and more beneath her calm exterior. He had quite obviously changed his mobile number; the old one appeared to be non-existent whenever she tried to ring or text it now. Either that or he had finally blocked her. What a coward he was (not to mention a fool) if he thought he could run away from her. She wouldn't allow him to treat her like this, they still had things to discuss. They had shared an intimate relationship and she deserved some respect from him at least!

Maxine shifted in her seat. She had been here for almost three hours now and it was getting extremely uncomfortable, not to mention cold and dark. Her back felt painful and stiff from being cramped in one position for too long and the thought of a hot bath and a glass of wine called out to her from across the shadows. The luminous figures on her car clock read 21:05. She pulled down the car's internal mirror and peered at her ghostly reflection. The gloom of the car enhanced the dark circles under her eyes and the weight she had lost in the last week had only added to the gauntness of her pale face, giving her a haunted look. Fingering the dry, stringy hair that kept falling into her face, she promised herself revenge. And it would come, but not just now. She started up the engine and decided to head home. She would come back tomorrow at the same time. The little girl had given her an idea.

★★★

"OK, Maria, that's great, Jess will be thrilled.

OK, no problem. Bye." Angela replaced the handset and re-joined Tom on the sofa.

"All set, Eva can stay next Friday. Do you think we're going to regret this?"

Tom took a sip of his tea and laughed. "Angel, how hard can it be? One extra little girl's not going to be that much trouble, is she? It'll probably be easier if anything, I mean you know how bored Jess gets having only us to play with. And anyway, we owe Maria, remember?"

"I suppose you're right. She'll be so excited, but they just seem so young for sleepovers. Why do kids have to grow up so quickly these days? When I was a kid we didn't have sleepovers until at least ten. Nowadays it seems they *end* at ten years max!"

Max, Max. Tom closed his eyes. He wished he could stop thinking about her. He couldn't help but be worried. Was she OK? Did she have another job yet? Was she putting it behind her now and getting on with her life? He really hoped so. Everything had gone quiet since he had changed his mobile and he knew that had to be a good thing. If nothing else, he thought, it would help her to get over him once and for all and finally move on.

***

Maxine pulled up at the top of the long private road, right at the edge of the large circular driveway and turned the engine off. This was perfect; no one could see her from here unless they were leaving the house, and the house was still in perfect view. She glanced at her silver-bangle wristwatch. It was only just gone six but the nights were beginning to draw in now and already the weak sun was setting in a cloudy grey sky. She would keep coming here for as long as it took to put her plan into action. She wasn't in any rush after all; she still had no job, didn't want one now, come to that. The benefits agency could pay for everything that she was entitled to, including her rent, and why bloody not? Everyone else did it, didn't they? No more dragging herself out of bed for anyone in the mornings, she thought smugly. *This* was her job now. Unpaid, yes, but worth every hour she would put into it. She would learn their routine if it killed her. Their business would become *her* business, and she would do whatever she had to do to make their lives a living hell. It could take months, years even, before the golden opportunity presented itself to her, but when it did, she would be there, ready and waiting. And if she had her way (and she usually did), after her plan had been brought to fruition, Tom and Angela would spend the rest of their lives forever looking over their shoulders, too scared to leave the house but just as scared to stay at home.

CHAPTER 35

Was it his imagination or did Amy keep looking over at him every time he talked to Sue?

Jack forced himself to get a grip. Ok, so Amy had overheard him in the kitchen last week calling her husband 'Pricky Dicky'. Big deal; so she now knew he wasn't that fond of her 'big-willied' other half. What man would be? He was quite certain though, that during his *kitchen-boiler faux pas*, he hadn't mentioned Sue's name once. However, unfortunately for him he knew that the exact words he *had* used last Saturday had deserted him and very annoyingly he couldn't be one hundred percent sure of what he had actually said. He had gone over and over it in his head but the words refused to let him catch them. Amy was still watching him. He tried smiling at her amiably but she looked away. 'Oh well, it wasn't you I wanted to fondle tonight anyway, love,' he thought bluntly, as he kept his other eye on Richard and Sue. *Why was she hanging around Richard again this week? Why couldn't he catch her eye?* He ached for her so badly.

Casually, he walked towards the cheese and onion crisps. Good grief, did Cheryl have no brains at all? These people would soon be sticking their tongues down each other's throats - the last thing they wanted was smelly breath wafting in front of their faces, spoiling the sexual ambience. He noticed, with no surprise, that they hadn't been touched so he snatched them up and took them into the kitchen to find a more suitable replacement.

As he left the room he tried once more to catch Sue's eye but it was no use. He had spoken to her a lot on the phone since Wednesday. She had told him not to worry; Richard might have a lot of 'equipment' but he certainly didn't know how to use it properly so there was simply no competition. She had told him that Richard thought the 'G Spot' was a breath freshener from the seventies and that orgasms were microbes. She said that she couldn't wait to be near him and that on Saturday she would be his again. The sex, she promised, would be better than ever. Somehow he found the latter an impossibility but he did like to keep faith in all things.

Picking up some ready salted Kettle crisps, some Hula Hoops and the two tubes of original Pringles he had found in the snack cupboard, he made his way back into the living room where the noise seemed louder than usual.

"So, how are you doing then, Jack?"

Turning around, he saw Amy standing beside him. *Shit. Why was she talking to him? Wasn't she in a mood? Hadn't she been giving him the evils all night? Maybe she hadn't been doing anything of the sort. Maybe his guilty conscience had just made him paranoid?*

"Hi, Amy, I'm well thanks, and you?"

"Yep, *I'm* great. Cheryl was saying that she has a

bit of a cold though. You should've cancelled you know – no one would've minded."

"Oh, it's just a sniffle, nothing that our Chez can't handle."

He glanced around the room looking for Cheryl. He hadn't known that she wasn't feeling well.

"Well even so," Amy continued, "she looks a bit rough to me. You should pay her more attention, Jack, you know what they say about women being like flowers, and flowers dying without water."

"What are you talking about?"

"Oh just 'women' stuff I guess. We girls notice these things you know. In fact you'd be quite surprised what we notice." She looked him squarely in the eye and glared at him, making him feel nervous.

Was she onto him and Sue? No – how could she be? He scolded himself again silently, for unwarranted paranoia.

"Um... hope you don't mind but I'm just going to see if Cheryl's OK."

Before Amy could get another word in, Jack turned around quickly and set off in search of his wife. He soon found her. She was standing in the hallway talking to Sue and Richard about the new colour scheme that she wanted for the bathroom.

"*IF* he ever bloody gets around to it!" She looked at Jack who had just appeared from nowhere, and smiled.

Sue and Richard laughed along politely with her as she hooked her arm through Jack's and snuggled up closely to him.

"Ooh, you knows I'm only joking, Jacky-Boy," she said in her childish voice, saved for special occasions – like showing him up in front of his mates.

Richard put his hand behind Sue and started rubbing her backside like a sex-starved teenager. Jack flinched.

"Well excuse us, you two lovebirds," Richard said, looking at Jack and Cheryl, "but I'm on the edge of desire and I need to escort this lady away... sharp-ish." He slapped Sue's bottom firmly with the palm of his hand and winked at Jack.

"Ooh, I'll tell the others that room's gone then, shall I?" asked Cheryl, excitedly.

Jack looked at Cheryl angrily. She was well on her way to Squiffy Land and wobbled as she quickly shooed Sue and Richard into the empty dining room and closed the door tightly. She slapped a yellow post-it note onto the door (their sign that the room was now taken) and then ran into the downstairs loo. Slamming the door heavily she mumbled something about a weak bladder and too much wine.

Jack stood alone in the hallway. He stared at the closed dining room door; the yellow Post-It sticker torturously mocking him.

"Hey there, you alright, mate?" Alan had breezed out of the kitchen with a fresh glass of wine in his hand. "You looked troubled."

"Me? Oh no, I'm fine. Just um, well... er, Cheryl's

in the loo and I just..."

"Are you sure you're alright, you look quite pale? I'll get you a drink, I brought some fancy import stuff with me tonight, beautiful taste, like nectar, mate."

As Alan turned around to go back into the kitchen, his tucked-in shirt rode up slightly and Jack noticed the belt around his waist. It was the black belt that Sue has spanked him with only days before. Just the sight of it tormented every fibre of his being and he glanced away quickly, back into the face of the hateful yellow Post-It note.

Alone again in the hallway his mind melted with confusion and jealousy. In front of him all that separated him from Sue and 'Pricky Dicky' for the second weekend running, was a partition wall and a wooden door. To his right all that separated him from Alan and his black belt was ten foot of wanting to kill someone.

He heard one of the couples in the front room mention a foursome and recognised Amy's voice saying that she was 'up for it'. To his knowledge it had never happened before and it was something that didn't appeal to him anyway. He was a 'one on one' man; the thought of group sex did nothing for him. He looked at the door in front of him yet again and, standing in tormented pain, he wondered if he would ever again in his lifetime feel as desperately sad as he did right now.

***

"Goodnight then."

"Goodnight."

The voices seemed far off and muffled. Jack lay on the bed, as he had done all evening, and the words drifted up the stairs and across the landing, into his and Cheryl's room.

"The last of the group's finally gone," Cheryl shouted up the stairs to him as she clicked the front door shut for the last time that night. "How's the head?"

He ignored her and closed his eyes. When she came up, he would pretend he had fallen asleep so that he wouldn't have to talk to her again until the morning.

He had been asking himself the same question all night; why had Sue done it? OK, so Cheryl hadn't exactly helped the situation, but even so, this was a free world and one of the rules they had in the swinging circle was that 'no' meant 'no'. No-one had to do anything they didn't want to do and Sue could have walked from that room with no questions asked. But she hadn't. She had stayed in there – with a man who had a penis the size of a prize winning Hungarian Frankfurter. And from what Jack could make out from the sounds that had drifted from the dining room right up into his bedroom directly above, she had stayed there with him for most of the evening too. Little wonder why.

Cheryl had been up to see Jack several times throughout the course of the night; *was he OK? Heavens that came on quickly! Amy said there was a nasty little bug going around.* Yes – *her fucking husband*, Jack had thought.

He reached out for the glass of white wine that Cheryl had brought him up an hour or so ago and downed it. It was warm but it still tasted good. There was only one thing for it – he had to speak to Sue as soon as possible, he wouldn't be able to function until he did.

Pulling the duvet up around him he closed his eyes tightly, as the sound of Cheryl's footsteps softly climbed the stairs.

CHAPTER 36

Andy held the phone in his hand and tried her number for the third time in two hours. Why hadn't she been in when he had phoned twice before? He had tortured himself all evening with that one single thought. But why *should* she be in? She was young, not to mention gorgeous, and it was a Saturday night for heaven's sake. Samantha was never going to be the kind of girl who would be short of a date or two. For all he knew she was with someone else now anyway, maybe someone she was serious about – maybe even *living* with someone. A lot can happen in eight months, he quickly convinced himself.

He cut the call quickly. Shit. Why hadn't he thought of that before? What would he say if a man answered? He re-filled his glass and poured yet another vodka down his dry throat. By the time he plucked up the courage to try her for the fourth time, he realised through the blurred edges of reality, that it might be too late in the day now for a courtesy call no matter how desperate he was to talk to her. The copious amount of 'Mr Vodka' that he had consumed, thought otherwise. It wrapped him in cotton wool and took him to a safe place where time was merely subliminal and where Samantha was patiently waiting for his call.

Hitting her name yet again, with fuzzy eyesight and a wobbly finger, he glanced at the vodka bottle and shook his head.

"I hate you!" He mumbled. "You take away all my common sense and reasoning, and I didn't have much of that to start with!"

As his squiffy brain reviewed the sense of the call, he wondered again for just a second if it wouldn't be better now to leave it until the morning. His finger hovered on the red circle to end the call.

"Hello."

Andy froze, unable to move any part of his body. It had only rung a couple of times and she had bloody well answered. *Shit*!

"Hello," she said again, concern in her voice now. "Who is this?"

"*Sam*?" was all he managed to whimper into the empty space around him.

"Yes?"

"Sam? Sam it's me." His heart was pounding now and he was sure she could hear it.

"Hello *me*," she replied with a croaky voice. "Do you mind telling me who '*me*' is, because after being woken in the middle of the night I'm not very good at playing Psychic Samantha."

Andy swayed in the armchair as he took in her sleepy voice. It was Sam! *His* Sam! Well, not quite *his* Sam anymore but Sam all the same. She didn't sound like she had changed at all, her voice was still sweet and soft, her manner still gentle and humorous. *Did she just say that it was the middle of the night? Shit.*

Why had he rung her so late? Of course. His friend, Vodka...

"It's me, Andy."

"Andy? Andy who?"

"Oh no," he mumbled in embarrassment, more to himself than to her. "Don't tell me you've forgotten me already." He could feel Vodka reacting badly with the greasy fish and chips he had had for supper. Vodka was winning.

"Andy? No way – not Andy Cooper?"

"Oh no," he mumbled on, concerned that because he had rung her at such a ridiculous hour he would now appear either drunk (which he quite obviously was), or just plain desperate.

"Nope. Nope. I don't care. Balls to it. It's late and I'm drunk and I'm not sorry," he rambled on. The room was beginning to move around him. "No, I mean I AM sorry. I AM sorry. Sam, I'm so fucking sorry. Lishun to me, just hear me out, that's all I'm asking."

"Of course I'll listen to you," she replied, yawning. "But you're drunk. Do you even know what you're saying? I haven't heard from you for, well, it must be nearly a year now and look at the time. What are you doing ringing me at this hour for?"

Andy hiccupped and before he could stop it, a small belch erupted from his chest, down the telephone line and straight into Sam's waiting ear.

"Er... thank you," she said, smiling to herself.

"Oh shit, I'm so sorry. Shit. Why is this all going

wong... I mean wrong? Bollocks, did I just say 'shit'? Oh no, did I just belch down the phone at you?"

"Andy," Sam sighed, confused, "it's really nice to hear from you and all, and I'm trying to ignore the fact that you've only called me because you're drunk but do you know what time it is?"

"Are you in bed?" he asked her suddenly.

"Me and every other sane person in the country, yes."

"You've got every other sane pershun in the country in bed with you?" he asked, deflated.

Sam was now wide awake and she giggled. "You know what I meant."

Andy covered his face with his free hand and closed his eyes. Everything seemed better like this, the room even stayed still – as long as he kept his hand there, supporting his alcohol-laden brain. If he could just stay like this a little longer he thought, then he would wake again very soon and realise that he hadn't just belched down the phone at his beautiful ex-girlfriend, hadn't said shit and bollocks within seconds of speaking to her, and was in fact just having another terrible dream.

"Andy?" There was no reply. This time she shouted. "ANDY!"

He stirred from his ten second reverie and jumped up from the chair, dropping the phone onto his wood flooring, where it clattered loudly. Making a quick grab for it, he realised now that this wasn't a dream after all. This was real. This was very real.

"Hello? SMANFA?" he wailed. "Are you still there?"

"Andy, what do you want? I'm getting worried now, is everything alright?" Her laughter gone, she was now serious. *Or was she annoyed?* He couldn't tell.

"It's great to hear from you, Andy, it really is, but..."

"Sam, I mish you." There, he had started it and he knew now that Mr Vodka wouldn't let him stop. "I mish you so so much. SO MUCH. I wanna see you, Sam, I wanna see you."

She laughed sweetly at the honesty that a good quantity of spirits could afford a person.

"I haven't heard drunken ramblings like this in... oh, I don't know... years. You'd better go, Andy, I think you've had waaay too much to drink."

"Noooo I haven't," he slurred.

"I'm going now, And, thanks for ringing, it's been good to hear your voice again, it really has. Even if it is... well... completely pissed."

She was going! No! Got to stop her. Say something, quickly! He looked at Vodka Bottle. "This is your fault, you bastard."

"I beg your pardon?"

"NO SAM! Not you! Oh no, I've fucked it all up."

"I'm ending the call now, And."

"NOOOOO! I LOVE YOU! SAM, I LOVE YOU. Pleash don't go... I... *I love you.*"

The line was so quiet that for a moment he thought

she had gone.

"Oh pissing perrrrfick," he spat into the silent line. "She's gone! She's fucking gone! Course she has – why wouldn't she? Jus' friggin' perrrfick! Now what, Mr Vodka? Got any more friggin' twatty ideas?"

"You're not going to remember any of this in the morning, are you?" The soft voice cut in unexpectedly.

Andy smiled soppily. *She was still there on the other end of the line!* He held the phone conspiratorially to his lips as he whispered back to her.

"Probly not, no."

He could hear her soft breath down the phone, almost warm in his ear, as if she were standing right beside him.

"Then I love you too, Andrew Cooper," she whispered softly. And then she hung up.

***

Opening one eye, he tried to focus on the room around him but shut it again quickly as the pounding in his temples began. Nausea swirled around heavily in the pit of his stomach as last night's fish begged to be released from the fairground ride within. Keeping his eyes closed, he took deep breaths and concentrated hard on not vomiting all over the duvet. *How much had he had to drink last night anyway?* He tried shifting into different positions in the bed to ease his self-inflicted misery but nothing helped. Giving up, he stayed on one side, completely immobile with an old clump of tissue he had found under his pillow, and held it closely to his mouth. Through the pounding headache, flashes of the early hour phone call slowly came back to him in dribs and drabs. *Oh no, what on earth had he done? What had he said to Sam?* He couldn't remember the details now but he knew one thing for sure – that it *had* happened and it hadn't been a dream. *Come on, think. Think!* Despite Vodka now laughing demonically as it clashed cymbals in his head, Andy refused to let it go. And then it came to him, fluttering into his mind like a golden ticket from Mr Willy Wonka himself. *She had told him that she loved him! Yes, that was it – she had actually told him that she still loved him.*

With his stomach still fighting for its right to throw up last night's vodka infused fish, he opened his eyes. A fuzzy image of Samantha proclaiming her love for him floated in front of him. Andy smiled and felt a grateful tear burning at the corner of his eye. His stomach didn't stand a chance now – how on earth could he possibly be sick at a time like this?

CHAPTER 37

"I'll phone Tom, shall I?"

Jack raised his head from the pillow an inch and opened one eye. "If you would, love," he croaked. "I still feel crap."

He had spent all of Sunday in bed feeling sorry for himself, going over the same thoughts again and again, and he intended to spend Monday sorting it out once and for all.

An hour later, with Tom deceived and Cheryl on her way into town, he got dressed and messaged Sue. She replied straight away; yes Alan was at work, yes she was in, yes he could come straight round.

As he stood at her front door in the pouring rain, half an hour later, he couldn't help but think how different this was to the other times that they had secretly met up. It was usually in anticipation of sex. This time all he wanted was to talk to her. To see her. To discuss a future; their future. Was that why he had used the front door instead of the back; because he was tired of sneaking around?

She answered the door dressed in a tight, pale yellow top and a pair of black, skinny jeans. She said 'hi' and smiled brightly at him but then turned and left him, leaving him to close the door. Jack followed her into the tiny kitchen and waited quietly as she filled two mugs with teabags and boiling water. Sitting himself down on one of the chrome chairs, he watched her closely. She seemed different somehow, distracted even. Something was definitely wrong.

"So... what did you want to talk about then?" she asked, pouring the milk into the tea.

He couldn't see the point in dragging it out any longer; time flew quickly enough when they were together as it was, so he might as well get straight to the point.

"Saturday night."

"What about it?"

"Well what do you think, Sue?" Her blasé attitude hurting him further. "You promised me."

"Promised you what?" she asked defensively, while frowning at his wounded face.

"You said that we'd be together but you were quite happy to saunter off with that bloody twat, Richard."

"Richard is *not* a twat," she replied, annoyance etched upon her face.

"Why are you defending him?" Jack was really pissed off now and could feel himself beginning to lose all control. "You promised me that you wouldn't go with him again."

"I promised you no such thing," she retaliated in disbelief.

"You said that we'd be together this weekend!"

"I didn't have any choice, did I?" Sue shouted back. "Your Cheryl pushed us into the room!"

"Of course you had a choice! You could've walked

from that room whenever you wanted."

"Oh yeah, and what the hell would I have said? 'Sorry Richard I'm having an affair with Jack and we've arranged to only sleep with each other from now on, is that OK?'"

"Don't be so ridiculous, you know what I mean."

"No, Jack, I don't know what you mean. I couldn't have got out of sleeping with Richard without causing a shitload of suspicion, even you can see that, surely?"

Jack paced the kitchen furiously. This wasn't what he had wanted at all; him and Sue at each other's throats as the green-eyed monster laughed in their faces.

"I'm sorry." The words were strained through gritted teeth, "I didn't come here to argue with you."

She slammed the mugs of tea down and glared at him. "Well what *did* you come here for then?"

This was all going wrong. Instead of pulling her in closer he could feel her slipping away from him and he hated it.

"I'm sorry. I'm finding this really difficult. I don't know how to say it."

"What do you mean 'how to say it'? How to say *what*?"

He thumbed the handle of his mug and looked into her face. The anger that only seconds before had engulfed him, drained away and all he wanted to do was hold her in his arms again.

"Are you happy with Alan?" he asked suddenly.

"What's going on, why are you asking me that?" She looked startled.

Jack thought about leaving it well alone. It wasn't too late. He could tell her to ignore him – '*it was nothing*', take her in his arms and within minutes might even be making love to her again. But he didn't. He couldn't. He had never felt this way about anyone before. This was his one chance and he wasn't going to blow it.

"What I'm trying to say is... well the thing is... I don't want to share you anymore." He could feel the first prick of tears forming at the back of his eyes. "I love you, Sue, and I don't want to share you with ANYONE. Not Richard, not Alan, not anyone." *There... he'd said it.*

If he thought he had seen Sue gob-smacked before, then he was wrong. Her mouth gaped open (*was it in horror or surprise... or both?*) and her eyes stared ahead unfocused, as though she were trying to see right through him.

"What on earth are you on about, Jack?" she whispered, finally. "*You want me to leave Alan?*"

This was it. This was the moment that he had really come here for. To throw caution to the wind for once in his sad little life and lunge forward to grab the star that dangled so tantalisingly close but had always been just slightly out of his reach.

"Yes. Yes I do. I'd leave Cheryl for you. I'd do *anything* for you."

Sue gawped at him as her brain tried to unscramble the confusing words and emotions that he had just thrown at her. She shook her head slowly.

"What about our friends? What about the group?"

"I don't *care* about the group, don't you get it? I *did*, *once*, but why can't you understand, all I want is YOU. With you I wouldn't need anyone else. Ever."

As his words hung in the air between them, the confusion etched on Sue's face slowly disappeared. Very slowly she smiled at him and moved forward so that she could hold his face in her hands and scan every detail of him.

"You'd do that for me?" she whispered, as the gravity of his words sank in. "You love me *that* much?"

"Yes, I love you that much, and more. I always will."

Sue reached for his hands.

"Think about it? That's all I ask," he pleaded.

She pulled him closer to her and held him tightly, rubbing her smooth cheek against the roughness of his, before smiling again.

"I'll think about it, Jack. I promise."

★★★

"Still alright for tonight?" James asked Andy, when Tom had gone into his office.

"Absolutely, yeah."

"I meant what I said last week, And – you don't have

to go through with this meal. Me and Charlie, well we understand if..."

"Hey? Oh no, I'm looking forward to it, really."

James looked across at his brother and smiled.

"Great. Well we're looking forward to it too. We just... you know... we don't want any... well, awkwardness."

"No, it's not a problem, really." Charlie was the past. He wanted Sam back, no one else.

"I'm happy for you, Jay, really I am," he continued. "There won't be any awkwardness. What time did we say again?"

"Anytime I suppose. Seven-ish? What do you think?"

Andy shifted his gaze a few inches and let his eyes focus on a nearby filing cabinet. He would be home by six tonight and he desperately wanted to phone Sam again before going out. He wanted to apologise to her for his ridiculous phone call on Saturday night and, more importantly, to see if she had meant it when she had said she loved him. *She must have meant it - you don't just tell someone you love them on a whim, do you?* Guiltily, he remembered the numerous occasions that he had done just that. *So many girls, so many whims.* He had been so drunk Saturday night that Sam could have said just about anything she wanted to and he probably wouldn't have remembered it the next day. But he *had* remembered it.

Stirring from his thoughts he realised James was still waiting for an answer. If he got to James' at seven that would be too early – he didn't want to rush the phone call to Sam. Hopefully they would end up talking for a couple of hours.

"Andy?" James looked confused. "Are we saying seven then?"

"Sorry. Can we say eight?" he asked, smiling. "I have something I need to do first."

CHAPTER 38

The phone rang six times before the voice he so badly wanted to speak to, clicked in for the fourth time that evening and asked the caller to leave a message after the bleep.

"Fuck," he shouted, throwing his phone down.

He had psyched himself up all day for this conversation. He needed to speak to her. NOW! Andy glanced at his watch. It was just gone half past seven. He had waited all day for this and now she wouldn't answer. *Was she busy or was she staring at her mobile and rolling her eyes in annoyance at seeing his number keep calling her phone?* He carried on pacing the living room floor - at least he was getting his steps up if nothing else. It was silly, he knew, but he couldn't help it. He would never get through this meal with James and Charlie if he couldn't speak to Sam first.

Andy looked at the time again and surrendered. He couldn't try her again tonight now, they wouldn't have time to talk properly. Stripping out of his work clothes he climbed into the shower and turned the pressure up as high as it would go. The hot and heavy spray hit his tired body like a thousand tiny fingers fighting each other to massage his skin. Soon the hard jets of water were stinging him but it felt strangely comforting. He rubbed a handful of shower gel over his chest and under his arms. *Was she seeing someone else* after all? She'd never said that she wasn't.

He finished his shower and dried himself off roughly before wrapping the towel around his waist and walking back into the kitchen. He needed a drink – badly. But not 'vodka-badly'. Dripping water onto the kitchen floor as he went, he yanked open the fridge door and pulled out a can of lager before throwing himself down onto the sofa. His wet hair dripped slowly off his floppy fringe and onto the soft hairs on his chest, and he left them there, like self-pitying tears.

One phone call in eight months didn't give him the right to an exclusive relationship with her, who was he kidding? He had no hold over her! Why had he been so stupid to assume that she would be sitting by the phone waiting for him to call her again anyway? It was only forty-eight hours since they had spoken. Was it really only forty eight hours? It felt like another eight months.

Andy had drunk half of the can's contents before the thought came to him. He slammed the lager down on the table and quickly snatched up his phone, a huge smile erupting onto his face as he realised he had misjudged his 'bad' fortune. *Why hadn't he thought about it before? She wasn't in! That was a good thing! He had been so caught up in his desire to speak to her again that he hadn't stopped to think that her voicemail was actually a godsend.* He could leave his message; apologise for Saturday - '*I was so drunk, you must think I'm such an idiot. I don't know what got*

237

into me, but hey, I really have missed you, which is why I rang you after all. So if you fancy meeting up some time then give me a ring.' Jackpot! A solution that would save them both any further embarrassment. It also put the ball in her court, he thought happily, even if that did make him a bit of a coward.

He reached for the remainder of the can and swigged it down with a lighter heart. Touching her name again on his phone, message already compiled in his head, his mind suddenly churned out thoughts that he didn't want to hear. *Had he forgotten the real reason that he had rung Sam in the first place; to talk to her and apologise for the way things had ended between them all those months ago? Wasn't this just being spineless? Was he really going to do this instead of waiting another day to speak to her properly? Yes, he was.*

As her phone rang for the sixth time, he waited for the voicemail to kick in yet again. But it didn't.

"Hello?" The out of breath but unmistakeable voice of Sam stopped him in his tracks.

"Sam?"

"Yes. Who is it?"

The line went quiet.

"Andy, is that you again?"

"Yes... yes it's me."

She waited for him to continue but he had frozen.

"Well, hello again," she said, filling the void. "How are you? Long time, no hear."

Andy looked at his watch, puzzled.

"Is it? I thought we only spoke on Saturday."

"I was being sarcastic," she replied.

"Oh right." He laughed - a laugh borne from nerves and embarrassment. She didn't laugh back.

"Sam, I... um, I really need to talk to you."

"Wow, I don't know whether to be flattered or insulted."

"What do you mean?"

"Well nothing for almost a year and then two phone calls in two days. What's this all about?"

"We need to talk."

"Well... OK, here we are talking."

"No, you don't understand. I mean, can you talk? Do you have ten minutes to spare?"

"Ooh," she said, seriously, "I can give you what... seven, maybe eight, but ten... it's looking doubtful."

Andy smiled with relief. "I'm so sorry about Saturday night."

The line went quiet for a moment. "Oh," she said eventually. "Are you?"

"Yeah of course I am. I don't know what got into me. I'd had too much to drink and, well, I've been thinking about you a lot lately and before I knew it I was making a complete dick of myself and at an ungodly hour too."

There was further silence on the line.

"Sam, are you still there?"

"Yeah, I'm still here. Well, thanks for the apology. I think."

"I just made such an arse of myself, I mean you must've wondered what on earth was going on."

"Well, it was strange to hear from you again, And, I'll give you that. All that time nothing and then wham, right out of the blue." She paused for a moment before continuing. "Andy, do you remember what you actually said to me on Saturday?"

He held his breath. This was it. This was the moment he couldn't put off any longer, didn't want to put off any longer.

"Yes. Yes I do." He took a deep breath. "I remember everything I said to you, Sam, and I meant every word."

"Oh."

"I'm so sorry for the way I treated you, the way things ended, it was unforgivable. I was a pig and that's an insult to pigs." He paused, waiting for her to object but she didn't. "Well what I'm trying to say, but making a bloody great hash of it, is that I'm sorry. I miss you, Sam, and if I'm completely honest I can't stop thinking about you." There he'd said it. *Now to seal the deal.* "Could we meet up sometime? Just for a coffee and a chat. It'd be nice, y'know, to catch up and..."

"Ohh, I don't know, And," Sam replied, quickly cutting him off. "Look, as we're being so open with each other then I might as well tell you."

Oh no! Here it comes – she's seeing someone else.

"It took me a long time to get over you, you know. In fact I've only just started getting my life back on track, and then you go and phone me out of the blue. Don't get me wrong, it's great to hear from you, it really is, but I don't think I can put myself through all of that again."

Andy clenched his teeth together. He could feel the bottom dropping out of his world and there was nothing he could do. He could hardly blame her after all.

"Yeah," he whispered, "I understand. You're seeing someone else, right?"

"No, I'm not seeing anyone. Not anymore anyway."

"You're not?"

"No, I'm not. I was seeing a guy for a few weeks but we've finished now. I told you, I've only just started to..."

"Well then why can't we meet for a coffee?" He waited and silently willed her to say yes but the line just hummed impatiently. "Please, Sam. At least give me the chance to explain things to you properly. There are things I need to say to you, things I need you to know. I'm not asking to pick back up where we left off, it's just a coffee. Meet me, that's all I'm asking."

The line remained silent. He glanced at his watch, it was 8.10. He was late. James and Charlie would think he wasn't coming again. They would think he was pacing the floor with a changed mind and a heart that yearned for Charlie but they would be so wrong.

"Listen, Sam, I promise you, I know what you're thinking but you're wrong. I won't hurt you again. I just want to see you that's all. Just give me twenty minutes and then you can walk away if that's what you want. I'll never bother you again. Just two friends catching up?"

When it came, it came softer and sweeter than he could ever have hoped.

"OK." Her voice coated the line like melted chocolate. "I'll meet you."

"You will? Oh wow. Well great. That's brilliant. I don't know what to say. Um... *thank you*." He thought he sounded pathetic but he didn't care.

He said goodbye and pressed the red circle to end the call, a huge grin spreading across his face as a rush of excitement flooded through him. He yelled 'YES!' as loudly as he could and punched the air. He was going to see his Sam again and already the euphoria was bubbling up inside him.

CHAPTER 39

Charlie handed Andy a glass of Sauvignon Blanc, smiled briefly when he knew James wasn't looking, and then sat back down in his chair.

"It's only Spanish Chicken out of a jar, so don't get too excited," said James, arriving from the kitchen with the casserole dish.

Charlie took it off him and began dishing up the brown, sloppy looking meal.

"This IS safe right, Jay?" he asked, eyeing it suspiciously. "I mean you DID cook it for long enough? I did say that I would cook. I love cooking!"

"Well I would've probably made a jam sandwich or something," Andy lied, picking up his knife and fork, "so believe me, this is going to taste great."

Charlie frowned. "Whatever! I bet you already had a sandwich at lunchtime, you have to get some meat inside you, you know!" He raised his eyebrows suggestively at Andy and pouted his lips effeminately. *Meat and two veg!*" he exaggerated. "That's what I say, it's the only way!"

Andy glanced at James, who was busy spooning green beans and peas onto their plates. If he noticed the double-entendre he didn't show it. Andy looked back to Charlie and then looked away again awkwardly.

"I didn't have a sandwich actually," Andy continued, trying to ignore Charlie's provocation. "I had a couple of bags of Pork Scratchings."

Charlie's face filled with horror. "Eughh! That's POSITIVELY REVOLTING!"

"Hey," James cut in, "how did you get on with Sam, did you make the phone call in the end?" He took his seat between Andy and Charlie, at the end of the small table.

Andy's face broke into the same huge grin that he had worn earlier when talking to Sam. "Yeah, I did."

"Well?" James asked, eagerly. "Don't keep us dangling. What happened?"

Andy finished a mouthful of food and looked at them both. He could see Charlie looking confused.

"We're meeting up."

"Really?"

Andy nodded. "Yep, really."

"*SAM*?" Charlie interjected. "Who the heck is *SAM*?"

Both brothers looked across to Charlie who had rolled the name off his tongue in obvious distaste.

"*Sam* is the woman Andy's been harping on about for days now," James replied, amused.

"*Woman*?" Charlie spat. "Sam's a *woman*?"

"Yes. *Sam-antha*," Andy confirmed. "And yes... she's a woman. At least she was eight months ago."

"Oh," Charlie said flatly. He held Andy's stare for a couple of seconds before looking back down at his plate. "Well... you look *very* happy about it I must say."

"Yes, I am. Very."

Andy concentrated on the food in front of him and stabbed a small potato onto his fork. "She's very special actually. I knew her a while back, she's actually an ex."

Charlie looked at him over his forkful of soggy chicken, through the black curtains of his floppy hair.

"OH NO! You're kidding, right? Exes are a big no-no!" He shook his head dramatically. "It'll NEVER work. You know what they say – 'if it didn't work the first time around then it damn well won't work the second'. Don't even *go* there, chick! Urghhh! There's nothing like sloppy second helpings to take the lead out of your pencil!"

"Yeah, well, that's why I don't usually go for 'sloppy second helpings'," Andy threw back, staring at him intently.

Charlie sucked his cheeks in angrily and looked away.

"But it was my fault that it didn't work the first time around with Sam," Andy continued, "and I intend to put it right now – the *second* time."

Charlie raised his eyebrows again and sniffed as he pushed some beans around his plate.

"Well we're really happy for you, aren't we?" James said, smiling at Charlie, who was feigning a sudden interest in his dull meal. "When's the big date?"

"What?"

"The date. When are you seeing her?" James asked. "I take it from the way you're floating between cloud eight and ten, that there *is* actually a date?"

Andy stared blankly ahead. *What the hell! They hadn't arranged a date!* James waved his hand in front of his brother's dead eyes.

"Hello? Earth calling Andy, come in, Andy."

Still Andy looked on, staring at the uninteresting space between James' and Charlie's heads.

"Andy? What's the matter?"

Andy felt his cutlery slip out of his hands and clatter onto his plate. "Bollocks! I think I hung up on her before we arranged it."

"Oh no, how totally clumsy of you!" Charlie smirked, stifling a giggle and cutting into his chicken with renewed vigour. "I must say, Jay, this meal is getting tastier by the minute."

CHAPTER 40

Maria bent down, kissed Eva goodbye and then watched with Angela as the two girls headed for their classroom door. Eva turned around at the last moment and waved frantically.

"Happy Birthday, mamma," she shouted happily for the fifth time that morning.

"I don't know what to do, Angela," she continued when they were alone.

Angela pulled her leather gloves onto her frozen hands and tried a comforting smile.

"He'll never find you, you said yourself that your cottage is a needle in a haystack."

"Angela, listen to me. If my brother said Adrio was released two months ago, then he was released two months ago. He is never wrong. And if my brother can track me down, then believe me, for Adrio this will be no problem."

"So what are you going to do?"

"I don't know. Move on again, what else can I do?"

"But you can't," Angela said a little too urgently. "What about Eva and her schooling? She's just settled in, Maria, it's not fair." They walked towards Angela's car and stopped when they reached it.
"Tell me what choice I 'ave?" Maria asked, sadly. Worry had already etched itself across her usually serene face. She was scared, Angela could see that.

Overnight, the fine lines on her face had deepened, as if invisible hands had been up all night with a hundred tiny chisels, immortalising the worry that she felt. Beneath her eyes were small, dark, baggy sacks; the haggard evidence of sleepless nights. Angela wondered how she would cope over the next few days and weeks if she looked like this after only twenty four hours.

"Let's not overreact," Angela said calmly. "If you do have to go then you'll have plenty of time to arrange something."

Maria laughed bitterly. "Plenty of time is one thing I do not 'ave. Do you know 'ow long it takes to move away and start over again with a small child?"

"You've done it once already, Maria, and you can do it again." Angela looked down at the cracked paving slabs beneath her feet. She didn't know what else to say to her to make her feel any better and she hated herself for being so inadequate.

"My brother says that Adrio won the appeal. He 'ad been telling anyone who would listen that he was coming to find me," Maria said shakily. "And now no-one 'as seen him for weeks."

"But he could still be in Spain. Surely he'll search every square inch of every Spanish Island before he even thinks of trying another country. And even then, why England?"

"Oh, Angela." Maria put her head in her hands and began to cry.

Angela eyed some of the other mothers who were now looking at them with interest. "Come on, get in the car. We can't stand in the street like this."

Once they were seated inside, Maria carried on through her tears.

"He will look in England for the same reason my brother did. Eet is the only other country I 'ave been to in my life. My father worked in England for a long while when he was still alive. Me and my brother, we came to stay with him a few times when we were very small."

Angela placed a comforting arm on Maria's shaking shoulder. "England is a large place, Maria. You said so yourself – he won't find you, you can't think like that."

Maria smiled appreciatively and dabbed her eyes with the sleeves of her coat. "Yes, I will be ok," she said bravely. "You 'ave enough worries of your own, I am sorry." She reached out to open the car door but Angela stopped her and smiled.

"Hey, where do you think you're going? You, my dear, are coming with me."

Maria looked confused.

"Well, you're not going to have much of a birthday on your own now, are you? I need to get you a present first and then later... well I've booked us in for lunch at a fabulous little restaurant I know."

Maria sniffed and smiled gratefully, before fastening her seatbelt. And Angela hoped against hope that

Nicco's wouldn't be fully booked.

CHAPTER 41

Dear Tom,

Oh dear. You're so predictable. How did I know that you would ignore my texts and letters? Just a hunch I guess. Thank you for proving me right yet again. As I write for a third time trying again (in vain no doubt) to reach out to you, I know that really I am just wasting my time; wasting more of life's precious sands of time on you, as if I haven't wasted enough.

Of course time for me now is no longer a commodity. I have so much of it on my hands since losing the job I loved, it becomes hard after a while to find ways to fill it. To someone like you of course, every second counts. I can see your face now as you read my words. What's the matter, Tom, have I interrupted something important? Oh what a pain I am, you must be sick of me! What a bloody nuisance. I bet you wish you could dispose of me, don't you, Tom? Do you? Do you wish you could wipe me away? Is that what I've now become; an inconvenience that you trod in for six months and now won't come off the bottom of your shoe? I'm sorry, I must be a dreadful annoyance.

I'm sure your new secretary isn't annoying though, is she, Tom? I've seen her a couple of times now. Has she settled in? Has she let you slide your hungry fingers into her knickers yet? Have you unclipped her bra and run your thumbs over her nipples, the way you did mine? Am I going too slowly for you, Tom? Maybe you've fucked her already, is that it?

Oh, Tom. Such a shame. We were so good, you and I. Do you remember? How could you forget? Did you really think I would just go away?

When I was a little girl I dreamed about someone like you. Except he wasn't married. Don't they say the good ones always get snapped up first? But he was different to you in other ways too. In my dreams I always came first. I'm used to that – do you remember? Of course you do – I always came first, didn't I? Just not where it mattered. Oh enough of that, I'm sure I'm making you very hard. Are you hard, Tom?

And then I wonder if you still think of me. Yes, you do. Of course you do. Because I haunt your every waking moment. I am the nightmare of your dreams. When the Bitch Wife wants it, you close your eyes and see me beneath your blood pink lids and your desperately hungry body, and when the Bitch Wife doesn't want it, you masturbate and think of me some more. Am I still good; as good in your mind as I was in the flesh? Does your memory serve you well?

I won't be ignored, Tom. I don't do ignored. But go ahead – you can ignore my phone calls, my texts, my letters even – but you can't ignore ME.

Maybe I'll send letter number four to your home – addressed to the Bitch Wife, of course. That might be good. That might be very good.

Maybe she'd like to know how you met me 'last night'

(you don't remember?). How you came to my flat and confessed that you hated her for trapping you into a loveless marriage. Oh you were so bitter, so angry. I already knew that of course; knew that you stayed with her out of obligation, pity even. For the child? Oh yes, that too of course. Such a dear pretty little thing that child of yours, Tom, I bet you love her so dearly, don't you?

Anyway, I'm digressing. Last night. Oh yes... last night. You still can't remember? Maybe Bitch Wife would like to know how you made love to me, madly, like a wild animal. You were rampant, you remember, Tom, surely? You couldn't wait to get inside me again, to feel my young, firm body next to yours, you said. So much more exciting than the premature sagging flesh your wife has, you said. That'll be the child, Tom. Children do that you know. They're parasites, and when they've stolen a woman's firm body for nine months, they go on to steal her beauty and youth for the next eighteen years. Such a shame.

Still... you have me, Tom. I'll always be here for you.

M. X

"Well?" Tom asked, impatiently. "What the hell would you do?"

Jack paced the carpeted floor of Tom's office, staring at the piece of paper as it flapped between his thumb and forefinger.

"Jeez, mate... I don't know what to say. Did you really see her last night?"

"What?" Tom looked at Jack disbelievingly and raised his voice. "Don't be a twat, of course I didn't. I don't know what the hell she's playing at but I'm seriously fucked off now. And how dare she refer to Jess, HOW DARE SHE!"

He waited for Jack's response but it didn't come.

"Well?" Tom prompted.

"She uses your name a lot, doesn't she?" Jack replied, re-examining the letter.

Tom was momentarily staggered. "I was hoping for something a little more constructive than that, mate, to be honest." He could feel himself begin to panic. This wasn't the Maxine he knew.

"Sorry. I just..."

"The first two were much the same," Tom interrupted, "but I threw them away, I thought they were one-offs." He got up and began pacing up and down the little office.

"How can *two* be 'one-offs'?" Jack asked, confused.

Tom looked at him angrily, daring him to be flippant again.

"Have you told Angela?"

"No."

"The police?"

"No."

"Why not? I mean to be honest, mate, if it was me getting these letters I'd be dialling 999 before you could say 'straitjacket'."

"And what will they do? For a start, mine and your fingerprints are all over the thing now anyway. I've read it and turned it over in my hands so many times that I've probably not only wiped all evidence of Max off it, but practically all of the bloody tree bark that it's written on in the first place. Look at it!" His voice was tetchy and tired. "All that's left of it is the ruddy ink."

Jack smiled faintly as he took in the thinness of the creased paper, rubbing it gently between his thumb and forefinger.

"Well it's blatantly obvious that it's off her, if you tell the police the whole story then they must be able to do something, warn her off at least." Jack frowned. He wondered what on earth could have driven the lovely Maxine that he knew so well, to do something as mind-blowingly insane as this. "She's cuckoo, mate," he continued at last. "That's all there is to it. She's gone loco. Maybe just ignore it? Once she realises she's getting no response from you she'll soon get bored and stop."

"I wish I shared your confidence," Tom sighed, "but this is the third one, remember?"

"Well what's the worst that can happen then?" Jack continued, putting the worn piece of paper down on Tom's desk.

"With Max, who knows?"

"Can't you ring her – tell her to stop?"

"You just told me to ignore her!"

"Well I don't know, do I?" Jack said, defensively. He flung his arms out. "She's a bloody fruitcake, mate. I wish I had a PhD in 'Bunny Boiling for the Mentally Deranged', but I don't."

"Oh for fuck's sake!" Tom muttered. He let his body slump down into his chair and his head sink into his clammy hands in defeat. "I wish I knew what to do for the best but I don't. I'm gonna have to go to the police, aren't I?"

"Sorry, mate, can't help you, I really can't." Jack walked to the door and opened it, turning back to Tom before he left. "But I'll tell you one thing, don't throw this one away, it's the only proof you have that she's been harassing you at all." Jack took a deep breath, nodded to Tom, and closed the door behind him.

"And I thought *I* had bloody problems!" he muttered to Sally as he passed her desk.

***

Tom fingered the letter for the hundredth time that morning. It was hard to believe that the same girl he had made love to for six months had penned the aberration that he now held in his hands. It was even harder to believe that she had a disturbing alter-ego; that of a psychopathic loose cannon.

Taking out his mobile phone from the jacket that was draped around his chair, he scanned through his contacts. Maxine's number wasn't there. Of course it wasn't. *What was the matter with him - he'd bought a new phone, hadn't he?* He had also deleted her number so it hadn't automatically crossed over. He walked over to the small filing cabinet, found her number on her employee information card and stared at the familiar digits. He had viewed them countless times before but they had never made him feel the way that they made him feel now. Was this all she was to him now; a row of random digits? Entering the numbers on his phone he stopped just before he reached the last one. *What the hell was he doing? He was using his new phone! Was he completely stupid? The last thing he wanted was for her to have his new number!* Putting his mobile safely out of reach, he punched the digits into his office phone and took a deep breath, acutely aware that with just one more press of his finger she would be there at the end of them, like Freddie Krueger at the end of Elm Street. Maybe Jack was right; maybe they really could sort this out if he just spoke to her again. But what if it simply served to fuel the rage that was already erupting inside her? Then again, could things really get any worse; she was already threatening him? It might escalate if he ignored her?

He thought about the moment that Angela had dragged her into their home to confront them both. What a shitty way to end an affair; *in front of the wife, under duress*. No wonder Max was mad at him. Had he really been that naïve to think that he could flush her out of his life, firstly by humiliating her in front of his wife (although that hadn't been his intention) and secondly by changing his secretary and mobile phone? What sort of idiot had he been to think that he could do that and she would simply go away quietly? Could things get worse? What could be worse than being pestered day and night by a psychotic blonde you'd had an affair with? He changed his mind and hung up quickly. Maybe he should just go to the police and stop this right now before it went any further?

He read the letter yet again. As far as he could see there was absolutely no reason for her not to carry on tormenting him like this. She had nothing to lose after all. She was living her life from day to day with anger and resentment dangerously bubbling away inside of her; a cauldron-full of hate and revenge. He would do as Jack had suggested and keep the letter, that was for sure - he would be a fool to throw it away as he had done the others.

Walking out into the main office, he told Sally not to disturb him for at least the next half hour and then he returned to his little room and nervously punched in Maxine's number once again.

★★★

Why did her phone always ring when she was washing her

hair, she thought furiously? She reached out blindly for the nearby towel and wrapped it haphazardly around her dripping blonde locks before running into the living room to answer it. She snatched it up without looking at the screen and spoke with annoyance at the untimely intrusion.

"Yes? Who is it?"

For a second there was no reply and she was just about to end the call when she heard his voice break through the silence.

"Max, it's me." Tom's voice shook slightly.

Maxine stood rooted to her living room carpet, her mouth ajar at the shock of the unexpected caller's voice.

"Max, are you there? It's Tom."

Still Maxine was rigid. She blinked her squinting eyes rapidly in disbelief and slowly turned her head from left to right as she tried to decide if she was dreaming. It wouldn't surprise her; it had happened before in the last couple of weeks – many times. She swallowed, her mouth suddenly devoid of all saliva.

"We need to talk, things can't carry on like this," he went on, authority rife in his voice.

Still speechless, Maxine gently lowered herself into the chair directly behind her. Her heart was thumping wildly in her chest but the phone was unwavering in her stiff hand.

"What the hell are you playing at?" Her silence was flooding his veins with anger now and he wasn't going to stop yet. "What the *hell* is wrong with you? This has got to stop, Max, do you understand? IT STOPS! Right here, right now!" He was shouting now but still Maxine didn't speak.

She looked around her well-furnished room, her small eyes darting from one random object to the next, never settling their gaze on any one thing for more than a second. *She was definitely dreaming. She had to be. Tom would never speak to her like this; it would be more than his life was worth.*

"You will *NOT* threaten me or my family anymore, do you hear me?" he spat savagely. "No more phone calls, no more texts and *NO MORE* letters, DO YOU UNDERSTAND?"

A knock at the door brought Maxine out of her confused state. She clutched the phone ever more tightly in her hand and walked to the window so that she could peek out through the little gap in the curtains. It was her best friend, Tina. *Of course. They had arranged to go into town for lunch today and she had completely forgotten.* She glanced at her watch. It was 12.00 exactly. *Shit! This meant that she wasn't dreaming after all.* Either that or it was the most convincing one she had ever had.

"Now listen to me and understand what I'm saying to you," he continued ruthlessly, and as if she were a child. "You just stay out of my life, Max. I'm not putting up with this anymore. I've done nothing to you, nothing at all, I ended an affair with you – an affair that we shouldn't have been having in the first place!

That's all. Get over it. Or I'll go to the police!"

Tina knocked on the door again, this time impatiently. For a moment Maxine was torn between wanting to stay on the phone listening to Tom's voice (no matter how angry he was with her) and ending the angry call to go and answer the door for Tina. It had started to rain heavily and Tina was now hopping from one foot to the other on the doorstep, as if it would somehow make Maxine open the door more quickly.

"Tom?" she whimpered softly, to herself more than to him.

But he was gone.

CHAPTER 42

Angela thanked the waiter and took a table near the window with Maria.

"Now this is MY treat, so no arguments," she said, as Maria scanned one of the leather-backed menus hungrily.

"Thank you so much, Angela," she said softly. "You 'ave made it a very special day for me. I 'aven't shopped like that for ages."

"Well it was about time you did then." Angela picked up her own menu hoping to see her favourite dish still on there.

"You know something? I 'aven't thought about Adrio or my brother the whole time we were shopping," she said gratefully. "This is the first time since this morning."

Angela reached out and placed a hand on Maria's arm. "Well you can stop again right now," she said kindly, "and think about what you want to eat. The Tortellini Alla Panna is wonderful by the way."

Suddenly, and without warning, the grey clouds that had followed them around all morning during their shopping trip, opened up and released their dismal offerings onto the street outside. A few seconds later they were expelling them with such force that the noise of the precipitation hammered heavily against the window pane next to them, making any speech in the restaurant almost inaudible.

Angela and Maria, along with everyone else in the restaurant, turned to view the bedlam outside. Car horns beeped and people dispersed and cleared the streets within seconds as the deluge soaked their coats to their bodies. A minute later the streets were flooded with inches of rain and the frenzied scattering of lunchtime shoppers had left the sodden pavements deserted.

"Wow," Maria said, looking at Angela in awe, "we were very lucky, no?"

"That's amazing," Angela replied shaking her head slowly as the first flash of lightning struck the pavement right outside the restaurant. "We were more than lucky."

***

Andy and Samantha walked through the park slowly, looking at each other every few seconds, unable to stop themselves from smiling. The pub lunch at Churchill's had gone really well. They had grabbed two squashy chairs by the lit fireplace, ordered a huge steak baguette each and then talked endlessly for the next hour in the quiet surroundings. He had taken her there on purpose, knowing full well that the usual bunch of town workies much preferred the more modern pubs or wine bars like The Toad & Pickle and Peter Peppers, to grab their lunchtime fill from.

The hour had flown by. Sam had filled him in quickly on her happenings in the last eight months and he had returned the privilege. She told him about the ex-boyfriend she had mentioned on the phone, who kept hanging around and pestering her despite her only seeing him a couple of times, and he told her about his string of failed relationships since they had parted, omitting Charlie completely. They had covered work, family and even food shopping; anything to avoid what he really needed to talk about.

Andy had booked the whole afternoon off work in the hope that lunch would go this well and he wondered if it was the right time to tell her that or if he would appear too pushy. He already knew that Tuesday was Sam's day off. She had told him on the phone last night when he had rung her back after making a quick exit from James' flat. He stopped for a moment and stared at the small haven ahead of them; the small park that he often spent his lunch breaks in was one of the last pieces of greenery left in the main town. Even this piece had been fought for, tooth and nail, over the last year by the local people, to stop the council from stealing it away like it had done with the rest of the common land. 'More flats' the papers had said.

"What are you thinking about?" She smiled.

He turned to look at her and slid his hand down her arm to finally take her hand in his.

"Sam," he said, playing gently with her fingers.

She responded by wrapping her hand warmly around

his.

"Yes?"

"Would you think me presumptuous if I told you that I'd booked the rest of the day off work in the hope that we could spend some extra time together?" He gushed it out quickly without taking a breath.

A smile played on her lips but she tried to hide it.

"Yes," she said, trying to adopt a modicum of seriousness. "I'd think you were an arrogant arsehole."

"Oh."

At that moment the clouds above them opened and the first splattering of huge rain drops fell on them like glossy, translucent jewels from the thick, grey sky.

"Shit!" Andy shouted, "Where did that come from?" He pulled her arm and they ran together down the street looking for shelter. "Are you OK?" he called to her but she couldn't hear him.

The rainstorm beat down on them heavily, stinging their skin with the force of small stones. Within a minute they were soaked through and their clothes clung to their bodies like an unforgiving second skin.

"I THINK THAT'S HAIL AS WELL!" he shouted to her. "WHERE ON EARTH DID THAT COME FROM?"

"I CAN'T HEAR YOU!" Sam shouted back, through the storm, as it hammered down upon them.

The first flash of lightning appeared and cracked loudly on the pavement in front of them.

"Quick," he shouted, "I've got an idea."

CHAPTER 43

Andy dropped his sodden suit jacket onto the kitchen floor and turned to click the kettle on.

"Two seconds and I'll get you a towel." He grinned, as Sam stood dripping next to the discarded clothing. "You might be drenched but my God you look beautiful." The words came out before he could stop them.

Grabbing a handful of her hair, she squeezed a puddle of rainwater onto the floor beside her and laughed.

"Sorry, And, but I think I'll need more than a towel!"

They looked at each other and laughed. Rainwater was dripping onto the floor from her soaked clothing and the puddle beneath her was growing. She shivered as the cold, wet fabric clung to her skin.

"Do you want a shower? I mean the heating's on and we can dry your clothes out in the tumble dryer – though they'll need a spin in the washing machine first. I mean, only if you want to." He looked away embarrassed and pulled two mugs from the cupboard.

"I see the place hasn't changed since I was here last," she said, changing the subject. "Still as spotless as ever. You still have Lynn come and clean the place?"

"Yeah," he grinned, "marigolds and a pinnie never did suit me!" He filled the mugs with coffee and turned back to her. "Still one sugar?"

She was pale and shaking, and her teeth were chattering. She smiled and nodded.

"You're really shivering. Sam, this is ridiculous, you've got to get out of those clothes, you'll catch your death as my old mum used to say. Go on, use the bathroom." He pointed her in the right direction, as if she had forgotten its whereabouts, and she smiled gratefully. "And help yourself to whatever you see, which being a sad git's pad isn't much. There's some Radox or something in there if you want a bath. There'll be a steaming mug of coffee waiting for you when you come out. Go on, go."

"Thanks, And, I won't be long."

Within seconds, he heard the taps being turned on and the sound of water gushing as they filled the white enamelled bath with steaming water. He rushed into his bedroom and took off the rest of his own soaking wet clothes and rooted about in his wardrobe for a clean pair of jeans and a top before going back into the kitchen.

The kettle had boiled but he thought of Sam and wondered how long she was going to be. From past experience 'a couple of minutes' from a woman could mean anything up to an hour. He decided against filling the mugs yet, just in case.

Ten minutes later he found himself pacing the floor waiting for her. He walked towards the living room window and watched as yet another flash of lightning lit up the now black sky outside. The streets below were deserted and flooded, and still the rain poured down relentlessly.

How had this all gone so well? He couldn't have improved on the present situation if he had sat down and planned it himself. Would Sam have come back for coffee if the skies hadn't benevolently opened for him? Well... maybe; they had been getting on really well after all.

The taps had been turned off and the apartment was suddenly flooded in silence. He turned to look at the closed bathroom door, just visible from where he was standing. Images began to flood his mind, like the deluged streets below him and he fought hard to keep them at bay. Within a few more seconds visions of her naked body sinking below the hot, soapy water in *his* bath, only feet away, only intensified. He plopped himself onto the sofa and gave in to them, letting a flurry of different scenes play themselves out to him, like lurid snowflakes lap-dancing in front of his eyes. Only a few minutes seemed to have passed, when the bathroom door suddenly opened. The gentle padding of her feet on the hard floor came next and when he looked up, she was standing at the doorway dressed in his bathrobe, looking at him awkwardly.

"I hope you don't mind, And," she said fingering the navy towelling, "but it was hanging on the back of the door and..."

"No, that's great," he replied, excited to see her body so close to something that he knew he himself would be wearing later. "I mean, that's fine. No problem."

"I've wrung these out as best as I can." She held up her clothes, still dripping, and shrugged.

"Give them here, I'll chuck them in the machine."

Sam smiled gratefully and sat down on the sofa next to where he had been sitting. "Are you sure I can't do anything?" She heard the spin cycle of the washing machine start up and the kettle being re-boiled.

"No, nothing at all."

A minute later, he walked towards her with the two coffees in his hands and sat down next to her. "Feeling better?"

She took one of the mugs from him and sipped at the strong liquid. A warm smile lit up her face.

"Tons thanks and thank you for a lovely lunch too." She beamed at him and he felt eight months of regret washing over him all over again.

Her mere presence was more than just a welcome addition to his lonely flat; it had been crying out for her, almost as much as he had. She filled it up and brought it alive. It was nothing more than four sad walls without her.

"Sam, how can you be like this?"

"What do you mean?" she frowned.

"Well, after everything, you know... the way I treated you, the way things ended. Don't you hate me?"

Sam looked down at her coffee. "Do you want me to hate you?"

"Of course not." He put his mug down on the table next to him and stroked her hand lightly with his fingers. "I've really enjoyed seeing you again. Thanks for meeting me. And for not letting me waste four hours of my Annual Leave," he added with a cheeky smile.

"Anything else?" she asked.

"For staying more than twenty minutes. For coming back here for a coffee."

"You *dragged* me back for coffee more like!" she laughed.

"Did you mind?"

"No, it was that or drown."

"I never meant to hurt you. I know I said it already on the phone but I just needed to tell you again to your face. I really am sorry for everything."

Just then, Sam's smile cracked and her features changed before his eyes. Her lips became thin and tight before she opened her mouth to speak.

"You only ever saw me when it suited you," she said.

Andy stared at her. Where had that come from? Was she finally allowing her true emotions to fight their way out through her battered bravado?

"I still hung on though, sad little lamb that I was, following you around like I didn't deserve better." Her voice trembled slightly and he could see the wet in her eyes; wetness from a painful past that had never really been laid to rest. "I couldn't do that anymore, And. I've changed. I'll never be like that again."

"No, I know. I wouldn't want you to. I was just a

dickhead who didn't know the best thing in his life when she was standing right in front of me. But I know now. And you're here now. That's got to mean something, hasn't it?"

Her eyes dropped to her lap and she played nervously with the robe tie that was tied tightly around her waist.

"Yes," she replied after a long pause, "I suppose it does."

***

Jack had thought of nothing else since Monday morning. This was it; this was the biggie. Running to the car, the torrential rain saturated him within seconds and he quickly clambered inside.

"You shouldn't have come in this weather, honey," he purred to her, "but I'm bloody glad you did."

Sue flung her arms around his wet neck and began kissing him wildly, breaking away only to nibble gently at his ear.

She had parked down one of the side roads and they had intended to drive off somewhere, anywhere, so that they could spend his lunch hour alone, but the unexpected storm that had had Sue cursing only minutes before was now evidently a blessing in disguise. The heavy curtain of precipitation mingled with lashings of hail stones, beat down so mercilessly that it covered the car in a constant streak of moving camouflage. With the engine and the windscreen wipers now turned off too, the windows were beginning to steam up and Sue felt they were as good as marooned on a desert island of their own. The streets had been completely emptied by the unforgiving storm clouds but that had little relevance now anyway. The outside world had become nothing more than an obliteration of life; a meaningless extra in the tapestry of living. They were as good as invisible.

"Sue," he breathed heavily, as her hand went inside his shirt, "did you think about what we said?"

"What do you think, Jack? I've thought about nothing else. Nothing else at all."

"And?"

"And I'm going to do it. I'm going to leave Alan." She was beaming at him and he thought she looked surprised, shocked even, at the words that were tumbling from her own mouth.

"Really? You're really sure? I mean... you've thought about it properly?"

"Yes," she laughed. "I told you, I've thought of nothing else. I want to be with you, Jack." Her eyes sparkled at the thought of the exciting prospect before them.

Jack grabbed her head and pulled her face close to his and then pulled her hair back so that he could gently bite her smooth neck. As he pulled up his shirt, she undid his trousers. And the rain beat down.

CHAPTER 44

The waiter led Tina and Maxine to a booth seat, took their drinks order and left them with the menus along with a charming smile.

"Friggin 'ell!" Tina breathed, hoisting her soaking wet coat off her cold body and squashing it into the space beside her. "He's a bit of alright! Shame we look like drowned rats. Look at the state of us just from a two minute run from the car park!"

"We couldn't wait in the car forever, Teen," Maxine replied huffily. "I'm bloody starving."

"I ain't never been in 'ere before. Looks a bit bloody expensive to me." Tina eyed up the framed black and white movie posters that adorned the walls around them. "Ere! 'Ow can you afford this place, I fought you didn't 'ave a job no more?"

"I don't," Maxine answered, shortly. "But I'll soon have enough money to come here every bleeding day of the week if I want to, and anyway, I'm paying. We're celebrating."

"Celebrating what?"

"The imminent arrival of money," she smiled.

"Hey 'ang on," Tina continued warily. "Is this that place your boss used to bring ya? It is, innit? What d'ya wanna come back in 'ere for?"

"Well why shouldn't I?" Maxine replied haughtily. "I'm entitled to eat where the hell I want, like everybody else. And anyway everyone knows it's the best place in town."

"Yeah but he could've been in 'ere, couldn't he?" Tina narrowed her eyes as the penny dropped. "Oh 'ang on a mo, that's why ya came here innit? You was 'oping to see him!"

"Don't be so bloody ridiculous," Maxine hissed across the table quietly while pushing her damp hair behind her ears. "I knew damn well he wasn't here! In fact I was talking to him ten minutes ago on the phone – while you were hopping around on my doorstep, you stupid moo."

"Are you serious?"

"Deadly. He wants me back," Maxine lied. "I told him to go swing from a tree and fuck himself. I wouldn't touch that man again if he was a cure for thrush!"

"Flipping 'eck! What did he say to that?"

"Not a lot. Men hate it when women have the upper hand, Teen. Said he wishes he'd never let me go, wishes I would go back to him."

Tina fingered the wet black tendrils hanging limply like thick string around her face, and gazed lovingly at Maxine.

"I loves your hair," she said, changing the subject. "Look how wavy it's gone in the rain, makes me dead jealous it does."

"Well, that's life, Teen, I'm afraid. We can't all be blessed now, can we?"

The waiter returned with their drinks and took their

food order. When he had turned and left them, Tina spoke in a hushed tone.

"Anyway, what money, what was you on about?"

"Pardon?"

"You said summink about the arrival of money. What money's that then? Granny died has she?"

Maxine watched Tina scan the room again in childlike amazement and it occurred to her that for Tina, this really was on par with The Savoy.

"Oh never mind that now, Teen. I shouldn't have mentioned it," she replied, trying to change the subject.

Tina lovingly fingered the indentations on the leather wine menu in front of her, and Maxine smiled at her childlike wonderment.

"Teen, have you ever eaten anywhere other than McDonalds and KFC?" she asked, rolling her eyes.

"Cheeky cow!" Tina replied. "You know I like that Harvester place too."

Maxine watched her as she stared at the décor in awe. The two of them were so different, people often wondered how on earth they had ever ended up as friends in the first place. Most people didn't know that she and Tina went a long way back; as far back as nappies. Their single mothers had lived next door to each other in council houses (where Tina still lived now) and with only a year between the two of them, they had spent most of their childhoods in and out of each other's houses. When they started school, it was Maxine, being the older and taller one, who looked out for Tina in the playground, and Tina, being short and skinny, had always been grateful for that. But whilst Maxine had bettered herself since childhood, Tina had not. Tina hadn't moved an inch away from the council urchin that she had always been, and Maxine could see now that she never would. Once so alike, she now silently cringed whenever Tina opened her mouth, and although she would never admit it to anyone, she knew deep down the reason why; Tina was a daily reminder of her own true past. She reminded Maxine of who she used to be, where she had come from and how she used to speak. And they were the few things in life that Maxine didn't ever want to be reminded of. No matter how many elocution lessons she had paid for since leaving school, or wherever (or *however*) she would manage to re-house herself in life, she would always know that she and Tina were peas borne from the same pod. Maxine had reinvented herself, acquired a decent accent and brought a new wardrobe, all of which had helped her onto the first steps of her desired transformation, but none of it had changed her roots. None of it could ever change her roots. If nothing else, the 'desired transformation' had paved the way for a decent job, good money, nice clothes and even a gorgeous pad. *So what if Tom had helped her with the apartment?* she thought flippantly, *she would have got there in the end on her own at some point.* Still, without him now, she would still be living in the council house with her mother, on the other, less desirable part of town, just as Tina was. Tina looked up to her now, with a degree of wonderment, and Maxine liked the feeling that gave her. With this in mind, Maxine contented herself with the fact that life had at least been kind to one of them. And thank God the 'one of them' had been her.

"Why don't you get yourself a job, Teen?" Maxine asked her suddenly, face screwed up, as she compared her perfectly polished nails to Tina's bitten down stumps. "I mean you've never worked, have you?"

"What do I wanna go and do that for?" Tina replied in a shocked tone. "I stacked shelves at Tesco once, cor, never again. Talk about 'ard work and we weren't even allowed to talk to each uvver when we was doing it!"

Maxine frowned. "How's your mother?" she asked, changing the subject.

"On 'oliday at the moment, fank gawd, she's a bloody nightmare! I'd move out but I can't afford it."

"Well there you go then – get yourself a job, Teen, then you *could* move out! I've worked hard for what I've got remember," she added, piously.

Tina sniggered. "Yeah, what, by shagging the payroll?"

Maxine closed her eyes in a show of distaste. "You're so coarse, Teen, you really are. I really loved that man. The apartment was a lucky bonus."

Tina looked across the table at her with ongoing admiration. "What was it like then; shagging a married man?"

"The same as shagging a single man," Maxine replied, rolling her eyes to the ceiling. "What do *you* think?"

"Yeah but you know what I mean. It must've been different. All that extra excitement, knowing it's dead wrong an' all that."

"Extra excitement?" Maxine scoffed. "You've got to be bloody kidding me. I can tell you've never bedded a wedded before." She looked at Tina and shook her head dramatically. "It's a bloody nightmare."

"How?"

"Stress! Knowing that he's going home to *her* every night, knowing that you'll only ever be his bit on the side, *no matter what he says to you.*"

"Well I did tell you they never leave the wife, didn't I?" Tina added this bit on with a smirk, pleased to have finally been right about something in her life. "I 'eard that on the telly once," she finished proudly.

"Well it's more hassle than it's worth, believe me. Way too much stress. I was a nervous bloody wreck half of the time."

"You used to tell me you didn't give a shit," Tina queried.

"When?"

"All the time. You used to say that it was just a bit of fun and that you didn't have a guilty bone in your body. You told me that he..."

"Oh shut up!" Maxine snapped.

"Ooh, pardon me." Tina put her elbows up onto the

white linen covered table and scrutinised her stubby fingernails before carrying on.

"Me mate Julie right, she was seeing a married man last year. Reckons it was bloody brilliant. Do you know what she told me?"

Maxine blinked slowly and sighed. "No, but I bet you're going to tell me."

"She said that he'd do her up the bum-hole, while his wife was up the shops like, then, later on, on the same night, do his wife too. He used to call it a Freesome by Proxy. Or was it a Poxy Freesome? Summink like that. Anyway, she said..."

"Oh Teen, shut up. Can't you talk about something else?"

"Like what?"

"I don't know. Anything other than... *that*."

Tina looked away frustrated but within thirty seconds broke the newfound silence. "Hey, Max, ain't that your boss' wife sat over there with that dark-haired woman?"

"Yeah, very funny, Teen. Don't piss about I'm not in the mood."

"No, I'm serious, look. I'm sure that's 'er."

"How the hell would you know anyway?" Maxine asked, craning her neck towards the window for a better look.

"I saw her that once at your office, don't you remember, when I came to meet you for lunch, about free monfs ago?"

A small group of girls on their lunch break walked

in and sat down at the last empty table, blocking the already dimly lit view.

"Well," Tina asked impatiently, "is it 'er then?"

"God knows," Maxine replied, mildly irritated. "A bunch of tarty office bods have just parked their arses in the way. Can't see a bloody thing now."

"Swap seats then," Tina suggested impatiently. "I swear to God, Max, that's 'er. Sit here and I'll go to the pisser."

Without further ado, Tina got up from her seat, pulled a '*fuck me, you're gonna flip*' face at Maxine, and walked towards the 'toilet' sign that she had spotted only moments before. Maxine pounced into Tina's seat the moment it became vacant.

IT *WAS* HER! The Bitch Wife! Sitting less than fifteen metres away in a window seat and talking animatedly with a dark-haired, foreign looking lady.

Maxine got up quickly and returned to her original seat. She could feel her heart thumping wildly in her chest as her mouth turned dry. Pressing her back deeply into the seat behind her she took a deep breath and closed her eyes. And she hoped with every fibre of her being, that Bitch Wife wouldn't walk past their table to use the toilets.

CHAPTER 45

Sam stood up and turned back to face Andy.

"Thanks again."

"Please don't go yet," he begged.

"I can't."

"What do you mean?"

"My clothes are still in your tumble drier," she laughed. "But they must be ready by now."

He retrieved her warm clothes from the dryer and she draped them over one arm.

"Won't be a tick. Can I use your bedroom?"

"Of course, it's all yours."

As the bedroom door closed, the pacing began again. Andy tried to think of something to do and decided to put the kettle on and make them both another drink. That might keep her here for a bit longer too, if nothing else.

By the time it had boiled and he had made them both another coffee, five minutes had already passed. He checked the time on his watch against the kitchen clock and saw that they were, as always, in sync. It would have taken Andy all of fifteen seconds to change his clothes - what on earth was keeping her? Maybe it was a woman thing, or was she quite simply going through all of his stuff? That was a woman thing too, wasn't it? His pacing took him outside his bedroom door on the pretence of using the bathroom opposite it. He stopped outside and tapped lightly.

"Everything OK in there?" he called out, trying his best to sound nonchalant. "I'm um, just using the loo if you wonder where I've disappeared to."

"Oh, yeah fine," she called back. "I won't be long."

Andy trailed into the bathroom, waited impatiently for two minutes and then flushed. When he came out there was still no sign of her. What should he do now? He couldn't knock *again*; she would think he was rushing her. He busied himself by stirring the coffees for the fifth time and then the door finally opened.

"Sorry I took so long," she said, walking into the kitchen and handing him back his bathrobe. "I guess I really should be off now."

"Oh no, don't go yet. One more coffee." He pushed the mug into her hand before she could refuse it, and with an arm around her waist, guided her back onto the sofa. "I've made it now, it would be an insult to the third world to chuck it."

Sam smiled and tested it. It was lukewarm, and she was able to take a huge mouthful.

"I've had a really nice time, And. It's been really good seeing you again."

"Do you have to say it like that?"

"Like what?"

"Like you're going in a minute."

"I *am* going in a minute."

"You don't have to."

"Yes, I do."

"But what about the rain?"

"What rain? It stopped half an hour ago."

His heart sank as he looked out of the window. Sam drank the remaining coffee in the next sixty seconds and got up from the sofa.

"I really have to get going. I've got a friend coming round later and the place is a tip."

"Oh, sure. Um, I'm sorry, I didn't mean to... well you know..."

"No, it's OK really. I just have so much to do that I really have to go and it's getting quite dark now."

She was right. The darkness of the thunderstorm had been replaced with the darkening of an early winter's evening sky, casting its grey cloak upon everything outside. The wind was picking back up again too and it looked dismal and cold.

"I'll drive you." It was more of an order than an offer.

"There's absolutely no need. I only..."

"No. I said I'll drive you. It's not open for discussion."

Sam smiled and kissed him on the cheek.

***

The wet roads squelched beneath the car tyres and reflected the incandescence of the street lights that shone down from above. The car's digital clock showed that it was 17:00 but outside it looked more like 9pm.

Where had this perfect day gone? The roads were quiet; the storm had sent any shoppers home hours ago and it was still a bit early for the workies to be on their way home just yet. Within ten minutes they were parked outside her flat, just over the other side of town.

"Looks like winter's here already, doesn't it?" she said, breaking the awful silence that had fallen upon the car since he had turned the ignition off.

"Yeah," he replied flatly.

"Right, well, thanks again. Sorry, I must've said that a hundred times today," she laughed nervously.

"It should be me thanking you."

Even in the darkness of the car, she could tell that he didn't want her to go.

"When can I see you again, Sam?"

She looked down and fixed her stare on the glove box just above her legs. "Oh, And, I don't know," the uncertainty rife in her voice. "Maybe it's best if we just leave things as they are for now."

"What? You're kidding me, right?"

"No, I'm not. We've had a great day, it's been the best, I just don't want us to go and ruin things."

"Ruin things? How can we ruin things, Sam? You just said yourself that we've had a great day."

"I know that, it's just that, well... I don't want to..."

"See me again?"

She shook her head slowly. "It's not that."

Turning in his seat he pulled her face round so that

she was facing him.

"Then what?"

Her expression gave him his answer.

"You think you can't trust me again, don't you? I'll spend the rest of my life proving that you can." He leant forward and kissed her softly on the lips. "If you'll ever let me."

She smiled and reached for the door handle. "Ok. Call me," she whispered.

**

Andy waited in the warmth of the car and watched intensely as she unlocked her front door. She turned and gave one small wave before stepping inside and slamming it shut.

"Come on," he muttered to himself impatiently, as he struggled to call up her number on his mobile. Finally he sat back and smiled to himself as her phone began to ring.

"Hello," she said, only seconds later and slightly out of breath.

"Hi."

"Andy, is that you?"

"Of course it's me," he said affecting a wounded voice. "Who else would it be?"

The curtains parted slightly and she appeared, a soft glow of yellow lighting behind, illuminating her. He could see her, phone in hand, shaking her head at him and smiling.

"Andy, what on earth are you doing?"

"You told me to call you, well... I'm calling you. When can I see you again?"

She held her hand up to the window and wiggled her fingers at him and he waved back. There was a small pause before she spoke again.

"I don't know. The weekend?"

"What?"

"I said, 'what about the weekend?'"

"The weekend? Sam, it's only bloody Tuesday, tell me you're joking."

"Well... Friday then?"

"Friday? Are you winding me up?" He exaggerated a tone of disbelief and she laughed.

"Well when do you want to see me then?"

"*Now.*"

"You're so funny," she laughed, and her light voice tinkled down the line. "I can see your lips moving from here you know."

"Close yes, but not close enough," he whispered back from the darkness of his car.

Her hesitation was deliberate; she wanted those words to hang in the air for as long as possible.

"Call me tomorrow then," she said at last.

Andy beamed and blew her a kiss from the car.

"Goodnight gorgeous," he said. And he knew he would sleep better tonight than he had in weeks.

CHAPTER 46

Cheryl put the two dinner plates down onto the table, sat down, and began eating her sausage casserole without a word to Jack.

"What's up?" he asked, reaching forward for some pepper. "You're very quiet tonight."

She looked up expressionless.

"I feel a bit tired, Jack, that's all, don't worry I'm fine."

"Are you sure? You look very pale to me."

He wondered if this was the form his guilty conscience was destined to take; showing long overdue concern and attention to his unassuming wife. After two mouthfuls of food, she got up and slid her uneaten meal into the kitchen bin.

"It's no good, I can't eat, Jack, I feel dreadful."

"Well go on up to bed then, love," he offered kindly. "I'll clear everything up down here."

"Oh you're an angel. Thanks."

Pushing another forkful of food into his mouth, he scanned her weary face.

"Do you think it's a virus or something then?"

Cheryl put her plate down on the side, the cutlery sliding off and clanking onto the worktops as she did so.

"Maybe." Instead of heading for the door, she turned and sat back down next to him. "Listen, Jack, I've been thinking. Maybe we should cut the Swinger's Night down to once a fortnight, or even back to once a month like it used to be. It all gets a bit much sometimes and I'm not always in the mood for it. What do you think?"

The suggestion surprised Jack so much that a bit of sausage went down the wrong way and he had to cough several times to clear it.

"Where's this all come from?" he asked, when he could safely breathe again. "Is that what the problem is?"

Cheryl shook her head. "No, not at all, but I have been thinking about it for a while now. I just feel like I want a bit of a break from it, that's all. It's becoming the 'expected Saturday night entertainment' isn't it?"

"Well of course it is," he answered unblinkingly, "it's what we've done for years. You've never complained before – in fact it was your idea in the first place, remember? I just don't understand the sudden change of heart."

She stared at him with a determination that he had seen many times before; usually seconds before she got her own way.

"Listen, Jack, I'm not saying I want to stop the club altogether, I'm only saying, do we really need to do this *every single weekend*? I think we'd all benefit if we cut it down. Most other swinging clubs aren't every week."

"Yeah, but we're not most other clubs, are we? Just

because they meet once a month, doesn't mean that *we* have to."

"No it doesn't, but you're not listening to me. I'm not saying we have to follow anyone else's code, just that *I* need some time away from it, that's all."

Jack put down his cutlery and stared long and hard into her drained face. "Are you sure you're OK, Chez?" His voice was tinged with worry and his heart was thumping wildly in his chest.

"I'm fine, Jack. I'm going to bed... but think about what I said, OK?"

He nodded and she closed the door behind her.

***

She knew. He was positive. The more he thought about it the more adamant he was that her shiny penny had finally gathered momentum and dropped heavily into the realms of reality. Cheryl wasn't stupid; she was as sharp as a razor in Patrick Stewart's bathroom cabinet. Did he really think he could keep insulting her intelligence by rogering Sue right under her nose every Saturday night without her taking note? But hadn't Sue been with Richard for the last two weeks? Why hadn't that put Cheryl off the scent?

He realised that it was irrelevant now anyway; he and Sue would soon be confirming her worst fears and starting a whole new life together. She was going to find out sooner or later and from the way things had gone with both Sue and Cheryl today, it looked set to be the former. He had to be careful now, at least until he had spoken to Sue again.

When he had finished eating his dinner, he washed and dried up and then returned everything to its original place in the kitchen. Then he boiled the kettle, made himself a strong cup of tea and walked into the living room, taking in the little bits of clutter that they had accumulated over the last four years. He reached up and took the wedding photo from the wall, holding it tightly in his warm hands. Could he really do this? Could he really throw everything that they had away just because another woman made him feel young and alive again?

Jack sat down, photo still in hand, and stared into the room around him. He already knew the answer to that.

CHAPTER 47

"What do you mean '*no*'?" Charlie was astounded and made no attempt to hide his disappointment.

"I mean NO," James repeated. "One, I've never been skiing before and two, I can't afford it."

"Well I've only ever been once before. You'll never learn if you never try," Charlie reasoned. He put his hands on his hips and pouted sulkily.

"But I don't *want* to go!"

"Oh for pity's sake, Jay," Charlie spat back. "Anyone would think I was asking you to climb K2 with me!"

"Well you might as well be," James replied crossly. "I don't 'do' extreme sports."

"Jay, skiing is *not* an extreme sport."

"Well I don't 'do' *sports* then."

"Oh GREAT! Is this the way it's going to be then is it?" Charlie bellowed, folding his arms across his chest. "What have I done – condemned myself to a life of boredom and telly watching?"

These last few words to spill from Charlie's mouth hurt James deeply. He was very content to sit and watch the telly in the evenings – he worked hard all day and he wasn't the 'do-er' type, what was wrong with that? Charlie's criticism stabbed him, like a knife into his comfort zone and it overrode any thoughts that he might have of knocking yet another argument on the head.

"Well if you don't like it then you know where the

door is." James regretted saying it the minute the words left his mouth.

Charlie stomped into the kitchen, grabbed his denim jacket from the chair and made for the front door without hesitation.

"Where are you going?"

"Out."

"Out where?"

He paused for a few seconds before replying. "You just told me to leave, Jay. I know when I've outstayed my welcome."

"I didn't say that. I said you know where the door is if you want it."

"Then maybe I *do* want it!" he snarled back.

"Oh, I see."

"You're bloody *suffocating* me," Charlie raged through clenched teeth. "I'm going out. I've got to go and see Paloma anyway, we still have things to sort out."

"Well how long will you be?"

Charlie's head jerked up and he threw his jacket onto the floor in full temper tantrum mode, his hands flying dramatically back to his slender hips.

"You're doing it *again*! You're stifling me, Jay, I can't stand it!"

"Oh stop queening it up, I only asked how long you were going to be." James felt exasperated. Living with Charlie seemed to entail suffering one huge drama after another.

"About eight inches!" Charlie shouted back, slamming the door behind him.

***

Andy stood still and waited for another noise. Not a sound. He moved and looked out of his living room window and saw Charlie finally come into view in the car park down below. He had a black denim jacket slung over one shoulder and stared up at the smart apartment block before getting into his car. Andy knew that it was James he was looking for, but darted out of sight regardless, behind the safety of his curtains. *Was James alright?* There had been a hell of a lot of screaming coming from down there and he was sure he had heard something about skiing too.

Pulling his jacket on he checked the time. It was only 7.45am. He might as well leave for work now, there was bound to be some stuff to do from yesterday afternoon and now that Tom was finally considering Flexi-Time, it would be a good chance to show him that it could work, even in an office as small as theirs.

Grabbing his keys and mobile phone from the kitchen worktop, he left the apartment and made for his car, texting Sam as he went.

CHAPTER 48

"A few people called for you. Here." Sally shoved a dozen sticky yellow Post-It notes forcefully into Tom's hand. "I told them all you'd call them straight back so don't disappoint!"

Tom looked confused, firstly at the clump of sticky square papers in his hand and then at Sally. He had never known anyone morph like she had; slowly, day by day, from shrinking violet to bossy Persian Ivy. Was this the same Sally that he had hired only last week because of her refreshing diffidence? The same girl who only last week had missed her first two lunch breaks because no one had told her she could go, and she had been too nervous to mention it? 'Hey we don't do things like that around here,' Tom had told her when he realised what had happened. 'Just go. It's a very relaxed ship, as long as the work gets done then I'm happy.' As she had passed him some letters to sign, he noticed her shy, rigid body tense up even further. 'We don't bite, honest,' he had continued, 'I want you to enjoy it here.' She had taken a big breath and smiled. The next time he saw her, the transformation had already begun.

Now at ease, the Ivy had begun to take root. She was reliable and worked methodically, but now she displayed more self-confidence than he thought he could cope with. He hadn't told anyone yet but she had already made complaints to him about Andy and Jack. They were unprofessional, she had said. Jack was sexist and they both used vulgar language in the office. '*It's 2019,*' she had complained sternly, '*and I shouldn't have to put up with this in a working environment*'. Tom knew it was true – it was probably the last remaining un-PC office this side of 1990, but Maxine hadn't cared. Maxine had loved it.

Sally's glossy black fringe had begun to flop over her dark brown eyes, but this only served to enhance, not hide them. She raised a cocky eyebrow at Tom, as if to say, 'Are you still here?'

"Uh... Thank you, Sally," he said, coming out of his reverie, "you're very... um,' he searched for the right word, "efficient."

He wanted a coffee now and knew he would be getting it himself; Sally had stopped making coffee on Day Three. '*It's sexist, not to mention demeaning to me as a modern woman. I don't plan on making my future husband coffees so why should I do it for you lot?*' she had complained.

As Tom turned, he saw that Jack had appeared behind him.

"Hey bud," Jack said, with a huge grin plastered across his face, "how's it hanging?"

"You look happy, not your birthday already is it?"

"Might as well be," Jack replied, bouncing on the spot with nervous energy. "Can't spare ten minutes can you?"

Tom looked down ominously at the dozen small, yellow squares stuck in his palm, lying on top of each other at odd angles. He could make out from one of them that Angela had rung twice.

"Yeah, course, as long as it *is* only ten though." He held his papered hand up. "Looks like I've got a busy morning."

"*You've* got a busy morning?" Jack laughed. "What it is to be top dog, eh. A couple of people to ring back and he's headed for a nervous breakdown!" He looked at Sally for camaraderie but she looked away.

"What's up?" he asked her, still beaming. Lost your sense of humour already? You've only been here two minutes!"

Sally ignored him and kept her gaze fixed firmly on her computer screen.

"Hey, what's wrong with you? You're about as relaxed as Michael Jackson at a PTA meeting." He chuckled at his own joke. "Not that time of the month already is it, Sal?"

Sally turned to Tom with a face of fury. "That's it! I don't have to put up with this! It's disgusting! What are you going to do about it?" she shouted.

Shock stamped itself over Jack's face, replacing his previous joy with confusion. Grabbing him tightly by the arm, Tom walked him into his office and slammed the door behind them.

"What the hell are you doing?" Tom whispered angrily. "You can't do this anymore, Jack! Max has left and no other woman within a hundred yards of the First World is going to put up with that kind of behaviour!"

Jack shook his head, dazed. "What are you ON about? What did I do?"

"She's made a formal complaint against you, which I'm not dealing with right now, but PLEASE - one psychotic secretary a year is enough for anyone!'

"OH COME ON! It was a JOKE! It was *blatantly* a joke!" His mouth hung open, astounded. "Hey, hang on, what complaint? About what? I haven't done anything!"

"I told you, Jack, I haven't got time for this now, we'll deal with it later. But she asked for HR! I told her we don't have HR. I'M HR!"

"That's ridiculous!" Jack shook his head, still reeling.

"What did you want to talk about that was so urgent?" Tom continued impatiently. "You've got ten minutes, starting..." Tom checked the second hand on his Breitling watch and waited a few seconds for effect. "Now!"

"No, I want to know about Sally! Come on!"

"Not happening, Jack, but you *will* be getting a warning for what you just said out there. It's not acceptable, things have to change."

"For fuck's sake, mate, come on!"

Tom glared at him for several seconds before looking away and pulling the Post-Its from his hand. Separating them carefully, he stuck each one around the edge of his computer screen.

"OK, I'll stop. I promise." Jack offered. "Just..."

Tom looked at his watch again. "Nine minutes, Jack..."

Jack resigned himself with a loud huff and put his hands on his hips. "OK. I'm leaving Cheryl."

Tom allowed a few seconds for the revelation to sink in and then shook his head. "And that's why you're so happy? I'm confused."

"I've been seeing someone else," Jack blurted out, sitting himself down in the chair opposite Tom's desk. "It's been going on for a while now."

Tom stayed silent. He had known Jack since school and it annoyed him how he still managed to throw surprises at him after all these years.

"She's amazing, mate. We're crazy about each other."

Words had momentarily deserted Tom, but his first ones were pointless ones.

"Well Angela's going to be gutted. I know we don't all get together as often as we used to but you know how much she loves Cheryl."

"That's not really what I was expecting you to say, mate, in all fairness," Jack said looking confused.

Ignoring him, Tom thought of the handful of times in the last few years that he and Angela had been to their house for drinks or meals, and vice versa. He had never thought for a minute that Jack would leave Cheryl. *Cheryl* leave *Jack* – maybe. She was never short of male admirers – Tom had seen her flirt many times with different men, including himself. But *Jack* leave

Cheryl?

"But you're our closest friends," he continued, as the announcement sank in. "I can't believe it. Are you sure you can't work things out? You don't *have* to leave her, surely?"

"You don't get it. I *want* to leave, I've never felt this way before, it's fantastic." Jack continued, all thoughts of a complaint against him momentarily forgotten. "Actually she's part of the Swinging Club," he added nonchalantly.

Tom's head shot up and his mouth fell open simultaneously. Sure, there had been some gossip about Jack and Cheryl taking part in such a club, hosting it even, but Jack had never so much as mentioned anything about it directly to him before, and his sudden frankness left him void of words.

"Come on, Tommo, you *knew*. Why so shocked? *Everyone* knew about the club, I heard the gossiping myself."

"No, I didn't know! And funnily enough you never mentioned it before either." Tom spluttered. "You never talked about any rumours."

"Ah, I know, but I never denied any either." Jack snatched a biscuit from the open packet on Tom's desk and smirked.

"Why didn't you tell me, I'm your *best* mate? I can't believe you never told me."

"Well I'm telling you now, aren't I?"

"OK. So... who is she? How long?"

Jack went on to give Tom a quick rundown on Sue and

the club.

"So," he concluded, "what Chezzer does with the club now is up to her I guess. It's her baby, not mine. Mind you I'm not complaining – I'd never have met Sue if it hadn't been for that club. I would've reached the grand old age of forty having only had sex with one woman in my life! Fuck me, mate, in that respect it saved me."

"But I thought you and Cheryl were good together," Tom said, perplexed. "I'm just surprised. How could you do it? Angela will be gutted."

"Hey, hang on a minute, you're a fine one to talk. What about Max? I thought you of all people would understand."

"My situation's nothing like yours."

"It's EXACTLY the same."

"I didn't leave Angela for a start."

"No, but that's the only difference!"

"Well then it's not exactly the same then, is it?"

"God, don't be so pedantic."

"Don't call me God."

They both smiled.

"I'm just stunned," Tom went on, "really I am. I had no idea."

"But I really love her, mate, it's mad. I've never felt like this before. I want you to be happy for me. The only problem is how do I tell Cheryl?"

Tom's eyes widened further and his voice rose two pitches in disbelief.

"You mean you haven't told Cheryl yet?"

"Of course I haven't told Cheryl yet. And Sue hasn't told Alan yet either. Did I tell you that she wants a baby? I've always wanted a baby. Cheryl doesn't 'do' kids. She's spent four years telling me that. Just think – I'm going to be a dad. Me. A fucking dad!"

"Woah, slow down! You're telling me she's pregnant now? You never said *THAT* in the rundown." Tom's head was spinning like an overpriced, vomit-laced fairground ride.

"No, of course she's not pregnant. But she's bloody well gonna be as soon as we move in together."

"But she might not get pregnant. There could be any number of problems, especially at your age. I mean we're both headed to forty on an express train and..."

"What are you saying? There's bugger all wrong with my sperm, mate, I'm telling you." Jack's virility was under attack and he would defend it at all costs. "Oh no, she'll get pregnant alright. She tried for years with Alan with no joy. But wait till she gets my Super Sperm flowing inside her."

"She already has, hasn't she?" Tom added dryly.

"Oh, yeah, but... well that's different, isn't it?" he answered, uneasily.

"Is it?"

"She went back on the pill a couple of years ago when Alan's sad little newts kept letting them both down. She couldn't handle it, month after month, realising he'd failed to hit the spot again." Jack was enjoying this - putting Alan down publicly gave him power and made him feel invincible. "She went back on the pill so that she didn't have to think about it anymore. Knowing nothing was going to happen in that department meant she could get on with her life again. That's what she said, anyway."

Tom looked worried. "I hope you know what you're doing, you're talking about starting a new life with someone who swings, for chrissake."

"You sound like my mum."

"You've spoken to your mum about it?"

They looked at each other for a moment and then smirked again.

"Seriously," Tom continued, "do you think that's a healthy environment to bring any kid into?"

"*Used* to swing, mate, *used* to swing." Jack's grin grew wider.

"Don't you feel remotely sad at the thought of leaving Cheryl? It's a huge decision. You're talking about leaving your wife and home."

"Well of course I feel *sad* about it," he said, a few dull clouds suddenly drifting across his bright eyes, "but there's something missing from the whole marriage thing. It's just not the same as it is with Sue. Do you know we haven't even had sex in months?"

"Oh come on, you're not going to tell me that this is just about sex, are you? You don't leave your wife just for good sex, I should know, remember?"

"No, that's just it, it isn't just the sex, it's the whole caboodle, the entire package. We're crazy for each other, man. I'd hoped you'd be happy for me."

"Of course I'm happy for you, mate, just go careful that's all. I just think that..." Tom stopped short. His eyes drifted to the writing on one of the Post Its and he pulled it from the computer screen quickly and stared at it before turning it over in his hand.

"What's wrong?"

Tom handed the small piece of paper to Jack before bringing his fist down heavily on the desk in front of him.

Jack read Sally's words from the slip of paper out loud.

"'*9.10am - Maxine rang. Urgent. Phone back by 9.30 otherwise don't worry, she'll phone Angela instead.*' What the fuck?" Jack handed the paper back to Tom. "What the hell's she playing at now?"

Tom looked at his watch. It was 9.35.

CHAPTER 49

"Bollocks, bollocks, bollocks!" Grabbing the phone off his desk Tom dialled her number as quickly as he could. It was engaged. He slammed the phone down, jumped out of his chair and paced his small office furiously.

"Shit. What are you going to do?" Jack asked nervously. "Can I help?" Panic was filling the room like dense fog and he felt useless.

Without another word, Tom left the office and found Sally by the photocopier.

"Sal, the message off Max - what did she say?"

"Sorry?" Sally looked confused. "What do you mean?"

"The message you took, what did she say?"

"What did WHO say? There were a dozen messages," she answered blandly, "I don't know which one you're talking about. Oh, hang on a minute," her eyes flickered with recollection, "do you mean the one off the weird girl?"

"Yes," Tom said without a second thought. "Yes, the one off the weird girl, what did she say?" He could feel the panic rising higher in his chest; his heart thumping wildly beneath his ribs.

"Um, well just what I wrote. I wrote down exactly what she asked me to. Why? Is there a problem?"

"No, no problem," Tom assured her, trying to dilute the adrenalin that he could feel welling up inside of him.

"She did sound as though she was in a rush though," Sally continued. "Slammed the phone down on me as soon as she'd finished talking. Who is she anyway?"

This last question threw Tom completely. Among his crazy, cluttered thoughts, he wondered why she would ask such a personal question to her boss of only one week.

"Sorry?"

"Oh, I just wondered who she was, that was all. She sounded quite young, and I know you have a daughter. I just thought that maybe she was..."

"NO. My daughter's only five. Why, do I look *that* old then?" Tom felt consumed with a sudden, unnerving vanity.

"Well..." she mumbled. "I'm sorry, I didn't mean anything by it. I just meant that she sounded as though she *could* be your daughter that's all. Actually," she went on, trying to dig herself out of a hole so big that she could have put a swimming pool in it, "I really thought more of a niece or something. I mean she wouldn't have called her dad by his first name, would she? But then some do you know."

"Sally," Tom interrupted in a bid to stop her digression, "what did she say about Angela?" He could feel himself rushing again and could hear the blood pumping loudly in his ears.

"I've already told you," she replied, annoyed now, "just what I wrote, that's all."

Tom sighed and turned to go back into his office. Jack had come out and was standing in the doorway just behind him.

"You OK?" he asked, throwing a wary glance in Sally's direction.

"Yeah," Tom replied with an unconvincing smile. "Let's hope so anyway."

**

With Jack back in the main office making small talk with Andy, Tom closed the door tightly behind him. He pressed the re-dial button on his phone and his heart lurched as, this time, Maxine's number began to ring. He glanced at his watch. It was 9.38am.

"Hello?"

The serenity that emanated from her voice infuriated him further and he felt himself about to lose whatever bit of self-restraint he had left.

"Hello, who is this?"

"It's *me*, who the hell do you think it is?" he hissed.

"Oh hiiiiii Tom, what a pleasant surprise," she sang. "I really wasn't expecting to hear from you. How *are* you?"

"Cut the crap, Max, what are you playing at?"

"Well that's no way to speak to an old friend now, is it? That's a real shame you know, I really had hoped that you'd have calmed down since you rang me last. Two phone calls in a week though, hmmm, I guess I really am in favour at the moment." She cooed happily as if without a care in the world.

"You know damn well why I've phoned you - because YOU rang me. What do you want? Have you phoned Angela? What the hell have you said to her?"

"Tom, really! One question at a time *please*! I haven't said anything to her – I've been on the phone to Tina. Her boyfriend just dumped her, by text funnily enough. I think she just needed to speak to someone who'd been there."

The line went quiet. Tom's breathing slowed down. *She hadn't phoned Angela.* He swallowed several times to try and relieve his dry mouth.

"Great timing though," she started up again, "cos I was just about to."

An alien hatred for her burned deeply into his soul. *He didn't have anything to hide from Angela anymore so why on earth had he been running around with a panic attack worthy of The Guinness Book of Records? Maxine had nothing to substantiate any claims she might make because everything she said now was a lie anyway.* He still had the third letter too – he would show it to Angela tonight, lunchtime even, and then she would believe him; one glance at the disturbing literary nonsense that was in his possession would be enough to convince anyone that she was talking absolute nonsense.

"I've shown Angela your letters, all of them," he lied. "Say or do what the hell you like, it won't make a blind bit of difference to us either way."

"Really?" Her voice was still light and breezy. "Well I guess we'll just have to wait and see about that, won't we?"

"I feel so sorry for you, Max," he said calmly now. "Actually no, I pity you." He knew this would infuriate her, even if she maintained her cool façade. "You're pretty pathetic, you know that?"

"So I've been told, honey," she replied calmly, before cutting him off. "So I've been told."

CHAPTER 50

"Anyone would think you were staying for a week," Angela exclaimed, eyeing the huge bag Maria had packed for Eva.

Eva's huge, dark, chocolate coloured eyes stared up at Angela, her glossy black hair framing her tiny face.

"Mrs Baxter," came her small voice, "I had to bring Bunny and if I bring Bunny then I have to bring Bear, and if Bear comes then I *have* to bring Toady."

"Toady?" Angela queried with a look of horror.

Eva pulled out a large, furry green and grey speckled toad, from the bottom of her large travel case. Angela smiled with relief.

"Sweetie, as long as it's soft and stuffed then I don't care what you've brought. Now you girls go and find some space in Jess' room for all of these things and I'll bring the rest up later."

Still holding on tightly to Toady with one hand, Eva pulled half of the case's contents out onto the shiny hall floor, rummaging around excitedly for Bunny. Within seconds Jess had found Bear and, clutching the toys as if their lives depended on it, they bounded up the stairs and into Jess' room, disturbing the silence that had settled comfortably there all day.

The front door crashed open behind her and Tom walked through it looking haggard and drained.

"Hey, you're home early," she said, walking over to

him. "Everything OK?"

"Hectic day. What's all this for?" He looked down at the muddle that she had just walked away from.

"Oh, that's Eva's stuff, she's staying, remember? Though where this all came from, God only knows. Maria said they escaped with hardly anything – that comment obviously didn't extend to Eva's stuffed toys!"

"I thought it was tomorrow night Eva was staying?"

"Well it was, but Maria rang today and asked if she could stay tonight instead. Said something about her brother coming over to see her at the last minute."

"Well he'd want to see Eva, surely?" Tom queried, having been told all there was to know about the Maria/Adrio situation. "He's had no contact with his little niece since they came here, surely he's dying to see her?"

"I'm sure he is, and he will do tomorrow, but they have a lot to talk about tonight and it's probably best if Eva doesn't overhear any of it."

"About Adrio you mean?"

"Bound to be."

Remembering Maxine's letter and unable to wait another minute, Tom put his briefcase down on the floor and took the envelope from his inside jacket pocket.

"There's something I need to show you." He pulled the thin blue sheet from its crumpled sleeve.

"Oh please not now, just give me ten minutes to sort this mess out and get the girl's tea on the go, then I promise I'll be all ears."

310

"Well I'll grab a shower then and we'll talk later," Tom said hiding his disappointment.

"You don't mind?"

"Of course not."

***

"Do you think she packed those extra clothes on purpose?" Angela asked curiously the next morning. "I mean it seems a bit of a coincidence that after packing two extra clean sets of clothes, Maria rings up this morning to ask if Eva can stay another night."

"I don't have a clue," Tom answered, pre-occupied with the TV.

"I'll bet I'm right. I bet she knew that Eva would be staying here tonight and that's why she did it. I mean I don't mind, but she could've just asked me, I wouldn't have minded."

Tom didn't reply. He stared at the patch of wall next to the flat screen TV.

"Tom," she called loudly, "are you listening to me?"

"Oh sorry, of course... definitely."

"Definitely what?"

"Definitely whatever you just said."

"I don't believe it, you didn't hear a word!"

"I'm sorry, I don't feel too good that's all."

"Why? What's wrong?"

Without looking at her, he held his left hand out and offered her the crumpled envelope that he had been holding onto all morning. She took it from him without a word.

"Go on, read it," he said, turning the television set off. "I tried to show it to you yesterday."

Angela silently pulled the thin letter from its snug but tattered home and began to read the words.

"None of it's true, Angela," Tom said when she had finished. "She's a psycho. A goddamn fucking psycho."

"And you only showed me this because she threatened to send the next one to *me*?" She looked up, annoyed. "Where are the others, why didn't you tell me?"

"You can see why I didn't show them to you; they were exactly the same. That one is just more of the same old shit. You shouldn't have to read that crap, so I threw them away." He nodded towards the letter in her hand. "It's all bullshit, Angela. She's sick in the head."

Angela refolded the letter and put it back into its envelope.

"What are you doing?"

"Nothing for now," she replied calmly, "but we're taking this to the police first thing on Monday morning."

"Wouldn't it be better to just put it in a drawer somewhere for now and wait?"

Angela looked up sharply. "This... this... *girl*, Tom, is threatening us and we are NOT going to sit on our..."

"Well I wouldn't say she's actually threatened us.

We don't want to overreact. I just don't think there's anything the police can do at this stage. If it carries on..."

"No. It HAS carried on. This is the third letter, Tom! We're going to the police first thing Monday morning and that's the end of it."

Tom swallowed and watched helplessly as she put the letter into her bag and walked away.

***

Andy waxed his hair and then appraised his reflection in the bathroom mirror. Was he underdressed? Overdressed? What would she be wearing? He hadn't given his appearance this much thought in a long time and he didn't want to get it wrong. He looked at his watch and knew he had better hurry if he didn't want to be late. He had booked a sofa at the local cinema to see a film that Sam had wanted to see. She had told him that it was about a famous actor being kidnapped, held to ransom and then bloodily tortured. He could hardly wait. If that didn't put them off their food, he had also booked them a table for afterwards at the new Thai restaurant that had just opened up over the other side of town. 'I've waited all week for the weekend to come round,' he had told her. She had burst out laughing and said, 'uh... obviously, you plonker!'

Pulling up outside Sam's house ten minutes later, he could feel the well of excitement opening up in the pit of his stomach. He had rung her every day since Tuesday, but it wasn't the same, he needed to see her, to smell her, to talk to her.

She took a long time to answer the door but when she finally did he beamed at her like a schoolboy on a first date and kissed her on the cheek.

"You ready then?" he asked excitedly.

"More ready than an Ever Ready battery," she smiled back.

CHAPTER 51

She had watched the house for only fifteen minutes when the front door suddenly opened and the little girl came out with a shiny red coat and shoes on. Bitch Wife was closely in tow.

Maxine shrank down further into her seat, despite already being well shrouded by the generous greenery around. The droopy branches of an old Weeping Willow tree, surrounded by dozens of other smaller, thicker trees, disguised her car perfectly. No one would see her here and she felt truly blessed. Someone was looking after her, she thought proudly; an angel of some sort even. *Was there an Angel of Revenge?*

Within a few seconds, she came to realise that there was certainly such a thing as an Angel of Good Fortune at least. Another child, a foreign looking girl, had come out to join them after a long struggle on the steps with her shoes. Bitch Wife had then kissed her own child, patted the foreign one on the head and then gone back inside. The door was still open. *Oh no! This was it! This was the moment. It had come around much sooner than she had ever imagined it would, but it was here, offering itself up to her like a willing sacrifice.* She probably only had seconds before the opportunity was gone and the thought of waiting endless weeks or months for the wheel of fortune to spin in her favour again was too much to bear.

Opening her car door and leaping out (toys clutched in her hands) Maxine ran amongst the trees as close to the house as their camouflage would allow. Reaching the edge of the copse, she quickly threw one of the dolls she had brought out into the driveway as far as she could but it landed quietly on the gravel and too far away from the girls for them to notice. *Shit. This wasn't how it had been in her imagination when she had played the scene out again and again, wallowing in the delight of an easy target.*

Clutching the second identical doll, she threw that too, but again it landed in the same fashion as the first and barely moved the gravel beneath it.

Maxine looked down at the last two items in her hands; a tennis ball and a packet of sweets. *She should have brought more, something heavier that would have drawn their attention more easily. Why had she been so under-prepared? But then it wasn't like she had ever done anything like this before,* she thought generously. *How was she supposed to have known?*

Suddenly there was movement from the house and once again she could see Bitch Wife attending to the children. This time she was sitting on the top step, pulling a pair of warm looking boots onto her feet and laughing with the girls over something one of them had said. Maxine waited impatiently as they watered the flowers around the outside of the house with identical blue watering cans. *Urghh! How horrendously perfect! What was this? Little House on the sodding Prairie?*

Maxine groaned inwardly.

It was a good five minutes before the small foreign girl said something to Bitch Wife that made her disappear once more. Maxine knew that this would be her last chance today.

The moment Angela disappeared from view, Maxine lobbed the tennis ball as far as she could, praying that it would reach its target. This time it crunched heavily on the gravel and when the girls turned to look, it bounced softly a couple more times before finally landing in one spot. Without hesitation the girls giggled and pointed, and within seconds they were chasing each other for the bright yellow ball. As they reached their target, the girl Maxine recognised as Tom's, bent down and retrieved it excitedly. Seconds later they spotted the two dolls lying side by side further along the driveway. They were now only feet away and Maxine, still shrouded by the trees and shrubs, knew that it was now or never. Glancing once more at the empty steps of the house, she emerged from the greenery quietly so as not to startle the girls.

"Hi, Jess," she whispered, waving frantically at the girls from the bushes. "Can I have those dollies? I dropped them, they're mine."

Jessie's surprised face softened and she smiled warmly before giggling with her friend.

"Quickly then, Jess, I'm in a real hurry," she said impatiently, one eye constantly on the house.

Jessie and her friend skipped up to Maxine without

further hesitation and trustingly held out the dolls for her.

"What are their names?" Jessie asked sweetly.

"Whose names?"

"The dollies' names."

"Oh, well that's a secret," Maxine replied, her face purposefully lighting up with excitement. "They're special dolls you see, otherwise I'd let you have them, but... hang on... I know! I have some more in my car right over here. Quickly! If you come with me you can have them. You'll have to hurry though or your mum might tell you off."

The two girls giggled and looked at each other excitedly.

"Well quickly, quickly then, or it'll be too late. My car's right here, we'll be two seconds."

Without delay, the two girls grabbed Maxine's hands and ran with her through the trees and into a gap that brought them out by the pine trees on the long, private road that led to the house.

"Oh no," Maxine exclaimed sadly when they reached her car. "Oh girls, I'm *so* sorry, they're not here! I'm sorry, I really am."

The girl's faces fell with disappointment.

"Look, don't be sad, I'll tell you what I'll do. I live right around the corner. We'll whizz to my house, that way you can choose whichever dolls you like and then I'll bring you straight back here before your mum even notices you've gone. What do you think?"

The nervous girls looked at each other for reassurance and Jess said no, with a shake of her head.

Maxine's stomach churned and she felt sick. Bitch Wife would be back outside the front of the house by now looking for the girls. If she shouted for them they would probably hear her, even this far from the house, and run off. *Shit! This was all going wrong!*

"Listen girls," she continued, feigning a confidence that had now deserted her. "I've got dozens of these at my house and you can take whichever ones you like. Come on, we'll be back in one minute. You can count. Can you count to twenty? I bet you five dolls each that we'll be back before you can count to twenty."

The girls looked at each other with their eyes and mouths wide open in delight. Excited once again at the prospect of new dolls, the girls began to giggle and, without further hesitation, climbed into the back of Maxine's car.

Maxine started the car up and drove away. And the girls began counting.

CHAPTER 52

As they walked out of the restaurant five hours later, a cold wind had picked up. The very last of the brown and red crispy leaves were being blown off the already half-bare surrounding trees, causing an artistic swirl of late autumnal colours to grace the air all around them, before winter truly set in.

"Wow, it's freezing. And there I was planning a midnight walk in the park." Andy wrapped his arm around Sam's shoulder and waited for her offer of a coffee.

He thought about James and Charlie in Switzerland, skiing in the Alps. A note in James' scrawled handwriting had been pushed under the gap of his door in the middle of the night, and when Andy had finally seen it lying there much later, he had read it with amazement and, if he was honest, a touch of jealousy.

Andy smiled to himself as he remembered James' words in the note. *'Charlie had already bought my ticket so it would have been a waste not to go. He's booked a beautiful chalet and apparently we hire everything we need when we get there'*. Yep, his brother, James, was about to have the first proper adventure of his life and Andy was filled with happiness for him.

"Well," Sam said finally, breaking him away from his thoughts. "You can come back to mine for a nightcap if you like. The place is a tip though, so I apologise now."

"No change there then," Andy grinned.

***

James had 'given in' to the pouts of Charlie and decided at the eleventh hour (when Charlie had called round with his fake Louis Vuitton case to say goodbye) that he would indeed go skiing with him. They had scrambled around wildly, chucking James' warmest clothes into an old, battered case that had once belonged to James and Andy's parents, before scribbling a note for Andy and pegging it as quickly as they could to Charlie's car and the appropriate airport.

James had never done anything remotely 'on impulse' in his life and halfway to Heathrow he had remembered that he actually had work the following week and that if he wanted a job on his return it might be a good idea to phone Tom and beg for time off.

"Haven't you got a slightly less hideous leather box than that?" Charlie had gaped in horror as he eyed the sixties, pea-green monstrosity with great distaste. "How could you even *use* such a thing, Jay? It's utterly humiliating! But never mind, Duck, we'll grab you a new one at the airport!"

CHAPTER 53

Detective Inspector Wainwright signed off from his walkie talkie and looked at Tom sadly. He was the older of the two men and his brown moustache twitched when he spoke.

"No joy at the secretary's house, sir. I'm sorry, but there's no-one there. We have a couple of officers staying put though in case something comes up. Please sir, sit down, we're doing all we can."

"What do you mean you're doing all you fucking can?" Tom paced the room hysterical with fear, as the two policemen looked on helplessly.

"I'm sorry, sir," Wainwright continued, trying to placate him, "but they're only young, they can't possibly have gone far in a couple of hours."

"What the bollocks are you talking about?" Tom shouted, pulling at his hair with his hands. "These are *five year olds* we're talking about, they don't GO anywhere! It's patently obvious that someone has taken them, and we all know who – you've seen the goddamn letter!"

"Sir, please, we're aware of that possibility and as I've told you, we're doing everything we can. We've got squad cars searching the entire area as we speak and dozens of other officers are performing door to door enquiries. It will be much easier in the morning though when we have daylight on our side."

"Daylight? Fucking daylight? That's my baby you're talking about, *my little baby*, what would you do if it was your daughter? Would you wait until the fucking morning then?" He grabbed Wainwright around the neck and yanked his head close to his own. "You listen to me, you bloody moron, you get out there and you find my girl right now. I don't care what you have to do, just bloody find her!"

"Now just a minute, sir," said the younger man, finally intervening with a superior air that belied his young age. "You have enough to worry about right now without us adding assaulting a Detective Inspector to your problems."

"Oh piss off," Tom shouted as he let Wainwright go and turned to face the young officer. "What would you know? You're what? Twelve?"

"I know it's frustrating, sir, but..."

"*Frustrating? FRUSTRATING?* Is that what you call it?" Tom turned around and smashed his fist into the living room door with such force that he blew a hole into the centre of it and instantly began to bleed. "Just piss off the lot of you and find my girl!"

He felt himself crumple into one of the armchairs. He had never felt so angry and sick in his entire life. So angry and so useless. He turned to look at Angela who was still staring into space in shock.

"Come on. If these bastards aren't going to find them then we'll have to. We can't just sit here doing nothing, this is insane!"

Still Angela didn't move or say a word and Tom felt like throttling her with his bare hands. Instead he got up to leave on his own.

"Sir, where do you think you're going?" Wainwright asked patiently.

"Where do you think I'm going? I'm going to that psycho bitch's house! And if she's not there then I'm going to scour the streets and bang on every single door until I find her."

"With all due respect, sir, that's really not a good idea."

"And what the hell would you know?"

"Sir, please. We really need you to stay here."

"Why? What for? To sit and go out of my fucking brain with madness? No way!" Tom headed for the bashed living room door.

"Sir, please, we really need you here in case they come home."

"*Come home*?" Tom looked at him in disbelief. "If you really think they're out there somewhere playing hide and seek at two in the morning you're more fucked up than I thought."

"Sir, listen to me," Wainwright said, deciding to change his tack. "If someone *has* taken the girls, they could be miles away by now. I don't want to worry you but they could be halfway to John o' Groats for all we know. We have helicopters searching the area as we speak and we really need you here in case we get any news. I'm sorry, I can only imagine how you're feeling.

I'd feel the same if it were me, but you have to trust us, you have to believe that we're doing everything we can to find the two girls and to get them back home safely and as quickly as we can."

It worked. Something inside Tom gave up and died and he slumped down beside Angela on the sofa and wept.

CHAPTER 54

The moment he walked into Sam's tiny flat the memories flooded back to him. Everything seemed to be exactly as it had been when he had last been here over eight months ago; the same furniture in the same places; the same photographs on the same shelves; the same DVDs in exactly the same piles.

"Bloody hell, Sam, don't you ever buy anything new? It's like going through a time-warp. I expected *something* to look different."

"I told you – my life stood still when we broke up." Her voice was cool and distant as she walked into the kitchen to fetch a couple of glasses.

He smiled to himself as he fingered a framed snapshot of him and Sam from over a year ago. They were on a beach in Brighton and had got a passer-by to take it. He had always wanted a copy of that picture but Sam had never got him one. Yet here it was, still in the same place.

"Yeah well, I guess eight months isn't that long after all," he called out.

"Not to some people, no," she called back. "Just because *you* carried on as if nothing happened, And, doesn't mean that I did."

"I'm sorry, Sam, I didn't mean to..."

He stopped short and frowned, picking up an unfamiliar photograph that was propped up on one of the shelves with the dozens of other familiar pictures in frames. This one was different though and it stood out completely from the others. It was the only loose photograph here that wasn't framed and the only one that he had never seen before. The person grinning back at him was a very handsome, foreign man and Andy felt a twinge of jealousy.

As Sam walked back into the living room, Andy quickly put the photo back on the shelf.

"This is all I could find, I'm afraid," she said, waving two glasses of golden liquid.

Andy took one from her and sniffed it.

"You keep this stuff in the house?" he asked curiously.

"Just for special occasions," she smiled. "Don't get excited, that brandy's been in my cupboard for eons. In fact you were probably the last person to drink it."

"Who's this in the picture?" Andy couldn't stop the words from escaping.

She glanced while she took a mouthful of the brandy and made a groaning noise. He couldn't tell if it was because of the brandy or the question.

"That's the ex I was telling you about. Marcos."

"Why did you finish?"

"Because it didn't work out."

"Why didn't it work out?"

"Because he was a jerk."

"Why was he a jerk?"

"What is this, Twenty Questions?"

"I'm sorry, I didn't mean to pry." He sat down on the sofa next to her. "I just don't like the thought of him pestering you and hanging around here that's all."

"Hey, I can look after myself you know. I'm quite capable of telling him to piss off whenever he turns up. He'll soon get the message."

"Yeah well, just as long as he does. Anyway, why do you even have a photo of him in here? I thought you only dated for a few months?"

Sam put her glass down onto the small table next to her and giggled. The wine that they had drunk in the restaurant earlier had gone to her head and she found his concern endearing.

"You're funny when you're jealous you know that?" she laughed.

"I'm not jealous."

"Yes you are."

"No I'm not.

"You are too."

"All I'm saying is that I don't like unwanted guys hanging around. I mean, you're here on your own, it's not nice."

"And your point is?"

"My point is," he paused before finishing. "He *is* unwanted, isn't he?"

"What's that supposed to mean?"

"Exactly what I said."

"Hang on a minute here." The playful glint in her eyes disappeared as endearment turned to 'cheek'. "You chased and chased me for months on end and when I finally relented and fell in love with you, hook, line and bloody sinker, you began to lose interest! You treated me like crap, and now, all this time later, you think you can just walk back into my life and tell me what to do! Forget it, Andy, cos it's not happening again!"

Andy looked on as tears sprang to her eyes. She picked up her brandy and knocked the rest back in one go. He was sure it was the alcohol talking; he felt quite light-headed himself. They had downed two bottles of wine in the restaurant and with or without the help or hindrance of booze, the past was bound to come back and smack him in the mouth again sooner or later.

"Come on, we've already been over this. We've had a lot to drink tonight. I feel like a shit already, there's no need to say all that stuff. You know how I feel about you and you know how sorry I am. How many times do I have to say it?"

"I don't care about Marcos, alright? He's an arse-hole." She got up to get herself another brandy. "You think I still like him? What would you know?"

"I know that you've still got his picture propped up on your shelf. That's got to mean something."

"Yes, And, it does, she shouted. "It means I'm a lazy cow! Why do you think yours is still there?"

The last comment stung him as if she had punched

him in the face. There was a long silence and Andy looked at her searchingly.

"I'm serious, And, look around you!" she continued. "You've just said yourself that time's stood still in my flat. If I haven't lifted a finger to take down *your* picture, then what makes you think I'd take down Marcos', who might I add I was still seeing up until a few weeks ago?"

"Yeah, OK, you're right. You're absolutely right – you *are* a lazy cow."

He grinned at her and no matter how hard she tried, she couldn't stop herself from smiling back.

"Want another brandy?" she whispered as he pulled her into his arms and kissed her slowly on the lips.

"Randy Andy would *love* another brandy," he whispered back.

"Well good," she said, before hiccupping.

Turning to leave for the kitchen, she caught her arm in his and fell backwards onto her small sofa, before hiccupping again loudly and throwing up all over her new dress.

CHAPTER 55

Andy waited on the other side of the bathroom door trying to stifle his laughter.

"Hey, you're doing me out of a job, I thought I was the one that threw up over your dresses?"

He could hear the water from the shower pounding down into the shower tray and it killed him not to be in there with her.

"What are you talking about?" she shouted back through the loud splattering.

"Down the alley in town," he replied, feeling more than a little miffed that she seemed to have forgotten about it. "I've thought about that moment over the last year more than any other. Don't tell me you can't remember."

The shower was turned off and he could hear her opening the shower door.

"You daft sod, of course I haven't forgotten. That dress cost me over a hundred pounds – I was trying to impress you."

"Well you certainly did that," he called back, his imagination running wild with images of the towel rubbing against her body. He tried to concentrate on his words in an effort to dispel all thoughts of her nakedness. "I went back down that alley last month. I could still smell it you know."

"What?"

"My sick. And the pee."

"I don't recall you wetting yourself as well."

"Well, no. I didn't say the pee was mine, did I?"

The door unbolted and Sam stood there with a pink bathrobe on and a white towel wrapped hastily around her head.

"Maybe I shouldn't have had that shower, it's made me feel worse. I think I should just go and lie down."

"Oh, do you want me to leave?"

"Well maybe, yeah. If you don't mind. I really need to lie down."

"Oh right. OK."

She hiccupped again and pushed past him into the kitchen. "Want some water first?"

"Yes please," he said, anything to stall the moment. He took the glass of water from her and glugged half of it straight away. "Sam, can I see you again tomorrow? We could have breakfast together."

"I don't eat breakfast, don't you remember?"

"Yes, I do, but I still want to see you. We could grab a coffee or something?"

"Well you could pick me up late morning if you like," she shrugged. "You could take me to Gilly's, they do the best Eggs Benedict and Smashed Avocado."

"I thought you didn't eat breakfast?" He looked confused.

"Well if it's late morning it'll be brunch won't it, not breakfast?

He watched her carefully, propped up against the

sink thirstily glugging down another glass of water.

"Whatever you say, Sam," he smiled. "I'm looking forward to it already." He walked over to her and kissed her on the nose. "I'd best grab a taxi and get going then. I've had a great night, thank you. I'll call for you about eleven then. You won't forget, right?" He kissed her again, this time on the lips, and then turned to open her door.

"Or," she said, as his hand touched the door handle, "my sofa's pretty comfy if you want to crash here?"

CHAPTER 56

A loud rumble of thunder woke Jack from his deep and satisfying sleep. He had been dreaming of Sue (again) and of a world where they were living together, just the two of them, in a small, cosy cottage on the outskirts of the town. In it, Sue had just revealed to him that she was pregnant and he had cried with joy at the tiny miracle taking place inside his lover's womb. He had kissed her and then tentatively placed a hand upon her gently rounded abdomen before being woken up by the storm.

For a split second he was dazed and wondered if the dream was in fact reality, especially when he realised that his right arm was outstretched and flat against soft skin. Turning his head though, he saw his hand placed squarely on Cheryl's stomach as she slept soundly, and he yanked it quickly away.

The clock glowed 03:10 and he quietly crept downstairs to fetch a glass of water. The dream had seemed so real, how on earth could he go back to sleep now? To make matters worse, he had an overwhelming urge to text Sue right now in the middle of the night, to tell her how much he had missed seeing her last night. There had been no swinger's night this weekend and it would be non-existent for the next few weekends too. Cheryl had done the deed and messaged everyone to explain that the club was to be less frequent and would now only be held once a month. He knew of course that he couldn't text her. Alan would be there lying beside her. Would they be curled up together or lying apart on separate sides of the bed? It killed him either way to envisage it.

Pacing the kitchen, it dawned on him yet again that it was irrelevant now anyway. Very soon he and Sue would be living together and they would be able to start over again, and with only each other for comfort. She had told him the last time he saw her that she had now done all the thinking that needed to be done; she was leaving Alan and the sooner the better. She had told him that they could start looking for a place together the very next week and that the minute they had found somewhere to go, she would tell Alan all about their relationship and she would move out. Jack had told her that he couldn't do that to Cheryl; a part of him would always love and respect her and he owed it to her to let her know what was going on as soon as possible. Sue was worried of course; Alan was bound to find out the truth sooner rather than later if Cheryl knew. But Jack had said that Cheryl would be fine and to leave everything to him. He went on to tell Sue that he planned to tell Cheryl everything on Sunday. He had told her that he couldn't live with the deceit any longer and the sooner he unburdened himself the better. If Cheryl kicked him out before he and Sue had found a place, then so be it. He could always stay at Tom and Angela's.

He looked at the kitchen clock. 3.13am. And then it struck him - *It WAS Sunday!* D Day had arrived in all of its inglorious glory. He felt sick but sat himself down at the table and prepared the speech inside his head, just as he had done over and over for the last few days.

***

The policewoman, who had only arrived half an hour earlier, handed Angela another cup of tea and sat down beside her. The thunder and lightning had brought with it even more fear and anguish; not only was their little girl and her friend missing but they were now missing in the middle of a huge storm where forked lightning crackled down to the ground every couple of minutes. Angela knew that they would be petrified and somewhere in her numbed brain she prayed that they were indoors somewhere safe and warm.

"Still no one at Maxine Carter's house, Mrs Baxter," the young policewoman confirmed, as she clipped her walkie talkie back onto the black belt around her waist. "Two officers are staying posted there though just in case."

"This is getting beyond a joke," Tom fumed, as Angela continued to stare into space. "Why haven't we heard anything positive?"

In the last few hours Tom had gone through every emotion imaginable, from panic, to anger, to shock, silence, disbelief (he had even laughed at one point, proper hysterical laughing as he waited for himself to wake up from the nightmare that never was), guilt, hysteria, depression and back to anger again.

"Are they going to break her bloody door down? How do you know that she hasn't locked them up inside her apartment? I mean, just because her car isn't outside!"

"Mr Baxter, for the third time, they are NOT inside the house. We've checked the entire property. If it *is* Miss Carter who has taken the children then it's very unlikely that she's going to take them back to her own place anyway. After the letters she's written to you it would be pretty obvious that that would be the first place we would go to, wouldn't it?"

Tom began pacing the floor once more. He couldn't rest, wouldn't rest, until the girls were back safe and sound.

"I think I'd better try Mrs De Silva again," the policewoman said, for want of anything better to say, before getting up and leaving the room.

"OH NO! Maria! I keep forgetting about Maria." Angela had broken her silence at last. "I'm so selfish. Here I am dwelling in my own grief when that poor woman doesn't even know that any of this has happened," she shrieked. "TOM, WHERE IS SHE? WHY ISN'T MARIA AT HOME?" Angela burst into huge sobs that shook her entire body, and with each breath gasped for air. "What are we going to do?" she screamed, hysterical now. "Where the hell is Maria, what's happening, Tom? WHAT'S HAPPENING?"

Tom went directly to her and pulled her to her feet, clasping both of her arms tightly in his hands.

"Listen to me, Angel," he shouted into her face, shaking her firmly. "Everything's going to be OK. I promise you. If I have to go out there and find them myself, then I will. DO YOU HEAR ME?"

Angela said nothing and continued sobbing loudly.

"DO YOU HEAR ME?" he shouted again, still shaking her wildly.

Wainwright put an arm on Tom's shoulder. "Come on now, sir, you must calm down, you'll be no good to anyone if you..."

"Calm down? CALM DOWN?"

Throwing Angela back down onto the sofa, Tom grabbed the Detective Inspector by the collar of his uniform.

"I'll give you bloody calm down," he raged, shaking him violently. "Why haven't we heard anything for chrissake? Hours have gone by and your lot haven't come back with anything at all! What the fuck are they doing? I could do better than that lot of useless twats, blindfolded and with my arms tied behind my back! That's it, I've had enough." Tom threw the middle-aged man onto the sofa next to Angela and made for the door.

"Mr Baxter, please! This is not going to get us anywhere, I promise you. Where are you going?"

"Where do you think I'm going?" Tom spat vehemently. "And I swear to God that if you try to stop me, I'll kill you."

CHAPTER 57

Maxine glanced up and down the street through the yellowing nets before moving away again and yanking the old floral curtains that covered them, tightly shut.

"You ain't gonna get away wiv this, Max," Tina scowled. "I dunno what the fuck you was finking of."

"Oh shut up," Maxine snapped back angrily.

"Even I know ya can't just go 'n steal someone else's kids. And my mum'll be back in a few days so ya can't stay 'ere forever."

"I said shut up!"

Maxine could feel her blood boiling and her heart thumping from the steady shots of adrenalin that her body was now pumping into her bloodstream. Tina stood up and walked to the lounge door.

"Want anuvva cuppa?"

Maxine remembered the sour taste of the two previous teas that Tina had made, and declined. She detested cheap teabags. She would have to send Tina to the shops at some point to buy something decent.

When Tina returned a little later, with only one chipped mug, Maxine relaxed slightly and sat back down.

"Ere, I just looked in on them girls again," Tina said strangely, as if they were a couple of P. T. Barnum's curiosities. "They ain't normal – all that crying! Fank goodness that funders finally stopped though, they're flat out now so don't worry."

"I'm not worried," Maxine exclaimed indignantly, "but I know a couple of people who will be."

"What ya gonna do now then?" Tina asked, still unaware of her best friend's plans.

"As I told you in the restaurant, Teen, this is where the money rolls in." Maxine rubbed her hands together slowly, visualising the wads of notes already in them.

"Money? What money?"

"Good grief, Teen, keep up. Are you bloody stupid?" She looked her slobby friend up and down before continuing. "Don't answer that. Isn't it bloody obvious what I'm doing?"

"Yeah, course it is. Nicking kids from your boss' 'ouse."

"For money, Teen, for money! You don't seriously think I'm doing this for the hell of it, do you? It's for money... well, and revenge. I've already prepared the letter, but bollocks to them, cos I'm not posting it for a few days yet. Let them stew."

"What, one of them ransom notes? Wow, let's see it then." Tina's eyes had widened to caricature proportions.

"Don't be so bloody stupid. You don't think I'm going to let you get your grubby little fingerprints all over it, do you? It would take them all of two minutes to link it back to me. Oh no. I've spent nights painstakingly preparing that letter, Teen, and there's no way in hell that I'm making it easy for them. I've put in a reference to some insurance swindle from years ago that went tits up, mentioned the names of the people involved, you know, that sort of thing. Tom didn't have anything to do with it, I know that for a fact but there were a lot of people out there who thought that he did. And the cops don't know that, do they? There's enough in there to put them off the 'Maxine scent', don't you worry. Even the details of where he's to drop the money off won't link it to me. I've thought of everything. There's nothing to link me to this kidnapping at all, not one thing. I've gone through every detail possible. I mean, just because I harassed Tom for a while and sent him a few dodgy letters, doesn't mean I'm mad enough to go and kidnap his kid, does it? Anything else is his word against mine and I'd like to see him try and prove it anyway."

"Max, I've just fought of sumfing."

"Oh yeah? That'll be a first."

"No, I'm serious. You say there's nuffink to link ya to the kidnapping right? Well... there is."

Maxine closed her eyes and raised her perfect eyebrows impatiently. *Why on earth did someone like Tina, who had left school at fifteen with no qualifications, could hardly read and had never had a decent job in her life, think for one minute that she could outwit someone like her?*

"Sweetheart," Maxine said slowly and patronisingly, "I love you to bits, Teen, I really do. You're my best friend, despite... well, everything. But I can tell you right now that I wore gloves and the same clothes every time I went near that letter. And when I'd finished it, I binned the clothes in a skip eleven miles away. I know all about fibres and DNA you know. I even used water to fix the bloody stamp with! And do you know where it is now? In a sealed plastic bag where it can't be contaminated and that's where it's going to stay until I post the ruddy thing! So don't try telling me that I've forgotten something."

"What about the girls?"

"Well, what about them?"

"They could tell the police everyfink that 'appened couldn't they? They're not babies ya know, they *can* talk."

Maxine paled and her stomach gripped itself into a tight ball. Her heart was racing again now as the adrenalin began re-flooding her bloodstream.

"Well," said Tina, taking another slurp of her weak tea. "I would've fought that was bloody obvious."

***

As Tom approached Maxine's road, he saw the white, marked police car parked outside the apartment. The thunder and lightning had finally stopped but the rain was still pummelling the already flooded streets. He felt so cold now that all of his clothes, including his coat, were soaked through to his skin. The clocks hadn't gone back yet and he could see that it was already getting lighter and that the night was almost near its end. As he got closer to the apartment he saw that all the lights were off and the front door had been forcibly opened. He could also see slight but definite movement in the police car.

The need to go into the apartment and see for himself quickly diminished. They were right – she wasn't here. Maxine was way too clever to bring the girls to her own place anyway and if he stopped here now he would not only infuriate the police further but he would be wasting precious time. Precious time that could be spent looking for the girls.

Tom turned around and ran back down the street the way he had come, and wracked his brains for inspiration on where to stop next.

CHAPTER 58

Jack turned over in bed and looked at the clock. It was nearly 11am and Cheryl had been up for hours. After spending half the night going over and over the same conversation in his head, he had finally dragged himself back up to bed at seven o'clock and had led still until Cheryl had got up and dressed, half an hour later. Now he could hear the banging and clanking of baking trays coming from the kitchen as she cooked a Sunday roast. *Could he really be that much of a greedy, selfish bastard to wait until he had had a good Sunday lunch inside him, before coming clean to Cheryl about his intentions?* There were worse things a man could do, for sure, he thought. And with that, he pulled the duvet tighter and turned over, before falling back to sleep.

***

He had intended to talk to Cheryl earlier, he really had, but the smell of the delicious roast beef winding its way up the stairway to his watering nostrils was too much even for him to bear. Anyway, he had told himself, it was surely better to do this thing on a full stomach considering that the anguish he was about to cause might yet stop her from eating for weeks to come.

As Cheryl cleared away the dinner plates in the kitchen, Jack wore patches in the living room carpet as he perfected his opening speech.

***

Sam pushed the plate away and patted her stomach.

"I told you the Eggs Benedict was the best, didn't I?"

Andy had spent the night on Sam's sofa hoping that she would eventually creep out of her bedroom and drag him into the bed with her. He had waited and waited, but she hadn't come. Not only had she not come, but the Sofa of Doom he had been forced to lie on had been so uncomfortable that it had left him with an aching back and a stiff neck. He rubbed the back of his neck firmly and looked around the bistro that Sam had chosen for brunch. It was freshly decorated in tangy lime and white paint and modern art hung from the walls. He liked it.

"So," he said, pushing his empty plate away, "where are we going for dinner?"

"Um... when you told me yesterday that you were taking me out on a date, you never told me that it would last for twenty four hours." Sam laughed.

"Are you complaining?"

"No, but I've never been on a date that lasted for four meals before."

Andy smirked and paid the bill and then they walked back to Sam's place silently, hand in hand, each lost in their own thoughts. When they reached the top of her road, Sam stopped still.

"What's the problem?"

"Nothing," she answered quietly.

Andy looked down the road to the steps of her flat and saw the figure of a man there, looking around impatiently. He looked back at Sam.

"Marcos?"

She nodded.

"Do you want me to say something to him?"

"No, it's fine honestly. Don't worry, I'll get rid of him."

Andy carried on walking but she pulled him back.

"Maybe it's better that you go home now, And, I can handle this. It's probably best if you're not here."

"Why?" Andy asked, annoyed. "I'm not happy about being the focal point of your life again for the last twenty four hours and then suddenly being dumped the minute ex-lover boy turns back up on the doorstep."

"Oh come on, And, don't be so ridiculous. He just needs a bit of convincing that it's over that's all."

"So why can't I do the convincing? If he sees us together then he'll KNOW it's over, once and for all."

"I said NO, now please let me deal with it in my own way," Sam said, annoyed.

"But, Sam..."

"Listen, And, I've coped on my own without you for most of my life, so please don't think that my world's going to fall apart just because you're going home."

"Ouch." He clamped his teeth together. "How long is this going to go on for, Sam? How many times am I going to have to listen to this?"

Ignoring him, Sam continued walking down the road towards her flat. Once there, she said a few words on the doorstep to Marcos, and Andy watched as they both walked inside and closed the door behind them.

***

Tom slumped down in the shop doorway. As was usual on a Sunday, the streets were fairly empty and no matter which direction he had taken, he had come up with nothing. At one point he had seen the back of a girl who he thought looked like Jess and had run up to her, pulling her by the arm to turn her around. It hadn't been her and the mother had screamed abuse at him and told him to get the hell away from her child before she called the cops. The girl had started screaming loudly and the few people that were hanging around, stopped to turn and stare at him as though he were a pervert. Tom had been to the office too. He didn't know why – it didn't make sense, but somehow he just had to go there and eliminate it from his raging mind. The place was locked up just as he had left it on Friday evening, and he had screamed out in desperate frustration. After hour upon hour of scouring the local streets over and over again, looking for the girls, Maxine's car, anything at all, he had ended up here in a piss-stained shop doorway with tears running down his flushed cheeks. He felt utterly exhausted and bereft of any more ideas. The police had been right; he was better off at home in case they turned up there. *Maybe they WERE at home now – maybe they HAD turned up.* Anything was possible. And after all, he had left the house over twelve hours ago.

His mind was made up. He would go home and without any doubt the girls would be there, safe and sound. And if they weren't then Maxine's life wouldn't be worth living.

CHAPTER 59

"So, what did you want to talk about then?" Cheryl made herself comfy in the armchair.

Rooted to the spot, Jack stood by the fireplace where he had been fingering their wedding picture over and over, all afternoon.

"Well?" she smiled, as she thumbed through the television magazine.

"Chez, I've gone over and over this a hundred times and there's no easy way to say it."

"Say what? Ooh look, the new series of Walking Dead starts tonight!"

This was it; the moment he had been waiting so long for, and also ironically, putting off. It was now or never. Fight or Flight. Look and leap and hope for the best. He cleared his dry throat and wished that he had a stiff drink in his hand to help the words flow.

"The thing is. Well, the thing is. This isn't easy for me you know." He turned away from her to face the mantelpiece again. "In fact this is the hardest thing I've ever had to do or say."

"Jack, whatever are you talking about?"

"I'm sorry, I'm so sorry."

"Whatever for?" Cheryl's voice cracked with worry and she dropped her magazine to the floor. "Oh no, Jack, what have you done? You haven't lost your job, have you?"

Jack turned around slowly to look at her. A vast crater had opened up inside the pit of his stomach and he felt as though all of his bodily organs were being sucked slowly and painfully into it.

"I'm leaving."

Cheryl stared at him and blinked.

"Leaving your job? Whatever for?"

"No. I'm leaving. Leaving you, the house, everything."

"What on earth are you talking about? I don't understand, what do you mean?" She stared at Jack, her face crinkled with incomprehension. "*Leaving?*"

"It's Sue."

"Sue? Which Sue? Alan's Sue? What's wrong with her?"

"We've, we've been... Oh Chez. I'm sorry."

"No!" Cheryl whispered barely audibly, her mind reeling from this new information. "You've been... you've... with *SUE*?"

Jack took another deep breath and sat down tentatively on the sofa. "I'm so sorry, Chez, there's no easy way of saying this... but we're... we're moving in together. We've been seeing each other for a while now and..."

Cheryl closed her eyes and stayed silent for several minutes. When she was ready, she opened them, stood up and walked to the living room door, only turning around when she reached it.

"When are you going?" she asked calmly.

"What?" Jack shook his head. He was now completely

thrown. In all of the different scenarios that he had acted out in his head over the last few days, and there had been many, this hadn't been one of them.

"Oh... well... as soon as we find somewhere I guess," he answered, puzzled.

"I see." Cheryl nodded slowly.

Jack felt an immense cocktail of distress and relief flurrying its way into the abyss of his stomach. She seemed so calm, so reasonable. He thought for a second and decided to go for broke.

"Thing is, Sue isn't telling Alan just yet, she wants to wait for the right moment."

"And is that what you did?" Cheryl asked curiously. "Is this the 'right moment' for you then, Jack?"

Jack looked at her and hated himself. *Why didn't he know what she was thinking and feeling?* She had put up a barrier and his ability to read her like a Peter and Jane book had disintegrated like the Dead Sea Scrolls, before his eyes.

"Well, if that's what you want," Cheryl said calmly. And then she smiled and left the room.

***

"Tom, where the hell have you been? I've been worried sick!" Angela screamed hysterically as he dragged his soaking wet, filthy, stinking body through the front door.

"Where are they?" he gasped, rushing past her and

throwing open the door to every downstairs room in the house.

"There's no news, we've heard nothing at all." Her tears rolled down her cheeks like a never ending waterfall of grief. "What are we going to do, Tom? I'm so scared!"

Tom tried to compose himself as he looked around at the new, unfamiliar faces in his home. The police had long since changed shifts and two shorter, younger policemen now sat in his living room, yet again assuming an air of authority that belied their young age. One of them was drinking coffee from Tom's favourite mug.

"And who the hell are you?" Tom barked, pissed off that they had made themselves so at home in his house in such a short space of time.

"I'm P.C. Williams, sir, and this is P.C. ..."

"I didn't mean literally!" Tom shouted in disbelief. "What are you doing here? Where are the others? Where's Wainwright?"

"We're covering until the next shift arrives, sir."

"I don't believe it," Tom raged, his entire body shivering despite the fact that he was now in from the cold. "They've sent two 'kids' less than half my age to babysit my fucking wife. Oh, and a useless maid to make the fucking tea!"

The policewoman, who had arrived earlier, shot him an angry look as she walked in with two more mugs of strong coffee.

"Get Wainwright on the phone NOW!" he barked to P.C.

Williams.

"That's not possible, sir," he replied politely.

"Not possible? My daughter's been kidnapped and has been missing for nearly twenty four hours so don't tell me it's not possible!"

"I'm sorry, sir, but it isn't."

"I said get him on the phone – NOW!"

"We can't do that I'm afraid, Mr Baxter," the quiet, spottier PC suddenly chipped in."

"Oh really?" Tom snarled, saliva spitting from his mouth like a rabid dog. "Give me one good reason why not."

"He's been rushed to hospital," P.C. Williams replied loudly. "He had a heart attack as soon as you left."

CHAPTER 60

The policewoman passed the phone to Angela and sat back down next to a distraught Tom. She explained the situation to Maria De Silva as best as she could and confirmed with her the hotel address that Maria had said she was staying at. She explained that an unmarked police car would arrive to collect her and her brother as soon as possible.

"Maria, oh Maria," Angela sobbed into the phone. "It's awful, this is a nightmare, I'm so sorry, I'm so, so sorry."

Maria had gone into shock upon hearing the dreadful news and kept repeating the same thing about Adrio, over and over.

"This is Adrio, I just know it," she cried down the phone. "My brother, Eduardo, he said Adrio 'ad tracked me down and there was big chance that he come to the house. I couldn't stay there, Angela, I was too scared. My brother, he check us into hotel. He said we be safe here. This is why I left Eva with you. I thought she would be safe..." She trailed off as more tears began to choke her words.

"Maria listen. It couldn't be Adrio. He doesn't know me, or where we live, and he didn't know that Eva wouldn't be with you. You must try and stay calm - we think we know who did this."

"You don't understand," Maria went on, the tears

choking her. "I don't put anything past him, he bad Angela, he so bad. I think maybe he been tracing my calls. Maybe he 'as detective working with him. Anything is possible. He 'as used them before and he would do anything to get Eva back to Portugal with him."

On hearing Maria's horrifying words, Angela began to hyperventilate and her arms shook in spasms at her side. Tom rushed over to her, his ghostly pale face crinkled with worry.

"SHE'S IN PORTUGAL!" Angela blurted out, hysterical again now. "Maria said..."

Angela's head burned in pain. Her legs trembled, before her feet gave way completely and she dropped to the floor; the cloak of unconsciousness draping itself over her exhausted body.

***

Tom felt utterly bereft. Not only had he caused a Chief Inspector to have a heart attack due to his outrageous behaviour and assault, but now his wife was being completely cared for by a policewoman, who only seconds earlier he had had the audacity to call 'a useless tea maid'. Whilst yet again he fell to pieces, the 'useless maid' had acted instantly; rushing around fetching cushions, raising Angela's legs and making her drink water. Tom didn't know the first thing about even the most basic first aid and felt so ashamed and useless that once more he began to cry.

***

The police arrived promptly at the hotel but instead of taking Maria and her brother, Eduardo, home, they spoke to the hotel staff who supplied them with a private room so that they could interview them there. They discussed various factors and felt that under the circumstances, Maria and her brother would in fact be safer if they stayed put for the time being. After several hours of questions being answered, statements being taken, and mugs of tea and coffee being consumed, the police gathered privately to come to the conclusion that they now had absolutely no idea where the girls were or even which country they might be in. Then they drew straws to find out which one of them was going to inform Maria and her brother, along with the Baxters, that the investigation was going really well and that they were doing everything they could to track down the girls and return them home safely.

***

They had long since stopped crying. Maxine had discovered since the early hours of the morning that the only way to stop the girls from sobbing for their useless mothers was to pretend that it was all just a game and that they would be going home very soon. It had certainly helped and finally they were beginning to settle. This morning though they had asked when their mummies were going to 'give up'. 'I've never played Hide and Seek this long before,' Jessie had said sadly. Eventually she had picked up some of the old toys and games that Tina had given them and dragged herself into the bedroom to play with Eva. They had been in there for most of the day, only coming down for the jam sandwiches and drinks that Tina had made for them at lunch time. Now it was early evening and Maxine had only just realised that no one had made the girls anything for dinner.

"They've got school tomorrow, Max, whatcha gonna do?"

"School? Of course they haven't got bloody school, they're kidnapped, you stupid cow!"

Tina put her finger to her lips as the girls walked into the room.

"We're hungry." Jessie complained, right on cue. She was rubbing her stomach and her tired eyes at the same time.

"Well go on then, Teen," Maxine urged, "knock something up for them."

Tina glared at Maxine, her mouth wide open in annoyance. "They're *your* hostages, Max, not mine. I ain't no good at cooking anyway. I dunno what kids eat, do I?"

"What's a hostages?" Jessie asked, her inquisitive eyes flitting from Maxine to Tina.

Somewhere deep in the pit of her stomach, Maxine's insides lurched with a tremendous guilt. She looked across and smiled as kindly as she could.

"Don't worry about it, Jess, it's a grown up word."

"What does it mean?"

"It means... it means, well when someone plays a game. Like us."

"Like Hide and Seek?"

"Yes," she said. "Like Hide and Seek."

Mouth still agape, Tina raised her eyebrows, mumbled 'unbelievable', and then left the room to see what offerings she could muster up from the kitchen cupboards.

"And what about you?" Maxine asked Eva, who was now standing two feet behind Jessie looking painfully small and vague. "You haven't even told me your name yet."

"She's shy," Jessie replied for her friend. "She doesn't talk as much as me, do you, Eva?"

"And you're both the same age?"

The girls nodded and Eva began to cry.

"What's wrong with her?" Maxine asked bewildered, as if being kidnapped at the age of five was the most normal thing in the world for any child.

"She's tired and she wants to go to sleep. And she wants her mummy to stop playing the game."

Maxine gritted her teeth and turned away.

Five minutes after eating the cheap and cheerful beans on toast that Tina had made, Eva fell asleep upstairs on Tina's bed. Ten minutes later, Tina crashed out on the floor next to her. The lack of sleep from last night had finally caught up with her. Maxine on the other hand was still running on adrenalin.

"What time do *you* go to bed?" Jessie asked as she and Maxine sat side by side on Tina's mum's gaudy green, floral sofa.

"Oh I don't know. A different time each night I guess. It depends when I'm tired."

"My mum *makes* me go to bed at seven o'clock every night," Jessie said flatly, her eyes bulging out as if she had been hard done by since birth.

Maxine turned slowly to look at her. It was the first time that the little girl had offered any personal information about her parents and it made Maxine feel strangely powerful. It suddenly occurred to her that she could find out almost anything she wanted about Tom and Bitch Wife, simply by talking to their little girl. *Why hadn't she thought about that before? She could delve into their lives more than she ever thought possible; she had her own little stool pigeon right here beside her... and she was free.*

"Can I stay up with you?" Jessie asked, her eyes suddenly sparkling. "PLEEEASE!"

"Oh sweetie of course you can," Maxine smiled back. "Actually, you know what? I'm really looking forward to it."

CHAPTER 61

Why wasn't she answering for chrissake? Andy ended the call and checked his messages again; *maybe she had messaged him and he hadn't heard it? No.* His two previous messages to her had still not been seen and now it was gone 9pm. *Was the jerk still there then? Was that what this meant?* Andy had had enough. He grabbed his car keys and started heading off towards Sam's flat.

By the time he got there his heart was racing and he was sweating so much that his clammy hands were stuck to the steering wheel. This was ridiculous, he knew that; he had never acted this way in his entire life – he wasn't the jealous type. *What had changed in him to make him behave like this? And what would he do if Marcos was still at Sam's anyway, flatten him? Hmmm, it seemed like a pretty good idea in the absence of any others.*

After the second knock, a small crack appeared in the door and Sam, in her pink bathrobe, peered out of it.

"Andy?" She looked surprised to see him, panicked even, he thought. "What do you want?"

Andy was momentarily dumbstruck. *What did she think he wanted, for heaven's sake?* He also now knew Marcos was still here; he had just seen the figure of a dark skinned man peek out of the living room curtain and upon realising that he had been spotted, he had quickly closed it again.

"What's going on?"

"What do you mean, 'what's going on?'?"

The last thing Andy wanted was to ruin his second chance with Sam but the green-eyed monster had been teasing him all afternoon and evening, like a provocative lap-dancer slowly wiggling her assets inches from his face. He had just about had enough. He was ready to grab the hairy little green-eyed bastard and smack him in the mouth as hard as he could.

"You know what I mean. What's that idiot still doing here?"

"I beg your pardon?" Sam had opened the door wide open now and stood on the doorstep looking horrified at the evil contortions that writhed around on Andy's face. "Calm down, whatever's wrong with you?"

"THAT," he pointed at the living room curtain that had just twitched again, "is what's wrong with me! If there's nothing going on with Marcos then what the hell is he still doing here at half past nine?"

"Talking," Sam said simply, "not that it has anything to do with you." She looked indignantly at him as she raked her fingers through her tangled wet hair.

"Talking? Just talking? Well you've got a lot to say, haven't you?" Andy asked angrily. "I could have done it for you, Sam, in two words. *Two* words. *GET. LOST*. Would've taken me two seconds! Quite simple really. And you've had a shower while he's here too, I see."

Sam glanced up and down the street, a veil of horror and hurt dressing her pretty face. "I'm not like that, Andy. I thought you knew me better than that." She shuddered and pulled her dressing gown around herself tightly. "And how dare you? It's MY house, I'll shower whenever I want!"

Andy stared at her with tears at the corner of his eyes.

"Stop it, Andy. What the hell is wrong with you?"

"Why are you doing this?" he asked, shaking his head slowly. "I love you, Sam. I'd do anything for you. I thought..."

"What on earth are you talking about? You've been back in my life for two minutes!"

"You. In your dressing gown, trying to convince me that nothing's been going on with that, that... moron!"

"How dare you!" she whispered, tears springing into her already red eyes. "I told you that I would deal with this in my own way, and I am!"

"What? For seven hours – in your dressing gown?"

"I don't have to explain myself to you. Who do you think you are waltzing back into my 'quite nice' life and trying to take back control of it?"

"I don't want control of your *quite nice* life, Sam, it's boring." He regretted the words as soon as they left his mouth. *What the hell was he doing?* He was buying a one way ticket to Self-Destruct Avenue and he couldn't stop himself.

362

"Yes you do," Sam retaliated, "who I see, when I see them, how long I see them for and even telling me what I should say. All of that and you've only been back in my life for two minutes!"

Andy felt ridiculous and ashamed. What the hell was wrong with him for chrissake? This wasn't *him* – this wasn't' Andy Cooper. This was some gobshite tosser about to destroy the one good thing that had finally come back into his life after all this time.

"No, Sam, no I don't. Just *him*. Just Marcus. I don't want to control you or your life. Just..."

"Just leave me alone." Sam began to close the door.

"NO! Sam, I'm sorry, please, I don't know what the hell's the matter with me."

"Well I do, you're jealous and you're crazy, and I've got two words for you too. GET LOST!"

"No, Sam, don't. I just..."

Sam slammed the door hard in his face.

Andy went back to his car, kicked it angrily and then drove home.

***

"Sam, I should go, I don't want to cause trouble."

"You're not, don't worry about it." She picked up her luke-warm cup of tea and took a mouthful of it as she sat back down next to him.

"From where I stand I think you wrong. He look pretty mad to me." He could see the tears at the corner of her eyes and she wiped at them quickly.

"He'll be fine," she smiled. "And if he isn't then he's not worth it."

"I really think I should go. I've caused more than enough trouble already, I don't want to intrude on you, that's not why I came here."

"I know that. You said you needed somewhere to stay for a couple of nights and I said you can stay here. You still can – end of story. It's my flat and my life, Adrio, not his."

Adrio smiled at her gratefully and began chewing at his little fingernail.

"By the way, who is *Marcos*?"

CHAPTER 62

Maxine handed her another glass of juice and laughed softly.

"So what did your daddy say to that? Bet your mum wasn't too pleased." Maxine fingered her tangled hair and re-joined the little girl on the sofa.

Jessie yawned and rubbed her eyes. In the space of half an hour, Maxine had managed to eke out all sorts of everyday goings on in the Baxter household. Although it would have all sounded rather mundane to anyone else, to Maxine every word that surfaced was another piece of buried treasure; another page of information painstakingly extracted from an unwritten diary. No matter how trivial the details that poured forth from their offspring's unassuming lips, every sentence produced a flurry of wonderful activity deep inside her chest cavity that was only ever equalled by the thought of her and Tom in her and Tom in bed together.

Thirty minutes became an hour. Maxine knew the things that Tom and Angela argued about, the programmes they watched, what they did at the weekends and even what they ate for breakfast and dinner. As the evening had drawn on, so indeed had the pace. The mere snippets that she had carefully extracted from the girl's mouth, like a dental hygienist carefully scraping away at plaque, had become small pictures inside her head which were now rapidly building themselves into one large collage. It was enabling her to do something that she had never been able to do before; to slowly, piece by piece, build a picture in her mind of their life together. And that way, slowly, piece by piece, she would be able to smash it down and destroy it.

Maxine glanced at the little girl's head, now nestled gently into the fold of her arm; like any other mother and daughter, she thought perversely. They had been up talking for hours now and Maxine had been surprised to find herself growing fonder and fonder of this sweet little person. No matter how hard she had tried to despise her (she had, after all, been half created by Bitch Wife and indeed lived inside her womb for nine months) she couldn't. *What was there to hate?* Jess was everything that she would have wanted in a daughter of her own and now, just being next to her, made something deep inside her yearn to keep this child for her own. She stared at Jessie's beautiful cherubic face. Her long, blonde curls bounced around the edges of her face when she moved and her dark eyelashes flickered as she tried to sleep. She loved her sweet and gentle voice and the way that some of her words came out wrongly when she tried to explain something that she didn't really understand. She loved the way she bounced on the sofa with an explosive energy when she talked, and the way she threw her arms about her wildly when she exaggerated something. She loved the way she giggled and then snuggled up into her for a cuddle every five minutes, as though Maxine were her best friend. But most of all, she loved feeling wanted and needed.

She glanced down again at the little body as it began to slump in the crook of her arm in exhaustion. Stroking the girl's silky soft hair with her long fingers, Maxine was now convinced more than ever, that Bitch Wife really WAS a bitch, and that she certainly didn't deserve such a beautiful little girl as Jessie.

***

"It was so bad that your letters was the only thing keeping me going most of the time."

Sam handed Adrio a bowl of cornflakes and sat down next to him with another cup of tea.

"That's nice."

"It is true. If you had not written me then I don't know what I would have done."

Sam smiled again and pondered on how she had got herself into this situation in the first place.

Abi, a lifetime friend of hers, had been writing to her boyfriend, Raymon, for four years. He had been locked up in a Portuguese prison for drug dealing. She had told Sam that he had a very good friend of his in there with him called Adrio, who was terribly lonely and desperate for someone to write to. For two years Abi had plagued her to write to him but Sam had refused; she didn't want to get involved with anyone who had the remotest dodgy background let alone a jailbird. And anyway, Andy had since come on the scene. But when six months ago she received a small blue envelope in the post with scrawny writing and a Portuguese stamp on it, she knew in an instant that Abi must have sent her address to Raymon, without her knowing, so that Adrio could make the first move and write to her.

After finding out that he was actually married with a child and really only in need of a friendly pen-pal, (and after being unceremoniously dumped by Andy only months before) she had finally relented and written back, more out of boredom than anything else. They hit it off instantly and no sooner had Adrio replied to a letter of hers, she would write straight back to him, time and time again. With each letter they exchanged, they seemed to have more and more in common and it wasn't long before she found herself waiting for the postman to bring the mail in the hope that there would be yet another little blue envelope about to fall onto her doormat.

It wasn't that she was attracted to him, she wasn't in the slightest. He had sent her a photo of himself with his second letter, the little one that still stood unframed on her dusty shelf with the other images of family and past relationships; the one she had told Andy was 'Marcos'. There was no Marcos. She liked Adrio a lot, but only as a friend, a confidante, as three minutes of sunshine (the time it took her on average to read his letters) on an otherwise dull and uneventful day. She figured it had a lot to do with 'ease';

it was so easy to spill your heart out on paper to a complete stranger who wasn't going to judge you. You had nothing to lose; no life-long friendship that went back to the cradle; no worries that what you said would be taken the wrong way – just a friendly mind at the other end of the post-box to share your thoughts and feelings with. Yes, it was his words of encouragement and support that sat so neatly on the blue prison paper that she found so inspiring. Words that had been so kind and uplifting, they had eventually carried her away from the dark shadow of Andy's ghost.

The letters had soon begun to talk of his release and how he would need somewhere to stay in England for a few nights so that he could sort out some unfinished business. Despite the trust that she now had in him, this had still worried her at first. Not only had she felt that he was hinting to stay at her place (what sane young woman would let a complete [ex-con] stranger into her home to stay with her?), but despite the fact that they had written to each other for months now, deep down she knew that she didn't actually *know* him at all.

"He could tie me up and molest me!" she had said when Abi had tried to convince her that it would be ok.

"You should be so bloody lucky! He's gorgeous – and anyway, I've met him several times when I've visited Raymon and he really is every bit a gentleman."

"Oh great, that's OK then! My best friend says he opens doors for old people so what the bloody hell am

I worried about? And there I was thinking I was going to be murdered in my sleep... you... you think he's gorgeous?"

Again, Sam had relented. She knew deep down that it was insane but the words in his letters came from somewhere deep within and made a connection with her soul that she felt could only ever come from a true soul mate. And anyway, she trusted her own judgement of character and so, she decided, she trusted him. When Andy had suddenly appeared in her life again, just days before Adrio's arrival, she was sure she had done the right thing by keeping it from him; she could just imagine what he would have thought about her having an ex-con she had never met before, staying at her house for a few days.

It was amazing, Adrio had said, how Sam lived in the very same town as the person that he needed to see. It was nothing short of 'miraculous' and, as he had said himself, 'truly meant to be'.

"What are you thinking about?" Adrio asked, worry spreading across his face. "You are not regretting this?" "I can book into hotel, eet is no problem I promise you."

Sam took a deep breath.

"No," she said at last. "It's no problem at all."

CHAPTER 63

Jack stirred as the noise from the kitchen grew louder. It was the most noise that had come from the house since his confession to Cheryl the night before. She had disappeared to the bedroom and stayed there and he had stayed put in the living room, hardly daring to move until he had finally fallen asleep on the sofa. Several times throughout the night he had woken and thought about going up to see her to make sure that she was alright. Maybe they should talk some more? She might even say something to make him feel less shit than he already did. But he didn't go. What was the point in talking to her if the only reason was to rid himself of a guilty conscience? Now he could hear the kettle boiling and he thought it was fairly safe to bet that she would only be making one cup of coffee this morning. The only way a steaming mug of caffeine was going to be winging its way to him right now, would be by long distance target practice.

By the time he had darted upstairs and quickly showered and dressed (all thoughts of being pelted with mugs of coffee forgotten), the front door slammed loudly and Cheryl's footsteps could be heard fading away down the path and out onto the street. Jack ran downstairs quickly and switched his mobile phone on while he waited for the kettle to re-boil. It beeped almost instantly and he sat down on one of the kitchen chairs to read the two messages from Sue. The first one said that she needed to see him urgently and could he ring her as soon as possible; Alan had left for work early today as he had a couple of meetings. The second one asked him if he had told Cheryl about the two of them yet. He checked the times and saw that she had only sent the last one five minutes ago.

"Hey gorgeous, what's up?" he chirped, when she answered her phone.

"Jack... thank goodness. I need to see you right now."

"Why, what's happened?"

"Don't ask, just come round as soon as you can."

"Don't ask? Sue, you sound upset, please - just tell me what's wrong."

"Just get here as quickly as you can."

***

As Jack pulled up outside the house, he noticed that the front door had been left open for him. What on earth was going on? He had to admit that it made a refreshing change from being ushered in around the back, as if he were a social leper but it was still odd. *Maybe she had told Alan everything too and maybe she was more than happy for the neighbours to see the 'new man' in her life?*

"Honey, what the hell's going on? I got here as quickly as I could. Are you alright, what's happened?"

His eyes darted anxiously across her blotchy face as they stood face to face in the small kitchen.

Sue stood momentarily without speaking and then without warning burst into tears. "It's over," she said simply.

"What? You're kidding right? You told him? Well that's great, that's fantastic! This means we don't have to wait another minute, it doesn't matter that..."

"No, Jack. It's over! You. Me. Over."

Jack stood motionless. "What are you talking about? Wh... what do you mean 'it's over'?"

Sue clenched her hands tightly together and stared at them, refusing to look anywhere else, even when he grabbed her arm and shook it.

"Talk to me. I don't understand," confusion flooding his flushed face.

Finally she looked up, her green eyes piercing into him. "I'm pregnant," she whispered at last.

For a short while time seemed to stand still. Jack tried several times to speak, but whilst his lips moved, no words came out. "Pregnant?" he uttered finally.

Jack stared wildly at the four walls around him. They seemed to be closing in, turning the already small kitchen into a tiny prison cell. The crown of his head felt like it had been ripped open. His brain felt burst out of its skull into intestine-like dreadlocks all over his hair. He clasped both of his hands over the top of his head and squeezed as hard as he could to steady himself. Finally he took a few deep breaths before moving his hands and looking at her once more and shaking his head.

"Pregnant?" he repeated slowly.

"I'm sorry, Jack," she said, starting to cry again.

"NO. This is *fantastic*!" Jack realised, as a metaphorical thunderbolt struck his dizzying head. "What am I thinking? This is GREAT!" He grinned widely, unable to contain his newfound excitement. "What are you sorry for? I've always wanted a child of my own!"

Sue wiped at her tears but they still came. "Alan always wanted a baby too."

"This could be the best thing to happen to us, don't you see that?" Jack continued, grabbing her arms.

"You don't understand. It's not that simple."

"Well it's that simple to me, babe. I'm here for you, I always will be." He smiled weakly at her and added, "I told Cheryl last night."

"You told her?" Sue whimpered like a tortured animal.

"Yes, I told her everything. So there's nothing to stop us now. You can talk to Alan and then..."

"It's Alan's," she interrupted, cutting him dead.

"What?" Jack looked at her in disbelief. "What are you on about?"

"The baby. It's Alan's."

Sue had never seen a smile evaporate so quickly from a man's face before and she felt physically sick.

"How can you say that?" The hurt all too evident on

Jack's strained face.

"Because it is."

"But how do you know that? How can you tell?"

"Dates!" Sue shouted irritably. "Ever heard of *dates*?"

"Yes, of course I have, but you've been sleeping with both of us, so how can you tell?"

"What's that supposed to mean?" She looked up angrily.

"Nothing, just that you must have the dates down to the day if you can say for a fact that the baby is Alan's."

"Yes, I have the dates down to the day, Jack! Down to the bloody hour and I'm telling you, *it's Alan's*," she shouted, as she shakily sat herself down onto a kitchen chair.

Jack raked his fingers through his messy red hair and sat down next to her, his thin legs twitching from nervous energy. He and Sue had stopped using any kind of protection long ago, unbeknown to everyone else in the swinging group. *Maybe it had been irresponsible. No... it had definitely been irresponsible.* Especially considering that they had still been members of the swinging group and had not taken into consideration anyone else's physical wellbeing. But it had been a mutual decision a while ago now and they had carried on that way since, regardless. Possible pregnancy hadn't been an issue; she had told him that she was on the pill.

"It's mine, isn't it?" he whispered after some time.

"No. I told you, it's Alan's."

"I don't believe you."

"Well believe, because it is."

"You're lying to me."

Sue pursed her lips together tightly and looked away. "You'd better go, Jack, I can't see you again."

"You what?" he laughed in disbelief.

"You heard me."

"NO! You could be carrying MY baby and you expect me to just get up and walk out of the door? After everything we've done, everything we've been through?"

"Just give me and Alan this chance, Jack please, I'm begging you!" She looked at him pleadingly.

"Chance for what? To play happy families with *my* bloody baby?"

"IT'S NOT YOUR BABY!"

"YOU DON'T KNOW THAT!"

He swallowed hard and put his head in his hands again. "For chrissake, I just told Chez I'm leaving her for you," he went on, pointlessly.

"I'm so sorry, Jack. But this baby changes everything, can't you see that?"

"It doesn't change anything for me. I still want to be with you just as I did ten minutes ago. I wouldn't be preparing to leave my bloody wife otherwise, would I?"

"Don't leave her. It's not too late. Just tell her that you made a mistake. Tell her that you changed your mind and that you've told me it's over. Tell her you want to be with her instead... to make a go of things. Tell her *anything*, Jack!"

"Why? To make you feel better about fucking me over?"

"That's not fair."

"Yes it *is* fair. If you felt the same way you wouldn't think twice about leaving Alan. We talked about it over and over, how does a baby change anything?"

"Don't be so bloody juvenile, it changes EVERYTHING."

"Not for me it doesn't."

"Well it does for me. I never promised you anything!"

Jack could feel the tears prickling at the corner of his eyes. He felt as if he was standing on the edge of a precipice about to fall in. *What was the use in saying anything more? She either wanted to be with him or she didn't. And she quite obviously didn't.* He stared at her intently.

"Look me in the eye and tell me that you don't want me anymore."

Sue sniffed awkwardly. "Alan can give this baby everything it will ever want, can't you see that?" she pleaded.

"And I can't?" His sparkling green eyes drilled into hers.

"I didn't say that, it's just..."

"Just that you would rather bring it up with Alan than with me."

"I didn't say that either."

Jack headed for the door. "You didn't have to."

CHAPTER 64

Jack drove to the common. It was a good few miles from Sue's house but he didn't want to go home. Not yet. He had been here several times before, usually with Cheryl on a hot summer's day; having a picnic, laughing and joking, planning their future. Today it was dark and grey and mirrored the heaviness that weighed down inside of him. He felt some relief when it began to drizzle, it seemed fitting somehow; the weather mourning with him when he should feel so much in despair. He had always liked the fine, dismal, drizzly rain. It refreshed him and he knew that he didn't look like a berk if he sat on a bench in it for hours on end. If you sit on a bench in a deluge, people look at you as if you're crazy. Or homeless. In drizzle no one cares. In drizzle you're invisible, he had always said.

Jack watched a couple of hooded people with dogs walk past him. Further in the distance was a man in a suit running as if his life depended on it. It probably did; it was 9.45am and Jack guessed that he was late for work. He knew that he should phone Tom and tell him that he wouldn't be in today, but a 'couldn't be arsed' feeling swept over his already self-pitying body and he switched his phone off instead, shutting himself off from the outside world.

"Are you OK there?"

Jack forced his body to move and looked up. An old

man walking a mangy looking dog had stopped in front of him. Jack's clothes felt cold and wet and were stuck firmly to his body. He looked at his watch. It was nearly 2pm. *How had he been here for over four hours?* He looked around and noticed that it was still raining lightly; the same steady, grey precipitation falling at the same steady pace. He felt numb. Numb from the steady cold rain and numb from broken promises – from the obliteration of a promised future that would now never be his. A numbness that made him feel he was no longer truly alive.

Jack pulled himself up, and, ignoring the man, wandered back slowly to the dryness of his car. Within seconds he began shivering. It was no good - he needed a stiff drink. And a pee come to that. Within ten minutes he had found a pub where he relieved himself on both counts, as his wet clothing continued to stick to his shivering skin.

As the afternoon drew on, Jack noticed the place had become empty. He knew that there would soon be some 'after workies' calling in for a swift one before heading home to their loved ones and he didn't want to be here when they did. The last thing he could stomach now were groups of buddies laughing and joking with each other when his entire world was crumbling in front of his eyes.

Leaving the car outside the pub, he began the long walk home, but now, with alcohol aiding his numbed brain, the thoughts and emotions that he had so far managed to quell, now threatened to escape, screaming from his cold, semi anaesthetised body.

What was he going to do now, for fuck's sake? What was he even going home TO? How could Sue do this to him? How could she carry on with her mediocre life with Alan, with a new baby that might not even be his? What would Alan say if he knew? He could go to Alan now and tell him everything but what was the point in wrecking their marriage just because she had fucked up his? Maybe he could do as Sue had suggested and tell Cheryl he had simply changed his mind? That way Cheryl need never know the truth. Or maybe Cheryl would tell Alan exactly what had been going on between them both, and if that was the case then Sue's bubble would burst soon enough anyway. Didn't someone once say that you reaped whatever you sowed in life?

It was nearly 6pm when he finally walked into the house and heard Cheryl moving around upstairs. His head hurt from all of the pointless thoughts and questions that had spun around inside it, like an unforgiving whirlpool of chaos. He still hadn't decided what to say to her and finally realised that he had nothing to lose by telling her one more lie on top of all of the others. What choice did he have now anyway? *He could always phone Tom and camp at theirs for a bit*? But was he that unhappy with his marriage that he would rather play gooseberry with his good friends over settling for second best with Chez on an evening? After all, he hadn't been *unhappy* with Cheryl before he had got together with Sue, he reasoned. *Maybe they could put this behind them, ditch the Swinger's Club once and for all and look to the future, albeit a puritanical one*? He was sure now, the more he thought about it, that once Cheryl believed that HE had ended things with Sue, given time, she would forgive him.

Jack reached the bedroom and sat down on the bed with a renewed sense of hope. He watched Cheryl carefully as she placed some of her best underwear into a small case.

"What are you doing?" He could hear the effect of the alcohol on his voice and knew that he must stink of beer.

"Tom's been ringing you all day, where have you been?" she asked, continuing with her packing and ignoring his question.

"Oh... I needed time to think things through. I couldn't face work, not today."

"And you didn't call him?"

"No, I didn't. I'll phone him later and explain."

"Well you'd better phone him now, Jack, little Jess has gone missing. He's in a terrible state."

"What do you mean 'gone missing'? She could be anywhere; that house is so huge she could apply to go on Hunted when she turns sixteen!"

"Don't be so bloody ridiculous. She's *GONE*. The police are round there and everything, they think she's been taken."

"Taken? Taken by who?"

"Just bloody ring him, Jack."

Jack's head hurt. He looked around the room and noticed all of the walls blurring into insignificance. He frowned and tried to focus on Cheryl's case again.

"What are you doing, Chez?"

"Packing," she said simply.

"I can see that, but why? Where are you going?"

"Well it hardly seems worth me keeping it a secret anymore, does it?" she said, more to herself than to him. "I'm sorry, Jack. Rob and I have been seeing each other. It's been going on for nearly a year now," she said matter of factly. "I didn't know how to tell you, but well... what with your news about you and Sue, I guess it doesn't really matter anymore, does it?" She stood at the foot of the bed beside him and smiled weakly. "It was a shock but I'm happy for you Jacky-Boy," she said tenderly, stroking his shoulder, "truly I am."

Jack frowned and half smiled as he scanned her face, before realising that she was deadly serious. Not only was she deadly serious but there wasn't one ounce of hard feeling or upset in her entire body. She was glowing in a way that he hadn't seen for over a year. And she was happy for him. So genuinely happy.

"What are you talking about, Chez? What do you mean 'you and Rob'?" His slurred words sounded hollow and sad and Cheryl looked at him with concern.

"I know it's probably a shock for you too, but at least we can all be happy now, I mean *really* happy,

Jack. Rob's taking me away for the weekend," she went on. "We're going to Dorset, a bit of peace and quiet. I think it's best for everyone."

"*Rob*? Jackie's husband, Rob?" Jack gabbled on, still trying to make sense of this latest revelation.

"Yes. Rob. I don't know any other Robs, do you?"

The abyss that had opened up in his stomach only the night before had re-appeared and began tugging at his internal organs once more.

"I don't... I don't understand, Chez. I thought we were happy, I thought we could work things out."

Cheryl smiled.

"Don't be daft, love, what's done is done. Come on, you've got Sue and I've got Rob. Even Jackie knows about it and believe it or not, she's given us her blessing." She put her hand on her chest and smiled. "God bless her heart."

"But I ended it," he blurted out desperately. "I ended it with Sue so that we could work things out. I don't wanna lose you. *Not to Rob anyway*," he added quietly.

Cheryl gaped at him as if he had suddenly sprouted another head. "Jack, what *on earth* are you talking about? Why would you DO that?"

A horn beeped outside.

"Look, I have to go, Rob's waiting for me outside."

"WHAT? I never saw him."

Jack walked to the bedroom window and glanced through the net curtains. Sure enough Rob was sitting outside in a brand new black BMW, looking towards the house. Towards him. Jack realised that he had walked straight past him only minutes ago.

"We're only going for a few nights," Cheryl continued, trying to calm him. "But when I get back we'll sort everything out."

"What do you mean?"

"Well, the house for one thing."

"The house?"

"Of course. Rob would like to move in as soon as possible. Well there's not much point in waiting now, is there? He thinks he'll be able to buy you out, love, but..." She dropped off and smiled again. "Oh, never mind about that now, we can discuss all of this when I get back. I really have to go. See you in a few days, yeah?"

"But what about me? It's over, Chez, – Sue and I are over. I finished it. For you... for *us*," he lied.

"I'm sorry, love, but ring her, yeah? I'm sure when you've explained the situation she'll be thrilled that you'll be able to be together after all."

"But I want *YOU*, can't you understand that?" The words almost choked him as they came out. Ironically, right now, now that he was losing her to Rob, he DID want her. He had already lost Sue and now he would have no one.

Jack heard a car horn sound loudly and he knew that it was Rob again. The urge to march downstairs, dismantle the entire steering wheel and make several attempts at shoving it up his goddamn arse was overwhelming.

"I'm sorry, Jack. We'll talk when I get back, OK? I really must go."

Cheryl zipped up the small case and left the room, pecking him on the cheek as she walked past.

"And don't forget to phone Tom," she shouted out, as she ran down the stairs.

CHAPTER 65

Jess and Eva had been missing for over forty eight hours. It was now Monday evening and it was cold and dark outside. The moment the knock came, Tom sprinted to the front door quicker than he had ever done so in his life, with one of the last remaining police officers following closely behind him. The majority of the police that had supported them in the first thirty six hours had now left him and Angela to it. They had told them that everything that needed to be done now could be done remotely. They would have Maxine's location the minute she turned her mobile phone back on, the minute she used her bank card or the minute she tried to leave the country. 'She can't stay off grid forever' they had told him. 'There are cameras everywhere nowadays, we'll have her the minute she drives onto a motorway'.

This hadn't helped ease Tom's suffering; *hadn't they said before that the girls could be halfway to John o' Groats 'for all they knew'? What if Maxine had ditched her phone? What if she didn't use her bank cards? What if she didn't try to leave the country? What if she didn't go on a motorway?*

'You're not on your own' they'd continued, 'You'll have some support here still, in case the girls turn up, and Mr Phillips will also stay here to support you should Ms Carter try to communicate with you'. It had been little consolation.

Jack stood on the top step between the regal looking pillars, pale and tortured. Tom had expected his friend to be horrified when he heard what had happened to Jess, but even *he* had to admit to being deeply touched by Jack's public display of shared misery. Tom ushered him inside, relieved to see him at last, and slammed the door closed. As they entered the living room, Tom's phone rang. It was Andy ringing to see if Tom had managed to get hold of Jack yet.

"He's here right now. Yeah sure... I'll phone you if there's any news."

"Fuck, man!" Jack exclaimed, as soon as Tom ended the call. "What the hell happened, mate? I've only just heard – I came straight away."

"Max has taken her," Tom replied matter-of-factly.

"*Maxine*? What the hell? You're joking? I don't believe it!"

"Well it's true." He waved his hand around the room, as if the remaining few officers and their iPads confirmed his theory.

Don Phillips, Head of Negotiations, clenched his jaw and shot Tom a look of obvious annoyance at the assumption that the kidnapper was Tom's ex-secretary. 'We have several leads, sir,' he had told Tom many times over the last few hours, 'and it is imperative that we keep them all open.'

Tom sat Jack down in the corner of the room farthest away from the officials and poured himself and Jack a large brandy, pretending not to notice the disapproving glance from Don Phillips.

"Are you OK?" Jack asked him.

"Of course I'm not OK. I've done the Psycho 'shower scene' thing," Tom replied, gulping down the amber liquid in one go. "Now I just feel cold. Cold and numb." He nodded towards Don Phillips. "He's been training me on how to answer my own bloody telephone – says he's from the Crisis Negotiation Team or something like that."

"They'll find her, mate, you've got to believe that everything will be alright in the end."

"I can't believe anything else, I can't afford to, but she could be anywhere and she's got my baby with her. Look at me I'm a fucking wreck." Tom could feel the anger begin to rise inside again and, trying to remember what the team had told him, took some deep, slow breaths.

"Well that's understandable. And they know it's definitely Max who took her, do they? I mean, did she write another letter? What does she want?"

"No. No letter, no demands. But I *know* it's her, I can feel it in my fucking bollocks."

Jack took a big breath, inflated his cheeks and puffed it out noisily.

"What else have they been telling you?"

"Oh you know..." Tom continued, "I've *'got to be strong, got to be ready in case she phones, if she does phone you mustn't say this and you mustn't say that'*, that sort of thing. They've been really good though, mate. I don't know what I'd do without them here. I'd probably blow it big time and make things a hundred times worse. If that's even possible."

"So the cops must think that she's involved then?" Jack asked, still unable to believe that Maxine was really capable of doing such a thing.

"Not really, they're just pacifying me. They think it's something to do with the insurance company."

"What, like a disgruntled ex-employee? That makes it Max again though, doesn't it?"

"No, they're thinking along the lines of someone who's had dealings with me in the past and saw an opportunity to make a small fortune out of me."

"They could be right though, mate," Jack said tentatively. "I mean to be perfectly honest I don't think Max would do something like this. I know she's as mad as a hatter at the moment but even *she* wouldn't kidnap a child."

"What the hell are you talking about?" The words were spat quietly from the corner of Tom's mouth, like a poisonous leak trying to remain unnoticed. "You saw the letter that she wrote to me, you know how insane she is at the moment, you said so yourself!"

"I did? You've showed them the letter?" Jack gave a sharp nod towards Don Phillips.

"Yeah, but they keep saying that they'll find whoever did this much quicker if they keep an open mind. But they'll have to admit sooner or later that the more time that goes by without tracking Max down, the more likely it is that she's got them."

"Them?" Jack looked confused.

"Jess' friend was here, she's taken them both. Deep down they must know something – they told me earlier that I can make a personal appeal to her if I really want to."

"To Max?" Jack asked, still trying to process the barrage of information that was being given to him.

"Yeah."

"And do you want to?"

"And say what? 'Hey you fucking bitch, you harm a hair on her head and I'll personally hunt you down and kill you with my bare hands!'?"

Jack squirmed and wished he had never asked such a stupid question. "Where's Angela?"

"Asleep hopefully, she went upstairs to have a lie down. We haven't slept for two days, she's not good, neither of us are, but what do you expect?"

"I didn't know *what* to expect," Jack confessed.

At that moment, Jack felt nausea washing over him. The events of the day, and now this evening, were beginning to take their toll on his sanity and he had an enormous urge to lie down on the floor in the foetal position and not move for days. He could feel his body rocking backwards and forwards, very slowly, in his chair but wasn't aware that it showed until Tom broke the short silence.

"Jack? Jack, what's wrong?"

Jack didn't reply. He remained rocking slowly and

rigidly as the grey fog closed in on him. What *was* wrong with him? *Was it self-pity for what had happened with Cheryl and Sue? Concern for his best friend's daughter? Guilt that he hadn't been here for Tom over the one weekend when he really needed him? He could have helped him scour the streets! He could have tried to make contact with Max and maybe found something to go on.* Jack stopped rocking and looked at Tom.

"Have you rung her?" he asked suddenly.

"Who, Max?"

"Sorry, that's another stupid question."

"Her mobile must be turned off," Tom answered, "because they can't get any location signal from it at all. And she hasn't been on social media, Nothing. She's not at home either; the cops have been outside her house since Saturday night and I've been there myself too."

"Well she didn't have too many friends, it can't be that hard to find someone who might have seen her."

"We've tried everything. They've been to her parents', no joy. Now they're trying to track down some friends of hers but even that hasn't proved easy. Why, what are you thinking?"

Jack stood up. "I need some fresh air. I'll be back a bit later."

"Jack," Tom called after him as he began to leave the room, "Do you think Cheryl would mind if you stayed the night? That's if you want to, I mean, I don't expect you to, you've got your own life, but I'd really..."

"No, she won't mind," Jack cut in. And then he left the room.

***

It was getting dark. Dark and cold. Despite the time of year, Jack felt sure they would get their first frost tonight. He got into his car; the stillness a blessed relief from the chaos that enveloped the house in his rear view mirror. He pulled away quietly. A quarter of a mile down the road he pulled over and turned the engine off. It was so peaceful that he felt he could sleep right here in the car but there were more important things to be done. Pulling out his mobile phone from his jean pocket, he called up Maxine's mobile number. Without ringing, her voicemail came on, asking the caller to leave a message. He knew there was no point. Like Tom had said, her mobile was turned off. Why would she leave it on if she knew that her signal could be traced? Jack slumped back into his car seat and put both of his hands over his face. Images of Sue and Cheryl, and the car crash that was now his life, swam into his mind but he dismissed them quickly and tried to focus on Maxine. From nowhere, a thought crashed into his mind. *Max still had his old phone! Did anyone but him even know that she still had it?* When she had smashed the screen on her old phone months ago, he had given her an old one of his, complete with his old Pay As You Go SIM card. She hadn't used his SIM card then, she had her own, but maybe she was using it now? It was only a thought and maybe he was clutching at straws but it was worth a try, he reasoned. He dialled the number and it rang several times before the voicemail kicked in.

"Max? It's me, Jack. I don't know if you'll even get this, but if you do, please call me, I need to talk to you, it's urgent." He paused for a moment. "Are you OK? I'm worried about you. No one can get hold of you and I need to know where you are. Please Max, talk to me if you're there. I'm your friend remember." He paused again before finishing, "And right now I think you need one."

He stopped, phone still connected, wondering if he should say anything else. "Just call me, Max. Anytime. I'm on my own, Chez has gone away for a while. Take care, yeah?"

Jack ended the call and drove back to the house to grab a shower and a change of clothes. When he got back to Tom and Angela's house, an officer he didn't recognise from earlier, stood stationed at the top of the steps, outside the front door. Jack waited in the cold while the officer fetched Tom for some kind of approval, and moments later he was plunged back into the sombre atmosphere of the Baxter household.

**

Maxine jumped as Jack's old phone rang for the second

time. This time it was Voicemail with a message for her. She listened to Jack's words as they swam one by one into her ear and echoed down into her nervous, jumpy heart. Then, without hesitation, she deleted it, before watching the local news about two little girls who had disappeared.

CHAPTER 66

Angela had been thrilled to see Jack in the house the following morning. She had smiled widely and then burst into fresh floods of tears, hugging him tightly and desperately. Tom finished speaking with Andy and put the phone down.

"They're fine," he said, tiredly. "Said they don't need you, Jack. Sally's being a 'PC pain in the arse' apparently, but she's doing whatever Andy asks her to."

"Good grief, the mind boggles!" Jack smiled, trying to lighten the mood, but no one smiled back.

"He's got her on claims," Tom continued pointlessly. "Apparently she told Andy that she won't tolerate a gender pay gap and wants the same pay as him. Total pain in the arse that girl. But I'd be knackered without her at the moment, what with James being away too." He looked at Jack and frowned, as if he had been talking to himself and had only just noticed him standing beside him. "Why didn't *you* go into work yesterday?"

The change in conversation took Jack by surprise and he struggled for an immediate reply.

"You didn't call the office, you didn't tell anyone," Tom continued. "Why?"

"Well what does it matter now?" Jack asked, astounded.

How could Tom even think about something so minor when his daughter had been kidnapped and he didn't even know if she was dead or alive?

"Well it *does* matter," Tom countered in a monotone voice. "What happened?"

Jack shrugged. "I was ill, I forgot to ring. Sorry, mate. I didn't know what you were going through until last night."

"Exactly. You didn't know. So why weren't you at work? Why didn't you call? I don't buy that you 'forgot'."

Jack was speechless. Yes, Tom was the boss but he had never acted like this before.

"What do you want me to say?"

"The truth."

"I was ill. That *is* the truth. I'll go in later, don't worry, I know how short staffed you are. I'll check everything's alright for you, it'll put your mind at rest."

"Ill? You recovered quickly," Tom frowned, not letting up. "What was wrong with you?"

Jack hated this. How could he burden Tom and Angela with his own problems at a time like this? He hated lying to him but he hated pretending that nothing was wrong too. Trying to be strong on the outside while his innards were being mulched just wasn't him.

"I know you, Jack, and I know when something's wrong. I won't let up until you tell me."

Jack swallowed hard. "She's left me."

There it was. The three words hung in the air between them but neither Angela nor Tom had the energy to do anything with them. They simply stared blankly into the space where they floated unseen.

"So," Jack continued, fractionally lighter now that he had minutely unburdened himself, "let's just leave it at that, eh?"

***

When Jack left Brandley House at lunchtime there had still been no news. He unlocked his front door and walked into the cold emptiness that he had left behind only the night before. There were no messages on the answer phone, not that he had expected any, and everything was still in its place. He had expected for some irrational reason, for the entire contents of the house to be gone. He didn't know why – no-one had been here since he had left it yesterday. He looked around the front room trying to imagine it raped of its possessions. He had seen couples on American TV in that situation a dozen times, squabbling in court over who the dog loved the most; ready to gouge each other's eyes out over a Rolling Stones vinyl collection. But hadn't Cheryl said something about Rob moving in here with her when she got back? She certainly didn't intend on going anywhere then, then again, neither did he. This was *his* house as much as hers and he wasn't going to sit back and let some bloke walk in and take it all away from him. Not without a fight anyway.

Remembering Maxine, he checked his mobile for messages. Still nothing. He sat down on the sofa and without further hesitation, called his old number up again and let it ring. Again it went unanswered and eventually went over onto the voicemail message. He rang her three more times before deciding to ring back yet again and leave her a second message.

"Max, I don't know if you're there but if you are, just ring me back, will you? We're friends right? Well, we *used* to be friends." He waited for a moment, before continuing. "I don't know what to say. Just tell me it isn't true. Tell me that you haven't done this, Max."

Images of her pretty, fresh face came into his mind. He and Maxine had hit it off from the minute she had walked into the job two years previously. They had struck up a brother/sister relationship and immediately joined forces in riling Andy and James as much as they possibly could. She always laughed at his jokes and he always laughed at hers. No matter how dreadful they sometimes were.

He thought back to the early days, before the rose-tinted glasses had found their way onto their boss' face, and how she had inadvertently annoyed Tom several times. It had always been because of some brainless, unnecessary mistake.

Once, he remembered fondly, Tom had handed Maxine a folder belonging to, he said, 'one of my *VERY* important clients'. When it went missing a few days later he made her empty the entire filing cabinet to look for it. Four hours later she found it filed under 'V'. 'What on earth was it under 'V' for?' Tom had asked, a look of disbelief on his face. 'For *Very* Important I guess,' she had replied, annoyed at his baffled expression. 'This is an *EXTREMLY* important file, Maxine!' Tom had said angrily. 'So should I have filed it under 'E' then instead?' she had asked innocently.

Jack smiled to himself at the recollection; just one of a thousand sweet memories he had of her. And then he remembered something else. He remembered her screaming at him in the office when she had arrived to collect her stuff. He remembered the crazy 'One Flew Over the Cuckoo's Nest' look in her eye when he had reminded her that Angela was Tom's wife. He remembered how heartbroken she was and most of all he remembered the despair and hopelessness that encapsulated her body in that final moment before she left. Suddenly from nowhere, clarity swept over him. *Of course* this was her doing, who else could it be? Tom was right. Jack had read one of the letters himself. He knew damn well that there was another side to her and in her current frame of mind she was *absolutely* capable of doing something like this. She was heartbroken, desperate and dejected; she would have acted without any rational thought. And right now he felt exactly the same way. He could quite happily go round to Sue and Alan's and tell him everything that had been going on. What was to stop him now apart from his conscience? If he was really honest with himself he would even go so far as to say that he could plunge a knife into Alan's chest without a second thought – *that would answer all of his problems, wouldn't it? Yes, he could then quite happily harass Sue relentlessly, beg her to live with him and then when she finally became sick and tired of fighting it, she would be only too pleased to have him help her bring up the baby. Wasn't that what he wanted? Wouldn't that make him happy?*

A small tear trickled from the corner of his eye and he silently stroked it away with his finger. Then, as if it was alien to him, he noticed the phone still in his hand and remembered that he was in the middle of leaving Maxine a message.

"Max. Oh hell." He sniffed quickly, trying to ease his runny nose. "I know how you feel – if only you knew just how much I know that." He took a deep breath before carrying on. "Chez has left me, she's been having an affair. I... I don't know what to do." Tears began to leak from both of his eyes once more. They contained so much hurt and pain that he could feel the heaviness of them on his cheeks. "I don't want your sympathy... I don't deserve any. I've been having an affair too. Her name's Sue. Truth is I was going to leave Chez anyway. She just beat me to it that's all, so serves me right, hey? Do you know what I feel like doing right now, Max? I'll tell you anyway. I feel like kidnapping them both. And that makes me as bad as you, right?"

The tears had taken on a life of their own and were now coursing down his face and falling onto his jeans; he was through with fighting them. His voice was trembling from the anger and pain that had been branded into his heart, like a burning hot brand searing into a thick, juicy steak.

"You don't believe me, do you? You don't believe that I could do that? I could stab him with a bloody kitchen knife and dump his body in a bastard river somewhere. And Sue, well, she's dumped me now, wants to stay with *him* – wants to play happy ever after all of a sudden. I hate them both so bloody much right now. I feel madder than I've ever felt in my entire life. I feel like I've become some insane person overnight who could do all of those terrible things that the real 'me' would never dream of doing in a million years." He took a deep breath and tried to compose himself. He wondered if Maxine would really be listening to this crazy message later on.

"But you know what? I'm not mad. And you're not mad either," he continued. "Love and hate, Max... it's a double-edged sword, it's one and the same thing. If there's one thing I've learnt in this shitty world it's that love is the most powerful thing in it. It can make you happy, it can make you sad, it can keep you sane or send you fucking mad!" He let out a small whimper that he wished had remained silent, but he carried on regardless. "It can drive you to heaven or hell, but you know what I've just realised? The destination is entirely *your* choice."

Jack's nose was dribbling in time with his eyes and he pinched two of his fingers together, one on either side of his nose, and wiped the clear mucus away. His red eyes were blurred through the stream of tears and they had begun to sting.

"I've chosen my destination, Max. I *choose* not to go to hell. Or jail." He looked around his warmly adorned room and swallowed. "What about you? What do *you* choose?"

Jack pressed the red circle on his phone's screen to end the call, then, taking a deep breath, he got up and washed his face in the bathroom before leaving the house once more.

CHAPTER 67

Jack walked into the office and filled Andy in on the latest goings on with Tom and Angela, which wasn't an awful lot. Andy already knew nearly everything that Jack told him but his face fell even further when he confirmed that Jess still hadn't been found. After a quick catch up, Andy went back to his ever increasing workload. Sally was still trying to work her way through a pile of claims and Andy was trying to keep on top of just about everything else. Jack watched them carefully. He could see that their hearts weren't in it and that not much actual work was being done. It wasn't long before he found himself hiding away in Tom's office doing little more than staring blankly ahead. He knew that he should be in control, for Tom and Angela's sake if nothing else. He should be out there for starters, helping Andy and Sally with as much as possible but he had big problems of his own and he needed time to think and to collect his thoughts together first.

Above all of his worries for Cheryl, Tom, and Angela, the only thing that his mind would really settle on was Sue. She was pregnant. She was possibly pregnant with *his* baby and she wanted to stay with Alan; one big, fat, happy family in the making. How could he possibly think about anything else other than the fact that she might be carrying his child? This had been 'it'; his one real chance of true happiness, flushed down the toilet by a few choice words. *Did she realise what she had done to him? Would she ever?*

His mobile buzzed and tinkled in his trouser pocket and he fought to get it out as quickly as he could. Sue had changed her mind, he just knew it! He should have had more faith that things would work out for him in the end, he should have trusted in her a little more.

Looking at his phone his heart sank. It was Maxine. And the rapid beating inside of his chest started up again as he read her words. 'I choose to win,'.

***

Maxine threw her phone onto the coffee table and, through the thick net curtains, glanced at the street outside. This was perfect. Far enough away from the madding crowd that she knew had surrounded her own home but close enough not to cause suspicion. She had watched the drama unfolding on the local news. At first she had been horrified to see the police and camera crew surrounding her little home. Who the hell did they think they were? They had no proof that she was involved in this? But the moment she had seen the shot of Tom's distressed face appealing for some news, any news, of his 'little princess', a perverted pleasure had coursed through her veins like a river of melted chocolate sliding down her throat.

Yesterday seemed a lifetime ago. 'Time to post that

ransom note, Teen,' she had said, smiling to herself, before packing Tina off to the local post box with the first class letter pressed heavily into her thick, woollen glove. A once innocent glove that was now laden with the invisible weight of sin. Maxine smiled to herself, wondering if Tom had received it this morning. Tina had said that it was very unlikely as she was sure that she had missed the last postal collection, but Maxine held out hope.

"Well," she said, calmly turning to Tina who had just left the girls in the kitchen eating yet more chocolate biscuits. "What do you think his face is like right now? Do you think he's read it a hundred times yet?"

Tina rolled her eyes towards the ceiling. "I don't fink 'e's read it once – I told ya, we missed the last post, 'e ain't gonna get it 'til tomorrow!"

"Oh for heaven's sake, Teen, you're such a bloody pessimist," Maxine retorted.

"Also, you know you said the uvver day when we was talking about DNA and stuff and you said that you'd even used water to stick the stamp down?" Tina squinted at Maxine's quizzical face.

"Yes. And what of it?" Maxine answered impatiently.

"Well I've been finking."

"Oh dear. Here we go again!"

"Well stamps are sticky nowadays ain't they? You don't 'ave to wet them, do ya? So what was you on about?"

Maxine rolled her eyes to the ceiling. "It was a turn of phrase, Teen, you dimwit! An expression. I was merely making a point, that's all!"

"Oh. OK." Tina thought for a moment before continuing in a tone that foretold a change of subject. "Max, you know you bin 'ere for free days now, well... when are you gonna leave?"

"Bloody hell, easy! Since when have you been any good at Maths?"

"You'll 'ave to go, you can't stay 'ere no more, you said it was only for a day or two."

"For chrissake what are you rambling on about? I can't *go* anywhere, can I? I haven't got *anywhere* to bloody well go! You've seen my apartment on the telly. It's besieged! Where do you suggest I go with two kidnapped kids?"

"Well you gotta go somewhere, I told you, you can't stay 'ere."

Maxine turned to her, impatiently. "You're supposed to be my friend, Teen, it's *your* obligation to look after me – I'd do the same for you and you know that!"

"My mum's 'oliday's over innit, she's coming 'ome tomorrow."

"Tomorrow?" Maxine shrieked. "Well... she *can't*! Why didn't you bloody tell me?"

"I did."

"You did not!"

"When you came 'ere I told you my mum would be back in a few days. Well you've 'ad a few days, it ain't my fault is it, don't get all lairy and take it out on me!"

"Well... I don't know, I mean, can't we just tell her that I'm staying here with two of my nieces or something?" Maxine asked desperately.

Tina rolled her eyes again and shook her head. "They're on every friggin' channel on the telly, Max, she ain't bloody stupid y'know."

"Shit."

Maxine clamped her jaw together tightly and swallowed hard. *Wasn't she supposed to be the clever one out of the two of them? The more intelligent?*

"Obviously being more refined don't mean you're more clever!" Tina added as if she could read her mind.

Maxine's jaw dropped open and she stared at Tina in shock, unable to reply. *Tina had never spoken to her like that in her entire life. Tina adored her, didn't she? Tina looked UP to her?*

"And anuva fing," Tina continued, a tonne of angst in her tone. "Why don't ya just give yourself up?" She was wringing her hands together tightly and biting her bottom lip.

Maxine turned around slowly, a horrified expression on her pale, waxy face. "*Give... give myself UP*? ARE YOU BLOODY INSANE? Do you know what they'll bloody well do to me if I give myself up?"

"I know what they'll do if ya don't."

"Like you know *anything*!" Maxine spat back.

"I've watched Orange Is The New Black y'know. I seen

what them lesbians do to ya in the showers. The cops are gonna get you in the end, don't you fink? I mean they're not stupid, Max, these people are gonna screw the hell out of ya!"

"I should be so lucky!" Maxine raised her eyebrows.

"I'm serious. And you can't stay 'ere, and you ain't got nowhere else to go, 'ave ya?"

"Well I'll have to find somewhere then, won't I?"

"But Max..."

"Look, I've just sent the bloody ransom note for heaven's sake!" Maxine shouted desperately. "I can't go and screw it all up now before I've even got a penny, can I? I *need* that money, Teen, it's only what I'm entitled to after all!"

"*Entitled to*?" Tina screwed up her face in disgust. "What about what 'e's entitled to? He's entitled to 'ave 'is little girl back 'ome wiv 'im, ain't he? It's not right, Max, I'm sorry, but it ain't right."

"Losing my job isn't right, Teen! Losing my only source of income and the man I love isn't right!"

"I fought you didn't love 'im no more."

Maxine fell silent. She didn't. She hated him. Well in truth she loved and hated him both at the same time. Jack had been right; love was a double-edged sword and if it stabbed you deep enough in the heart, you were fucked. She felt her bravado slipping and fell into a moment of panicked paralysis.

"Them girls are goin' 'ome. *TODAY*!" Tina shouted, jabbing her finger into the air in front of her.

"NO. They can't... I..." Maxine felt herself crumbling. One more suggestion to blow her plan and she would surely spiral out of control. She could feel her body wet with sweat, her clasped hands trembling as she realised she was no different now to an animal caught in a trap.

Tina picked up her mother's white cordless phone and held it out towards Maxine. "Ring the cops now... or I will."

"You don't mean that," Maxine whispered. Her baby blue eyes pierced deeply into her friend's, like a laser burning into a cataract. "You wouldn't dare!"

"I was up wiv 'em 'alf the night, Max – asking for their mums they was, while you snored on like sleeping friggin' beauty." Tina waved the phone in her face again, impatiently. "I can't stand it no more. Now phone the cops."

Maxine felt the heat burning inside her body; heat from hurt, heat from rage. Heat from losing control. It consumed her entire being like a forest fire raging out of control, scorching every inch of her flesh and bones, leaving no internal nook or cranny untouched. Heat. Burning heat. Heat from love, heat from hate. Heat from fury, heat from shame.

Tina placed the phone into her friend's hand. Maxine looked at it woefully for a moment or two. And then she dialled Jack's number.

CHAPTER 68

Jack held his arms out in front of him, and Angela slid between them, collapsing into a huge blob of nothingness once again. He could feel her sense of helplessness and knew that there was nothing that he could do to ease the suffering that enveloped her.

"It's like grief," she finally spluttered. "It's just like grief except there's some hope there hanging in the air... hope that they'll come back, but that just makes it double the torture – the not knowing."

Jack stroked her hair and held her tightly. "That's nonsense, Ange and you know it. Jess is fine, absolutely fine. I know it, I can feel it in my bones. I promise you, it's just a matter of time." He could feel his mobile in the back pocket of his jeans silently vibrating but ignored it.

Tom stood in the doorway of the kitchen watching quietly for a moment before joining them. The kitchen had become their one true sanctuary in the last three days. Don Phillips, Head of Negotiations, had now permanently set up his laptop in the living room and wanted to be around as much as possible in case Tom and Angela received a call. There was a regular police shift change on the front door and sometimes a third officer would turn up to check that everyone was OK, stay for a short while and then leave. But the kitchen had been a sanctuary from the bedlam that had surrounded them in the first twenty four hours, and a sanctuary it remained. It felt womb-like. Comfortable. Comforting. Quick and easy snacks were close to hand (neither of them had eaten a proper meal in three days) and the kettle was on an almost permanent boil, and so it made it a good choice of place to stay around.

Tom pulled out a chair and sat down quietly, not wanting to intrude on the wonderful job that Jack was doing of comforting his distraught wife. He knew that it should be himself standing there holding Angela, keeping her strong, but he was filled with too much grief and he had no strength in him left to give. It was moments like this in life, he thought, that ripped couples completely apart. Maybe, sometimes, if you were strong enough, it might pull you together; united in grief. But how could you possibly be there for each other, be strong for each other, when you were both being ripped apart by actions that were completely beyond your control? Tom didn't understand. He looked up and nodded at Jack appreciatively and Jack replied with a sad smile.

"Will you stay with us again tonight, Jack?" Angela whispered, drying her eyes on his sleeve but still holding onto him tightly. She didn't mind asking him now that she knew Cheryl wasn't in the house alone waiting for him.

Nothing further had been mentioned about Cheryl's disappearance. Angela and Tom still didn't know anything more about why she had left. The three words that

Jack had uttered yesterday, '*she's left me*', were the only ones that had been spoken on the subject.

Jack looked at Angela and then to Tom, and Tom in turn looked from Jack to Angela. They knew that they were all thinking about Cheryl. But only Angela knew the words that would encourage Jack to talk.

***

"You know what they say, Jack," Angela said sadly, as she placed two mugs of strong coffee in front of him and Tom. "If you love someone, set them free. Then if they come back to you..."

"Plunge a twelve inch blade into their head?" Jack finished. He thought he saw a flicker of amusement in Tom's dead eyes.

"If she doesn't come back," Angela continued, sitting down beside them both, "well what I'm trying to say is that, well that's the hardest part of loving someone, isn't it?"

"What? Letting them go?"

"Letting them go if they *want* to go, yes."

Jack sat in silence for a few moments mulling over Angela's wise words. It wasn't long before he could feel his own words, the ones he had been desperately restraining, about to burst out of the pressure cooker that was now his head. He tried to stop them; these two people had more than enough on their plate without having to endure his chaotic love-life dilemma, which by comparison, was pathetic. But the gate had been opened and the horse was bolting. He looked at Tom.

"Sue's pregnant."

From the silence that enveloped the room, and the look of quiet acceptance on Angela's face, Jack knew that Tom must have told her about his affair with Sue and his plans to leave Cheryl. Jack shook his head slowly.

"I'm sorry Ange," he smiled weakly. "I did love Chezzer, I really did. I still do in my own way."

Angela smiled back faintly but said nothing. Shock had taken her words away. Her un-made face looked haggard with the strains of the last three days and she had enough to deal with without judging Jack for his bad life choices. Jack looked over to Tom who was also speechless, so he fiddled nervously with the handle on his mug and carried on.

"I was thrilled, mate, absolutely thrilled." His voice began to break up, but already he could feel the relief at the thought of tossing this giant albatross from around his neck, into the open, so he soldiered on. "She wants to keep it, of course. Just doesn't want to keep me."

"Is it yours?" Angela asked.

"I don't know, Ange, it's too soon to say. She says it's Alan's, I think she even wants it to be Alan's."

"But what if it isn't?"

"Makes no difference, she wants to bring it up with him regardless. She hasn't even told him about us."

"So what happened with Cheryl?"

Jack shook his head slowly. "I'd told her everything, even told her that Sue and I were moving in together." He looked at Tom. "She confessed that she'd been seeing someone else anyway, can you believe that? Cheryl's been seeing someone else too! What a bloody mess."

"And now she's leaving you... for him?"

"Well I think she's expecting me to move out actually."

"And the baby? What did she say about the baby?" Angela continued. To think about something else for just a few minutes was a short escape from her own dreadful reality; a welcome relief.

Jack took a glug of his coffee and fought back the tears. "Cheryl doesn't know about the ba..." The word caught in his throat and he dropped his head in his hands. "I'm sorry. I shouldn't have said anything. You two, with everything you have going on. Shit, I'm so selfish. So *fucking* selfish!"

Tom swallowed hard. He had never felt so useless. He couldn't be there for Angela and now he couldn't be there for Jack. But did he want to be there for Jack? *Their child was missing for heaven's sake - what could possibly be worse than that? Certainly not Jack's 'love troubles' that he had, incidentally, brought upon himself. But hadn't Tom brought HIS mess upon himself too? If he hadn't messed around with Max then Jess would be here right now.* He hung his head in shame.

Angela reached out across the kitchen table and clasped her hand over Jack's.

"You can stay with us for as long as you like. We need you here, Jack, you're a rock for both of us."

"Yeah, some rock," he countered dryly.

Jack's mobile began vibrating once again in his back pocket. This time he stood up and took it from his jeans and upon seeing that it was Maxine, shielded the display from them both. He gaped from Tom to Angela and then back again.

"Um... it's um..."

"Cheryl?" Angela finished for him.

"I'm really sorry but I've got to go."

CHAPTER 69

For once, Jack drove without any musical assistance. He loved his music. In fact he lived for it in many ways. Tonight however, it would have been a terrible distraction from the already terrible distractions in his life.

The streetlights were already illuminated and their soft, yellow glow reflected drearily by contrast into the dark, wet roads beside and ahead of him. As he pulled into the car park just outside town, he saw her already waiting there for him. Just making out her silhouette behind the wheel of her car, Jack drove up to the far corner of the old disused car park and parked his car next to hers. No sooner had he shut his car door, than he was opening hers, and with adrenalin making his heart thump loudly inside his chest, he sat down in the front passenger seat. The words that he had rehearsed on the way down deserted him the moment he looked at her.

"Chrissake, Max!" he blurted, astounded at her dishevelled appearance.

She smiled wearily. "Thank you."

"What for?"

"The insult."

"I didn't say anything."

"You didn't have to."

For the next few moments they sat muted in the

stillness. He couldn't believe that his words had deserted him; he had rehearsed them over and over. He waited, hoping that she would break the painful silence, but she didn't. Instead she stared ahead at the wet windscreen as the inside darkness of the car surrounded them.

"Max, what's going on?" he asked eventually. He waited for a reply but nothing came. "MAX!"

"I didn't know what else to do," she mumbled. "I didn't know who else to call."

She looked calm, almost serene, but he guessed that deep inside she must be trembling. *Maybe the gravity of what she had done was finally sinking in? Maybe remorse would soon flood her veins and she would beg Tom and Angela for forgiveness?*

"You said on the phone that you've got the girls. Where are they? Are they OK?"

"They're with my friend, Tina." Still Maxine stared straight ahead, detached from everything around her, except Jack's voice. She had yet to look at him. "And yes, they're OK. I'm not a murderer, Jack."

"No... but you're a kidnapper." He saw her flinch in the darkness. "Max, what the bloody hell were you thinking of? WHY? Why on earth did you do this?"

Without warning she turned and looked at him, an expression of horror on her pale face. "You haven't told anyone have you? You promised!"

"I told you I'd meet you and speak with you, but I'm not going to lie to you. When I leave here I'm going straight back to Tom and Angela's. There are police there, Max!"

"What do you mean, 'back to Tom and Angela's'?"

"There's just a couple left, granted, but there WAS an entire investigative team to start with."

"What do you mean, 'back to Tom and Angela's'?" She repeated, ignoring him.

"I've been there, supporting them. What did you expect? He's my best mate!"

"But I'm not going to hurt those girls!" she declared in a wounded voice. "I wouldn't harm a hair on their heads!"

"Yeah, Tom and Angela really know that, don't they?"

"The only people I wanted to hurt were Tom and that Bitch Wife of his!" she screamed furiously, finally letting the anguish inside her erupt.

"Well, bloody well done, Max!" he shouted, her selfishness pushing him to breaking point. "CONGRATUFUCK-INGLATIONS! Cos you know what? You did that alright!" Jack slammed his fist down hard on the dashboard, causing her to jump and then burst into tears.

"DON'T EVEN GO THERE!" he yelled. "Just don't fucking go there – your tears won't work on me." He shook his head furiously and grabbed his red hair in his fists. "What is the *matter* with you, are you fucking *insane*? You kidnapped two kids, TWO LITTLE KIDS! I hope you like prison food, Max, cos I'm telling you what, mate, that's *exactly* where you're headed any time now!"

Maxine felt cornered. She was well and truly trapped. *What could she do now? Push Jack out and drive away? Hardly! She had asked him here to help her. And anyway he would only go straight to his car and drive to Tom's to tell them everything!* She punched the dashboard of her car repetitively with her two small fists.

"FUCK! FUCK FUCK FUCK FUCK FUCK!" she screamed angrily into the darkness, her face saturated in tears and her breathing short and sharp. "I thought you were my friend, Jack. I thought you would help me, you bastard!" She sobbed wildly, mascara running down her cheeks.

"I AM your friend, Max, but hey... GUESS WHAT? I'm Tom and Angela's friend too - their BEST friend, so what the hell do you want me to do, eh?" he pelted back. "Go on tell me, what do you expect me to do? You want me to go home quietly and shut the fuck up and pretend that I don't know where those girls are? If you think that then you ARE fucking insane!"

"STOP IT!" she screamed, rocking backwards and forwards in her seat with her head in her hands, trying to drown out his words. "JUST STOP IT!"

"No, I won't. I won't stop it. Tell me where the hell those girls are and we can get them back home with their parents where they belong!"

"I did it for love you know, Jack. LOVE! What a joke that is!"

"Love?" Jack looked bewildered. "That's absolute bollocks and you know it!"

"It's not bollocks! I thought you understood how I

felt. If not then why did you leave that shitty message on my phone, Jack, huh?" She tilted her head and stared at him. "Oh wow, you didn't mean it at all, did you? You don't know how I feel! That was just bullshit to get me to meet you, wasn't it? Of course it was! How the hell could *you* ever know what I feel like anyway? I shouldn't think you've ever really loved anyone in your entire life, not REALLY loved them! Not unconditionally. Not so as you'd do anything for them! Not so as you'd *die* for them!"

"And how the hell would you know that?" Jack shot back.

"Because you and Cheryl are a goddamn joke and you know it! And before her you'd never so much as dipped your stick anywhere NEAR anyone else! Loved? You haven't even lived!"

Finally, Jack had been silenced. He stared directly in front of him, into the gloomy night that existed outside the warmth of the car, his mouth open, but definitely silenced. Maxine stared at him and took deep, loud breaths, filling her lungs with as much oxygen as possible, preparing herself should he suddenly decide to lean over and strangle her. When he looked back at her she whimpered. *Was she having a panic attack? Did he care*? Her words had cruelly sliced into his already wounded heart, and he slumped backwards into his seat, feeling tears prickling at the back of his eyes. He breathed softly and neither of them spoke again for several minutes.

"I'm sorry," Maxine mumbled eventually, when the atmosphere in the car had died down to such un-dramatic proportions that she feared he was no longer breathing.

He didn't reply.

"Jack, I..."

Jack reached for the car door handle. In that one moment he couldn't bear to be anywhere near her.

"Please," she pleaded. "Please, I beg you, don't go, Jack. I need you!"

For a while longer his hand stayed put, until eventually she saw it slide effortlessly away as his body slumped back into the seat beside her. He looked down into his lap.

"I'll take the girls back. Tonight. As soon as we leave here. I promise, Jack. I promise I will. Just stay with me in the car for a little while longer. Just give me some time in here to get my head sorted out."

Still he said nothing.

"I'm sorry for what I said. I was angry, I didn't mean it. I can't control myself sometimes – it's my biggest fault."

Still he didn't speak. She didn't mind; he was staying in the car with her and right now that was all that mattered. In here she could clear her head. In here she didn't have to think about what was going to happen to her in the next few hours. In here, for a while at least, she was safe and she could pretend that everything was fine.

"You're wrong you know," he said finally.

"Wrong?"

Even in the gloom of the car, she could see that he was reliving a memory; probably one of many that he had that would help to keep him warm at night when he was an old man, she thought.

"Wrong about what?"

"I *have* lived you know." Then he turned to her and smiled softly. "And I've loved too. And despite what you think, I DO know what you're going through."

"What *am* I going through, Jack?"

"Torture, pain... a living hell."

"Yeah, tell me about it!" she mumbled.

So he did.

CHAPTER 70

Bolognaise pizza was just about the best you could get, he reckoned. The hunger pains had come with a vengeance and instead of steadily pacing himself, he finished the twelve incher in four and a half minutes.

Andy knew he hadn't eaten properly for days, but was it any wonder? Sam hadn't contacted him, and after the dreadful 'doorstep display' on Sunday evening, he had absolutely no intention of calling her either. OK, so he had acted badly, he knew that, but what on earth did she expect him to do under the circumstances? *Shouldn't she have been flattered that he appeared to still give a toss after all these months? Couldn't she have just invited him in to meet Marcos so that he could see for himself that there was nothing going on between them? She had been in her dressing gown for heaven's sake! And Marcos had kept peeking out of the curtains!* Nothing about that seemed 'innocent' to him. *If she had nothing to hide she would have let him in, wouldn't she?*

The last two days had been almost unbearable. Images from a real-life hell had invaded his every waking thought. It was bad enough that half of them were X-rated scenarios of Sam and Marcos together, but the other half, which were of Jess and her face-less little friend, were quite simply horrifying. Andy had seen the news too; knew that the police had been to Maxine's house and ransacked it. *Why on earth would they suspect Maxine of all people of doing something like this? Neither Tom nor Jack had told him that Maxine was a suspect. What on earth was going on*? The newsreader had said something about a letter but he hadn't caught it properly and he had been trying to ring Tom and Jack ever since to get the latest. So far he had had no luck. He could only imagine the depths of despair that Tom and Angela had reached.

His thoughts finally drifted to James and Charlie, and the wonderful time that they were no doubt having in Switzerland. What he would give for a holiday right now, away from everything. Despite himself, he now realised that he was missing James' presence in the apartment below. How many months had gone by before now when they simply hadn't found the time to pop in to see each other outside of work, even for five minutes? That lately they had both made so much effort, only seemed to enhance the fact that James was now miles away across the sea, having a fabulous time with a man that only weeks ago, he himself had been crazy for. How strange it was now that the entire episode felt like it had happened in another lifetime.

Andy threw the empty pizza box into the bin and slumped back onto the sofa, shattered. The last few weeks had drained him entirely. They had eaten at his sleep, his energy and his humour. He rubbed his eyes roughly, trying to stay awake, and flicked through the television channels mindlessly, stopping only when he stumbled upon Sam's favourite film, Somewhere in Time. He had missed the beginning but he paused for a while to watch it as he thought about Sam.

Christopher Reeves was playing Richard, who had just travelled back in time to meet Elise McKenna, the woman he had become infatuated with.

What would he change if only he could go back in time? He would never have got involved with Charlie for a start, he was sure of that. He would go back a few weeks and decide not to ring Sam up after all those months too... or maybe he would still ring her but not make a prick of himself on her doorstep. He thought some more. No - actually he was glad that he had done that. But he would have changed something; he would have barged into her house and walloped the little twat instead of exchanging harsh, futile words with the woman he loved. Andy looked back at the film.

Richard had found Elise. She was walking along by the riverside and he was rooted to the spot, mesmerised by her flawless beauty. Finally, he plucked up enough courage to go and talk to her.

Andy thought about the courage he had plucked up from God knows where (he seemed to recollect it was from a vodka bottle but couldn't be too sure) to phone Samantha after all those months. His eyes flicked back to the screen.

They exchanged a few pleasantries; she had no idea who he was, and she was turning now and walking away from him.

He remembered how Sam had walked away from him on Sunday evening; in her pink dressing gown, back into the warmth of her house... and a waiting 'Marcos'.

Elise's manager had arrived as if from nowhere, and was trying to shoo Richard away; she was going to be a famous actress one day and he didn't want men like Richard loitering around her, thank you very much.

Andy thought of Marcus loitering around Sam. He changed channels but the same film was on the next channel too, only this time the film was further along.

Richard had managed to get himself into the hotel where Elise was staying and he was trying to dance with her on the hotel dance floor. She flinched and began to move away but he stopped her with Sam's favourite line from the film, 'Wait! You have no idea how far I have come to be with you.'

"What bollocks. I always hated this crappy film," Andy moaned aloud, trying to turn the channels again. But still the film played on, even further along into the story.

They were now madly in love and completely inseparable. Richard had hummed Rachmaninov to her, blown out the candle and, by the look on Jane Seymour's face the next morning, and the comment, 'You'll have to marry me now' - had made mad, passionate love to 'Elise' throughout the night.

Andy bashed the remote on the table in front of him and the channel changed again, but still the film continued.

"What the actual hell?" he shouted, throwing the remote control at the wall, angrily.

She was laughing at his suit. He had got it from a costume shop before he had gone back in time. It was supposed to make him 'fit in' to that time, but the shop keeper must have got the dates wrong because even for 1912 it was outdated. Despite this, Richard loved the suit and he began pointing out all of the hidden pockets inside the jacket, trying to show her just how fabulous it really was.

"Oh no, not the coin, please! Not the bloody coin!" Andy shouted at the television, now detesting the film more than ever. This was Sam's favourite part.

Andy walked over and turned the television off but it defiantly stayed on. Confused, he pulled the plug from its socket but it made no difference.

Richard pulled a handful of money from the suit's inside pocket but one of the coins was from the 1970s; his own time, and it had buggered up the entire time travel phenomenon, causing him to whiz forward in time... back into his own time; back to the seventies – leaving Elise sobbing in an empty hotel room in 1912, heartbroken.

Andy detested the next part of the film most of all. Watching the pitiful figure of a man that he had always admired in the Superman films, reach such a desperate low that he would compromise his own self-respect just to be with the blasted woman again, was at best sickening.

Now firmly back in the seventies, Richard had gone back to the hotel and booked himself into the same room that they had shared together in 1912. Through meditation, he desperately tried to throw himself back in time again; back into her arms.

"How desperate can a man get?" Andy shouted out, annoyed that there was no way out of the film now. "I would *never* let myself get into a state like that over a bloody woman, no matter who she sodding well is! You played Superman for heaven's sake! Yes, she's Jane Seymour, but still... get a life!"

Well aware of the heaviness in his own heart but denying it absolutely, he picked the remote control up from the floor and hurled it once more as hard as he could at the living room wall. *Why wouldn't the sodding channel change over*?

The image changed to the final scene of the film.

Richard sat in the hotel chair, unmoving. It hadn't worked; he was still in the seventies. He had been there for days, perhaps weeks, without eating a thing, without thinking of anything other than his lost love. Andy's childhood superhero, dead in a hotel room. *Dead from a broken heart.*

***

The voices swam into his ear and buzzed around in his head for the longest time before he forced himself to open his eyes. He was lying on the sofa and the voices were coming from the television set in front of him. The remote control was on the table in front of him and not in bits on the floor as Andy distinctly remembered only moments earlier. He looked at the television. A man was interviewing a woman in her forties with pink hair and a nose stud.

"The trouble is," she said animatedly, "there are still not enough people who care about actual recycling. You've got your Greta Thunbergs, sure, bunk off school if you must. You've got your Extinction Rebellion, sure, play on the bridges in London. But do we still care about *recycling*? Do we care *enough*? No, we don't!"

Andy sat up and looked at his watch. It was 10pm. He turned the television off and then, taking a detour through the kitchen, he moved the pizza box from the bin and put it into the recycling bag. And then he went to bed.

CHAPTER 71

Maxine pulled her hand away. She didn't know how long it had been resting on Jack's knee for; she couldn't even remember putting it there. Jack hadn't seemed to notice either. It had been the saddest story that she had heard for a long time, bar her own, and she felt genuine compassion for the man sitting next to her, who by his very own admission, was still her friend. She had no idea how long they had been sitting there for in her cramped car; she had just let him talk for as long as he needed to about Cheryl and Sue, spilling out his heart as he proved to her beyond doubt that he did indeed feel her pain.

"What are you going to do now?" she asked him tentatively, when he had finally finished speaking.

He thought for a while before replying.

"Do you know what I'm dreading the most?"

Maxine stayed silent and let him talk.

"I have this image of Sue and Alan walking through the park one day with my child. They look happy and they're laughing and I'm walking towards them... and I can't get away." He stopped and turned to Maxine. "That's stupid isn't it? I mean, it'll probably never happen."

"If it ever does, I promise I'll be there for you, Jack."

He smiled at her gratefully and then, without warning, jolted in his seat and looked at his watch.

"What the hell am I doing?"

"What do you mean?"

"I'm sitting here telling you my useless problems while Tom and Angela are at home not even knowing whether the girls are alive or dead! Come on, we've got to go." He strapped his seatbelt around himself hastily and waited for her to start the engine up. She didn't. "Max, *come on*, I mean it. We have to go. NOW!" He shouted impatiently.

Maxine held her bunch of keys tightly in her hand and showed no sign of moving them towards the ignition. The only movement was her body trembling slightly.

"He's going to hate me," she whimpered, her face crumpling.

"Who?"

"Tom. Who do you think? What am I saying? He already hates me!"

For a moment Jack was lost for words. He was torn between sympathy for her, and wanting to slap her so hard across the face for only thinking of herself. *How could she be so bloody selfish?*

"JACK!", she wailed, wiping at the fresh tears that were now falling onto her already blotchy face. "Oh no, what have I done, what the hell have I done? Tell me I'm going to wake up. Tell me that this is all a bad dream." She banged her fist on the steering wheel in torment.

"Let's go, Max. It's nearly over." He placed a hand

over hers. "Everything will be fine."

"I sent him a ransom note. He probably hasn't even had it yet!" she cried, pointlessly.

"You... you WHAT?" Jack's eyes bulged from the latest revelation. "You wanted money?" he asked in disbelief.

"Well no, not really. I just wanted to hurt them, I wanted to hurt *him*. I took the girl because I couldn't think of anything more precious to take from him. Her friend just happened to be there and..."

"There *wasn't* anything more precious to take from him!" Jack replied flatly. "AND you wanted money?"

"I lost my job! I might lose my home – he paid a huge amount towards that flat of mine, did you know that?" She shouted irritably. "What am I saying? The next time I step out of this car I'm done for and I'll lose everything I've got anyway. That's irony for you!"

"What does that matter now?" Jack asked, confused.

"I don't know. I guess it doesn't."

"Those things don't matter a toss, can't you see that?" he shouted at her. "You can get *another* job, a *better* job, and with the extra money you can make the payments on the flat yourself. Have a bit of self-respect, Max, for goodness sake!"

"But I love him," she cried. "*I really love him* and I don't think he'll ever really know just how much. He broke my heart, Jack."

Jack grabbed her shoulders and turned her around to face him. "People break each other's hearts all the time, Max. In time someone else will come along and mend it for you, I promise. That's life."

She rubbed furiously at her face as each new tear contaminated her with emotions that she didn't want to feel. She smiled sadly at Jack and tried to put the key into the ignition but she was trembling so much that she was missing time and time again.

"Oh shit, will I go to prison?" she screeched suddenly, dropping the keys to the floor. "I'm so scared. I've never done anything wrong in my life before."

"Max, get out of the car!"

"What?"

"Give me the keys and get out of the car."

"No!"

"I said, give me the keys. You're not fit to drive." He raised his eyebrows and held his hand out authoritatively until eventually she reached down slowly to get them and dropped them, defeated, into his waiting hand. Once they had swapped seats, Jack fired the engine to life. The radio came on suddenly, making them both jump.

"I'm sorry. I always leave the radio on for company. But then it comes on automatically when you start the engine up and I..."

"SHHH!" Jack held up a hand to silence her.

The newsreader had said something about the two missing girls. He had missed what it was, but now they were saying that the net was closing in on the kidnapper since new evidence had come to light.

"What the hell does *that* mean?" Maxine wailed.

"That they probably know where the girls are. We have to get there as quickly as we can. Direct me. Where are we going?"

"WHY RUSH?" Maxine shrieked, hysterical now. "If they know where the girls are then they're probably already at the house. They'll probably be waiting for me when we get there, handcuffs at the ready. I'm not in any rush to do Porridge, Jack!"

"Don't you get it?" Jack asked, astonished, squinting his eyes at her. You were about to take those girls home all of your own accord. Who the hell do you think is going to believe that, once the police have turned up and stormed the place?"

"You."

"Yes ME! But no-one else! It could double your sentence, Max."

The last few words slapped her across the face. She barked the directions to Jack as quickly as she could, never letting her eyes rest for one moment on anything but the dark night outside. It was starting to sleet and she could see the petrol light shining brightly with all of the other lights on her dashboard. She knew she should have filled up earlier; the light had been on this morning too when Tina had borrowed it to go shopping. She could only pray that there was enough petrol to get them back to the house. Why had she used her car tonight anyway, let alone leave it parked outside Tina's house for days? Maybe that had been her downfall; maybe it had been spotted? How could she have been so stupid?

The traffic was heavy for the time of night. The bad weather had made everyone on the roads slow down and she knew this could easily add ten minutes to their journey time. They drove on in silence. The only noise to be heard was the drumming of Jack's fingers on the dashboard every time the car came to a complete stop. She watched them drumming again and again. When they finally turned the last corner, Jack stopped at the end of the road and glanced down the quiet street for signs of life. It was nearly 10.30pm, it was wet, dark and cold and the road was silent. The only light to be seen was from the lampposts that graced the outside of every tenth house or so. Moving slowly forward, he managed to park right outside the house, into the space that Maxine had left there hours before. When the engine died, the frenetic atmosphere in the car died with it, and they sat momentarily in silence, staring into each other's pale faces before Jack turned away and took his phone out of his pocket.

"I need to ring Tom right now and let him and Angela know what's happening."

"WHAT? NO WAY!"

"I have to, we can't just turn up with the girls, cheering 'surprise, surprise!' They need to know, Max. The cops need to know. I could get into real trouble otherwise."

"But they're going to find out anytime now anyway,

what does another ten minutes matter?"

"It matters a lot!" Jack looked at her worried face and took a deep breath. "Max... look, I just want to say that... well, whatever happens..."

"Yes?" Her eyes were wide and her breathing heavy.

"Well... whatever happens..."

A banging on the car window stopped him mid-sentence and they both looked up sharply. Tina was standing at the kerb in a thick, bobbly jumper and a pair of faded baggy jeans, looking anxious.

"Where the hell have you been?" she shouted to Maxine as Jack wound the window down. "You said you was only gonna be 'alf an hour!"

"Why, what's happened?" Maxine looked nervously from Tina to Jack, before clambering out of the car.

"Nuffink's 'appened," Tina replied, looking Jack up and down suspiciously. "I was worried that's all. The girls were crying earlier an' I couldn't shut 'em up. One of the neighbours came round to see what the noise was."

"Oh shit." Maxine closed her eyes and tried to steady herself. "Did the neighbour say anything? Did she see them?"

"No, just what I said. Why, what's 'appened? What's the matter wiv ya?"

"She's fine," Jack said, answering for Maxine. "Just get the girls and put them in the car."

"'ang on a mo, who d'ya fink you are?" Tina barked, frostily. "You can't tell me what to do!"

437

"Teen, just bloody do it. NOW!" Maxine hissed. Tina blinked slowly and looked back to Jack before swallowing hard. And then she rushed inside to do exactly as she was told.

CHAPTER 72

As they pulled away from the petrol station, Jack felt the stirrings of bad feeling building up inside of him.

Firstly, the man behind the counter had seen the two girls, he was sure of it. It had happened when he had been paying for the petrol to top up Maxine's car. He had only put a fiver in – it might have seemed a bit tight, but he knew that Maxine wouldn't be driving her car around for a long time to come, and a fiver was going to be plenty to get them to Tom and Angela's. In his haste he had forgotten the number of the petrol pump he had used, and the guy had glanced outside for a moment – onto the brightly lit forecourt, where Maxine's car stood, as if on a gleaming pedestal for all to see. The girls' sleepy faces could be seen quite clearly and as they had been on every local news programme, every social media site and in every newspaper for the last few days, he was certain that the man had recognised them. If not, then why was he now talking on his mobile phone while watching them pull away? *And why the hell had he used the closest pump to the building anyway?*

The second dose of bad feeling came from the first. *Could he now be seen as an accomplice in all of this? Wasn't this what they called 'aiding and abetting'? But hadn't he only aided in getting the girls home, not taking them away? Did it make any difference? The cops probably wouldn't think so; they would say he had taken the law into his own hands. Tom probably wouldn't think so either. He would be furious to know that Jack had known (albeit for a short time only) that Maxine did indeed have the girls and hadn't told him.*

As soon as he drove out of the station, he pulled over to the side of the road and tore his phone from his jeans, perspiration breaking out over his body.

"What are you doing?" Maxine asked nervously.

"What do you think I'm doing?

"Phoning someone?"

"I'm phoning Tom and Angela. I should've phoned them earlier, before we got petrol. I told you – they need to know what's happening.

"But we'll be there in two minutes, what's the point?"

"THE POINT IS, MAX, THEY HAVE A RIGHT TO KNOW!"

"Are we going home now?" Jess piped up from the back seat.

The light, tinkling voice shocked them both. Of course they knew that the girls were there; they had helped Tina pluck them from their beds, half asleep and put them there themselves. But they weren't supposed to be awake. They looked around and saw the two girls wide-eyed, with hope dancing across their faces.

Jack turned to Maxine, his eyebrows raised, waiting for her to answer.

"Yes honey, you're going home," she answered sweetly.

"Is the game over?" Jess continued excitedly, smiling and nudging Eva.

His eyes still on Maxine, Jack frowned. Ashamed, she looked down.

"Yes. The game's over."

"When will we be there?"

It was Maxine's turn to frown. "Just as soon as Jack can drive us there!"

Jack clenched his teeth and put his foot down on the accelerator as his phone fell to the car floor.

***

As the car came to a stop on the wet, glistening gravel, Maxine was reminded of the last time she had been here. She had been forced here by Angela and made to look like an idiot in front of Tom. Now she knew that she really was an idiot and she had no-one but herself to blame. She looked at the cars that were already here. Tom's familiar silver Mercedes sat neatly on the drive next to Angela's dark blue one. It looked black in the eerie light that shone from the outside security lamps. There were two other cars there too. A black BMW and a Police car in all of its neon glory. She winced and turned to Jack.

"Can I stay in the car?" she asked him pointlessly.

"No you can't."

"I won't run, what's the point? They'll get me in the end, and anyway, where would I run to?"

"I'm sorry, Max, but no," he repeated.

Maxine grabbed his arm as he opened the car door. "I can't do this, Jack. How can I? I'd rather die."

Ignoring her he climbed out of the car, into the night and opened the back door to get the girls out, before shutting it with a loud slam. He waited for Maxine to get herself out.

Very slowly, as if she might suddenly collapse, Maxine eased herself out of the safety of her little motor. Moving to the other side of the car, she stood silently next to Jack and the girls. As she looked around nervously, she took several deep lungfuls of fresh air and wondered when she would get another chance to do something so beautiful and simple. The lights from the house shone dimly onto them all and she realised that the most awful moment of her life had finally arrived. There was nowhere to run to now. She was a pig about to have an apple thrust into her mouth before being forced onto a barbecue. A lamb being led to the slaughter. A free bird about to be thrown into a cage.

Jack reached out, took her by the hand and led her slowly to the stone house in front of them. It loomed upon her like a great foreboding castle and the only way she could keep moving towards it was to look away. Holding onto his other hand, was Jess, and holding onto her, was Eva. But he held Maxine tightest of all.

Despite the lights filtering through every window from the downstairs of the house, it was only when they reached the stone steps that Maxine noticed a policeman standing at the top, by the front door. He looked cold and tired and she thought he was probably wishing that he had been posted indoors in the warmth.

"Good evening," he murmured to them all, before realising that the small figures in front of him were indeed the missing girls. "Good Lord above!" he exclaimed loudly. "What have we got here then?"

And he opened the front door and followed them all inside... into the warmth at last.

CHAPTER 73

Eva shifted from foot to foot shyly but Jessie screamed excitedly the moment she walked into the familiar hall. Her yelps of 'mummy, mummy' were soon recognised as Angela and Tom looked at each other in dazed confusion before darting out of the kitchen, their euphoric faces flooded in ecstasy when they saw the girls with their own eyes. They were closely followed by two policemen and Don Phillips, whose faces contained almost as much joy and relief as that of the parents.

Angela threw herself around Jess' little body, screaming in an agony of ecstasy that was unrecognisable to her usual voice. Tom, who so elated that he felt sure he was dreaming, ran to mother and child and wrapped himself around the both of them as completely as he could. He could hear himself crying and could feel himself shuddering from the sobs that shook his entire body. He could never have imagined that anyone could experience such overwhelming joy in one single moment.

Raising her head, Angela noticed Eva standing next to them all with a police officer at her side, and she pulled her forward to join them all. Within seconds the little girl had become part of the great communal hug of love and the four of them stayed there for a while, not one of them wanting to move.

The officials stood silently, watching the beautiful scene before them. No one dared speak for the longest time. No one dared to intrude on such a special moment in time. No one had noticed Jack and Maxine standing by the front door.

For the shortest, sweetest moment, Maxine dared to believe that she might not get into trouble after all. *The family were re-united, that was the main thing, right? She had brought them home! OK, with Jack's help, but still, why wouldn't they be lenient?* They all looked so happy to be together again that she felt sure that once they had noticed her and heard her sad and sorry story, understood the desperation she had felt and seen how sorry she was for her actions, that they would feel compassion for her and let her go. *Was it up to Tom and Angela or the police? If they didn't press charges then she would get off, wouldn't she? Or was it a different story when kidnapping was involved? It certainly was with murder but then she hadn't murdered anyone, had she? She hadn't even harmed anyone – well not physically anyway.*

Maxine looked at Jack who was, along with everyone else, watching the magical scene in front of him, a tear glistening in his eye for his best friend's moment of joy. Then she turned and looked at Tom. *Really* looked at him. She had never seen him so happy in all the time that she had known him. She had never seen him cry and had never seen that ecstasy in his face before; not even when they had been having what he had said was the best sex he had ever had in his life, which, she now realised, probably hadn't been. *This had to be what love was really about, wasn't it? What was it that she had said to Jack in the car? That he had never really loved anyone, not truly, not so as he would die for them?* In that moment she knew that Tom would die for his little girl; that he would even kill for her if necessary.

In the second it took for that thought to run through her mind, Tom looked up to see her standing still, staring at him with tears in her eyes. She knew that once the numbness and shock at seeing her there had worn off, he would kill for little Jess sooner than she had first thought. He would kill *her* and *now* – with his bare hands.

"You fucking bitch," he whispered through gritted teeth.

It was barely audible and Jack had to swing around to see that he was actually talking to Maxine.

Angela looked up and saw in a moment what was happening but was so stunned that she couldn't speak. Within seconds Tom had run across the hall and lunged at her. His beautiful hands that had once stroked the curves of her body so softly, so full of love and lust, had found their way around her neck in an instant, and without any rational thought he squeezed his fingers as hard as he could.

"You bitch, you fucking bitch! I'll fucking kill you for this!"

Tom's face was crimson and the veins across his

temples were bulging so much that she thought he might die at any moment. Maxine tried to pull his hands away but he was too strong for her and she knew that without the help of the people around her, he wouldn't let go.

The officers and Jack were around him in an instant, pulling him off her and trying to calm him down but there was a monster inside Tom now that wasn't going to give up that easily. He held his hands up in surrender but the moment they released their grip on him, he lunged at her again. This time she screamed loudly as he grabbed her hair and banged the back of her head against the hallway wall. Once again the officers restrained Tom, this time however, no one dared to loosen their grip on him.

"Come on, mate, calm down." Jack blurted, horrified. He looked at Tom as though the outburst had not only been unexpected but also unjustified. "You don't want the girls to see this, surely."

Tom looked across to Angela and nodded, and she quickly grabbed both girls tightly and dragged them into the living room with her, closing the door firmly behind them all.

"Problem sorted," Tom panted, as he tried in vain to lunge at a sobbing Maxine again.

"Sir, please," one of the officers said calmly, "we don't want to have to use force but if you insist on attacking the girl then we'll have no choice." He pulled out a pair of handcuffs to show Tom that he meant business.

Tom stared at the cuffs in disbelief. "Are you taking the piss? This bitch kidnapped my kid and did God only knows what to her and you're gonna handcuff *ME* for getting angry?"

"I didn't do anything to them," Maxine sobbed in defence.

"Shut up!" Tom screamed back. "Don't you *dare* talk to me, don't you even look at me!"

"Tom, I'm sorry, I'm so, so sorry," Maxine bawled, now unable to stop herself. "If only you knew how bad I feel."

"I SAID 'SHUT UP'!"

"I was never going to hurt them. I just wanted to hurt *you*. It's like I was possessed. I wanted you to hurt like I was hurting..."

"I SWEAR TO GOD IF YOU SAY ANOTHER WORD, MAX, I'LL FUCKING KILL YOU!" Tom was foaming at the corners of his mouth now and spittle was flicking onto her with every word he shouted.

Jack looked on helplessly. He knew that Maxine deserved everything she had coming to her but it didn't make him feel any less sorry for her. He didn't enjoy seeing her being torn to pieces as she bared her soul in front of strangers.

"Mate," Jack tried again, "the girls are back – they're safe and sound. Nothing's happened to them I promise you."

"And how do you know?" Tom turned to look at Jack in surprise. His eyes were wide and fierce. Like a wild animal being attracted to fresh meat, he turned his attention to Jack. "How in hell's shit do you know fucking *anything*?" His eyes narrowed. "You were with her tonight, weren't you?"

"She sent me a text. I went there so I could help her to bring the girls back, that's all."

"And you never told me?"

"Of course I never told you. Look at you! What would you have done?"

"And you never told the police?"

"You would've killed her."

"Yes, I would have. And I'll never forgive you for taking that opportunity away from me!"

"Jess and Angela need you at home with them, mate, not locked up in a prison somewhere for the rest of your life, can't you see that?"

Tom didn't answer. He was looking at Maxine in disgust and she knew that if looks could kill, he wouldn't have needed his bare hands at all.

"I was going to ring you on my way back," Jack continued defensively to the curious faces of the police officers that now seemed to be closing in on him and Maxine. "It just didn't work out that way. I only found out tonight myself what was going on. I did what I thought was for the best. The best for everyone involved." He looked at Maxine, but she was staring at the floor.

Before Jack knew what was happening, handcuffs were being locked around his wrists. The second officer was locking a pair around Maxine's.

"What's going on?" Jack asked, dumbfounded. "Tell them, Tom. I've helped bring the girls back, that's all."

"I'm sorry sir," the officer said bluntly. "I'm arresting you for aiding a kidnapper and withholding vital evidence."

"But I only *aided* her in getting the girls *back* for chrissake!"

"You do not have to say anything, but it may harm your defence if you do not mention when questioned, something which you later rely on in court. Anything you do say may be given in evidence."

"I haven't done anything wrong!"

"You have the right to a solicitor. If you do not have one or cannot afford one then one will be appointed for you."

"This is ridiculous, what have I done but help bring the girls back?"

"You withheld important information about the girls' whereabouts, sir, now if you'll come quietly it'll make it easier for everyone."

"But I didn't *know* of the girls' whereabouts!" Jack continued in vain. "I met Max in a car park for fuck's sake!"

"Sir, you can answer all of our questions down at the station..."

The rest for Jack was a blur. He only vaguely remembered Maxine being read her rights. He less vaguely remembered the look on Tom's face. The look that burned deeply into him and told him that things would never be the same again.

CHAPTER 74

Maria and Angela had spent a lot of time together while the girls were gone. It had been a time of shared anguish, tears and pain, but this time it was different.

Maria and her brother had been flitting between the hotel, the cottage, and the Baxters' home for the last couple of days, never really settling at any one of them. No sooner would they arrive at Tom and Angela's than they had been wishing they were at home – *what if Eva turned up?* As soon as they got through the front door of the cottage (regardless of the police officers with them) they had been unable to rest, and after finding Adrio in every shadow of every room they would go back to the hotel where much of their clothes and other personal belongings still remained. Once there however, they would consider it a waste of time, time that could be spent helping to find the girls, and therefore would find themselves back at Angela and Tom's house again. The tiring police officers had escorted them wherever they had decided to go (despite suggesting that it might be better if they stayed in the same place) and they had been at the hotel for the third time in twenty four hours, for only minutes, when they had received the call that the girls had been returned safe and sound. They had immediately rushed to Brandley House to be re-united with Eva, and finally in the early hours of the morning, when Don Phillips along with one of the police officers had left them in peace for the first time in days, the two girls had eventually fallen asleep on the sofas with them. Tom, Angela, Maria and her brother however, hadn't shut their eyes for a second, despite their recent lack of sleep, and had spent the rest of the night talking in hushed voices about Maxine and Jack. The only signs that complete normality had not yet been restored was a fresh-faced officer posted on their doorstep to deal with the media, and a police woman assigned to the house who had promised to remain in one of the back rooms unless she was needed. She had told them that she needed to remain in the house until the girls had been interviewed tomorrow, and if necessary, examined.

Luckily for Tom, Chief Inspector Wainwright had been released from hospital only an hour after the girls' safe return. The suspected heart attack had turned out to be a severe panic attack brought on from Tom's attack, and as soon as the hospital were satisfied that he wasn't about to keel over and drop dead, they were only too pleased to let him go home. They needed the bed after all. However, Chief Wainwright had refused to go home. Instead he had jumped in a cab and gone straight round to the Baxter's home, only to find himself ensconced into the happy family with the greatest of pleasure. Wainwright had assured Tom that he wasn't pressing charges and then he had ensured that they were left in peace, for a few hours at least. Had Wainwright continued to have been kept in for observation, Tom knew only too well that the girls' interviews and physical examinations (he still held out hope that the latter would in the end not be needed) would not have been held off for a moment longer than deemed necessary.

"I cannot believe that a girl could do such a thing," Maria said, breaking into his thoughts, as she stroked her sleeping girl's black, glossy hair. "Eet is unthinkable. I 'ope she goes to prison for a very long time."

It was four in the morning and the heat of the open fire was warming Tom nearly as much as the whisky. He let a large amount of his favourite malt sit in his mouth for just a moment longer than he usually did and then he closed his eyes, took a deep and satisfying breath, and allowed it to fight with the fire on warming the rest of him.

"I can believe it," he said, cutting into the short silence before it settled itself too comfortably amongst them. "I always said it was Max who did this."

His eyes strayed to Angela as he said the name. It seemed strange to him now. Strange that he could mention it so easily when for so long he had hidden it away and tried desperately not to utter it. How different it all felt now. It seemed unimaginable to him that only weeks ago he had been laughing with Maxine, crying with her... sleeping with her.

He stared into the long, yellow, flickering flames

that danced and spat in the open fire. Its warmth caressed and nuzzled him, mesmerised him and released him from the reality of the recent past. He knew that in only a few hours the girls would undergo their videoed interviews with plastic dolls (Wainwright had warned him) and thereon, possible medical examinations. But when a horrified Maxine had looked him in the eye in the hallway and swore she hadn't laid a finger on them, he knew without hesitation that she was telling the truth. Maxine was no pervert, he knew that. Mad, yes, but not perverted. It was patently obvious to everyone, and also quite unbelievable, that the girls didn't appear to have been harmed mentally or emotionally. Five minutes after Maxine and Jack had been carted away by the police, Jess had asked him, 'I like Max. Where is she going? When can we go and play there again?'

Again, Wainwright had informed them that a child psychologist would in time confirm just how much (or how little) the girls had been affected by the entire episode.

Thinking briefly about work, Tom realised that he hadn't called Andy to update him on the safe return of the girls and to tell him not to expect Jack. *Jack. Poor Jack.* As much as Tom believed Maxine he truly believed Jack too. He was the best friend Tom had ever had in his entire life; they would have done anything for each other. There was no way that Jack could have known a thing about what was going on, at least not until very recently. *He had been staying here with them anyway, hadn't he?* Tom remembered clearly the look on Jack's face when Tom had told him that he was convinced Maxine was behind everything; the shock and disbelief that had swept across his features at the entire concept had infuriated Tom at the time. *Maybe Jack had contacted her once the awful possibility had reared its ugly head? Maybe she had contacted him?* Until he spoke with Jack again, he could only guess.

"You mustn't blame yourself for this," Angela said to Tom, interrupting his thoughts.

"No. No one could possibly 'ave known this was going to happen," Maria's brother, Eduardo, chipped in. "I saw a film once, it was called Fatal Attraction and..."

"Yes, I saw that one too," Tom smiled back.

"Saw it and lived it, yes?" Eduardo smiled.

"Yes."

Tom leant over to top up both of their whiskies. He liked Maria's brother. He was younger than Tom was, probably late twenties, early thirties he guessed. His English was very good, and whilst Eduardo definitely had an accent, Tom puzzled at the difference between Maria's stilted English and Eduardo's well-structured and often humorous sentences.

"Maria's English is..."

"Shit?" Eduardo chipped in, laughing.

Tom laughed back as Maria looked on amused. "No, it's very good, but, well, yours is..." Tom struggled for the right word.

"Better?" Eduardo laughed again. "Ah, yes, it is

better than Maria's and that always drives her insane."

"This is true," Maria confirmed with a smile.

"I 'ave lived in England you know," Eduardo continued. "When I was a lad I was at school here for five years – while our mother taught Maria how to be a good little housewife."

"That is not funny," Maria said, whacking him playfully on the arm.

"Different generation, sis, that's the way it was then."

"What do you mean, *then*? Eet is still like that in the village we grew up in, Eddie. Tom, you feel better now? Eet is good that we can all laugh again, yes? Eet has been the worst week for all of us."

"I can't explain how I feel – it's crazy. But I don't blame myself, not anymore. Not really."

He looked across at Angela as she ran a finger over Jess' soft, plump cheek. Jess stirred and then turned over on her lap before nuzzling into her mother even closer and re-starting her subtle snores. Angela grinned at Maria.

"I don't even feel mad at Max anymore," Tom continued. "I'm just so relieved to have Jess back safe and well, that nothing else matters. The thoughts that went through my mind... I can't begin to tell you. But the relief... well it just sort of overrides everything else, even the anger, it's completely gone. It's crazy."

Before anyone realised what was happening the sound

of mail being forced through the letterbox was upon them and they all commented at how quickly the night had passed. Angela and Maria were in the same positions as before, with the sleeping girls draped across them.

"I really need the loo now," Angela groaned, shifting around on the sofa.

Maria pulled her arm slowly from under Eva's neck and looked at the time. "I can't believe that eet is nearly eight in the morning," she said, shaking her head.

Tom got up from the floor, where he had been firegazing for most of the night and stretched out blissfully. His neck felt stiff and he rubbed the back of it as he padded into the hallway to fetch the post. He was sweaty and unshaven. His short, coarse, dark hair had, over the last few days, become lank and lifeless and he silently cheered that he would at last be able to enjoy a long and relaxing bath, now that things had returned to normal.

"Look at this lot! Nothing for days and then a tonne of the stuff!" Tom came back into the room glancing at each envelope in turn before putting it at the back of the pile in his hand. "I must call Andy. We haven't got Jack at work now so we're going to need an extra pair of hands," he said, momentarily forgetting about the mail. "I wonder how long they'll keep him in for? I might phone up the agency, see if they can't send over someone half capable to help out for a few days." He looked back at the post. "Hey Ange, this one's for you."

He placed a small white envelope into her free hand. "Don't you think it's odd that some days we get no mail at all and then on others we get ten envelopes chucked through?"

Tom smiled at how wonderful it felt to have things finally return to normal. How quickly you slipped back into the mundane aspects of life when distractions and stress finally left you, he thought. He saw a brown envelope and put it to the back with the others.

"I've got a theory. I reckon that because they're so short staffed down at the sorting office they have days where no one actually delivers any post at all in this area. I mean, we are a bit out of the way, so to speak."

Angela pulled a face but he carried on.

"It's true I'll bet you anything." Tom paused to open up an addressed envelope that didn't look like junk mail. "Then what they do is, they save up two or three days of mail and then deliver it all together. Think about it – it would save them hours of manpow..." He stopped short and stared at the paper in his hand.

"Everything OK?" Angela asked him.

He didn't reply.

"Tom? What's wrong?"

Tom carried on reading until he reached the last word and then he silently handed the letter to Angela.

CHAPTER 75

MR BAXTER,

I HAVE YOUR DAUGHTER AND HER FRIEND.

FOR THEIR SAFE RETURN I REQUEST THE SUM OF £100,000 IN USED BANK NOTES.

NOT TOO MUCH TO ASK FOR. PLENTY MORE WHERE THAT COMES FROM I AM SURE.

I REQUEST THAT AT EXACTLY 1PM ON FRIDAY OF THIS WEEK, THE ABOVE SUM BE LEFT AT 'LOCATION 1' - DETAILS OF WHICH ARE ATTACHED TO THIS LETTER - YOU WILL THEN WALK TO SUSIE'S BAR - MARKED ON THE ENCLOSED CORRESPONDENCE AS 'LOCATION 2' - AND THEN BACK TO 'LOCATION 1'.

AT 1.05 THE GIRLS WILL APPEAR THERE UNHARMED IN ANY WAY.

I TRUST YOU REMEMBER THE NUTTALL CASE MR BAXTER. PAUL AND ALEX WOULD BE PLEASED TO KNOW THAT RETRIBUTION IS TAKING PLACE AFTER ALL OF THESE YEARS.

THE GIRLS ARE UNHARMED AND WILL REMAIN SO AS LONG AS YOU COMPLY **EXACTLY** WITH THESE WISHES.

IF THE POLICE ARE CONTACTED HOWEVER, THE SITUATION WILL HAVE TO CHANGE.

The tranquillity that had embraced Tom's shattered body was gone. Angela trembled as she tried to make sense of it all.

"I can't believe that she expected £100,000! What the hell is wrong with that girl?" she breathed.

"Wasn't it bad enough to do what she did to us without expecting thousands of pounds into the bargain?"

"I thought she did it to mentally torture us, not to... she's *bloody evil*!" Tom raked his fingers through his lank hair.

"To take our little girl," Angela went on, "and then ask for *money* to get her back... well it's just, it's just..." The tears slid from her eyes as she heard herself say the words.

Angela knew that the pressure of the last few days had taken its toll on her mind and body and that really this was just an outlet for the pure relief she now felt; relief for the fact that their hell was finally over.

"Why did she mention Alex and Paul?" Angela continued, confused. "We haven't seen them since, well since we found out about them. I didn't know that she was still in touch with those sharks."

"She isn't. It's all bullshit. She mentioned them to cover her tracks that's all. The crazy cow really thought that she was going to get away with this." Tom could feel himself struggling to stay calm. "She thought that if she mentioned them, then we'd automatically think that one of their dodgy pals was behind the whole thing and not her. Unfortunately for her, Jack dragged her here before we fell for that load of crap."

Tom looked at the postal date on the envelope even though he knew it was irrelevant now; Max had taken the girls with the absolute intention of extracting money from them, that had been her real motive all along. How could he ever feel sorry for her now? She hadn't done this on a whim. This hadn't been orchestrated purely because of a broken heart, or from a case of momentary mania, no, she had seen her chance to make a fortune out of them and she had gone for it. *This had been calculated, premeditated, she had known exactly what she was doing, the crazy bitch! But then what did any of it really matter now anyway? She had been arrested and it was all over, wasn't it?*

Tom found the female police officer in the kitchen sipping coffee from a mug. He handed the letter to her and then turned his back and re-boiled the kettle.

CHAPTER 76

Maxine looked around the miserable cell that she had been placed back into. She had been brought here momentarily last night upon her arrival, before being taken into an interview room with a single plastic table and four chairs. One male and one female, both uniformed, had taken their places on one side of the small table and signalled for her and Mr Watkins, her middle-aged, overweight solicitor, to take the remaining chairs on the other side.

The interview seemed to Maxine to have lasted half the night. They had started at the beginning. At first she had felt nervous of the small black recorder gently humming away in the background and she had also found herself unable to keep from staring at the small CCTV camera that was hanging from the corner of the room. However, both things soon disappeared into obscurity once she had started reliving her affair with Tom. Giving a detailed account of their relationship had brought back all of the old feelings that she now had to admit she still harboured for him. The forty-something policewoman pushed forward a box of tissues for her to use as the policeman continued unaffected, with his invasive questions.

"Look, you know I'm guilty," Maxine cried desperately, "so do you really have to do this to me? I could understand it if I was pleading my innocence and you had to try to break me down to get me to confess, but I admit *everything*, so what is the point in all of this?"

The man looked up at her as though she were a complete imbecile. "Look at it more like giving a statement. We know you're guilty but we still need all of the details."

His long face had pinched features and his thin, black hair was receding. She stared at his glowing scalp every time he looked downwards. It made him look a lot older than she was sure he really was and she cringed inwardly as she realised that he couldn't have been much different in age to Tom. *Wasn't this embarrassing enough without having a bloke the same age as her ex-lover, staring puritanically across a grey plastic table at her?*

"What's my crime? I fell in love and made a bloody huge prat of myself, so sue me!"

"Your crime, Miss Carter, is kidnapping two small children."

A tap on the door interrupted them and another, much younger policeman entered the room holding something in a clear plastic bag. He walked over and handed it to the male police officer sitting opposite Maxine, who scrutinised it before turning it around and holding it in front of her face.

"And, it would seem, holding them to ransom. Extortion is a serious crime. As is kidnapping."

Maxine paled further.

"I didn't hold them to ransom!"

"Are you saying that you didn't type and send this letter to Mr Baxter and his wife?" His eyebrows shot upwards.

"Well, no, I'm not saying that. I typed the letter yes, but..." She stopped herself.

Would it make any difference if she told them she had got her friend to post it? If they could prove that Tina knew *what* she was posting then probably yes, it would make a difference to Tina at least. But getting Tina into serious trouble would be all that she would achieve. *Perverting the course of justice? Aiding and abetting a criminal? What was the point in that? The last thing she wanted was to implicate one of the only friends that she had left.*

"Would it make any difference if I told you I got Sadiq Khan to post it on his way to a planning meeting?"

"No." His humourless face looked at her sternly, and as if reading her mind, he changed direction. "The house where you stayed with the girls, wasn't it a friend of yours?"

"No," Maxine fired back quickly. "No... it was, well it was her mum's house."

"And she sheltered you and the girls there?"

"Well, she let us stay there with her yes, but..."

"So she protected you then?" His dark, beady eyes narrowed and a faint smile finally danced on his lips.

"No! She did *not* protect us. She didn't know a thing."

"What do you mean, Miss Carter? Could you be more specific?"

"I mean I lied to her. I told her that they were my nieces. Tina has nothing whatsoever to do with any of this so please leave her out of it."

The man scrutinised her features further before continuing. "Well we're out of sync here now anyway, let's backtrack to where we were."

"I'd rather not."

"You said that after the scene with Mr and Mrs Baxter at their home, you left your job."

"Please let me go now," Maxine pleaded.

"You have to give a statement of accounts."

"This isn't a statement, it's an interrogation."

She looked to her solicitor for help, but he said nothing. His grey and faded, pin-striped suit had seen better days and Maxine wondered if he would be offended or thrilled if she offered to take it on a much needed day trip to the recycling bin at her local car park, when this interview was over with. *Or would she be going straight back into that tiny cell again?* The trousers stretched unforgivingly around his huge waist and the sleeves were an inch too short, as were the trousers. His eyes kept closing and he shook his head to keep himself awake. Maxine jabbed him in the side sharply with her elbow and scowled at him. He opened his eyes widely but looked straight ahead at the policewoman's bust. *Wasn't he supposed to say something? Anything? Wasn't he supposed to tell them to go easy on his client? Wasn't he supposed to agree with her that they were unnecessarily interrogating her? That's what they did on the telly wasn't it?*

"Look at it like an interview. It will be combined with the evidence from the two girls and used to help decide your sentence when you appear in court," the officer continued. "You'll have to go in front of a judge, Miss Carter, in the next day or two, and that's when they will review all of the details." Finally he smiled. "You've pled 'guilty' so it will all be over a lot sooner than you think. No trial. Just a sentence hearing."

What would be over? Her life? She felt her stomach lurch and looked at her solicitor again, in vain.

"How long?"

"Well, like I said, a day or two and then..."

"No, I mean... how long... in prison?" Maxine swallowed hard as she heard herself say the words. Her hands began to shake and she put them under the table in an attempt to hide them.

"Well now," the officer continued briskly, "like I said, Miss Carter, that is completely up to the judge."

***

As Maxine looked around the cell, she took several long, slow and very deep breaths. She had plenty of time to cogitate now; far more than she wanted. They had officially charged her with kidnapping and attempting to extort money. How could things get any worse than this? *How could she ever feel more wretched and desperate than she did now?* She was going to prison in a handcart and there was no way out of it.

Amid all of the black thoughts of prison bullying and lesbianism that Tina had warned her about, Maxine wondered how Jack was. Was he being charged with aiding her? Perverting the course of justice? Poor Jack. She wanted to see him more than anyone else; she needed to speak with him, to see if he blamed her, hated her. She hadn't seen him since they had both been arrested and taken away from Tom's house by the police, and even then they had been put into separate cars. She had been allowed a phone call and as she had no family nearby and Jack had been placed in a cell next door to her, she had given up that right. There was no one she wanted to call. She could have phoned Tina, but what was the point in that? She had just spent three long days crammed into a tiny house with her; she was the last person she needed to speak to. The police had appointed a solicitor for her and what a waste of space he had turned out to be.

Maxine sniffed self-pityingly as she looked around the small room. She had been searched, photographed, fingerprinted and grilled for hours on end. They had taken everything in her possession including her mobile phone and she felt lonely, vulnerable and scared. *Where was Jack now? What was he doing?* She had asked the police who were looking after her but they would only say that they couldn't inform her of anything at the moment. She wiped at her wet face with a sleeve and took a deep breath. Despite being on her own, the air around her was heavy and sweaty. The smell of previous occupants – assorted bodies from assorted homes, fighting for their place among the previous repulsive scents that lingered here, had all coagulated into one hideous stench. Suddenly the door was opened and a woman handed a sandwich to her on a chipped plate.

"Someone else will bring you another cup of tea in a minute, lovey," she said, as she picked up Maxine's cold, untouched tea from earlier.

Maxine winced at the sight of the stale cheese and tomato sandwich and also at the thought of another cup of rancid tea. It had tasted worse than Tina's cheap tea-bag tea and that was saying something. She could see that she was going to have to lower her standards significantly if she were to survive the next few years of her life without starving to death. Deciding that she could afford to be fussy for at least a little longer (she had intended to shift a few pounds before Christmas anyway) she pushed the sandwich to one side, ignored the tea, and sipped at her glass of water. That was another depressing thought; she was going to be spending Christmas in prison.

It was getting late in the day now and she beginning to feel cold. She looked around the cell for something to wrap herself up in but there wasn't anything around except the tatty old, discoloured blanket that they had given her an hour ago. Why the hell hadn't she thought ahead? She could have brought her thick chunky knit sweater in with her, if only she had thought to grab it before she and Jack had left the house. Well she wasn't to know, was she? She had never been in a police cell before. And if this was what it was like in a police cell then what the hell was prison going to be like? From what she had read in the papers though they were pretty nice nowadays; 'a home from home', her local paper had once said. She had heard people talk about them as if being there was better than spending time at a holiday site; pool tables, satellite TV, ala carte menus.

Maxine pushed the thoughts away. Her teeth were chattering now and she needed to get warm. *Surely they would have to send someone to her house soon to fetch her some clean clothes?*

"Don't worry, love," a voice piped up as if reading her thoughts. "Heating's gone on so it'll warm up in a bit."

"Oh wonderful," Maxine replied dryly. "Until then I'll just try and fend off double pneumonia!"

She closed her eyes and let her thoughts run wild. Jack. Tom. Jess. Tina. All of their faces swam in and out of focus and bashed each other for a prime spot in her mind's eye. Even Angela was there and Maxine was surprised to find that she no longer thought of her as the Bitch Wife, but as a real person. 'Angela', she thought again. *That wasn't so hard was it?* Since seeing her a few hours before with her husband and daughter in the hallway (just minutes before Tom had turned and tried to attack her) she had realised that Angela was no different to any other woman on the planet; doing her best to just get by. Maxine had watched Angela display a love to Jess that she herself could only dream of giving to a child. In fact they had something in common; they had both loved the same man. The only problem was that it had been at the same time.

Maxine heard hushed voices coming from outside her cell but kept her eyes closed tightly. She didn't want to open them. If she did then she would only be reminded of where she was and what she had done; far better to stay in her private world where no one could hurt her, and where anything was possible.

The door of her cell made a sudden clanking noise and she realised that it was being opened. This was all she bloody needed, some drunken scumbag or teenage shoplifter imposing on her small space just when she was getting used to being on her own. *Wasn't there another room that they could put them in? The cells weren't exactly packed out and this wasn't exactly sodding Butlins!*

Maxine opened one eye slowly and saw the tea lady holding out a cardboard cup to her.

"And what's *that*?" Maxine asked disdainfully. "Sorry to be ungrateful but if it's more pissy tea, thanks but no thanks."

The woman ignored her and smiled. "Who's the lucky

one then?"

"Lucky?" Maxine scoffed, sarcastically. "I might be some things today, but lucky is not bloody one of them."

The woman handed Maxine the brown cup. "Well I'd call being bought a hot chocolate by a nice young man, when you're only normally given 'pissy tea' in here, *very* lucky indeed."

CHAPTER 77

Jack took the long route back to Tom's house. It was a pleasant enough day considering that it was winter, and he wanted to savour every lungful of fresh air that was willing to be inhaled by him. Only hours ago he had doubted the fact that this moment would be happening at all but now it was a reality and it felt great. They had believed him and now he was free. Of course, the fact that Maxine had admitted everything to the police, confirmed his story word perfectly and therefore exonerated him completely was more the real reason than that they had simply 'believed' him. But still, his faith in justice had been restored either way. The only dampener to Jack's high spirits was that he hadn't been allowed to see Maxine before he left. Despite the fact that she had pleaded guilty to all of the charges, he had been told that there was still a small chance that he could be called as a witness, and so to see her or speak to her would be out of the question. He really hoped that she got the hot chocolate he'd sent for her; the tea in that place was dire – it was the least he could do.

He had decided to take the long route and savour his time with fresh air and private thoughts, and as he strolled down every back street that would eventually take him to the private road that led to Tom and Angela's beautiful house, he tried to make sense of the last few days and hours. At the end of the next road he turned and walked past a grimy looking newsagents nestled snugly between a row of terraced houses, and noticed a thirty-something looking man sitting outside what would have been the original entrance but was now blocked off. The shop had long been deserted and thin strips of paint were flaking off its entire ageing body. Once upon a time it would have been a house just like the identical houses that were wedged either side of it. It would have been loved by its owner and cared for with pride. Now it had been forgotten about. Any love that anyone had once held for it had long gone and the building looked as sad and desperate as Maxine had when he had last seen her.

The man in the doorway wore a grey hoodie and torn, faded jeans. His once white trainers were black and grimy, and his long dark hair fell in greasy strands around his face. His head was bent forwards in sleep or shame, Jack couldn't tell which, and a brown mangy looking dog was lying on a blanket beside him, looking up at him woefully. Jack realised, shamefully, that he had never given any money to a homeless person before. *What was the point? Did it ever really make any difference? Didn't they just go straight into the first corner shop and spend it on cheap booze? Or blow it on drugs? That was the drill, wasn't it?* As he stared at the figure in front of him he wondered just for a moment if one person could really make a difference to another person's life. *Could one random act of kindness really change someone's life forever?* Putting his hand deep into his pocket, Jack rooted about and pulled out a selection of loose change. He stared at the paltry offerings in his palm and shifted some of the coins about as he looked for a couple of pounds to give to him. Dropping the coins onto the man's lap, Jack thought briefly about the twenty pound note that he knew was in his back pocket. He paused and thought about his life. It had so very nearly taken a turn for the worst; he really could have ended up in prison. *Jack Preston. Thirty nine years old. In prison.* Never in his life had he ever done anything wrong before – other than sleep with other men's wives but they had known about that (most of the time) so that didn't count, did it? *He had a job, his health, friends, a home (just), a wife (just about). What did this poor sod at his feet have, apart from a mangy old dog and clothes that even a charity shop wouldn't want? Who knew what the future held for anyone? Maybe one day he would even have a son of his own and if God forbid anything happened in his son's life that ever caused him to end up on the streets like this, then he would like to think that someone, somewhere, would have an epiphany, just as he was having now.* Without another thought, Jack pulled the twenty pound note out from his back pocket and knelt down in front of the man.

"Here, buy yourself something to eat and drink, clean yourself up a bit."

The man saw the colour of Jack's money and looked

up in surprise.

"Life's too short, mate," Jack went on, looking around at the filthy shop doorway. He got up to leave but stopped himself and knelt back down. "Can I ask you something? Is this what you really wanted from your life? Is this what you imagined it would be like when you were small?"

The man scrunched up his dirty face at Jack. "You trying to be funny?"

"No," Jack said sadly, "I'm deadly serious. There's only one person who can change it, mate. We're all in control of our own destiny."

"Fuck off," the guy mumbled back. "I'm not your mate. And you can take your fucking money back an' all, if all you're gonna do is lecture me. You don't know anything about my life, you don't know anything about me." He threw the twenty pound note back at Jack.

Open mouthed, Jack looked at the note lying on the pavement between them and grabbed it quickly before a gust of wind decided to take it away from both of them.

"But I don't want it back, I want you to have it."

"It's alright for you, in your nice clothes," the guy sneered, peeking at Jack through his ripped hood. "Got a good job have you? Got a nice house?"

"Just about, yes."

Jack stood up, annoyed. All he had wanted to do was help the guy for goodness sake; offer him a bit of advice and maybe say something that would inspire him. He hadn't meant to sound patronising. He decided to try again.

"All I'm saying is that it doesn't have to be like this. You can turn it around. You can change it."

"What – with your twenty quid?" The man scoffed.

"Like I said," Jack continued, annoyed now, "we're all in control of our own destiny."

"I'm not in control of anything."

"You've still got your pride, that's a start isn't it?"

"Yeah, and I won't even have that if I take *that* back." The man nodded towards the twenty pound note that Jack was holding out to him.

"Pride's good, mate, but don't be an arsehole."

They stared at each other for several seconds before the man clenched his teeth together and very slowly reached his hand out to finally take the money.

"Thanks," he muttered, embarrassed, scrunching it in his fist and thrusting it straight into his pocket.

Relieved, Jack turned to walk away but stopped himself again and turned back.

"Hey, just one more thing. Two little mice fell into a bucket of cream. The first mouse quickly gave up and drowned. The second mouse fought and struggled so hard that he churned that cream right into butter and he crawled his way out." He waited for a reaction but got none. "I heard that in a film once," he continued, smiling, more to himself than to the man. "Guess I've just always wanted to say it to someone. Take care, man." Jack smiled wistfully and walked away.

CHAPTER 78

"I'm sorry, mate. I knew about it, but only because she mentioned it last night, just before we came back with the girls."

"She told you what it said, that she wanted £100,000?"

"£100,000?" Jack swallowed hard. "No... I had no idea."

"That psychopath kidnapped my kid, sent me a ransom note for a hundred grand and I bet she's *still* acting like she's done nothing wrong!" Tom jabbed his finger into the air in front of him.

"But she's admitted everything, she knows what she's done. One thing you can't say is that she's acting like she's done nothing wrong," Jack argued.

"Maybe, but don't forget, if it hadn't been for you then my daughter would still be with her. She only brought her back by force."

Jack sighed and rubbed his head. There was no denying that, whichever way he looked at it. He tried to recount to Tom his conversation in the car with Maxine. He had played the reels of last night's memories over and over again in his mind, trying to remember all of the conversation between them; he had already done it once for the police statement but now it was beginning to blur.

"She's still a psycho bitch," Tom remarked, when he

had finished. "Still, it's good to see you, mate. Thanks for coming.

"How long do you reckon she'll get then?" Jack asked, keeping the subject on Maxine.

"Well if it was up to me she wouldn't get out at all, but knowing this pathetic society... I dunno, a couple of years. Hey, can I ask you a favour?"

"Of course."

"Well it's just that, y'know, everything's going to come out now, isn't it?" Tom asked.

"How do you mean?"

"At the office. When word gets out, everyone is going to wonder why on earth Max would kidnap my little girl. It doesn't make sense, does it? Everyone's going to want to know why she did it."

"Do you want me to tell them the truth?"

Tom thought it through. It would be easy to make something up, people cracked all the time for all sorts of reasons and it could make them do the weirdest things. Still, it would go to court eventually and all sorts of things would come out, including their affair, and then the local news and press would have a field day as the true cause came to light. No, it was pointless lying now; everyone would find out eventually anyway. He had cast his stone of fate the very first time he had succumbed and kissed those soft, plump, red lips.

"Yes," Tom nodded slowly, resigned to his fate. "Tell them. Tell them everything."

Angela walked into the room and put the last of the plates down onto the dining table and announced that lunch was ready. Maria, Eduardo and Eva had left hours ago with the two remaining police officers, once the girls had been interviewed and checked over. The only one left now was the 'doorstep duty' copper who had been left to satisfy the local press and TV cameras with a statement written by Tom and Angela. And Angela hoped that when he was gone, things would finally return to normal.

CHAPTER 79

Maria kissed her brother on both cheeks and hugged him tightly.

"Do you 'ave to leave so soon?"

"The train is booked, little sis. This week has gone quickly, yes?"

"Yes and no," she replied. "Eet doesn't seem like you 'ave been here more than two days and yet... eet 'as been the longest week of my life."

"You'll be fine, I will be back in a few days, it is not like I am leaving the country."

"But you 'ave not had a chance to spend time with Eva. Please Eduardo, I don't want to be on my own, not yet, eet is too soon. Please stay with us another day or two in the cottage. I don't want to be here on my own."

Eduardo smiled and hugged her once more. "I told you, you will be fine. I have things that I need to sort out while I am here. Adrio is not here, sis, my contacts say he 'as been spotted in Spain."

"And what if they are wrong, what then?"

"They won't be wrong, they are the best. I will see you in two days, sooner if I can, OK? Why don't you telephone Tom and Angela – stay with them for a couple of days, just until I get back?"

Maria knew that he was trying to keep her at ease and that exposing her worries to him wasn't helping anyone. He had lived here before, she reminded herself. Most of his schooling had been in England; he'd had a life here once, of sorts, and he had people to see and things to do while he was here. If she didn't pull herself together then he would feel unable to leave her at all; he would feel obliged to stay with her and that would be worse. She forced a smile onto her scared and pale face.

"Sure, you go. You are right, of course we will be fine."

As Eduardo picked Eva up and pulled her into his arms for a farewell hug, Maria quickly wiped away the tiny tear that was forming in the corner of her eye and smiled again.

***

Adrio watched, mesmerised, from his usual hideout at the end of the lane. He could hardly believe his luck.

For a week now he had idled away hours, days and nights, waiting in vain for a glimpse of his wife or child. He had spotted a few police cars hanging around on a couple of occasions and he had wondered if indeed they were onto him, but there had never been any real reason for him to think that to be true. When the police had been here, he had disappeared and come back later, and on another occasion, simply hidden himself in the thick bushes and foliage that surrounded the little cottage. It had been easy to hide out here, much simpler than he had ever imagined.

When one of his prison mates had bragged about having a friend on the outside that could find just about anyone, anywhere, for 500 cigarettes, it had been the perfect opportunity to hunt them down. It hadn't been too difficult; he had friends who owed him and they had owed him big time. With his release imminent, the time had been perfect to pull in all of those favours, and, with the help of Mr 500 Fags, bring his long thought out plan to fruition. It had been difficult at times. At one point he had begun to wonder if he had the wrong address but on one of his visits he had spotted a small photograph of Eva as he peered in through one of the little windows. This was the right house after all. It was meant to be a case of straight in and straight out, with as little messing around as possible but he hadn't banked on wasting a week simply trying to find them.

Also, there was Sam. He had only intended to stay with her for a night or two; get his bearings, find the house, take Eva and go. He had been with Sam for a week now and things were getting awkward. If he had been even remotely interested in her he would have tried his luck in the bedroom department, but she was too western and bolshy for him. He liked his ladies to put him on a pedestal – and a bit of subservience wouldn't go amiss either. Also Sam had been questioning him a lot. He couldn't blame her for that; how many ex-cons have a social life to rival the Spanish Royal Family, the minute they get out of the slammer? He had played the nice, charming and misunderstood Portuguese man for a week now and was finding it increasingly difficult to sustain. No, it hadn't gone the way he had planned at all. But rules were made to be broken and plans were made to be scrapped and re-written at a moment's notice if needs be. It was nothing if not challenging but he loved a good challenge. Oh, the hours he had wiled away outside this cottage in the last week were nothing compared to the months of planning that had gone into this little expedition. Now however, when he had least expected it and dare he say it, was finally feeling defeated, here she was. Here *they* were. Right before him.

The man who had just turned and left them was now walking in his direction. Adrio moved back and crouched down into the undergrowth once more, hardly daring to breath. As the man walked close by, Adrio took the opportunity to take a quick peek. *Wasn't he that pretty boy brother of hers?* He couldn't afford to worry about such things now; the man had a bag and hadn't he just kissed them goodbye? Luck finally seemed to be settling on his side. Time was precious and he had already wasted more than enough of it. Once the man was out of sight, Adrio walked up to the front door, determined not to waste another second.

CHAPTER 80

Maria picked up her brother's woolly hat from the living room floor and stroked it fondly.

"Uncle Eddy left his hat," Eva laughed.

"Yes, trust Eddy to do that," Maria shook her head. "He has always been the same, even when we were small children, he was always losing things. But he will be back for eet. Eet is too cold in England for Uncle Eddy, he won't go far without his hat."

In the tiny entrance hall, the front door handle was being pushed down but to no avail.

"Ah, here he is, he has come back for eet already, he didn't get far!" Maria laughed. "The door is locked, Eddy," she shouted out. "Wait, I come and open eet for you."

As soon as she had turned the key and heard the clunk of the lock, the door was pushed open from the other side, hitting her hard in the chest. When she saw that it was Adrio, she screamed and scrambled to push the door shut again, but he was too strong for her and he pushed her back, stepping inside easily and slamming the door behind him. The dull thud of the gnarled oak door hitting the door frame made her gasp and for a second, silence fell upon them.

Maria cowered on the floor, slowly sliding backwards on her backside towards the living room where she knew Eva would emerge any second now.

"You chose well, baby," Adrio panted. "No neighbours to hear you scream."

"What are you doing here, Adrio?" she cried. "What do you want?"

"You mean you don't know?" His dark eyes looked huge and menacing, his face sweaty and unshaven. He wore a dark, heavy wax jacket and a grey beanie hat that covered his mass of dark, greasy curls.

Maria knew only too well that he had come for Eva. She had feared since the day he was sent to prison that this day would arrive. Feared, but not really expected it. It was a fear that was never meant to materialise; a fear that had been bound to her conscience from the moment she took a man's child from him, despite her reasons for doing so. But what a fool she had been to think for one minute that she could hide out here forever and that Adrio of all people would never find her. It had been hope; a hope that had been as real as her fear, but not as forthcoming.

"Adrio, please. I always mean for you to see Eva. I was going to contact you as soon as you were released from prison. I 'oped that we could sort something that would be good for all of us. Eva belongs to both of us after all."

"Eva doesn't *belong* to anyone. But if she does, then she belongs with me – her father!"

The little girl appeared in the living room entrance. Maria had reached it and held out a hand to her. The little girl took it.

"Mummy, where's Uncle Eddy?" she asked, eyeing Adrio suspiciously.

"I *thought* it was 'im outside!" Adrio sneered. "Still as pretty as ever I see. And what business has he got coming here?"

"He's my brother, he has every business to see his niece if he wishes," Maria spat defiantly.

"And I 'ave no business seeing my daughter?" he boomed.

"Mummy," Eva's voice wobbled. "I'm scared."

"YOU SEE!" he bellowed. "She does not even know her own father!"

"Stop it! Stop shouting. You are frightening her half to death."

At this, Eva burst into tears and crouched down, hiding behind Maria.

"She is coming with me!" Adrio spat. Running out of patience he reached behind Maria to grab the girl's arm.

Eva screamed even louder and clung on to her mother's neck as tightly as her little arms would allow.

"Enough! You do not belong here, you belong home with me. Back in Portugal."

"Please Adrio, don't do this," Maria begged.

"SHUT UP! I did not come here to 'ave a discussion about it. I am taking her and that is that."

"Leave me alone," the little girl cried, as he tugged roughly at her arms. "I want my MUMMY."

"You see, Adrio, she does not want to go!"

"She is too young to know what she wants," he spat back. "She 'as no choice, I 'ave wasted a week already waiting for you, I am not wasting another minute." Adrio reached down and clamped both of his hands around Eva's small body and snatched her up quickly.

"That is kidnap, Adrio. She has been kidnapped once this week already!"

"What are you talking about?"

"That is why we 'ave not been here. I 'ave only just got her back and now you are going to mess with her mind and take her away again!"

"*Kidnapped*? You expect me to believe this rubbish? And what did *you* do to her?" he shouted. "*YOU* KIDNAPPED HER, MARIA! You took her away from ME!"

"YOU KIDNAPPED HER, ADRIO! That's why you were in prison in the first place!"

"She belongs with me."

"You can't do this. How do you think you are going to get her to Portugal when you don't 'ave her passport?"

"Are you crazy? I been in prison, baby. I met people that make fake passports in their sleep!"

He walked to the door with Eva crying and wriggling in his arms as Maria got up from the floor and kicked at his legs as hard as she could. Putting all of Eva's weight on his one arm, he quickly opened the front door but as he made a move to leave, Maria kicked the door shut.

Adrio turned and laughed at her.

"You think this is going to stop me?" He put Eva down and held her hand tightly, opening the front door again with his spare hand. "You are pathetic, Maria. I cannot believe that you thought you would get away with taking my baby away from me."

"WAIT!" she panted as she tried to catch her breath. "If you are going to take her, then at least let her take her favourite toy."

"She don't need no toys, I will buy her new ones."

"Please!" Maria begged.

"I said NO!" He turned and started to walk down the short pathway.

"MONEY!" she shouted as if her life depended on it.

Adrio stopped and turned around. "What did you say?"

"I said, 'money'. Let me give you some money."

Again he smiled. "That is a first!" he said, an amused expression on his face.

"She has a lot of money here. Eet is cash, you know, *proper* money. If I get eet you can change eet at the airport."

"We don't need money."

"Several hundred pounds would help you both."

"And why would you give me money?" he asked suspiciously.

"Eet is Eva's money... eet should go with her. If you take eet then at least I will know that she will be ok."

Adrio remained still for a moment and then turned

to leave again. "We do not 'ave time for this, we must go."

"Eet is in the kitchen, I will only be a minute."

Maria ran into the kitchen as quickly as she could. She could see Adrio had stopped and was waiting for her, as she knew he would. Within seconds she had dialled 999 and left the phone on the side ringing for the emergency services. Then, grabbing the largest knife from her knife block she quickly made her way back to the front of the house to join them.

"Well?" Adrio asked impatiently. "Where is it then?"

Maria carried on walking until she stood right in front of him. "I never thought this day would come, Adrio," she whispered.

"Where is the money?" he asked again.

Maria let the knife slide out from the sleeve of her top, down into her hand.

"Oh very clever baby, but not clever enough." With one sharp hand movement the knife lay on the ground, and before she could grab it again it was in Adrio's hand. "You will regret doing this, you stupid whore!" he shouted, before spitting in her face.

Eva screamed as he tightened his grip on her.

"And you, Adrio, will regret ever hurting my sister."

Adrio turned around sharply to see Eduardo standing behind him with a six inch hunting knife in his hand.

CHAPTER 81

Jack's stomach clenched at the mixed feelings conflicting inside him. On one hand it was wonderful to be climbing back into his old car so soon after thinking he might never get to drive it again. On the other, it was hard to believe that it was less than forty eight hours since he had left it in this dingy car park and openly spilled out his heart to Maxine. He wondered pointlessly what would become of her car now. It had still been sitting on Tom and Angela's drive the last time he had been there – he guessed that it would soon be taken away and disposed of, in the absence of anyone collecting it for her. Jack looked at his watch. He was aching to get home and get into the bath; he felt sweaty and was convinced that he could still smell the police station on himself.

After leaving Tom and Angela's house he had spent a good couple of hours at the office. He had only intended on popping his head around the door to make sure Andy hadn't strangled Sally or any of the temps yet, and of course to do as Tom had asked and tell them everything before they heard it on the news. But things hadn't gone as smoothly as he had hoped. No sooner had Jack climbed the stairs to the small office, he could hear Sally's indignant voice bouncing off the office walls from the top of the stairwell.

"Well if you didn't display so many anti-millennial

traits then you would totally get what Greta Thunberg is trying to do!" Sally was shouting.

"She's a kid! She should be in school. End of!" Andy retaliated.

"Fascist!"

"You millennials are a smug pack of narcissists, aren't you?" Andy carried on his defence under attack. "You abhor anyone who existed before you did!"

"Shut up, rapist!" Sally snarled.

"Rapist?" Andy's face screwed up in horror and incomprehension.

"Well... every man has the ability to rape a woman."

Jack opened the office door and looked on in shock. Andy and Sally were standing in the middle of the room as three young temps stood to the side watching the 'show' in amusement.

"WHAT? And how does that make me an actual rapist? I could call you an ignorant minded snowflake but... oh wait a minute..." Andy put his forefinger on his chin sarcastically.

"I find your comments extremely offensive."

"Of course you do! That's my point, dimwit! Keep playing Millennial Victim and we might even hear some violins in a minute. But probably some vegan friendly ones!"

"You're a millennial too, you bloody idiot." Sally retorted, raising her eyes to the ceiling.

"No, I'm not!"

"When were you born then?"

"None of your goddamn business."

"Covert wanker!"

Jack finally found his tongue. "ENOUGH! What the hell is wrong with you two? Cut it out right now!"

Andy and Sally, who had been completely unaware that Jack had walked in, turned in horror to face him.

"Jack? How long have you been standing there for?" Andy asked, embarrassed.

"Long enough!"

"Well I'm not putting up with it anymore!" Andy shouted to him, embarrassment quickly gone. "She's tapped in the head! She's got a bloody screw loose!"

"Mental health is a serious issue actually," Sally said smugly, crossing her arms. "You would do well to remember that, in the current climate. But the only mental health issue I currently have is working with you! Tosser!"

Jack looked around the room and saw the young temps faces illuminated in fascination. They had quite obviously not witnessed such excitement since the news broke on Gwyneth Paltrow's Vagina Candle, and they were relishing every second of it.

"You and you" Jack pointed to Andy and Sally, "in Tom's Office. Now!"

The only thing that Tom had told Andy, was that Jack was still 'indisposed' and so he should go ahead and get more temps in if needed. Jack's revelation, that Maxine had been arrested and was possibly facing kidnapping charges of little Jess and her friend, Eva, left both Andy and Sally, for the first time that day, speechless. Andy had seen her flat on the news and mention of her name but he didn't think for one minute that she had actually done it.

Jack took a deep breath and then, as promised, to Tom, told them about Tom and Maxine's six month affair. Sally hadn't known Tom long but was still surprised to hear that such things had gone on before she had arrived at the company.

"I can't complain though," she said flippantly. "I mean that's obviously the reason I have a job here in the first place, so I'm kinda grateful... in a bizarre way." She looked at Andy and threw him a nasty look.

Andy was numb and couldn't speak. Never in a million years did he think that Tom would do such a thing to Angela. Never once had he suspected in the slightest that anything was going on between Tom and Maxine. And never did he imagine that Maxine was capable of kidnapping. And to send a ransom note? *What the actual fuck? What would James say when he got back from skiing?*

Andy missed his twin more than he cared to admit. *Shouldn't he be back from skiing by now?* This had been the longest few days he had ever known and he needed him here.

Once Sally had left the room, Jack filled Andy in on the finer details of the night, including a graphic account of meeting Maxine in the car park and taking her to Tom's, as well as his own short spell in custody.

Andy shook his head, still struggling to process everything.

"Can I go now, without you and Sally killing each other?" Jack asked as he was leaving.

"I'll do my best," Andy finally muttered, "but I can't promise anything."

***

As Jack climbed back into his car, he decided to take a leisurely drive through the main town. There was, he decided, no better way to feel utterly free than this; to immerse yourself in a huge crowd, be that walking on the pavement or driving on the road. He could turn left, or he could turn right. He could stop at the amber light or take his chances and try to make it through just as it turned red. He could stick to the speed limit or do what he usually did, which was to drive ten mph over it. The simple choices filled him with unsuppressed excitement. How wonderful freedom of choice was; *why had he never really appreciated it before? Why did it take a close shave (and prison flashing in front of your eyes) to make you appreciate the simple things in life?*

As he drove on, he thought about the house that he and Cheryl had bought together only a few short years before. He remembered carrying her over the threshold on their return from their honeymoon, and the day that they had christened every room in the house. It wasn't long after that that they would be christening every room in the house, with different partners every Saturday night, but he hadn't known that then. In those early, heady days, Cheryl had been enough for him, and he enough for her.

As he pulled up outside the house, he turned off the engine and stayed in the driver's seat for a while longer. He scanned the outside of their marital home. It was a good house as far as houses go. OK, so it looked like every other three bed, red-bricked house in the street, but still, it was a good house. Maybe when Cheryl got back from her little jaunt, they would be able to sort something out after all, or if worst came to worst, maybe he would be able to buy her out. *Now there was an idea.*

Jack walked towards the house before pausing for a few seconds on the doorstep and inhaling a few deep lungfuls of fresh air. Finally he let himself in and ran straight up the stairs to do what he had really been looking forward to doing since his arrest; run himself a deep bath. Tom and Angela had been fantastic but there was a certain comfort that you got from your own house that you didn't get anywhere else and he intended to get it in the form of a hot, bubbly, two hour long soak. Once he had discarded the last of his clothes he remembered the clean towels that were stored inside the airing cupboard in his and Cheryl's bedroom.

"Jack, is that you?" a voice called from the very same bedroom seconds before he reached it.

It was Cheryl. *She was back! She must be unpacking.*

"Yeah, of course it's me," he shouted, as he walked, naked, into the room. "I didn't realise you were ba..."

Jack stopped mid-sentence as he saw Rob sitting in their bed with embarrassment reddening his face. He was fiddling nervously with his hands, trying to pull the duvet up and over his chest. He was also open mouthed in shock at Jack's naked body, but Jack didn't care.

"Um... hi, Jack. Alright?"

"Not really, mate, no."

In that most hateful of moments, Jack felt his world crash back down around him. Adrenalin shot around his body in an instant and he wanted to smack Rob once and for all, as hard as he could; smash any sign of life from his vile, smarmy little face.

"We weren't expecting you to just *turn up*," Cheryl intervened gently, as though she could read Jack's mind.

"Oh I'm sorry," Jack countered sarcastically. "Do forgive me, I thought for one stupid minute that this was *my* house." He glared at Rob until Rob had no choice but to look away.

"Yes, we had a lovely time, thanks for asking," Cheryl sang, inappropriately. Her face showed obvious amusement at Jack's oblivion to his own nakedness.

"Well, that's just wonderful then," Jack replied dryly. "Why don't I pop the kettle on and you can tell me all about it."

"Oh cheers, mate," Rob answered, surprised.

"Are you taking the fucking piss?" Jack stared at him in disbelief.

"No, really, I'm absolutely gagging. We got here an hour ago and we came straight upstairs, so I haven't..."

"Had a cuppa yet?" Jack finished for him.

"Yeah," Rob smiled, pleased that they now appeared to be on the same wavelength.

Without warning, Jack lunged past Cheryl and onto the bed, grabbing Rob around the throat.

"What the fuck do you think you're playing at?" Jack shouted. "I come home to find you in my bed, ON MY FUCKING SIDE OF IT," he added bitterly, "fucking my wife! And you want me to go and get you a cup of fucking tea?"

"But... you offered!" Rob answered, confused. "You said, 'why don't I pop the...'"

Rob didn't finish the sentence. Jack punched him twice in the face as hard as he could, and, leaving Cheryl screaming at the sight of blood dripping off Rob's face and onto the duvet, he left the room to have his bath.

***

Jack smiled with amusement. It wasn't just that he had finally smacked Rob in the kisser, and with it, released a lot of the pent up emotion that had clung onto him over the last few weeks – that had helped, but no, it was more than that. It was that he couldn't stop thinking of his own bare dick dangling inches away from Rob's face as he had bruised him with the two best punches he had ever thrown. The look of horror on Rob's face, as it dangled ever closer to him, made Jack wish he had shoved it into his mouth and rammed it down his throat. *That would've shut the fucker up – for a while at least*, he thought.

He chuckled again, took a deep breath and then immersed himself completely into the steaming water and stayed there for as long as his lungs would allow, completely missing Cheryl's sobbing, as Rob kissed her and said goodbye.

CHAPTER 82

Eduardo stood face to face with Adrio, his own, bigger knife at the mad man's throat. He jerked his head towards the house as a sign to Maria to take herself and Eva into the quiet haven only feet away. She didn't need to be told twice. Adrio released his grip on little Eva's hand and she quickly disappeared with her mother.

"You fool," Adrio spat at him. "You will never beat me, you 'ave no right to stop me taking my own child. Hijo de puta!"

"I have every right, Eduardo snarled. "Now give me your knife!" His free hand squeezed Adrio's fist as he tried to loosen his grip on the blade that he was clinging onto for dear life.

Adrio let his knife drop to the ground. "Get it yourself."

Eduardo pressed the edge of his own knife closer still to Adrio's throat. "I said 'give me your knife'."

Feeling the blade beginning to cut his skin, Adrio crouched down very slowly and felt around on the ground for the knife. He handed it lamely to Eduardo who in turn slid it down into the inside of his boot.

"Now you listen to me," Eduardo said, keeping the blade of his knife firmly against Adrio's unshaven throat, so that the first signs of blood appeared. "You will leave now and never come back, or I WILL kill you, do you understand me?"

Adrio closed his eyes and swallowed hard. "I shall go, do not worry," he mumbled.

Eduardo moved the knife slowly away, never taking his eyes from Adrio's, but in that second Adrio saw his chance and punched Eduardo hard in the chest causing Eduardo's knife to fly through the air, close to the cottage. Within seconds Adrio had run to retrieve it and Eduardo grabbed the other knife back from his boot and quickly ran to stop him. He was too late. The two men now stood facing each other only feet apart, both of them with a knife in their hand once again.

"Come near me and I will not only kill you but your sister too."

Eduardo took a step closer, brandishing Adrio's small knife with a confident air. "I would like to see you try."

"Good, stay around and you shall see with your own eyes."

For a moment the two men stayed in their positions, neither moving their eyes from one another, and then without warning Adrio lunged forward and struck out at Eduardo, slashing him across his jaw. Eduardo retaliated and lashed out quickly with his knife, cutting Adrio across his chest and, making him lose his footing, he fell to the ground. With Adrio's knife temporarily lost in the long grass that surrounded them, he smiled. Sliding his knife back into his boot, Eduardo punched Adrio hard in the face. Blood poured from his nose and mouth but Adrio opened his eyes slowly.

"You think this will stop me? he laughed, blood filling in the cracks between his teeth.

With the force of a man possessed he threw Eduardo off and scrambled quickly to his feet. Eduardo panicked; he knew that he was a strong, fit man but even *he* doubted that he would be a match for Adrio, one on one.

"Come now," Adrio taunted as if reading his mind. "We can fight like men, this is good, yes? I do not need a knife to kill you."

As Eduardo finally rose to his feet, Adrio threw himself at him and they both landed heavily, back down in the long grass. Adrio, now sitting on top of Eduardo, smiled menacingly before punching him several times in the face. Eduardo could feel his nose bleeding and the pain that accompanied it suggested it was broken.

"Fode-te imbecil!" Eduardo panted, and with all the strength that he could muster, threw Adrio off him.

Within seconds Adrio charged at him again. This time, as Adrio reached him, Eduardo kicked out at Adrio's stomach with both feet, in one giant thud. Adrio fell back to the ground, winded. While he had the advantage, Eduardo leapt up quickly and kicked Adrio twice more in his sides, causing him to roll around on the grass and curse. Catching his breath as the blood from his face dripped onto Adrio's, he waited for him to move again, and when he did he kicked him as hard as he could between the legs. Twice more Adrio moved, and twice more Eduardo kicked him mercilessly, until at last he heard the siren of a police car coming down the lane.

CHAPTER 83

"Well you must think I'm bloody ruddy blind then!" Charlie threw his fake Louis Vuitton case down onto the bed and his hands onto his hips, in his usual dramatic manner. "I saw the way you looked at Daniel, every single time he helped you with your skis. You're a born flirt, James, I don't know what I ever saw in you!"

"Oh I get it," James sighed. "This is the bit where we have a massive row, so that you can walk out and go back home to Paloma with a clear conscience."

"Paloma? Who mentioned Paloma?"

"Charlie, you phoned your wife every single day of the trip, two or three times a day in fact, I don't know why you didn't just take her instead of me."

"Oh merry hell!" Charlie sang, his hands now flying into the air. "Here we bloody ruddy go again!"

"And what's that supposed to mean?"

"You know full well what it means. It means that every single day of our trip was spent with you not only hanging onto Daniel's every word, but harassing me about Paloma! She's my wife for heaven's sake, Jay, you can't expect me to act as if she doesn't exist!"

"No one's asking you to, but did you really have to phone her three times a day? And this jealousy over Daniel – wouldn't happen to be because *you* fancied him would it?"

Charlie left the bedroom, flounced over to the small

mirror that hung on the far living room wall and squinted at his unhealthy reflection from all angles.

"The trouble with you, Jay, is that you only ever see the bad in people."

"What? What on earth are you talking about now?" Feeling exasperated, James turned into the small kitchen to fill up the kettle.

"I went skiing with Paloma every year throughout our marriage and yes, I admit that at times I missed her, but only because we always had so much *fun* when we went! With you... well, all you did was bloody ruddy moan!"

"Will you stop saying that?" James shouted from the kitchen.

"What?"

"Bloody ruddy! I notice that you only started saying it after the hundredth time it came out of Daniel's mouth! And hang on, I thought you said you'd only been skiing once before?"

Charlie span around, sucking his cheeks in, in exaggerated offence. "There you go again you see! You've got some sort of major prob going on."

"What?"

"Serious jealousy issues, Jay. You're on par with that Bobbit woman!"

"Who?"

"You know... the one who cut off her husband's thingy after he'd had an affair." He pointed between his legs.

"Now you're being ridiculous."

James felt drained from the drama of the last week and slumped down into his favourite chair. From the way Charlie was talking he would have thought that he was referring to someone else entirely. James knew he wasn't any of the things that Charlie painted him as, and never had been. Despite his age and status he wasn't the horny philanderer that Charlie liked to think he was. He was grey and old for his thirty five years; he ate oxtail soup, wore slippers and watched Coronation Street for goodness sake! He was laid back and placid; his idea of a great holiday was taking a week off work to catch up with The Chase. Yes, whilst Charlie had revelled in every second of the skiing holiday, James had hated it. It just wasn't him and never would be. He wasn't the type to go gallivanting along the slopes, feeling 'at one' with nature. He couldn't get used to the skis for starters. Whilst every other novice there appeared confident and scooted off within minutes, he had never quite got the hang of it and had spent the entire week willing time to fly quicker than the Virgin flight that had taken them there in the first place. But it hadn't. For most of the week, James had stood and watched. The skis were on his feet, yes, but he wiggled around in them in a patch of snow two metres square, rather than actually attempt any skiing. The more James thought about it the more he knew deep down that he and Charlie were more mismatched than Hillary Clinton and the Pope.

"It's no use, Charlie," he said, realising that their friendship needed putting down like the dying horse that it was. "There's no point in us carrying on like this."

"Exactly!" said Charlie brightening. "So you'll go to counselling?"

"What?"

"You'll go to counselling?"

"Counselling? What on earth for?"

"Well to sort out your 'jealousy issues'," Charlie replied, using his fingers as inverted commas. "Why else?"

"I'm not going to counselling, there's nothing wrong with me! And we've only known each other for six months."

"OH!" Charlie answered in a clipped tone.

The last week had proved to Charlie too, beyond doubt, that he and James were not the best match in the world. He liked to live life to the full; to seize every opportunity with both hands and hang on for the ride. Life was for living not existing, and the thought of living a dreary 'vanilla' life with James was not what he had had in mind when he had left Paloma.

Charlie walked back into the bedroom and picked his Louis Vuitton case back up off the bed and headed towards the front door.

"Where are you going now?" James asked tiredly.

"Away," he replied simply.

"Away?

"Yes, away."

"You can't just say 'away'! Away where?"

"Away ANYWHERE!" Charlie shouted venomously. "Anywhere where you ARE NOT!" He jabbed his bony finger in the air.

"Charlie, this can't go on. You can't just walk out on me every single time we have words. I'm sick of it and I'm sick of your constant dramatics. It's like living at the local playhouse!"

"I'm going away for good, Jay. I don't know where – back to Paloma even, if she'll have me. At least she'll let me catch up on Drag Race and Strictly, while she gives me a damn good 'welcome home' blow job!"

"You don't love Paloma." James shook his head sadly.

"Right now that doesn't matter a polar bear's knacker to me! I don't love you either so what difference does it make?"

And with that, Charlie opened the door and walked out, slamming it shut behind him.

CHAPTER 84

Maxine looked around the tiny prison cell in shock. If she had thought she was hard done by at the local police station then she had been clearly misguided. Also, the first appearance in front of the judge hadn't gone as well as she had hoped, though just how well she thought an appearance on the charge of kidnapping could go was hard to comprehend.

Firstly, she had been refused bail. This had been more of a surprise to her useless solicitor than to her – *why bail a kidnapper anyway? So that she can go and kidnap more kids?* Of course she knew that that episode of her life was well and truly over and that she would be no more of a threat to children now than Mary Berry. But she had never understood the logic of that 'bail stuff' anyway and who would pay for it if he *had* granted it? Not Tom and Angela that was for sure, and she had no money of her own to speak of – certainly not the thousands that most definitely would have been requested. She certainly wasn't going to lose her home just to spare herself a few months in the clink.

Secondly, the judge had hinted that the trial date could be months away and wouldn't be confirmed until the Preliminary Hearing in a few weeks' time. Talks of so many different hearings were drowning her in despair. *Why the hell couldn't the judge have just got it over and done with and sentenced her there and then this morning in two seconds flat?* No wonder the waiting lists for these things were so long if they wasted precious time on useless hearings!

The only good thing that her hopeless solicitor had told her was that as she had pleaded guilty and everything seemed to be fairly clear cut, the trial wouldn't take too long and that meant that the date shouldn't be too far away. He had said that a few months was nothing to wait compared to most high profile cases that, though admittedly more complicated than hers, could take anything in the region of eighteen months to two years. He had also said that any time she served in prison now would be deducted from the final sentence. This was good news to Maxine, until she started thinking of the sentence in multiples of ten years. *A few weeks spent in prison now wasn't going to make much of a dent in those sorts of figures.*

Maxine also wondered what Jess had told her parents. She had looked after the girls pretty well considering, she thought, and no obvious harm had come to either of them. OK so they had cried a bit, especially at first, but they had come to see the whole thing as a game and they had known that they were going to go home eventually; she had promised them that, and as Maxine had told them, she never broke a promise.

As she bit her nails for the first time in years, she supposed that at least one bit of good fortune seemed apparent at the moment; the small cell had bunk beds but so far it appeared that she had the place to herself. It was sparse, it was grey and it was cramped, but it was hers and hers alone.

As if the female guard along the corridor had sadistically read her mind, the barred door to the cell was suddenly unlocked and then pulled across on runners. In the next second and without a word of warning, another female was being ushered inside, before the door was closed and locked again.

Maxine stood motionless as she raised her eyebrows and took in the woman's appearance. She was about the same age as herself but the comparison ended there. She was short and very muscular, butch even, and peeking beneath the sleeve of her grey t-shirt Maxine could see a tattoo on the top of her arm that looked like two crossed revolvers. Her dark hair was cropped very short, almost into a skinhead, and she had a pointed, silver stud in each side of her nose.

"Hiya, I'm T. K.," she said smiling, eyeing Maxine up and down.

Suddenly, Tina's warnings of all things lesbian behind bars, flashed through Maxine's mind, and she swallowed hard, looked away and said nothing.

CHAPTER 85

Sam kicked her shoes off and called out for Adrio but there was no reply. She knew that he wouldn't leave without saying goodbye and anyway, his things were still here.

After a difficult day at work she needed something stronger than a cup of coffee. She walked over to the cupboard that she kept the emergency wine in, and thinking of nothing except the task in hand, uncorked the bottle as quickly as she could. Of course it hadn't just been work that had got to her, the entire week in general had been exhausting. Not only had she been missing Andy badly (and the git hadn't even phoned or texted), but with Adrio coming and going at all hours of the day and night, she just couldn't feel settled in her own place anymore. However, that was soon to change; Adrio had told her last night that he planned to leave today, so she raised her glass of wine to the ceiling in a solitary toast to imminent normality.

It wasn't that she hadn't enjoyed Adrio's company, she had, when he had actually been here. Just as their letters had proved, they had a lot in common and talking to him was easy. She knew beyond doubt that when he went back home they would continue to write to each other, but there was something strange about him too that she couldn't quite put her finger on.

When he had first written and told her that he would

like to come and visit her he had only vaguely mentioned knowing other people in the same town, and yet since he had been here he had spent more time away from her than with her. That was fine to a degree – she was thrilled that he hadn't got the wrong idea about their friendship, which was what had worried her when he had first turned up on her doorstep. The thing that had confused her was why he never mentioned the people he had gone to visit. When she had asked him he had simply said that these were just people that he knew; old friends of his who he just wanted to catch up with. Sam took another swig of wine. Something didn't make sense; if they were old friends of his then why hadn't he arranged to stay with them instead? *Why would he dump himself on a 'pen pal' that he quite obviously wasn't in the least bit interested in, conversationally or sexually?*

More confused than ever, she sighed and emptied the contents of the glass into her mouth before quickly re-filling it.

* * *

Just a short distance away, Andy was still at the office. The first signs of a sniffle had soon turned into a full blown cold and now his nose was streaming badly. One of the office temps had left early with flu symptoms and Sally, who also had a bad cough and cold, had told Jack that it was inhumane to keep her here when she was so ill.

"I'm entitled to go home!" she had whined.

"You're 'entitled' full stop! Andy had snapped back, before Jack had stepped in to diffuse things yet again.

Tom had popped in for a few hours to make sure the place was still standing but he hadn't stayed long enough to add any real value and they were now sinking under the sheer volume of work. Jack had hung back late to help out but the fact was that it was now seven o'clock on a Thursday night and everyone had left but him.

There came a point, Andy figured, that no matter what, you had to face reality. Reality for him at the moment had arrived in several guises. Firstly, the amount of work to the amount of staff was verging on tragic, and secondly, he still couldn't get his head around Jack's shocking news of Tom and Maxine's affair. Lastly but definitely not least, Sam hadn't phoned or texted him and he was quite obviously still a single man with a papal social life. For just one moment he thought about ringing around some of his mates to arrange a major drinking session. The thought lasted all of three seconds before he realised that in actual fact that was the last thing he really felt like. His body was hot but he was shivering, and he realised that maybe his 'cold' was the beginning of flu after all.

As he prepared to lock up behind himself, he remembered that James and Charlie were due back today from skiing, although he couldn't for the life of him remember what time their flight was. He would check them out when he got home and fill James in on everything that had happened while he had been away.

Andy wrapped his scarf tightly around his neck and pulled the collar of his coat closer together. When he had left the house this morning the weather had been pretty good. That, combined with an effort to clear his head of Sam (and his cold), he had decided to walk. Now however he bitterly regretted leaving his car at home. It was dark already and the wind blew freezing air around his catarrh filled head. As if to mock him, large raindrops started to fall and despite really not wanting to go past Sam's house, he knew it would cut a good ten minutes off his walk home. His only worry was that she might see him and think that he was spying on her, but as the raindrops came thicker and faster, he thought first and foremost of his warm apartment.

As he approached Sam's street he crossed onto the opposite side of the road to her house. It was dark, wet and windy but that wasn't the only reason his pace was quickening; if he was going to walk down this hellish road then he would get it over with as quickly and as painlessly as possible.

Despite his best efforts to power walk through the dull aching inside his chest, he slowed his pace as he came in line with her house. He didn't want to do it but he knew that no matter how much he tried not to, his head would turn and he would indeed glance towards her place, searchingly. And it did.

Nothing. Nothing except a faint glow of light shimmering out from the sides of the drawn curtains. Finally he stopped completely and paused for a moment, considering for a second whether he really had it in him to stir things back up and knock on her door, to sort this out once and for all. A part of him wanted to, desperately, but his ego was bigger; his stubbornness stronger. *Anyway, Marcos was probably in there with her. They were very likely back together by now, if they had even split up at all.*

Andy waited and watched the closed curtains for a few more moments and then turned away, dropped his head, and carried on walking in the wind and the rain.

CHAPTER 86

Maria and Eduardo sat comfortably in the warm and safe haven of Brandley House. Maria was already on her second glass of wine while Eva played upstairs with Jessie. Eduardo's eyes and nose were bruised and swollen but it was a small price for him to pay to save his sister and niece. Tom found it difficult to comprehend.

"Like we haven't all been through enough!" he blasted. "No matter how much he loves or misses his child, why would he put her through the torment of dragging her from her mother to make her live abroad?"

"You do not understand him," Maria explained. "He doesn't think like a... um..." she struggled for the right words but couldn't find them. "...like you or me."

"You can stay here for as long as you like," Angela confirmed, kindly. "All of you. I mean it."

"Thank you, Angela, you are a dear friend, but eet is safe to go home now. He is with police and they say he not be free now. But we stay for tonight? Is OK?"

"Absolutely, I wouldn't have it any other way." Angela smiled.

"Does he have money?" Tom asked, following his own line of investigation. "He must have hired a pretty good private investigator to find you that quickly."

"He 'as friends that you and I would not want to know, Tom," Maria answered. "Even more now that he 'as been in prison again. They are not the sort of people we would want anything to do with, you know what I am saying?"

"Oh yeah, I know alright," Tom replied. "Well let's hope that they lock the pair of them up together and throw away the key."

Everyone knew he was talking about Maxine and they silently agreed.

CHAPTER 87

Sam downed the last of the wine and looked at her watch. It was almost eight o'clock. She didn't usually drink alcohol mid-week but what the hell, she was in no mood to be wholesome tonight. As she hadn't eaten much, the effects of the wine quickly took their toll and she decided that should Adrio come back any time soon she might just flirt outrageously with him. She was quite obviously a free agent now, after sending Andy away with a flea in his ear. He hadn't been in touch with her since and as it had taken him so long to make contact with her the last time around, this time, she decided, she wasn't going to waste any time hanging around waiting for him.

She hiccupped, giggled and then pictured herself with Adrio on the sofa; her tongue in his mouth and his hands on her breasts. It was something that she knew she would never allow to happen if she were sober and not quite so desperately in need of some T.L.C.

Smiling, she skipped into the kitchen looking for the brandy that she and Andy had shared just recently. There was only a small amount left.

"That'll do," she said aloud, knocking it straight back from the bottle.

There was a noise at the front door. She smiled, undid two of the buttons on her top, flicked her hair back and waited for Adrio to walk in. All week he had knocked briefly before letting himself in. She didn't mind, in fact she thought it was a good idea. Whilst not really comfortable with the idea of him just letting himself in, but at the same time not expecting him to stand on the doorstep waiting for her to answer each and every time he came back, she had thought it a good compromise.

Instead of Adrio's footsteps however, there had been a long pause before the knocking came again. Sam got up and wobbled slightly as she made her way to the door.

Andy stood on the doorstep soaked through from head to foot. His hair was stuck to his head and the rain ran off him as if he had just stepped out of a shower. He wore the expression of a lost boy as he stared at her through the rain that continued lashing down upon him. It pulled at her drunken heartstrings and for one moment she wanted to pull him into the warmth of the house and smother him with kisses. *Hadn't she lied to him and led him to believe that Adrio was an ex-boyfriend called Marcus, that she was willingly letting hang around?* She swallowed hard and then hiccupped.

"Hello. What..." She didn't finish the sentence. Instead she stood back and, her resolve weakening once more, waved him on through into the dryness and warmth of her home, but he stayed where he was.

"Andy?" She frowned.

"I didn't come here to worm my way back into your life," he said at last.

"Oh," she replied, disappointed and confused.

"I've been walking up and down this road for an hour trying to decide whether I had it in me to knock on your door and speak to you."

Her heartstrings tugged again but despite his sentiments, she could feel herself getting cold and wet as the rain lashed down.

"Andy, just come in. The weather's horrid, we can't stand here talking like this," she said, buttoning her top back up as high as it would go.

Andy ignored her and sneezed before carrying on. "I haven't got much to say, Sam, so just let me say it. I might be a twat sometimes but I'm not so much of a twat that I can't see further than the end of next week."

"What?" Sam was confused. The alcohol was fuzzing her brain and right now she could only cope with straightforward conversations; nothing cryptic or too thought provoking.

"Marcos," he said flatly.

"Marcos?"

"Yes. If you're with him then that's fine, it really is. I..."

"What?" Sam shook her head.

"Sam, I pictured myself as an old man."

"Andy, I can't do this. I don't know what you're talking about. Don't do riddles with me when I've drunk a bottle of wine and brandy, *please*."

Andy raised his eyebrows and glanced at his watch. "Wine AND brandy? It's not even eight o'clock."

"So are you my mother now?"

"Sam, just be quiet for one minute and then I'll go." He sneezed again loudly. He looked pale and was shivering.

Sam moved further back inside the door but despite the shelter she was getting wetter. The cold wind was blowing the rain into the hallway and it was beginning to splash onto her walls.

"I didn't intend on ever seeing you again," Andy continued. "I know I'm stubborn, it's my worst fault, but I'm not stupid and I'm not an idiot. I pictured myself as an old man, rocking in a chair, maybe in an old people's home – the whole works. And the one thing that I knew I would never forgive myself for, the one thing that I knew I would regret one day would be never straightening things out with you. All that bad feeling between us just seems like the wrong ending somehow. Don't you think we shared something special, no matter how short, to treat each other like that? Don't you think life's too short and that people's paths cross for a reason? Don't you think that most people are too stupid or stubborn and get to *be* that old man before they even think about it, and then it's too late?"

Sam could feel the tears at the back of her eyes pushing themselves to the fore. The tears in Andy's eyes had brought them forward and stolen her words.

"So I came to say 'hello, and that I hope you're OK'," he continued. "And I came to say, 'I *did* love you, Sam, and I still do'. I came to say 'I'm sorry for ever hurting you', and you know why? Because I'm bigger and better than the guys who don't know how to apologise. I'm bigger and better than some twat who has so much pride that it's suffocating him. And I'm bigger and better than that old man who has nothing to do but look back on his life with regrets. It's not going to happen to me, Sam." He paused for a moment and smiled. His tears and the rain were one. "When I'm an old man, moments like *this* moment *right now* will keep me warm at night because I'll know I didn't let pride get in the way of saying what I was really thinking and feeling." He paused again. "I love you, Sam." He turned to leave but then stopped suddenly and looked back at her.

"Thanks for listening," he said simply, before sneezing again. And then he turned and walked away into the wet and windy night.

CHAPTER 88

Jack heard a noise downstairs and stirred. After more loud banging and several clanging noises, he opened his eyes and looked at the bedside clock. Still fighting the urge to go back to sleep, he sat up and stretched himself out. Last night he had had the wonderful long soak that he had promised himself (three hours of it – with a constant letting out of tepid water and topping it back up with steaming hot), and had finally tumbled out of the bath looking more like Baby Yoda than the red headed Bradley Cooper that he had been hoping for. Once he'd left the bathroom he had heard Cheryl on the phone downstairs to her mother, revealing the state of their 'perfunctory' marriage. Jack had fought the urge to charge down the stairs, grab the phone from her hand and scream the truth out to his empathetic mother-in-law; not only had Cheryl been having an affair behind his back too but that she thought it quite the norm to bring him home in the middle of the day for a quickie in their marital bed. *'Oh and by the way 'mum', we're swingers!'*

As so often was the case in marital breakdowns, only one side of the truth was being told and Jack resigned himself to the fact that her mother wouldn't believe him anyway. He had flopped himself down onto the bed and listened in silence as the whole sorry story of him and Sue came to light. He could only imagine what curses her mother was wishing on him down the telephone line, in reply to that little lot.

When the torturous phone call had finally ended he had thought about charging downstairs and having it out with Cheryl but he knew that it would be futile and instead he lay on the bed until eventually he had fallen asleep. Now he looked at the clock again; it was 8pm. Good grief, had he really been asleep all that time?

The clanging sound came again so he got dressed quickly and went downstairs to see what was happening. When he reached the entrance of the living room he stopped. The once beautiful but knick-knack ridden room had been stripped of every plant, ornament, picture and DVD that had ever been bestowed upon it. The bareness of it all reminded him of every New Year when somehow the room looked empty once the Christmas decorations had been pulled down. This time it was different. The room really was empty, bar the sofa, chairs and television set. She was even unplugging the CD player in front of his eyes.

"Chez?" he asked stunned. "What the hell do you think you're doing?"

Cheryl ignored him and carried on wrapping the speaker wires around themselves.

"I said 'what the hell do you think you're doing?'"

"What does it look like, Jack?" she replied coldly.

"It looks like you're dismantling the CD player."

"I can't carry on like this," she continued, ignoring his sarcasm. "I thought that we could act like adults in all of this, but..."

"Are you saying that this is all because I twatted that jerk earlier?"

"If you're talking about Rob, then yes. How dare you do that to him!"

"So you're telling me that it's the most normal thing in the world to come home and find another man in your bed with your wife then?"

"Don't act holier-than-thou with me!" Cheryl shouted back. "You've been with Sue behind my back for God only knows how long! Look me in the eye and tell me you've never been to their house when Alan wasn't there?"

"Yes, Cheryl, I *have*, but that's the fucking point! Alan *wasn't* there!"

"And you *weren't* here, Jack. Not when we first got here anyway. How were we to know you were going to come home, it was a Thursday afternoon – why weren't you at work anyway?"

Jack was momentarily stunned. "Is it just too much to ask that you have a bit of respect for me and don't rub my face in it?"

"Respect?" she laughed. "How can I have any respect for you?"

"I've done nothing to you that you haven't done to me," he answered bitterly.

"Really? Did I tell you that I saw Sue earlier on?" she said dryly. "I popped into the supermarket to grab some bread and milk, I didn't think there'd be any here when I got home, and I was right." She looked at him intensely. "You didn't tell me that she was *pregnant*." Cheryl left a deliberate and lengthy pause before finishing. "Or didn't you know?"

Jack paled and felt nausea whipping up in his stomach.

"I think I heard something about it, yeah," he muttered as casually as his voice would allow.

"Alan's thrilled to bits by all accounts, couldn't wait to tell everybody," she went on, "says he's always wanted a baby *of his own*. He thought he was firing blanks." She narrowed her eyes at Jack. The expression on her face spoke a thousand more words, some of them being 'if I ever find out it's yours your life won't be worth living'. Jack pulled his eyes from hers and fixed his stare on the far end of the room.

"Well I'm sure they'll be very happy," he said finally, through gritted teeth.

The words had almost choked him. *What man on this planet could want this baby to be his own more than he did now?* He didn't know what was worse – the thought of the baby not being his or the thought of it being his but being raised by Alan. He was knackered either way and a sense of injustice enveloped him in an invisible black cloak. Just the thought that the baby might be Alan's, hacked into Jack's internal organs like a psychopathic surgeon with a blunt and rusty knife. And the thought that it might be *his own* flesh and blood calling Alan 'dad', tore into them even further.

"Well," Cheryl said, finding her voice again, "I'd rather thought that Sue and I were at the age where babies were a non-entity. It's a shame that *you*... I mean '*life*' was never so kind as to grace *me* with a bundle of joy."

If Jack thought a moment ago that Cheryl had hurled jagged daggers at him, this time she had clearly bludgeoned him with his own golf clubs.

"YOU NEVER WANTED KIDS," he shouted angrily. "You never *wanted* them so don't blame me for the fact that your eggs are now on a bullet train to Menopause City!"

"You bastard!"

For a moment neither of them spoke. Cheryl put the speaker down and fell into the springiness of one of the chairs, a small tear trickling down her cheek.

"I'm sorry," Jack said, rubbing his red eyes with the heel of his palms. "I shouldn't have said that."

Cheryl didn't reply.

"We've both done wrong, we have to accept that," he continued. "There's no point in blaming anyone else and no point in blaming each other. Can't we just accept that we're both to blame for the shitty state that we've got ourselves into? At least that way we might just get somewhere."

"I'm going to my mother's," Cheryl said suddenly, ignoring him. "Until me and Rob can find a suitable place to live."

"Oh no, come on, Chez," Jack pleaded.

"I'm sorry, Jack, it's the only way."

He thought for a minute. *Wasn't Cheryl only doing what he had planned to do with Sue; set up a new home, a fresh start? How had this all backfired so terribly on him? He could cause a scene but what difference would it make now?*

"You wanted the house," Cheryl continued bluntly. "If you can afford to buy me out, it's yours. I don't want it, there are too many memories."

"Well we obviously have a lot to talk about then," Jack continued in retaliation. "Like the fact that you're not going to bleed me dry by taking everything in the house that isn't nailed down! You're the one leaving so I don't see why I should be left with four bare walls."

"I've got nothing more to say, Jack. Think about it and let me know as soon as possible, otherwise an estate agent will be here with a For Sale sign within two weeks."

"Two weeks? Two weeks does NOT give me enough time to sort out a new mortgage – IF I can afford it, which I very much doubt."

"Two weeks," she repeated calmly. And with that she wiped her eyes, stood up and began wrapping the wire around the second speaker.

CHAPTER 89

After Andy had dragged himself out of the luxury of a hot bath, he chucked on the first pair of jeans that he could find and pulled a clean top from his wardrobe. Pulling the tab on a cold beer from the fridge, he marvelled at how much lighter and happier he felt. Despite his cold having spiralled (walking in the wind and rain for what had felt like an age was only ever going to make it worse) he had done what he had to do with regards to Sam. On reflection he realised that he had never before done anything like that unless he stood to gain from it. He had never risen above his ego and pride before and now that he had experienced it he was astonished at how great it made him feel. A huge weight had been lifted, as if by magic, from his shoulders and he now knew that for once in his life he had done the right thing. He had done something that he would never regret; something 'good' and 'right' and self-cleansing. He could now move on. *Maybe this was what the Americans called 'closure'?*

Feeling lighter than he had in days he decided to finally call on James. He knew him and Charlie were back, he had heard noises coming from James' apartment directly below him.

As Andy reached his door to leave the apartment, there was a sharp knock on it and he quickly yanked it open.

James stood momentarily in the doorway before walking straight past Andy and sitting himself down on his sofa.

"Hey bro, I was just on my way to see you," Andy said, smiling. "How did the trip go?"

"Shit as it happens, word of warning... don't go skiing with a married gay man."

"Oh." Andy closed the door and joined James in the living room. "What happened?"

"Just about everything other than the obvious."

"Which means?"

"Charlie's gone, and he's not coming back."

"Whoa! Gone where?"

"I don't care, back to Paloma I expect."

"Paloma? But I thought they were over."

"So did I."

Andy walked to the kitchen area and, leaving his unfinished beer, opened one of the cupboard doors. He pulled out a bottle of rum and some coke, and grabbed two glasses before re-joining James in the living room.

"We need a drink," he said, slamming the glasses onto the table and filling them.

James didn't argue and began relaying the week's series of unfortunate events to Andy. It didn't take long before they were onto Andy's news and he filled James in on the drama that was Maxine, Tom, Angela and Jess.

"Woah! That's the first and last time I'm going away, I can't believe it - nothing exciting ever happens around here and then the minute my back is turned... WOW." He shook his head as if the action would somehow make everything make more sense. "And how come I never knew about Tom and Maxine?"

"I don't think anyone knew, except Jack. But it'll be over every newspaper this side of town now so I guess he wanted it all out in the open. You can't blame him."

"Wow," James said again. "I can't believe Max really kidnapped their girl, it's unbelievable. Is she really going to prison? Shit."

"What do you think? She's locked up ready and waiting. It's a shocker alright." Andy emptied his glass into his mouth and poured another rum.

"So," James said eventually, when they had exhausted every avenue of office gossip, including Andy's showdowns with Sally, "what about you and Sam, things hotting up?"

"No mate, it's not happening."

"What do you mean?"

"She's got some other bloke – some ex that kept hanging around, I was a fool to ring her again after all that time, it was never gonna work out."

"Well you didn't know that, did you? Not when you phoned her I mean."

"No, but hey, I really don't wanna talk about it right now." He leant over to refill James' glass but James put a hand over the top of the tumbler to stop him.

"I'd love a cuppa, bro."

"Course you would!" Andy smiled and got up to switch the kettle on.

"Works been shite," he shouted from the kitchen. "I can't begin to tell you. Temps not knowing their arses from their elbows, despite apparently working for insurance companies before. God only knows if Jack'll turn up tomorrow, Sally's off sick and I'm full of it."

"What? Shit?" James smirked.

"A cold, you cheeky fecker!"

"I'm supposed to be off until Monday," James called out as Andy made his tea, "but I can come in if you need me, sounds like it's been chaos."

"You don't have to offer twice - I'll see you at nine!"

"Great," James groaned. "Something tells me I'm going to regret this."

CHAPTER 90

Maxine's first day with T.K. hadn't started off too well at all. Being holed up together in the confines of the small depressing cell had not only taken away her privacy, but it seemed, her right to the top bunk, the rationed toilet tissue and also the solitary chair that was next to a small table on the opposite side of the room. She had failed to be assertive and stand her ground, when it had become clear that T.K. was not someone to be messed with. Within minutes of the guard leaving them, she had told Maxine that she was inside for GBH on her ex-lover, with intent to kill. Maxine couldn't think of anything to say in reply to that and so stayed silent. She wanted to ask if the ex-lover in question was a man or a woman but one look at the sinister glint in T.K.'s eye was enough to satisfy her curiosity. She decided there and then that she would really rather not know, and besides, what difference would it make anyway? T.K. was quite obviously a psychotic bully, probably capable of murdering man, woman or beast, and for once in her life Maxine wished that she *had* watched Orange Is the New Black. Maybe it would have given her some tips on what to expect from inmates like T.K., or better still, how to survive them. But then it was only a drama after all and this was real life. *Could the two be compared?* Tina had always said that anything could happen on T.V. but as far as Maxine was concerned anything could happen in real life too and she certainly wasn't ready for any form of 'prison reality' in hers.

As T.K. began to commandeer the top bunk, she asked Maxine the question that she had been dreading.

"So," she grunted, "what you in 'ere for then? A pretty fing like you don't belong in a place like this. Nicked some teabags from the corner shop for granny did ya?"

Inwardly Maxine trembled. She couldn't remember when she had last felt so terrified in her life. If she had thought being dragged to Tom's house in Angela's car or the idea of going to prison had been bad, it was nothing compared to the reality of sharing a cell with a 5'4", fifteen stone, lesbian rhinoceros.

"Well?" T.K. barked. "You gonna answer me or what?"

Maxine thought for a second. She had to answer, of that there was no doubt, but did she have to tell her the truth? Maybe not; it wasn't as if they were going to be in here together long term. They would eventually have their different cases heard and be given different sentences and then who knew what would happen. *Then again, was it worth lying in a place like this? Surely T.K. would find out sooner or later; people talked, especially the guards.*

"Kidnap," she said quietly.

"Do what?" T.K. barked again. "Did you just say 'kidnap'?"

Before Maxine could reply, T.K. was laughing, a

loud, barking laugh that Maxine felt sure the entire floor could hear. One thing that she had noticed since she had been sent here was that the place echoed terribly, just as she imagined it would.

"Listen," T.K. said when she eventually stopped laughing. "One fing you ain't never gotta do is lie to me, see?"

"I... I'm not lying," Maxine stammered.

The smile left T.K.'s face and she slid down from the top bunk and walked over to Maxine, who was now cowering between the chair and the table. When T.K.'s face was only inches from her own, she pulled out a cigarette from her pocket and lit it, keeping her gaze fixed on Maxine.

"I really would rather that you didn't smoke," Maxine squeaked pathetically. Her lapse from cigarette restraint after Tom had dumped her, had been short lived. All seventeen cigarettes had given her a tight chest and, realising that Tom wasn't worth lung cancer, she had thrown the rest of the packet in the bin.

Without answering, T.K. blew the smoke directly into her face. Maxine winced and coughed but didn't move. She was too terrified to move.

"Kidnap eh?" T.K. said as she took another long drag on her cigarette. "*YOU? Kidnap?*"

Maxine said nothing.

"Who d'ya kidnap and why d'ya do it?" she asked bluntly.

Maxine could feel the familiarity of tears prickling

at the back of her eyes. She so desperately didn't want to show how scared she was but it was a battle and she could feel the tears were winning.

"A girl," she answered simply.

"*What girl?*"

"Well two girls," she corrected herself.

"Oh TWO girls now, is it?" T.K. continued staring at her before inhaling, and then once again blew her cigarette smoke into Maxine's face, but this time Maxine held her breath and turned her head away. "So why would I believe that someone like you would kidnap two girls?"

Maxine felt the first tear sliding down from the corner of her eye.

"I SAID," T.K. continued angrily, "WHY WOULD I BELIEVE YOU?"

"I... I don't know," Maxine stammered. "I really can't see why you should. But it's true. Why else would I be in here?"

T.K. tilted her head and looked at Maxine as if she were suddenly a curiosity. This time she dropped the sharp edge to her voice.

"OK. So why then? Why d'ya do it?"

Maxine took a deep breath. She knew she wouldn't have long before T.K. became angry again. There wasn't time to make anything up; she had never been good at thinking on her feet and the Rhinoceros would only find out eventually anyway.

"I had an affair with my boss."

"AND?" T.K. shrugged, unimpressed.

"And he wouldn't leave his wife for me," she finished.

T.K. laughed. "What, so you *stole* his kids?" she mocked.

"Well... yeah, his girl and her friend."

"Why her friend?"

"I don't know for chrissake, she just happened to be with her," Maxine snapped angrily. "Who the hell do you think you are anyway?" she asked, finally finding a foolish amount of bravery. "And what business is it of yours why I'm in here? What were you going to do to me if I hadn't told you? Beat me up?"

Maxine tried to steady her shaking arms by folding them in front of herself. She knew that people like T.K. could smell fear a mile off and if she was going to survive in here then she would have to grow some, and quickly. Even if it did get her a bloody nose.

"Maybe," T.K. replied, smiling in amusement at the sudden outburst.

"Well it wouldn't look good at your trial and it would only add time to your sentence too."

T.K. roared with laughter. "You fink I give a pig's shit about that? Are you for real, Barbie?"

Maxine looked T.K. up and down and realised that a person like her really wouldn't care less about serving a bit of extra time in exchange for the satisfaction of holding a reign of terror over some insignificant prison fodder like herself.

"Go fuck yourself," Maxine blurted suddenly. "I'm not cowering to you!" She had now given Rhinoceros a good excuse to beat ten bells of shit out of her but she also knew that someone like T.K. didn't need an excuse. No, if Maxine was going to get beaten up then she might as well go down with some pride, she reasoned.

"Well, well, well. You do have a bit of spunk in ya afta all." T.K. smiled. "Still think you're lying to me though."

"Why else would I be in here? If I'd *stolen teabags* as you put it, I shouldn't think that would warrant me being in here with all these hardened crims, do you?" Maxine saw something register in T.K.'s eyes.

T.K. slowly chewed the inside of her cheek, until at last she seemed satisfied with Maxine's confession.

"OK, so maybe I do believe ya after all," she said, stubbing out the butt of her cigarette on the wooden table beside her. "I mean who would be so stupid to make up 'kidnapping' in prison?"

"Well... good." Maxine said, feeling some relief for the first time since T.K. had been brought here.

"Trouble is," T.K. continued, rubbing her fist with the palm of her other hand, "we don't like kiddie fiddlers in 'ere, know what I'm saying?"

"I beg your pardon?" Maxine screeched; horrified at the picture that was no doubt forming in T.K.'s mind. "I did no such thing, what the hell do you take me for?"

"Well now I wouldn't know, would I? Don't know ya

from Adam. 'Ow do I know you ain't done a Hindley on 'em?"

"What the hell?" Maxine gasped, horrified.

Suddenly feeling sick she turned around to gag into the small, stained basin beside her but nothing came out. She splashed her face with cold water and then moved to sit on the chair but T.K. pulled it away from her and sat down on it herself, lighting up another cigarette. Maxine watched her in fascination. She wanted to ask her why they let the inmates walk around freely with matches and lighters but decided it would be safer if she didn't. After all she didn't want to rub Rhino up the wrong way anymore than she already had.

"See the fing you don't seem to understand is that people like you ain't welcome 'ere by the rest of us."

"Well believe me I'm not here out of choice! And I never did *anything* to the girls – apart from look after them, feed them, you know, that kind of thing. I'm not like that. Believe it or not I'm a good person."

"Yeah right, chick. Whatever."

"It's true. I'M NOT LIKE THAT!" Maxine's quivering innards had now been stirred up enough to erupt once more into mild hysteria. "I AM *NOT* A PERVERT," she screamed, slamming her hand down on the table in the same spot that T.K. had stubbed out her cigarette. "SO DON'T YOU *DARE* CALL ME ONE you... you... COW! I did it for revenge that was all, to get back at him for bloody well hurting me so much!" Her tears had burst through their temporary dams and T.K. was now looking at her with renewed interest.

"I wish I hadn't done it but I did!" Maxine continued. "I also wish to God I'd never laid eyes on him and that I'd never let myself fall in love with him but I BLOODY WELL DID, AND THAT'S LIFE! And the mad thing is that I *still* love him, STILL STILL STILL – even now. How's that for a joke? I hate him too but most people say it's the same difference! IT'S SHIT AND IT STINKS AND IT'S A GREAT BIG FUCKING MESS BUT THERE YOU ARE! LIFE *IS* SHIT! LOVE *IS* SHIT!" She banged her fist on the table again.

T.K.'s mouth gaped open, allowing her cigarette to hang loosely from her lips. She blinked several times at the open display of deep emotion that filled the little cell.

"So," Maxine continued quietly now. "whatever you're going to do to me just do it. Kick me, punch me, flush my head down the toilet, stub your cigarettes out on me, bend me over in the shower and shag me up the arse with a great big dildo!" She looked at T.K.; her great piercing blue eyes, now red and sore, sore from crying, sore from heartache like she had never before felt in her life. "Just do what you like to me, because you know what? NO-ONE WILL *EVER* HURT ME AS MUCH AS HE DID!"

T.K. didn't speak. Her mouth was still open and she took the cigarette slowly from her lips. With the heel of her hand, she wiped at her wet eyes.

"T.K.?" Maxine stared in surprise.

T.K. got up from the chair and before Maxine knew what was happening, had put her arms around her in a tight hug.

"Shhhh. It's OK. I know where you've been, kid," she said quietly, stroking Maxine's hair. "I've been there too."

CHAPTER 91

When Jack walked into the office he was more than a little surprised. Not only were James and Andy at their desks but he soon found Tom in his little office too.

"Wow, like the old days or what?" he smiled, shutting the door to Tom's office behind him and sitting down.

"Thought I'd better get back to it," Tom grinned, as he made a coffee. "But now that I know you're all here I might just bugger off early." He handed his coffee to Jack and made himself another one, before deciding whether to confide in him or not.

"Go on," Jack said suspiciously.

"What?"

"You look like you've got something to tell me. Go on, what is it?"

Tom smiled and chewed his bottom lip.

"Me and Angela..."

"Yeah? You and Angela what?"

"We're having another baby."

Jack sank back into his chair, his mouth open in amazement. "What? You've gotta be kidding."

"Nope," Tom smiled, "I'm not, I'm deadly serious."

"But... but, after everything that's happened, surely that's the last thing on your mind?"

"How do you mean?"

"Well you've both been through so much, I mean, it

just sounds kinda mad, why don't you wait for a bit, you know, get over everything that's happened."

"Jack, we're not *trying* for another baby – the baby's already here. Angela's pregnant."

"Good grief."

"It just happened, it wasn't planned, and well... we're thrilled, new start and all that. Doctors reckon she's about three months gone, and we never even knew, how's that for mad? Mind you what with everything that's been going on it's hardly surprising. Still, we have the scan next week so we'll know the dates for sure then."

Jack thought of Sue and felt instantly saddened. He hadn't contacted her and he hadn't heard from her either, but then again why should he have? She had made it quite clear the last time he saw her that she and Alan were making a go of things. He had no right to contact her now, not if he wanted to do the right thing. He felt discomfort in the pit of his stomach and wondered whether she was having morning sickness. *Had she had a scan of her own yet?*

As if he could read his mind, Tom groaned. "Mate, I'm sorry, I didn't think. Any news?"

Jack shook his head. "No, none. I don't suppose I'll hear anything either, it's not really anything to do with me anymore, is it?"

"Hey, we've got our fortieths coming up," Tom said, deliberately changing the subject. "What d'ya reckon – joint party?"

"Cheryl's gone, cleared the house out completely. Really don't feel like partying, mate, if it's all the same to you."

"What are you going to do?"

"Don't know yet, try and buy her out I guess, or start looking for something smaller. She knows about the baby – saw Sue in the shops."

"If you need anything, anything at all..."

"I'd better get back to work, there's enough of it." Jack pushed his untouched coffee away and got up to leave. "Congratulations by the way," he said sadly, despair washing over his aching heart. "And give my love to Ange."

And with that, Jack and his heavy heart left the room.

CHAPTER 92

The ex-lover that T.K. had performed G.B.H. on and also attempted to kill, had been Dan, her boyfriend of five years. Because of him, not only had she endured years of mental and physical cruelty but also had at her lowest, lost the will to live. Maxine listened intently as T.K.'s story unfolded. She heard how her boyfriend would drink himself to oblivion, drug himself up to the eyeballs and then cripple her. Not only did he cripple her physically and verbally but he would deliberately bring home different women for her to 'catch' him with, crippling her emotionally and mentally. When she didn't 'catch' him, he would leave photographs about the place for her to find. When one day she finally plucked up the courage to tell him that she didn't care anymore, he broke her nose and two of her ribs. Over the five years that she had been with him he had also broken her jaw, her arm and her pelvis. But worst of all, he had broken her heart and her faith in men.

As T.K. finished telling her heart-breaking story, Maxine found herself feeling numb from the shock of it all. *How on earth could this ever happen to someone like T.K.?* T.K. was big, she was strong, and just one look at her would be enough to send most men running to their mothers. *Why didn't she just leave him, tell him to go to hell?* T.K. had tried many times of course, and Maxine knew only too well how tightly love could bind two people together. It could take years for a person to walk out of a violent relationship – she knew that was true; *how often had she watched Jeremy Kyle?* Sometimes people put up with the most horrendous situations for huge parts of their lives, but at the end of the day people had their limit. *Everybody* had their limit. They might not know where their limit was until they reached it, but it was always there for sure.

Maxine reflected on the differences between herself and T.K. Though their lives had been completely different, some similarities were definitely there. Like T.K., Maxine would have done anything for the man she loved, put up with almost anything, but also like T.K., only up to a point. T.K.'s limit had taken five years to reach (not much compared to some of the sights she had seen on Jeremy Kyle) and when she had indeed reached it, she took a knife from the knife block and stabbed him three times. He didn't die and T.K. had ironically thanked the heavens that he didn't, or now she would be facing a murder (manslaughter if she was lucky) charge instead. T.K.'s solicitor had told her that she was doing everything in her power to get her off without a sentence. Courts were more sympathetic than ever nowadays to victims of abuse, she had said, but T.K. was still expecting the worst. For more than a moment Maxine had wished that she had T.K.'s solicitor. She sounded interested, committed, confident and above all 'highly experienced', unlike her own useless half-wit.

And what about herself? Where was *her* limit? *Had*

she reached it when she kidnapped Jess and her friend? If she had then why did a part of her still love Tom so much? Maybe a part of her always would – isn't that what they say – true love never really dies?

Later on when they were eating lunch together at one of the long benches in the food hall, T.K. told her that Dan was the only person she had ever slept with, and ever truly loved. Maxine coughed on a slice of carrot and told her that she had assumed that if not a lesbian, then she was at least bi-sexual. This made T.K. laugh incessantly but for Maxine it was no laughing matter. She was annoyed with herself for judging T.K. by her appearance, something that she had spent most of her life doing to people.

In that moment, as she and T.K. ate a tasteless beef casserole together, Maxine decided that she was going to change. Not only was she going to change, she was going to get out of this place and enjoy the rest of her life. She was going to finally put Tom behind her, get a new job, start meeting new people and make some new friends. Life was for living after all, not for spending in limbo, or in the past.

When they got back to their cell, Maxine's solicitor was waiting for her.

"Good news," he breathed excitedly. "The courts have set a date for the pre-trial. Bad news – it's tomorrow."

"WHAT?" Maxine blurted. "You've got to be kidding."

"No I'm not, wish I was."

He looked shorter and fatter and balder than she

remembered and he was sweating a lot too. She even wondered if he was the same man.

"This means that I have to stay up half the night preparing our Plea-Bargain, can't have you serving a long stretch when it's the first time you've ever put a foot wrong."

"Yeah but I didn't put a foot wrong, did I? I put an entire acre wrong!"

Mr Watkins laughed and coughed at the same time, his chest sounded wheezy and his face had turned red.

"Are you OK?" she asked, looking him up and down with worry.

"Yes, fine, no time to worry about me."

"You said that as I was already pleading guilty we couldn't use a Plea-Bargain, or whatever it's called."

"Well not exactly, no, but we can still try out a bit of bargaining regardless. Now, hearing's at ten sharp, so I'll meet you here, say eight?"

"EIGHT? Is that really necessary?"

"If you want any hope of getting out of this place, yes," he said, wheezing as he looked around the cell. "Eight sharp it is then, we can go over everything, we'll ask for leniency due to the circumstances."

"What and say that I'm mad and '*God told me to do it*'?"

He laughed again and wiped his sweaty face on the sleeve of his jacket. "No no. Don't worry, leave it all to me, we'll go over it all in the morning before the hearing. All we need now is a bit of luck."

With that, he turned around, and with his overweight body wobbling inside his brown suit, he disappeared down the corridor.

T.K. looked at Maxine worriedly. "With him on your side, kid, you're gonna need all the luck in the world."

PART TWO

Whatever your true wish is it can be yours, but force not your will upon nature to grant your request. Rather, expand your wish and let it be envisioned as happenstance, flowing gently with nature. Thus, that which you envision becomes reality. Reality, hence, not formed of your own will but of the will of nature, which makes it so.

Author not known

CHAPTER 93

As Maxine stood before the judge, she could feel her insides trembling. She smoothed down the skirt of her two-piece suit and looking across to Tina, thanked her once again with a warm smile, for bringing it in for her.

She thought back to two months ago when her solicitor had arrived at the prison, hot and bothered from the short notice of the pre-trial hearing. That was when the judge had first set the date for today's trial. She had expected to wait a lot longer than two months but the judge had explained to her that her guilty plea meant that the trial was pretty straight forward, would not need a jury, would not take long to get through and that this in turn meant that it could be heard a lot sooner. This had been great news for Maxine; the end was in sight and one way or another this nightmare would soon be over.

The judge opened the case and Maxine looked around the court room quickly. It was pretty much empty. She didn't know why she had expected it to be any different. Who did she think was going to fill it? She guessed that particular pre-conception was either borne out of watching too many television courtroom dramas in her time, or merely that not that many people were really interested in the case. Or in her.

Much to her surprise and relief there was no sign

of Tom or Angela. Much to her distress, no sign of Jack. She couldn't blame him really; he was Tom's best friend after all and could hardly turn up to show her support.

She had written to her parents and confessed the entire tale to them in the hope that if no one else came, *they* at least would be here for her. Two weeks later they had simply sent a card to her from Mauritius wishing her luck. '*Got your letter before we left, darling, but we've had this break booked for six months now,*' it had said, '*can't possibly cancel at the eleventh hour*'.

It was true. The only people here besides the judge, herself, her solicitor and Tina, were two reporters from the local newspaper, a representative for Tom and Angela, some court staff and a couple of policemen who were ready to give evidence if need be. Her solicitor had told her that the judge would already have read the written statements, including Jack's.

As Maxine stepped up near the judge and entered the dock a short while later, she re-lived the last two and a half years of her life, starting at the beginning when she had first started working for Tom. With help from her solicitor, she told the judge all the details of their love affair and the circumstances that culminated in the girls' kidnap. This time she didn't feel embarrassed, just thoroughly ashamed.

When she had finished her detailed account (which whilst having taken two and a half years to.live it, had taken only twenty five minutes to re-tell it), and answered every question that the judge had thrown at her, her solicitor stood up and once more asked for leniency. He reiterated that she was only nineteen years old and that whilst she took her share of the blame for the affair and regretted deeply any distress that she had caused Mrs Baxter, Mr Baxter, now forty, had been the more mature of the two by a long way; old enough to be her father. It was indeed *he* who was married and *he* who took advantage of a young girl who was not only his employee but '*barely in the first stages of womanhood*'. The judge reminded him that they were not here to discuss the moral issue of affairs but to decide on a sentence for a kidnapping that Miss Carter had already pleaded guilty to.

"However," he went on, "I *shall* take into consideration all of the details that have been presented to me."

With that, he adjourned the court for thirty minutes. It was the longest thirty minutes of Maxine's life.

***

When the judge finally walked back into the courtroom, Maxine felt wrung out. Mr Watkins, her solicitor, had bought her a coffee during their thirty minute reprieve but she had been unable to take more than a sip of it. The realisation that any moment now she would be going to prison for possibly a very long time had churned and knotted her stomach so much that she felt she could vomit at any given moment. She had hugged and kissed Tina, begging her to visit in prison and not to forget her, and of course Tina had told her that she would always be there for her.

"All stand," the Court Clerk called, and they all stood.

Maxine watched the judge intently, looking for clues in his demeanour as to what her sentence could possibly be, but there were none. Mr Watkins had told her that she could be looking at around five to eight years. It was a ball mark figure and no one could be sure what was going on in the judge's mind, but, he had told her, without wishing to raise her hopes too much, it was much more likely that 'under the circumstances' it would be a lot less.

As Maxine tried to calm herself by remembering all of the things that Mr Watkins had told her, she realised that the judge had already started talking. What planet was she on for heaven's sake? *Here she was about to have the book thrown at her and all she could do was daydream like an extra in a Coldplay video!* She tried to make sense of what he was saying but found it difficult now that she had missed the beginning of his speech. There was something about 'sad and desperate case' – *was he talking about the court case – or about her?* Then she heard 'such a shame for a girl of that age'. *Was he talking about her or Jess?* She tried to focus on what he was saying but the sound around the courtroom had become echoed. Her ears were buzzing and her head felt light and detached.

"Miss Carter," the judge called out suddenly, "are you feeling alright?"

Maxine remembered shaking her head slowly before hearing no more, and, feeling only the coldness of the floor on her face, everything went black.

***

Maxine had eaten half of a chicken sandwich and drunk two glasses of water before the judge came back into the court room. This time she was seated and she nodded to the judge when he asked if she was sure that she was quite alright and ready to begin again. He told her that he understood how she must be feeling and that she wasn't the first to faint in his courtroom and almost certainly wouldn't be the last. Then he adjusted his red robes and peered at her over his half-moon glasses, smiling kindly at her. She smiled back. He reminded her of Santa Claus. She silently thanked the heavens that she didn't have an angry, judgemental Judge Judy screaming at her right now.

"This is a particularly sad case," he began, and Maxine wondered if this was how he had begun his original summing up.

"I have heard your confessions, Miss Carter," he went on, taking on his officious tone once more, "and

I have also read all of the statements from all of the parties." He looked at her, a serious expression settled upon his face. 'Santa' was gone. She was reminded of her ninth birthday when her parents had told her that Father Christmas didn't really exist. Nice birthday present.

The judge continued, outlining the details of the case once again and told her that it was a huge error of judgement on her part to think for a minute that kidnapping would be the answer to her problems; indeed it had magnified them. Despite her young age, she was an adult and old enough to know that what she had done was illegal. This wasn't something that she had carried out on the spur of the moment as she had happened to drive by the Baxter's home, suddenly struck with mad, senseless and irrational thoughts. This had been a 'calculated act', he said, and it had taken careful planning. This she proved by turning up at the house armed with toys with which to tempt them. And of course, she had admitted everything.

"There is also the charge of attempting to extort money for us to deal with, Miss Carter. Again, this was calculated, well thought out, not something that one does on a whim."

The judge paused for a sip of his water and Maxine thought she would die while she waited for him to finish. Seconds seemed like minutes and minutes like hours and she wondered, not for the first time, who invented time anyway? *Wasn't it man-made? Wasn't it just a stupid way of making a day or a week make sense to senseless human beings?*

Finally the judge coughed and carried on. "However, Miss Carter, I must also take into consideration a lot of other factors in this case. You are only just nineteen years of age, eighteen when you first began seeing Mr Baxter. He was thirty nine years of age and also your boss. I don't believe for a minute that you agreed to the affair for fear of otherwise losing your job. As you have admitted in your statements and also in front of me in person today, you became smitten with him, so much so that you believed that one day he would leave his wife for you. Affairs of the head, as quite often happens, become affairs of the heart. I believe that you were distraught when Mr Baxter ended the relationship and I believe that you acted as you did because you were depressed and wanted to hurt him as much as he had hurt you." He pushed his glasses to the end of his nose and once more peered over the top of them at her. "Miss Carter, I know that you are fully aware that what you have done is terribly wrong and as you told me earlier, you regret your actions deeply. Can you imagine for one moment please what the world would be like if we all acted on our less humane instincts?" He frowned at her and she nodded back, as a little tear trickled slowly down her cheek. "I for one, Miss Carter, wouldn't be sitting here now passing judgement on YOU. I would most probably be in prison myself."

She thought she saw him smile at his humorous statement - chuckle even.

"I also take into account that the girls were not harmed," he continued, officious once more, "physically at least. And also that they appear to have been well looked after and on video they have confirmed this. This I believe has helped prevent any emotional damage to either of the girls involved. I am also aware that, albeit with the help and encouragement of a friend, you returned the girls and even came back with them to face the music. For this I applaud you." His expression became stern as he peered at her intently. "It was a very sensible thing to do, Miss Carter."

In that instant she realised just how much she owed to Jack. If it hadn't been for him she would never have brought those girls back when she did, and in fact as she knew only too well, Jack had practically dragged her there kicking and screaming. She thought for one moment about admitting this to the judge but knew in her heart that somewhere in the midst of all this crap she was being thrown a Chance Card and she wasn't going to lose it now.

"I also take into consideration the fact that when you took the girls back you must have been well aware at that point, that the money you had attempted to extort would no longer come to pass. By taking them home you in effect forfeited any money that you *thought* you might hope to gain. I also believe you when you say that by *that* time, you deeply regretted ever having written the ransom note or ever having taken the girls in the first place. Why else would you have returned home to face the music? You have also pleaded guilty to all charges against you and as I have already explained to you, this has made the entire episode, if I may call it such, far easier to deal with."

At this he paused for a moment and took a long hard look at her. Maxine now felt stronger and stood back up.

"I am aware that this is your first offence. The court has heard how sorry you are for your actions and for the heartbreak and worry that you have caused Mr and Mrs Baxter."

Maxine was crying again. Not great dramatic sobs put on for effect but small silent tears that slid effortlessly down her pale cheeks. She sniffed and wiped them away quickly, trying to salvage some dignity.

"I do not believe you to be violent or a danger to society and I also do not believe you to be insane, which is why I will not request a mental health assessment of you. This has been an emotionally charged incident and I believe that you acted completely out of character in a time of great depression and distress and that for that, you are truly sorry. However, despite all of this, Miss Carter, you committed a terrible crime, and there must be consequences for what you did. We may never know the damage that you have caused to those two girls emotionally or mentally. I am imposing a four year prison sentence upon you." He peered over his glasses at her again. "I hope you realise I have been lenient today. I can see that you realise the gravity of what you did."

He stood up to leave, the Court Clerk barked 'All rise!' and it was over.

Maxine stood dumbfounded. Her scrambled brain tried to make sense of the judge's order. Four years? That was good, right? *But four whole years in prison? Did that mean she would be out in two years? People only served half of their prison sentence, right?*

PART THREE

In your search for Yourself you must trod a path which is like the path that a bird makes in flying through the sky. The path is used but no other can follow it, as no sooner is it made than it is gone. All other paths leave their marks for the convenience of others to follow... but your path is yours alone...

Author unknown

CHAPTER 94

Just like the winter, the spring days with their unpredictable breezes and showers had long gone. The sun, just like himself, had become stronger, the breezes calmer and the clouds in the sky less noticeable. In fact, as Jack walked slowly through the park he noticed that on this beautiful afternoon, summer was in full swing.

He walked on, closing his eyes for a moment and relishing the feeling of the sun's warmth upon his face. Despite several people walking and talking around him, he heard nothing but the faint twittering of birds overhead and the heaviness of his trainers pounding on the pathway beneath him. When he opened his eyes again, colours appeared more vivid, people seemed happier and the air around him more energised. People wore t-shirts and some even had vests and shorts on. Kids licked their ice-creams as their parents held their hands. Women chatted while their men listened happily. How different things were when the sun came out, he thought.

Jack reflected on the last two years; the worst of his entire life. He had spent them travelling a winding pathway very much like the one he was walking on now, except *that* pathway had been a spiritual one from which he had learned many things.

It had been twenty five months since Maxine's case

had gone to court and she had been sentenced. He had seen it all over social media as well as on the local news and had felt torn between conflicting emotions. His first thought had gone out to Tom and Angela and he had phoned them instantly. They had been upset. Tom had said that there was no justice left in the world, ('She'll be out in two! What a joke!') and complained that he had lost all faith in the British legal system. 'Still,' he had said, 'we're off that path of hell now, we have a new baby on the way and we've got to look to the future.' Four months later Angela had given birth to a healthy baby boy and Jack couldn't remember when he had last seen Tom so happy.

His second thought had gone out to Maxine. Despite everything, he was glad that she had been given a fairly lenient sentence. After their conversation in the car that night, before they had set off to get the girls and take them home, he had seen a side to her that he had never seen before. Love had consumed her, used her and spat her back out with green vomit. It had tormented her and destroyed her, as it had done him. It had left her so completely exhausted that he had feared for her sanity. He'd wanted to call her - but say what; congratulations? Congratulations for what? For getting away lightly with kidnapping two young girls? Still, he had desperately wanted to speak with her and let her know that he was there for her should she need him. When a few months had passed he had thought about visiting her in prison. But he hadn't. He hadn't because he couldn't be there for her. He had to be there for Tom. His mate. His buddy.

Two whole years had now passed and despite his heartbreak over Sue, Alan and the baby, he had managed to avoid all three of them completely. He had asked the universe to grant him that one wish and so far it had complied.

After eighteen months of animosity, he and Cheryl had finally managed to put their differences behind them. Seven months ago after bumping into each other at a local supermarket during a snowstorm, they had both reached for the last loaf of bread. He had grabbed it quickly from her hand before she turned and he realised it was Cheryl.

"Why are you here?" he had asked, annoyed.

"Rob and I are moving back here," she had told him. "I'm sorry, Jack, but I miss my friends."

Jack had been unable to speak. She had taken almost everything from the house eighteen months before and they had argued by WhatsApp almost every week since, about the house, the divorce or one thing or another.

"We've had eighteen months of hurting each other, Jack," Cheryl had continued, "can't we just move on now?"

In that moment Jack had felt tired. Tired of hating and tired of fighting. Slowly, he handed her the last loaf of bread and smiled, and after taking it from him, she hugged him. The next day they had gone for coffee and talked. They agreed to clear away the baggage that they had hung on to for so long and by the end of the afternoon they had taken a childish oath to be good friends to each other forever. Now they would look out for, and help each other whenever they could, they had promised. So far they had kept to their word. Whilst Jack had helped Cheryl and Rob raise money for their JustGiving fundraiser for Cheryl's fertility treatment (she had now become hell-bent on having a child one way or another), Cheryl often messaged him to see if he wanted a plated-up Sunday roast if she 'made too much this weekend'. She would then deliver it to him before rushing back to the new house that she shared with Rob. Jack had visited Cheryl in hospital every day when she had been rushed in with pneumonia in January, and, once home, Cheryl had saved Jack all of the newspaper tokens for a hugely discounted cruise for two. He didn't have anyone special in his life now, she'd said, 'but you never know what's around the corner, Jack.'

Yes, he had learnt many things during the last two winters, mainly that life was too short and precious to hold grudges against people you cared about.

He thought of Angela and Tom, whose second child was now twenty one months old. They were happier now than Jack could ever remember them being. Jess had insisted on her parents hosting an eighteen month birthday party for him because, 'how can you expect me to wait another six months?' she had stomped. Jack had been invited round to help finish all of the remaining jelly and ice cream without a fuss. Which hadn't been a problem to be fair. Angela had told him that afternoon that Maria and Eva had now moved away from the small wooded cottage with its flaking paint and shadowy trees, and were now settled into a modern town house not more than ten minutes away from Brandley House.

Looking around the park now, Jack's thoughts finally turned to Andy and Sam. The day after Andy had called round to Sam's in the pouring rain, for 'closure', she had been horrified to see Adrio on the local news and even more horrified to learn that he had tried to kidnap a little girl. Apparently, so the news had said, she was his daughter, but that did nothing to ease the ill feeling coursing through Sam's body. She still had some of his clothes at her house and she had felt sick to the stomach that she had harboured such a horrible and dangerous man without realising it. After quickly packing his stuff up and taking it to the local police station, she had called round to Andy's, unannounced. She told him the entire story; that Marcos was actually Adrio, who was the man who had been in the local paper and on the local news for trying to kidnap his own daughter, Eva. She also knew now, thanks to Facebook, that 'Eva' was the other girl who had been kidnapped alongside Andy's boss' daughter, Jess. *Local girl kidnapped twice in a week!*' the headlines had said. Sam had become distraught as it all sank in, and Andy had put his arms around her and taken her into his apartment. Within ten minutes she had told him that no one had ever said anything so moving to her in her entire life as he had said to her the night before, on her doorstep in the pouring rain. She loved him and she missed him and she wondered if there was any way they could give things another go. They got engaged on Valentine's Day, after Andy had dragged Jack around five different jewellers on four separate lunch breaks asking for his advice on this ring or that. Jack smiled at the memory.

It was during one of those 'lunchtime trips' that Andy had confided in Jack about his brother, James. After James' failed relationship with Charlie, James had been thinking of moving away and had now undoubtedly made up his mind that he would. Andy had been shocked at first; this wasn't exactly the sort of thing he had expected from his hermit brother, James, but after speaking with him about it, it became clear that James' brief relationship with Charlie, despite its trials and tribulations, had left him realising that there really was more to life at thirty five than crosswords, Countdown and Coronation Street. If nothing else, Charlie had shown him that there was a world out there waiting to be experienced and explored; there were endless opportunities to try new things and there was lots of fun to be had while doing so. James hadn't exactly grasped the fun and enjoyment that life had to offer while he had been with Charlie, but he intended to do it now – for himself. He had told Andy that he had given a month's notice on his apartment and had already booked tickets to Greece and Croatia. 'From there on, who knows?" he had told him. All Andy knew was that despite his own personal happiness with Sam, he would miss his brother terribly.

As Jack continued to reminisce through the small but beautiful park, he saw two figures walking towards him. He could hear their faint laughter trickling into the air around him and, as they got closer, he could hear a toddler screaming at and teasing the two parents.

When they were about twenty metres away, Jack realised with alarm that the two people were in fact Sue and Alan and for one terrifying moment he stopped walking and stood rooted to the spot. He knew that regardless of his sudden immobility, they would soon be upon him as they chased the toddler to keep up. Jack felt his heart begin to race. *He thought he had a deal with the universe? Wasn't it supposed to be keeping them apart? Wasn't it supposed to be helping Jack to move on with his life? This wasn't supposed to happen!*

In that moment time began to slow down. The sound of the footsteps and laughter that belonged to the couple became distorted and alien to him. Their pace had slowed down so much that he felt suddenly transported to another place, another planet, where time as he knew it simply didn't exist. He could see them walking ever closer yet still they never seemed to reach him. The birds had stopped chattering, the children had stopped yelling and all he could hear was a muffled and distant screeching noise like that of brakes being applied heavily. This was his worst nightmare come true. This could NOT happen. The universe had shat on him from a great height and screamed, 'the deal's off!'. And so here it was; the moment that Jack had always dreaded; the one that he knew one day *might* happen but never wanted to believe ever really would.

And then, like a steam engine suddenly chugging back into life, he was back in the real world, back on his planet, with time as he knew it. And the two figures were once again walking at a normal pace towards him. The toddler's laughter had resumed its normal speed and when he next looked up, they had all stopped right in front of him. All three of them.

For one horrible stomach wrenching moment no one spoke, and then Alan, still blatantly unaware of his wife's infidelity, broke the silence with great gusto.

"Jack? Oh my goodness, Jack! How are you, mate? Haven't seen you around for such a long time."

Jack tried to speak but couldn't.

"Hi Jack," Sue said softly. She smiled a faint, nervous smile and then dropped her stare to the ground.

Still Jack didn't speak. He felt frozen to the core. He hadn't seen Sue since the day she had told him that she was staying with Alan. Was that really two years ago already?

"Jack?" Alan sounded worried. "Is everything alright?"

And then it happened. As if from nowhere, it came to him. Not easily (it was the hardest thing Jack could ever remember doing in his life) but he reached down, deep down inside of himself to find it and pull it out, like a rat hiding fearfully in a sewer. It didn't want to come – this 'greatness', this 'goodness' that was buried inside him, but Jack had grasped it with both hands and yanked it screaming into the daylight – and it was there.

"Hey guys, how are you? Jeez, Alan, it's been," he shook his head with awkwardness, 'I don't know... ages. How are you both doing?" The huge smile on his face hid overwhelming agony but he hoped it didn't show.

"Just great, things have been just great," Alan laughed. "And we've got a new addition as you can see." He waved dramatically towards the toddler, pride etched in every tiny crevice of Alan's face.

Jack's eyes drifted unwittingly to Sue's, but they were already staring at him in dread. For one electrifying moment they locked in united horror at this truly awful moment; a moment that should never have arrived, but it *had* arrived, recklessly and fatefully.

"So I see." Jack said, feigning as much joy as he could muster, as he tore his eyes away from Sue's and forced himself to look down at the child.

And there it was. A boy. With a shock of red hair and a face that had walked straight from the pages of a photo album from Jack's childhood.

"His name's Ben, after my father, don't worry he doesn't bite! Well, only when he doesn't get his own way." Alan roared at his own joke and all Jack could do was look on muted and in pain. His insides twisted and writhed in a moment of utter agony as he realised the lad was indeed *his* lad, and that the boy would never know it.

"What d'ya reckon then, eh? Isn't he a beaut?"

Sue stood silently biting on her bottom lip. She didn't want to look at Jack, she *couldn't* look at him again.

"Well," Jack said quietly, after forcing his tongue to work again. "I don't know what to say, he's uh, well... he's," he struggled for a word. "Amazing," he finally whispered.

"Yep! Yeah he certainly is. You've missed the 'wetting of the baby's head' I'm afraid, two years too late," he roared again at his own joke, "but still, we'll have to catch up sometime, yeah? Can't believe it's been so long."

"Oh... Yeah, sure."

"Daddy! Daddy! Swing! Swing!" the toddler screeched, and Alan picked him up and put him on his shoulders.

Jack watched in awe. The perfect child in front of him was his; his own flesh and blood, his own little miraculous creation. He had created a new life and silently prayed that wondrous possibilities would unfold for him. The only problem was that it would be Alan giving him the wondrous possibilities and not himself. It would be Alan witnessing the wondrous possibilities and treasuring every memory they made together. Jack suddenly became aware of how wet his clothes were with perspiration, they were stuck to him and he felt sick.

"You OK, Jack?" Alan asked him, concerned. "You really don't look too good. Sue give him some water, will you?"

"No, I'm good, I'm... yeah, all's good man. Just hot."

Jack took some deep breaths as Alan rummaged around in their backpack for a drink. Jack took the chance to look at Sue once more. She was looking at him sadly and shaking her head, mouthing 'don't'.

"So uh... how are you, Sue?" Jack swallowed saliva from his already dry mouth. "You look great by the way." He could feel the sweat now dripping from his forehead and wiped it quickly with the back of his hand. Then he took another deep breath and turned back to Alan. "Congratulations, mate, he's a smasher, he really is. Don't worry about the water, I have to go, I'm uh... really late for an appointment."

Alan stopped and looked up. "Oh, sure thing. Look, mate, let's not leave it so long next time, let's catch up soon yeah?"

"Absolutely, we will do, yeah." And without another word, Jack walked away.

"We'll wet the toddler's head together, yeah?" Alan shouted after him, obliviously.

Jack kept on walking.

573

***

As soon as Jack came upon the next available bench he walked over to it and collapsed back onto the hard ridges, enjoying the discomfort that it gave him. He hurt like hell inside, why shouldn't he hurt just as much on the outside? Perversely it made him feel better; he wanted to feel uncomfortable, wanted to feel dreadful and wretched. The devil had shat in his face yet again, why should he feel any different?

He didn't know how long he had been sitting there for, staring into the vast space in front of him. The only thing registering in his brain for the entire time was the fact that he had a child. He ran his fingers through his own shock of red hair and pictured the boy again. He had a son. He had created a little boy. A little boy who was named after a grandfather who wasn't really his grandfather. *When would he see him again? In a few months? Another two years? When he was a teenager? Never?*

Since the collapse of the swingers' group he had seen none of the other members and he hadn't expected to either. He had only ever forged friendships with these people from circumstance. Whilst they had all played at being great friends they really had very little in common with each other and therefore had no real reason to see each other anymore. As far as he knew, Cheryl felt the same way. Apart from Rob of course. And even now, he had only bumped into Sue and

Alan by accident. *Is that when he would see his son again, by accident?* Only moments ago nature had played one last cruel trick and thrust a beautiful son upon him when he had least expected it. A son that he could have nothing to do with... not if he wanted Sue to be happy. And he did want her to be happy. Just moments ago his life had changed forever. Or was that hours ago? He looked around at the near empty park. The sun was low now and had cast a beautiful orange glow around the trees in front of him. He could see a man walking a dog and a woman pushing a buggy with a toddler at her side, other than that he could see no one else. Jack got up from the bench and started to walk back the way he had come. He looked at his watch. It was 17:45 – *so he HAD been here for hours*. It was beginning to feel chilly and he quickened his pace.

As he got closer to the park gates he saw a woman up ahead, sitting on a bench, exactly as he had sat on 'his'. She was leaning back hard against the uncomfortable wooden slats and had her eyes closed with her face tilted up towards the lowering sun, determined not to miss a bit of it. It wasn't long before the hairs on the back of his neck were standing on end. He blinked several times to be sure and even looked away for a moment before staring back for confirmation that the woman sitting in front of him was indeed Maxine. She looked different; younger and fresher. Her hair was different too. It was longer, more carefree somehow. Long blonde waves danced around her shoulders and back as she tilted her head from side to side, enjoying the last of the day's sunshine. Yes, the bob might have gone, but it was definitely Maxine.

When he reached her, he stopped and stood in front of her. His shadow blocked out the dying sun's light from her face and she frowned. Her face scrunched up and she opened her piercing blue eyes in annoyance. It took just a moment to register.

"Jack?" she asked softly. "Oh wow, is it really you?"

Jack smiled and sat down next to her. "How are you doing, honey?" he asked gently. "Stupid question, you look amazing."

And then she couldn't talk. Her eyes circled his face over and over, as if it was too good to be true and she should make the most of the vision while it lasted.

Jack laughed. "Don't look at me like that, you'll go dizzy."

"It's just so... so... so damn good to see you." She beamed at him and pulled him down onto the bench beside her, squeezing him tightly. "How have you been?"

"Oh you know... OK I guess." He looked at her intensely before deciding to elaborate. "I'm sorry I didn't visit you... I..."

"No matter," Maxine smiled, "I was a mess, I'm glad you didn't come."

"Cheryl and I split," he continued.

"Oh no, I'm sorry, Jack, really I am."

"Don't be. It's for the best and we're fine, still friends and stuff, y'know."

"Oh, well that's great, that really is."

"Well, it's not *great*," he smirked, "but yeah, I know what you meant. And how about you – how have you been? I wanted to ring you, Max, really I did. It was just so... well, *difficult*."

"I'm fine... you know."

"How long have you been out?"

"A couple of months. I'm finally able to put the past behind me. It's taken time, God only knows how I got through it all, but I did and I feel stronger every day."

"That's great, Max, good to hear."

"I've got myself a new flat and I'm looking for a new job too," she added smiling. "I'll get there."

"Yes, you will," he beamed.

"You were right, Jack, it's going to feel so good to pay my own way. I've got some dignity and pride back and no amount of money can buy that."

"I don't know what to say, Max. I'm happy for you, I really am. You look amazing and you obviously feel it. Hey, did you ever get that hot chocolate I bought for you when you were in the police cells?"

"Heavens, that seems so long ago now," she laughed. "It was the best thing I'd drunk all week!" A flash of sadness crossed her face. "Jack. How's Tom?"

She hadn't wanted to ask, she hadn't meant to, but something inside her had pushed the question out before she could stop it. She felt embarrassed but carried on.

"I mean, um, well I heard he had another baby."

"Yes, yes they did. A boy. Not a baby anymore though. He's fine, well, *they're* fine."

Through the sadness Maxine smiled. "Good. That's good. I really am... well... that's just good." She smiled. "I like the word good."

"Good," Jack replied, grinning.

She laughed and crinkled her nose at him.

Jack felt strangely proud of her. She had been through so much in the name of 'love', just as he had, and despite the fact that he could still see Tom's shadow lurking faintly in the back of her eyes, he knew that she had ventured a long way through a very dark and gloomy tunnel and that the end of it was now in sight.

"You know, Jack, all the time we worked together, I always knew when there was something wrong with you."

"How do you mean?"

She looked at him and smiled softly. "Oh, I don't know, I just always sort of knew if something wasn't right. I guess I just kind of sensed it from you. Just picked it up off you, y'know?"

Jack looked puzzled.

"Like now," she said. "What's wrong?"

He frowned and then paused for the longest time. And then, suddenly, without even thinking about it, he told her all about Sue and about his recent meeting with her, Alan and the boy. Maxine sat in silence until he finished.

"I'm so sorry, Jack, I don't know what to say, I really don't. I'm useless in a crisis, I told you before, it's all bravado with me, it's just a cover. What are you going to do?"

Jack thought for a moment before answering. "What can I do? If I do anything, then I destroy whatever happiness they have together."

"What about *you*? What about *your* happiness?"

Although he smiled, the sadness that pained him was clear.

"Max, as long as that child is happy then I'm happy. If I break up the only stable home he has then how long do you think he's going to be happy for? I've been hurt by all sorts of different people in my life, in all sorts of different ways, it's not going to happen to him." Jack looked down at his feet, bit his lip and wondered once more when he would see his son again.

"Are you alright?"

"Hey," he said, trying to lighten the mood and avoid answering the question, "I was stabbed once, did you know that?" He lifted his t-shirt and showed her the one inch puncture wound in his side.

"Jack, you and I both know that physical wounds heal a hell of a lot quicker than the emotional ones." She looked off into the distance. "Inside, deep inside, you carry on hurting for an age. The wound gapes open, all bloody and raw. It seems to take forever to heal... but it *does* heal, Jack. Physical wounds, emotional wounds, so different to each other, but it's all the same thing in the end. One day they DO turn to scars, and if you have scars then at least you know you've lived. That's what I tell myself anyway. One day I'll wake up and know that it's true."

Jack picked up her hand and held it gently in his, before moving it up to his lips and holding it there for the longest time with tears in his eyes. Finally he kissed it, but he didn't let it go. He held it to his face and stroked it across his wet, cold, rough cheek.

"You're right," he whispered. "I know you are. And then I guess the trick is to reach out and trust in love again."

"Love is what brings all the heartache in the first place," Maxine answered sadly, light tears straining at the corner of her eyes.

"And it's what takes it away again too," Jack replied. And then he brushed her tears away, tilted her chin upwards, and kissed her.

***

Jack and Maxine walked hand in hand through the park in the direction of what they hoped would be the nearest open café. Jack looked around him. Despite the time of day, the sky was still cloudless and seemed to be blessing everyone's life in one way or another. He breathed in deeply. An overwhelming sense of peace seemed to pour down over him.

Just ahead he saw a man, about the same age as himself, holding a woman's hand and kissing it, just as he had done to Maxine only moments ago. She was wearing a similar summer dress to Maxine too and was leaning against an oak tree, not more than ten feet away. The man stood in front of her, his feet on the pathway. He was stroking her hair and she was smiling at him.

As the man turned his head, Jack thought for one moment that he recognised him, but couldn't think where from. He could see he was a good looking guy and his hair was cropped short and had been styled, similar to his own, with hair wax. He had on a shirt that Jack himself had admired in one of the high street shop windows only two weeks ago. The pretty woman with him put her arms around him and slid her thumbs through the belt hoops of his jeans, pulling him closer to her. A dog sat happily on the ground next to them. They were talking and kissing.

As he and Maxine got closer to the couple, the man turned and saw Jack. He frowned and then stared at him intensely before dropping the girl's hand. Feeling awkward, Jack quickly looked the other way.

"Do you know that guy?" Maxine asked. "He's looking at you really weirdly."

"No. No, I don't think so."

When they were level with the couple, Jack made himself look at the man again.

"Jimmy, are you OK?" the woman was asking him. "You're worrying me, what's wrong?"

The guy ignored her and continued staring at Jack.

"I'm sorry, mate," Jack said, stopping in front of him, "do I know you?"

The man said nothing but continued to stare.

"I feel sure I know you from somewhere," Jack said awkwardly, "but I can't think how."

Still the man said nothing.

"Come on, Jack," Maxine whispered. "Please let's go. He's giving me the creeps."

Jack frowned, took her hand once again and, tearing his eyes away from the man, continued their walk out of the park.

"TWO MICE FELL INTO A BUCKET OF CREAM," the man shouted out.

Jack and Maxine stopped and turned around.

"The first mouse quickly gave up and drowned. The second mouse fought and struggled until he churned that cream into butter... and he crawled his way out."

With grateful tears in his eyes he smiled at Jack.

"I am that second mouse."

THE END

In existence itself, there is no time...

this is the meaning of eternity. If man were not here on earth, 'time' would disappear immediately. Trees would grow, the sun would set, the moon would rise, and everything would continue as it is... but there would be no 'time' because time is only a concept of the human mind, and it does not come with the present; it comes with the memory of the past and the imagination of the future.

Author not known

BOOK CREDITS
'Two Mice' - Catch Me If You Can, by Frank Abagnale and Stan Redding

Printed in Germany
by Amazon Distribution
GmbH, Leipzig